For Tomasz

Our homeland is on the verge of collapse . . . The atmosphere of conflicts, misunderstanding, hatred causes moral degradation, surpasses the limits of toleration. Strikes, the readiness to strike, actions of protest have become a norm of life.

Citizens! . . . I declare, that today the Military Council of National Salvation has been formed. In accordance with the Constitution, the State Council has imposed martial law all over the country.

General Jaruzelski, Communist Leader of Poland,
speaking on December 13, 1981

The winter is yours, but the summer will be ours.

Solidarnosc graffiti during martial law,
Poland, 1981–83

Prologue

If I can just crawl to the bottom step, I might be able to reach the stair rail, pull myself up with my good arm. My legs are useless – the fall must have broken something in my back.

I knew the risk. I knew when I told the boy who I was that he might kill me, but I had to do it – how else could I bring up the matter of our mutual friend? At first, he didn't believe me, didn't remember my face. I had to raise my voice then, remind him what had happened to him – incredible that he should need reminding!

That did the trick. Something in his eyes changed.

I told him I regretted his sacrifice, tried to explain what a dangerous time it had been for the country – if we had lost our nerve, well, there would have been tanks on the streets again – and not our own ones this time.

He didn't see it that way. So I ended up in a puddle of my own piss on the cellar floor.

It was worth it. The boy read the document. He wants revenge – I saw it in his eyes – and that means I'll get mine.

If I can just make it to the bottom step.

One

Janusz slammed the younger man so hard against the flat's freshly painted plasterboard that he heard the fixings pop, and twisted the neck of the guy's sweatshirt around his throat.

'Honest to God, Janusz!' Another shove. 'Sorry. Panie Kiszka. The contractor didn't pay me yet, but in two days I'm getting a thousand, I swear on the wounds of Christ.'

As Janusz paused for breath, his free hand propped against the wall, he caught his reflection in the triple-glazed window next to Slawek's shoulder. It showed a big man in early middle age, wide-shouldered and lean, and with a strong jaw, yes – but with the unmistakable beginnings of a stoop, and a scatter of grey in the thick dark hair. *Naprawde,* he was getting too old for this kind of thing.

Straightening his spine with caution, but keeping a grip on Slawek's collar, he scanned the room, a newly fitted 'luxury' studio apartment in a tower block overlooking the moonscape of the Olympic construction site.

Floor to ceiling windows framed the black skeleton of the half-built main stadium, which sat like a giant teacup, ringed by attending cranes, seventeen floors below. When the block was finished, the view would put an extra forty, maybe fifty thousand, on the fat price tag.

Unbelievable. From what he'd seen of Stratford – and he saw far too much of it for his liking, now so many Poles were working around the Olympic site – the place was a dump. After the Luftwaffe had flattened it, along with most of the East End, the town planners had decided to recreate the town centre as a poured concrete shopping mall on a giant three-lane roundabout. It reminded him of the stuff the Communists had crapped out all over Poland in the fifties and sixties.

Slawek was two weeks late with payment and as full of bullshit as ever. The power hammer Janusz had supplied over a month ago, still labelled *'Property of the Department of Transport'* stood propped against the cream-coloured bulk of an American-style Smeg. Janusz knew that the fancy fridge – along with the rest of the gleaming kitchen appliances – was missing the manufacturer's serial number, because he had removed it himself with an angle grinder before delivery.

'The quicker I finish this job, the quicker I get paid – and you get paid,' said the young man, taking advantage of the pause in hostilities.

Janusz had spent enough of his youth on building sites to see past the superficial gloss to the flat's shoddy finish. He'd have got a bollocking for the slapdash plastering, and for using non-galvanised screws in the cooker hood, which would rust solid at the first blast of kitchen steam. All the same, it did look almost finished. He sighed. As much as he needed the cash, he had to admit Slawek had a point.

He thumped him once more, half-heartedly, against the wall. 'Slawek, you are a pointless fucking hand-job.' But Slawek caught the change of tone, and sure enough, the big man suddenly dropped him with a gesture of disgust.

'One more week – and you screw me around next time, they'll have to pull that jackhammer out of your arse.'

'*Tak, tak.* I really appreciate it, panie Kiszka.' Slawek practically skipped as he followed Janusz to the door. 'Maybe I can do some small job for you, to say thanks?'

That brought an explosion of laughter from Janusz. 'I wouldn't let you build me a cat flap!' he said over his shoulder. Slawek's renovation of a three-storey Georgian townhouse in Notting Hill was infamous in the Polish community: he'd knocked down a supporting wall and created W11's first Georgian bungalow. The local council – not to mention the client, an unhappy Russian billionaire – was still looking for him. Slawek's face crumpled in protest.

'One mistake doesn't make me a bad builder,' he shouted down the corridor after Janusz as the lift doors closed behind him.

Three floors down, a laughing group of young men piled in, carrying tools and paint kettles. Janusz saw that they all wore number one crew cuts – the ultra-short cut that had once been the badge of a recently completed stint in the military. Many young Poles apparently still favoured it, even though compulsory national service had been abandoned a year or more back.

On seeing the older man, they quieted and bobbed their heads: '*Dzien dobry, panu,*' using the respectful form

7

of address. Good lads, thought Janusz. But within seconds, their chatter, the closeness of their bodies, and the press of the lift wall at his back started to stir the old feeling of dread in the pit of his stomach. His breathing grew shallow and the vaporous tang of solvent seemed to suck the air from his lungs.

As the lift plunged, the tallest one met his eye, grinned, and with an unpleasant jolt, Janusz saw his younger self reflected back at him, the unfinished features and gangly limbs, the absurd optimism. Then, without warning, another image, pin-sharp and even less welcome: Iza's face, freckled, laughing as she clattered down the stairs of the university. He squeezed his eyes shut, willing away the other memories.

The helmeted ranks of ZOMO advancing through blizzarding snow, the obscene thump thump of lead-filled truncheons striking human flesh.

His breathing ragged now, Janusz hit the button for the next floor and pushed past the startled boys to the door, muttering some excuse. He took the remaining five flights down to the lobby at a run. Out in the street, he sucked in life-saving lungfuls of the chilly spring air.

Kurwa mac! Was he constantly to be reminded of the past by this deluge of young Poles?

'Bloody foreigners,' he said out loud, startling an old lady waiting at the bus stop. Suppressing a grin, he murmured an apology and headed to the café across the street.

Janusz inhaled the savoury aromas emanating from the café's kitchen as he studied the menu, chalked up on a blackboard.

'Dla pana?' asked the fair-haired, plump-cheeked girl behind the counter, pen and pad poised.

'Your *bigos*. Is it homemade or out of a tin?' he asked. She made as if to cuff the side of his head. He ducked, grinning, and took his glass of lemon tea – the real thing, not some powdered rubbish – to the only empty table, beside a window made opaque by the café's steamy fug.

The *Polska Kuchnia*, or Polish Kitchen, was a good half mile from the commotion of the Olympic site, but the place was packed with groups of construction workers in cement-stained work clothes filling up on the solid, comforting food of home: *pierogi, golabki, flaki*. These were the men turning the architects' blueprints into reality: the stadium, the velodrome, the athletes' village, as well as the high-rise apartment blocks shooting up around the edge of the five-hundred-acre site.

The young couple who ran the place had tried to make it more homely than the standard East End greasy spoon: there were checked tablecloths, brightly coloured bread baskets, even a crocus in a jam jar at every table. If it weren't for the growl of passing lorries, thought Janusz, you could almost pretend you were in a little restaurant somewhere in the Tatra Mountains.

Just as the girl set down his hunter's stew – and it looked like a good one, with slivers of duck, as well as the usual pork and *kielbasa*, poking through the sauerkraut – the street door crashed open and Oskar arrived.

Short, balding and barrel-chested, Oskar scoured the café with a belligerent stare, and found his target – a group of young guys in a corner laughing and joking over the remains of their meal. Planting his legs apart, he let fly with a volley of Polish.

'What in the name of the Virgin are you still doing here, you sisterfuckers?' he boomed. 'What did I tell you yesterday? If you are late back again I'll have the contractor on the blower cutting my balls off.'

The lads scrambled to their feet, a couple of them falling over their chair legs in their haste to get to the door, amid a barrage of laughter from the café's other occupants, who'd stopped eating to enjoy the show. But Oskar was merciless.

'Don't try to hide your ugly mush from me, Karol, you cocksucker. Maybe your mummy did name you after the fucking Pope, God rest his soul,' he made the sign of the cross without pausing for breath, 'but I still haven't forgotten that granite worktop you wrote off and I'm gonna fuck you up the *dupa* on payday.'

As the last of them scurried out, heads down, Oskar subsided, satisfied. Then, seeing Janusz, his face split in a grin. '*Czesc*, Janek!'

Janusz stood to greet his friend and, without thinking, put out his hand. Oskar roared with laughter and, ignoring it, embraced his mate in a full bear hug, kissing him on alternate cheeks three times. Janusz cleared his throat: between Poles the effusive greeting was no big deal, but after two decades in England, it made him squirm.

Oskar put a hand on one hip and mimicked an effete handshake as he sat down. 'You've been in England too long, mate. Soon you'll be wanting to fuck with men!' He chuckled delightedly at his joke.

Janusz smiled wearily. He loved Oskar like a wayward kid brother – a friendship that dated back to their first day of military service in 1980 – but he could be a pain in the ass. He could picture it still. A rainy day behind the barbed wire of Camp 117 in the Kashubian Lakeland,

and the line of new conscripts, heads newly shorn and uniforms at least two sizes too big, looking more like bedraggled baby birds than soldiers. Even now the memory prompted a flare of anger. At seventeen, he and Oskar – *all* those young men – should have been full of hope. Instead, all they'd had to look forward to was endless months training for the threat of invasion by Western imperialist forces – and then what? Martial law, curfews and rationing . . . the dreary *realpolitik* of the socialist dream.

Oskar waved a pudgy hand at the table where his dawdling workers had sat. 'Seriously though,' he said, 'these kids don't know how easy their life is these days. Do they have any idea what site work was like here in the eighties? Twelve-hour shifts, no "*health and safety*". Never mind an hour off for lunch, we didn't even get a fucking tea break.'

Janusz grunted his agreement. 'And if you wanted goggles or ear defenders, you had to buy them yourself,' he said, tearing apart a piece of bread.

Oskar used his sleeve to wipe a porthole in the condensation of the window and peered out at the traffic. 'Remember that *chuj*,' he mused, 'The Paddy foreman on the M25 job – the guy who treated us like dogs?'

'The one whose thermos you pissed in?' asked Janusz, raising an eyebrow.

'Yeah, that's the one,' said Oskar, a beatific grin spreading across his chubby face.

'Fuck your mother,' he said, peering at Janusz's plate. 'What is that shit you're eating?' – then, to the girl who had just arrived to take his order – 'The *bigos* for me, too, darling. It looks delicious.'

After she had left, Janusz finished his last mouthful and pushed the plate away. 'Too much paprika, perhaps, and the duck was a little overcooked, but not bad,' he said with a judicious nod. He pulled out his box of cigars, then, remembering the crazy no smoking laws, reached for a toothpick instead.

'Listen Oskar, I still want the booze, but I've got a problem. Any chance of you waiting a couple of weeks for the cash?'

Oskar, mouth full of good rye bread, mumbled: 'Don't tell me – that donkey Slawek made a *kutas* of you?'

He helped himself to a slurp of Janusz's lemon tea, shaking his head. 'I can stand you half a dozen cases, mate, but not much more than that. I've got no slack right now.' A secret smile crept along his lips. 'I just sent five hundred home so Madam can buy a new living room carpet.'

'I thought you were saving up so you could go home for good?' said Janusz. 'You'll be here for ever if you let Gosia spend all your *smalec* on carpets.'

Oskar belched philosophically. 'Like my father used to say: "The woman cries before the wedding; the man after."'

The girl put a plate of *bigos* in front of Oskar, whose eyes rounded with childlike greed. 'Duck!' he exclaimed indistinctly through his first mouthful.

Ever since Janusz had known him, Oskar had worked like a navvie to support Gosia and the kids. They had slogged together through the night building motorway bridges in the eighties – back-breaking twelve-hour shifts – but come next day's rush hour, when Janusz was still in bed, Oskar would be standing in a lay-by on the A4, flogging hothouse roses to motorists heading home. Even now, alongside his job as foreman for one of the biggest Olympic site contractors, he still found time for what he called his 'beverage import business'.

It amounted to half a dozen clapped-out Transit vans that plied the cross-channel ferry routes, bringing in cases of cheap booze and cartons of cigarettes to sell on to traders like Janusz. The bottles of spirits ended up on optics in private clubs where no one questioned the 'NOT FOR RESALE' label, especially since the bottles carried another reassuring promise: 'EXPORT STRENGTH'.

'Listen,' said Oskar, with a mischievous look, 'if you're short of cash, I could always get you a shift on the site.' Dropping his fork he grabbed Janusz's hand, and turning it over to check the palm, chuckled. *Kurwa!* All this *wheeling and dealing'* – he used the English phrase – 'gave you hands like a schoolgirl's! You wouldn't last five minutes on a real job.' He scooped up another tottering forkful of *bigos*. 'You want to come over later, watch some football?'

'I can't tonight,' said Janusz. 'I've got a ticket for a lecture at the Royal Institute – one of the physicists from the CERN project.'

Oskar frowned. 'That big metal doughnut in Switzerland – the one that keeps blowing a fuse?' he asked. 'Something to do with the First Bang?'

Janusz nodded – it was easier.

'They say the universe will collapse one day, you know,' said Oskar, adopting a scholarly air. He clapped his hands to demonstrate: *'Pfouff!* Down to the size of a beach ball.' Before he could offer any further cosmological insights, the café door rattled open to admit three lanky buzz-cut youngsters, dwarfed by their rucksacks.

Their loud voices exuded confidence, but the way the trio hung close together, shoulders almost touching, told the real story. First-timers, thought Janusz, straight off the 0830 Ryanair flight from Warsaw. When the tallest one spotted Oskar his relief was palpable.

Joining the men at their table, the boys greeted them politely. Oskar balled his checked napkin and after wiping the grease from his lips, punched out a number on his mobile.

'*Czesc*, Wassily, you old hedgehog-fucker,' he bellowed. 'You still looking for ground-breakers? I've got three beauties for you – real musclemen.' He winked at Janusz. The youngsters exchanged apprehensive glances, shrugged. 'I'll bring them over now.'

Oskar levered himself up from the table on powerful arms with a sigh. 'Some of us have man's work to do,' he told Janusz. 'I'll put your name on a dozen cases, *kolego*, but if you can get cash for more by tomorrow, let me know.'

Oskar departed, trailed by his clutch of new recruits, but at the café's threshold he turned.

'Remember what we used to say when we were skinny-arsed conscripts shivering in the barracks?' he shouted to Janusz. 'Life is like toilet paper . . .'

Janusz finished the saying for him: '. . . very long and full of crap.'

The rectangle of oak slid open and Janusz bent his head to the aperture.

'I present myself before the Holy Confession, for I have offended God.'

He shifted in his creaking seat and coughed, a bassy

smoker's rumble. Through the wire mesh, he could make out Father Piotr Pietruski's reassuring profile, topped by his unruly shock of white hair.

'It has been, uh, three months since my last confession,' he said.

'Six, *faktycznie*,' corrected the priest. 'I did hope that we would see you at Midnight Mass, at least.'

'I'm sorry, father. I've had a lot of . . . business to attend to.'

Unconsciously, he clenched his right hand, stretching the grazed knuckles white.

The priest tugged at his earlobe – it was a familiar gesture, but whether it signalled resignation, or exasperation, Janusz never could tell. He felt a surge of affection for the old guy: Father Pietruski had always looked out for him, from that first morning more than two decades ago when he'd showed up here after a 48-hour bender, rain-soaked, wild-eyed and stinking of *wodka*.

Back then, before every inner-city high street had its own *Polski Sklep*, homesick Poles had beat a path to St Stanislaus, hidden away down an Islington back street. English Catholic churches, all modern steel and concrete, were unappealing, but St Stan's was solid, nineteenth century, its stone structure curvaceous as a mother's cheek, and since the mass was conducted in Polish it had felt almost like being at home. And the shop in its crypt where you could buy real *kielbasa*, cheesecake and plums in chocolate, didn't hurt either.

These days he wasn't even sure he still believed in all the mumbo jumbo, so why did he still come? Partly, he supposed, because the church felt like the last remaining pillar of the old Poland, a place where respect and honour were valued above all else. Or maybe because he'd never forget how Father Pietruski had found the drunken boy a bed, fed him lemon tea, and later on, put him in touch with a foreman looking for site labourers.

Even if it meant the old bastard never got off his case.

'Have there been any recent incidents of violence?' asked the priest.

'One scumbag who was beating his wife. She came to me for help.'

'And?'

'I like to help women. I helped her. He decided to get another hobby,' Janusz shrugged, pressing a smile from his lips. Better not to mention the woman in question was his girlfriend.

The older man sighed. It was never straightforward with this one: his methods might be unsanctionable, but his instincts were often sound.

'Anything else to trouble your immortal soul?' Janusz detected a trace of sarcasm.

'Sins of the flesh, father.' A sudden image: a rumpled bed, the rosy S of a woman's naked back, Kasia's, framed by an oblong of light. 'The normal things.'

'These "things" are not *normalne*. You are a married man: that sacrament is indissoluble!' The priest actually rapped out each syllable with his knuckles on the mesh.

The old fellow had – unusually for him – raised his voice, stirring up a little rush of whispers from outside the box, where, Janusz knew, a bevy of old dears would be waiting to confess their imagined sins. Maybe the priest was right, but what was he supposed to do? He and Marta had read the last rites over their marriage long ago, and he wasn't cut out to be a monk.

'Yes, father,' Janusz bowed his head a fraction. The exchange didn't alter much with the years. It was a pain, yes, to be lectured, but like the church's smell – incense, spent candlewicks and ancient dust – it was strangely comforting, too.

'I know you and Marta have been estranged for many years,' Father Pietruski continued, his voice lower, but still firm. 'Nonetheless, you *must* try again – for the sake of the boy, at least. Build some bridges with her, hmm?'

Janusz moved his head in a gesture that he hoped might pass for assent. The priest waited for something less ambiguous – in vain.

'Say three Hail Mary's and the act of contrition,' he said, blessing Janusz with his right hand, 'And I'll meet you at The Eagle in half an hour.'

Janusz stood and stooped to leave the box, the step loosing off a gunshot crack. The ladies outside rustled with excitement, like birds disturbed at their roost.

'*Dzien dobry, paniom*,' he bowed, recognising many of the faces. They chirped greetings back, but one, sitting in the middle of the pew, grasped his arm as he tried to pass.

There was no escape. Pani Rulewska's upright posture and the deference of the other women marked her out as their leader, even though she was in her late fifties, a good couple of decades their junior. He paused, bowing his head a fraction.

She wore a dark red skirt suit of some rich, soft material, which even he could see was beautifully tailored. He recalled that she owned a designer clothes factory in the East End, and never let anyone forget that a gown created by her Polish seamstresses had once graced the shoulders of Princess Diana.

'Now, panie Kiszka, I hope that we can count on your support in the forthcoming patriotic event?' she demanded in her rather grating voice.

Patriotic event? He felt a flutter of panic, as though he was eight years old again, and unable to remember the next line of his catechism.

'The election?' she prompted. 'The older people, of course, can be relied on, but the youngsters, the ones here, they are another matter. They are away from home and family, they are led astray by *straszne* English habits. Drinking, sex, drugs . . .' Pani Rulewska shook her head. 'This is no longer the England we once loved.'

The other women bobbed their heads, murmuring assent. He nodded, too, and not entirely out of politeness: the England he'd found a quarter of a century ago might have been duller and greyer, but hadn't it also been gentler, and more civilised? *Or am I just getting old and cantankerous?* he wondered.

'You are known, and respected – mostly . . .' she qualified. 'You can reach the young ones, tell them how the new president will rebuild the country and give them all jobs back home where they belong.'

Despite Janusz's instinctive distrust of politicians, the Renaissance Party candidate did seem to offer Poland a way out of the predicament it found itself in after twenty years of democracy. Sure, the economy had bounced back after decades of Communist mismanagement, but there still weren't enough well-paid jobs to prevent the exodus of a million or more young people overseas, most of them to the UK. The country's graceful Hapsburgian squares were fast disappearing beneath a deluge of fast-food chains and gangs of stag-partying Brits, and unless

Poland's exiled generation could be lured back home soon, he feared for his country's identity.

Janusz liked the *Partia Renasans'* big idea, a massive regeneration programme to create jobs and attract the exiles home – and the way it reunited the alliance of the church, unions and intelligentsia, which in the eighties had defeated the Communist regime under the Solidarity banner. The Party had already won the *Sejm* and the Senate, and now its leader, Edward Zamorski – a respected veteran of *Solidarnosc,* a man who'd endured repeated incarceration and beatings during the fight for democracy – looked set to become president.

Which was all well and good, but knocking on people's doors wearing a party T-shirt wasn't really up Janusz's street. So after murmuring a few vague words of support, hedged with protestations of masculine busyness, he gave the old dears his most gallant bow, and made a quick exit, feeling their eyes on his back all the way up the side aisle.

At the last alcove, he paused under the gentle gaze of a blue-gowned plaster Mary, lit by a shimmering forest of red perspex tea lights, and, asking forgiveness for his white lie, crossed himself.

With an hour or more to go before the evening rush, the only sound in The Eagle and Child opposite Islington Green was the clink of glasses being washed and stacked.

Janusz ordered a bottle of Tyskie for himself and a bisongrass *wodka* for the priest. When he'd first arrived in London these drinks were exotic, practically unheard of outside the Polish community, but the mass influx of young Poles that followed EU membership changed all that. It still made him chuckle to hear English voices struggling to order Wyborowa, Okocim, Zubrowka.

He took the drinks out to the 'beer garden', a stretch of grey decking pocked with cigarette burns, ringed by a few wind-battered clumps of pampas grass. He chose a table under a gas heater: it was a bitter day, but a drink without a smoke, well, wasn't a drink.

'More sins of the flesh?' asked Father Pietruski, clapping Janusz on the shoulder just as he was lighting his cigar. The old man's manner was friendly, mischievous even, now he was off duty.

'To your health,' said the priest, taking a warming sip of *wodka*. 'So how is . . . "business"?' – the sardonic quotation marks were audible.

'Not so good. A few cash-flow problems – till I collect from a couple of bastards who owe me.'

The priest locked eyes with Janusz over the lip of his glass.

'Using no more than my persuasive skills, father.' A conciliatory grin creased his slab-like face.

'To think you were once the top student in your year. And not just at any university: at Jagiellonski!' mused the priest, for perhaps the hundredth time.

Janusz permitted himself a brief glance skywards.

'*Such* a fine brain, you had – Professor Zygurski told me,' said the priest, shaking his head. 'Of course, theology would have been more fitting than science, but, still, what a waste of God-given talent.'

'It wasn't a time for writing essays,' shot back Janusz. 'How could I sit on my backside in a cosy lecture theatre talking about Schrodinger's cat while people were getting beaten to pulp in the streets?' Pushing his free hand through his hair he added in a brooding undertone, 'Although maybe I should just have carried on fucking about with Bunsen burners.'

The priest pulled at his earlobe, decided to let the profanity go. The early eighties had been a disruptive and dangerous era for everyone, he reflected – especially the young. The protests organised by Solidarity adhered largely to the principle of peaceful protest but were met, inevitably, by the batons and bullets of the Communist regime. In more normal times, Janusz might have gone on to match, or even outshine, the achievements of his father, a highly regarded professor of physics at Gdansk University, but soon after General Jaruzelski declared martial law, the boy had abandoned his studies to join the thrilling battle for democracy on the streets. Then, just as suddenly, he had left for England – abandoning the young wife he'd married just weeks before. When Janusz had turned up at St Stanislaus, he was clearly a soul in torment, and although Father Pietruski had never discovered the root of the trouble, one thing was certain – whatever happened back then cast a shadow over him still.

He studied the big man with the troubled eyes opposite him. This child of God would never be a particularly observant Catholic, perhaps, but the priest was sure of one thing: he was possessed of a Christian soul, and when the new government was elected – by God's grace – it was to be hoped that men such as he would return home to rebuild the country.

He leaned across and tapped Janusz on the back of the hand.

'I may have a small job for you,' he said. 'Something *honorowego* – to keep you out of trouble – and use that brain of yours. A matter that pani Tosik brought to me in confession.'

Janusz raised an eyebrow.

'And expressly permitted me to take beyond the sacred confines of the confessional. One of the girls, a waitress in the restaurant, has gone missing.'

'With the takings?'

'No, no, a God-fearing girl,' said the priest. 'She always attended mass. She'd only been here a few weeks, waiting tables, plus a little modelling work.' Janusz raised an eyebrow and grinned through his cloud of smoke.

'Yes, a very beautiful young woman, but a good girl and a hard worker. She disappeared two weeks ago without a word, and pani Tosik is worried out of her skin. She doesn't want to call the police, *naturalnie*.'

Janusz inclined his head in understanding. Maybe Poles were insubordinate by nature, or maybe it was a reaction to forty years of brutal foreign rule – either way, they didn't roll out the welcome mat for the cops.

'So? She's found a boyfriend who's getting rich doing loft conversions,' he said, flicking a fat inch of ash off his cigar.

'Maybe so, but the girl's mother back home hasn't heard from her and pani Tosik feels terribly guilty. She wants her tracked down,' he met Janusz's eyes, 'And she'll pay good money.' Janusz couldn't help smiling at the old man's transparent look of guile as he delivered his trump card.

Finding a missing person was hard work and involved lots of schlepping round on the tube, which he loathed – but it was common knowledge that pani Tosik was loaded, and he could certainly do with the cash.

Father Pietruski drained the last of his drink and stood to go to the bar.

'Anyway, I suggested you – God forgive me.'

Two

The sky over the Thames was a milky, benevolent blue, but a freezing wind raked Detective Constable Natalie Kershaw's face as the fast-response Targa tore over the steely water. As the speedboat swept under Tower Bridge, engine noise booming off the iron stanchions, the uniformed helmsman sneaked a sideways look at her profile, the blonde hair scraped back in a businesslike ponytail. He wondered if he dared ask her out. Probably not. She might only come up to his armpit, but she looked like a ball breaker – typical CID female.

Kershaw was miles away, thinking about her dad, scanning the southern bank for the Bermondsey wharf where he had hauled coke as a warehouseman in the sixties – his first job. He'd pointed it out to her from a tour boat – an outing they'd taken a couple of years ago, just before he'd died. She finally clocked his warehouse – harder to recognise now its hundred-year-old patina of coal smoke had been sandblasted off. Fancy new balconies, too, at the upper windows: all the signs of the warehouse's new life as swanky apartments for City bankers – *Yeah, a right bunch of bankers,* she heard him say. He'd be pleased as punch to see her now, a detective out on her first suspicious death.

When her DS had dropped it on her that morning she'd been a bit hacked off – she already had to go up west for a court case, and this job meant her racing straight back to Wapping. Anyway, surely a floater pulled out of the Thames was a job for a uniform? But telling the Sarge that, however diplomatically, had been a bad move, she realised, almost as soon as the words were out of her mouth. Worse, she was on early turn this week, so this had all gone off at 0730 hours, and DS Bacon, known to his constables, inevitably, as Streaky, was *not* a morning person. He had torn a big fat strip off her in front of two of the guys.

'Let's get one thing straight, Kershaw – you'll do whatever fucking job I throw at you and say thank you, Sarge, can I get you a cup of tea, Sarge. If I hear any more of your cheeky backchat I'll have you back on Romford Rd wearing a lid faster than you can say diversity awareness.'

Streaky was in his fifties, old-school CID to his fag-stained fingertips, and Kershaw suspected that in his book, female detectives were good for one thing: interviewing witnesses in rape, domestic violence and broken-baby cases.

Of course she could complain to the Guv, DI Bellwether. Streaky's Neanderthal management style – the swearing, the borderline sexism, his old-school insistence on addressing DCs by their surnames – it was all a total no-no these days, but she'd rather keep her mouth shut and get on with it. You needed a thick skin to be in the job. If she got stick now and again for being a young, blonde female – and therefore brainless – she could give as good as she got. Anyway, everyone copped it for something. Being fat, thin, Northern, ginger, having a funny name, having a boring name, talking posh, talking Cockney, anything. At her first nick, one poor bastard had made the mistake of letting on that he did karate, and the next day his desk disappeared under a deluge of Chinese take-away menus and house bricks. She couldn't even remember his real name, because after that everybody – even the girls on switchboard – called him Chop Suey.

Giving – and taking – good banter was about bonding, fitting in, being part of a unit. If you couldn't take friendly abuse from fellow cops you were finished, game over. One thing she was sure of: Natalie Kershaw wasn't going to end up one of those sad cases moaning about sexism at an employment tribunal. If she hadn't made Sergeant by the time she turned thirty, in three years' time, she'd pack it in and do something else.

Anyway, once she'd had a proper look at the job Streaky had thrown her, she thought maybe it wasn't so lame after all. The floater had come up naked, and you didn't have to be Sherlock Holmes to know that suicides don't generally get their kit off before chucking themselves in the river. So maybe it was a good call to send a detective to have a look before the pathologist started slicing and dicing – Streaky might be a dinosaur in a bad suit, but occasionally he showed signs of being a good cop.

The Targa overtook a tourist boat – the occupants craning to check out the cop at the helm and his attractive plain-clothes passenger – and within seconds, they were pulling up at a long blue jetty on the north shore in front of Wapping Police Station. Kershaw gave the uniform a smile, but ignored his outstretched hand to step down from the bobbing boat unaided. She headed for the nick, a Victorian building with more curlicues and columns than a footballer's wedding cake, but after a few steps his shout made her turn. Grinning, he pointed across the jetty to an oblong tent of blue tarpaulin, then, revving the Targa's engine unnecessarily, he sped off.

He was cute, she thought. Why don't guys like that ever ask me out?

She pulled the tarpaulin flap open and ducked inside. Just at that moment two river cops were unloading the contents of a black body bag into a shallow stainless steel bath, about twice the size of the one in her flat. The darkly slicked head of a girl, followed by her naked body, slithered out of the bag in an obscene parody of birth.

'Fuck,' muttered Kershaw, caught unawares. It wasn't her first stiff – as a probationer she'd been sent on a call to a tower block in Poplar after some neighbours reported a foul liquid seeping through their ceiling. In the upstairs flat she'd found the remains of an old guy who'd been dead in his armchair for two weeks in front of a two-bar fire. He looked like a giant half-melted candle.

But she had to admit this one was a shocker. The girl's skin was purplish and mottled, the breasts and stomach bore gaping slashes, and here and there were raw patches the size of a man's hand, as though someone had taken a blowtorch to the body. The face was fairly intact, except for the eyes, which were now just two blackened empty pits.

One of the PCs left, and the other gave her the rundown.

He was a middle-aged, lifelong-plod type: a bit world-weary, but straight as a die, which was a relief, because she hadn't anticipated the sheer embarrassment factor of looking over a naked female with a guy old enough to be her dad.

'A runner spotted her on the foreshore at low tide,' he told her. 'Just this side of the Thames Barrier. We get quite a few floaters washed up on the sandbank there.'

Kershaw pulled out a notepad and pencil. 'She didn't necessarily go in the water round there, though?'

He shook his head. 'Could have drifted anything from fifty yards to ten miles downstream – all we can say is she went in somewhere on the tidal section. They can travel a mile a day, or more,' giving her more than he needed to, info she could file away for future use.

'What about the eyes,' she said, nodding toward the empty pits. 'I'm guessing . . . rats? Birds?'

'Eels, probably,' he said. 'Greedy buggers. The type people eat jellied. Personally, I prefer a prawn cocktail . . .'

They shared a grin over the eyeless head.

'And the injuries?' asked Kershaw. 'Any chance they could be pre-mortem?'

He bent to examine the deepest wound, through which the pale glimmer of the girl's ribcage could be seen, and twisted his mouth sceptically: 'Hard to say. Boats and barges can do a lot of damage, and she's probably been in over a week. When it's cold they stay under longer – the stomach gases take more time to build up.'

Moving up to the head, Kershaw bent to study the girl's face, trying to ignore the yellowish foam bubbling out of her nostrils. The skin was puffy from prolonged immersion, which made it hard to tell what she might have looked like in life, but from her slim figure Kershaw guessed she was in her mid to late twenties – making them round about the same age. She was seized by a sudden need to know the girl's identity.

'Will we get prints off her?' she asked the PC.

With a latex-gloved hand, he turned the girl's left wrist palm-upwards to reveal the underside of her fingers, which were bloated and wrinkled, the skin starting to peel.

'Washerwoman's hands,' he said, with a shake of the head. 'You'll get bugger all off them. We'll take DNA samples, though – maybe you can get your budget manager to approve a test. The reference is DB16.'

Kershaw scribbled on her pad. 'The sixteenth dead body you've found this year?' she asked.

'Yeah. And we're not even four months in yet.'

The smell emanating from the body filled the tent now. A not-unpleasant riverine tang, but with a darker under-note that reminded Kershaw of mushrooms left in the fridge too long. She felt deflated, disappointed not to find something more . . . concrete. But then she thought: don't be daft, Nat, did you really think you'd pitch up and spot something to solve the case, *Prime Suspect* style?

'There's no way she'd be naked, is there, if it was just suicide?' she asked, suddenly anxious that the girl might turn out to be just another random jumper. 'I mean her clothes, they couldn't have come off by themselves, in the water?'

He turned his mouth down at the corners. 'I've never heard of a current removing a bra and pants.' They avoided each other's eyes. 'No, I'd say she was definitely naked when she went in,' he went on. 'And this time of year, I shouldn't think she was skinny dipping.'

He bent to reach into a bag at his feet. 'I'd better get on with the samples while she's fresh,' he said, and started to line up plastic vials on a nearby trestle table.

Left alone with the body, Kershaw noticed that the girl's shoulder-length hair was drying at the ends, turning it a bright coppery gold. It was a shade her dad used to call *Titian*, she remembered, out of nowhere.

Her gaze fell on the girl's left hand. It lay as the cop had left it, palm-up on the stainless steel, fingers slightly crooked, suggesting helplessness – or entreaty. A gust of wind whipped the tarpaulin flap open with a crack, making her jump.

'I almost forgot,' said the cop, returning to Kershaw's side. 'There is one bit of good news.' Cupping his gloved hand under the girl's hip, he tilted her body.

Near the base of the spine, just above the swell of the girl's buttock, Kershaw could see what looked like a stain beneath the waterlogged whiteness of the skin. Bending closer, she realised it was a tattoo – an indigo heart, amateurish-looking, enclosing two names, obviously foreign: *Pawel* and *Ela*.

'Gives you a head start on ID-ing her,' the cop said, setting the body back down with surprising gentleness.

Three

The rectangle of plastic snapped open as the last coin clinked through the slot, and Janusz stooped to his peephole. Beyond it, in the centre of a dimly lit windowless room, a slender naked girl writhed around a floor-to-ceiling pole under a shower of multicoloured lights.

Every trace of her body hair had been shaved or plucked away, making her nakedness absolute, apart from a single stud in her navel. The girl's movements, timed to the grinding rock music, had a natural grace, but her made-up face was expressionless and her gaze focused on some distant point. Her long fingernails struck the only incongruous note – painted not the usual scarlet, but jet-black.

Janusz watched just long enough to make sure it was Kasia, then straightened and checked his watch, frowning, and tried to block out the alkaline reek of old semen in his cubicle. The music came to an end, only to be followed by another, smoochier number. Cursing softly, he glanced up at the ceiling and reached into his pocket.

He could still hear the smoke alarm wailing as he leant against the club's rear wall enjoying his smoke – his fourth, or maybe fifth, cigar of the day. The last punter, a paunchy guy in his forties wearing a chalk-stripe suit, stumbled out of the fire exit, head bent as he finished fastening his fly. Noticing the big man in the old-fashioned trench coat, he straightened, and pulling out a pack of cigarettes, asked for a light.

Janusz sparked his lighter, although the guy had to bend forward to reach the flame. Then, blowing out a stream of smoke, the punter planted his feet apart and jabbed his chin over his shoulder. 'Did you see the bird in there?' he asked, with a man-to-man chuckle. 'I'll bet that's a road well travelled.'

Janusz's face remained impassive, so the guy didn't notice his right hand clench reflexively into a fist, nor realise how close he was skating to a broken jaw.

'I wouldn't know,' said Janusz, taking an unhurried draw on his cigar. 'I just work here sometimes.'

The guy gave him an assessing look, trying to work out the accent – posh-sounding, but some foreign in there, too. 'Yeah? You a bouncer then?'

Janusz shook his head.

'Work behind the bar?'

Another shake. Then Janusz looked the guy in the face properly for the first time.

'Look, it's supposed to be hush-hush,' he said, 'but what the hell, today's my last day in the job.' He ground his cigar stub out on the wall and discarded it, then leaned closer. 'I rig the hidden cameras in the peepshow booths,' he said in a conspiratorial murmur.

The guy stared at him: 'Cameras? I've never seen a camera in there.'

Janusz shrugged. 'That's because I'm pretty good at my job.'

The guy's face was going red now. 'So you're telling me . . . they *film* the blokes watching the shows?'

Janusz dipped his head sideways in regretful assent.

'Why the fu . . . ?' the guy's voice held a mixture of anger and foreboding.

'It's a live feed to the internet,' said Janusz. 'Apparently, a lot of people will pay good money to watch guys . . . you know . . .', and with an economical gesture he demonstrated the activity he was too polite to put into words.

Now, the guy's mouth was opening and shutting like a Christmas carp, and Janusz wondered if he was going to have a stroke or something.

'It's a . . . It's a . . . *disgrace*,' he croaked. He waved a finger up at Janusz, 'I'm going to . . .' and then brandished it at the back door of the club, 'I'll report them to . . .' Then he wheeled around and went off down the Soho alleyway, still ranting and waving his arms.

Just then, the girl emerged from the club, wrapped in a black towelling dressing gown. She peered at the retreating figure, who was shouting something about the Human Rights Act, and then up at Janusz.

'What's with that guy?' she asked.

'I don't know,' he said, with a shrug. 'London is full of crazy people.'

She shot him a suspicious look. 'You haven't been telling the customers stories again?' He shook his head, avoiding her eyes, but had to suck in his cheeks to keep from grinning.

Kasia pulled the robe tighter around her – it was cold – and reached into the pocket for cigarettes. 'You think you're so funny, Janusz,' she said. 'But if the boss finds out he'll kick your *dupe*.' She raised her chin in the direction of the smoke alarm, which had now settled to a strident beeping: 'And I suppose that's nothing to do with you either?'

The unchivalrous daylight added ten years or more to her face, he thought, but she could still pass for thirty-five, thirty even, no problem.

'I got bored,' he said.

She widened her eyes in mock reproach. 'Oh, a nice compliment. You don't like my show?'

'Nice body. *Piekne*,' he said. 'But then I knew that already,' levelling his amused gaze at her. She held the look, trying to look stern, but one side of her mouth lifted, despite herself: the crooked smile that filled his daydreams.

She bent her dark blonde head to his lighter, steadying his hand a beat longer than she needed to, making his stomach trip. It was funny, but he could never quite connect the woman in front of him with the one he'd seen pole-dancing minutes earlier. That girl was hot stuff, no question, but she didn't make his insides polka like Kasia did. His jaw tensed as he noticed the yellow tidemark of an old bruise that her make-up couldn't quite conceal along her cheekbone.

'Listen, Kasia. I paid that *chuj* Steve a visit this morning.'

Kasia's hand jumped to her face.

'*Kurwa!*' the curse slipped out before her lips could catch it, '. . . and?'

He looked amused: she hardly ever swore, and was

34

probably making a mental note to take her misdemeanor to confession.

'I made the case to him that a man does not strike a woman, not even his own wife.' The words were old-fashioned and his deep voice was reasonable – but his eyes had suddenly gone cold.

She pulled the lapels of her gown closer. 'What did he say?'

'My impression was I left him a reformed character,' he said. 'But he knows that I am happy to continue our . . . discussions if necessary.'

She said nothing, but reached out and briefly touched her cold hands to the sides of his face.

He pulled back a fraction: he didn't know why, but the gesture made him angrier than her pig of a husband and his wife-beating habits. Why did a woman like her stay with such a man? Kasia came from a good family and was as smart as a fox – she had a degree from the film school where Polanski and Kieslowski had studied, for Christ's sake! But he'd already heard her answer to that: 'love can die but marriage lives for ever.' And this sleazy job of hers was the couple's only income. Half a million Poles managed to carve out a living here, but born and bred Londoner Steve could never find work. It was too easy to get by on benefit in this country, he reflected, not for the first time.

No point telling her to leave him, anyway. Like all Polish women she was obstinate as hell, and would tell him to go fuck himself. To cover his expression he dropped his cigar stub and ground it underfoot.

As Kasia turned away to blow a stream of smoke down the street, he let his eyes rest for a moment on her half-averted profile, her long, beautiful nose. It was what he'd first noticed about her that day, when he'd been lugging boxes of booze from the van to this same door.

'I could come to your place tomorrow?' she said, still turned away, a trace of uncertainty in the upward inflection.

His anger slid away at that, replaced by more complicated emotions. Maybe that night they'd spent together two weeks earlier hadn't just been a one-off. He pushed his hands in his pockets and gazed up at the roofline.

'Sure, why not. And tell Ray I've got a delivery of Wyborowa coming in next week if he's interested.'

What the hell. Like his mother used to say, he always ran to meet trouble halfway.

An hour later, Janusz made his way north eastwards along Essex Road, head down against a biting wind. He was heading for pani Tosik's restaurant to follow up the runaway waitress story Father Pietruski had told him about. As one of the best-connected people in London's *Polonia*, Janusz had picked up more than a few missing persons jobs over the years. His near-perfect English helped, even if his language primers – British war movies he'd watched as a kid, and later, eighties US cop shows – had spiced his vocabulary with some colourful and outmoded phrases.

This job sounded like all the rest: parents back home fretting because their daughter hadn't phoned home for a few weeks. It was always a young girl, invariably 'God-fearing and steady' – he'd never once heard a runaway described as *kaprysna* – and the outcome was always the same, too. He'd find her living in sin with a boyfriend in some godforsaken bedsit. She'd cry a little, grieving her lost virginity, and after a few stern words, would promise to phone home to Mama.

It occurred to him that this was pretty much how Kasia's life in London had unfolded when she'd come over after her film degree. She told him she'd been a Goth back then – one of those kids who dressed like zombies and put metal bars through their tongues – but a respectable, educated girl all the same, with a job in a Polish patisserie in Kensington. She'd been learning English at evening classes with the aim of getting a job as a runner in the film business – her goal was to become a director one day. But then she'd met that big mouth Cockney *idiota* Steve. Reading between the lines, he'd persuaded her to chuck it all in and go live with him – they would start their own business, he'd buy her a Super 8 camera so she could make her own films, blah blah. Worse still – because her family back home disapproved of the match, she had lost touch with them.

Naturalnie, Steve's big plans came to nothing, and Kasia progressed from working in a pub, to serving drinks in Soho clubs, and then to her current job as – laughable euphemism – an exotic dancer. Even a decade ago it would have been unthinkable to find a decent Polish girl doing such a job, Janusz reflected, but she said it paid her three times as much as bar work, and it was undeniable that her sketchy grasp of English limited her options.

Restaurant Polka stood on the corner of an elegant Georgian terrace a few streets north of St Stan's, its wide front window and green and white tiled facade revealing its original incarnation as the neighbourhood greengrocers. Now the windows were hung, somewhat incongruously, with ruched, plum-coloured silk curtains.

The doorbell sounded a grating three-chime peal. The elderly lady who answered – aged about seventy, he estimated, maybe seventy-five – wore a ruffled cerise silk blouse, a similar shade to the curtains, and tinkled with gold. He would bet that the artful crown of permed blonde hair was the work of Hair Fantastic, the local salon that doubled as operational HQ for North London's fearsome Polish matriarchy.

'*Dzien dobry*, pani Tosik,' said Janusz making an old-fashioned bow. He'd made a mental note to watch his manners, uncomfortably aware that the courtesy drummed into him by his parents had become coarsened over the years, first by life on a building site, and more recently by the uncouth behaviour his current line of business some-times demanded.

'Come in, darling, come in!' piped pani Tosik. 'How lovely to have a man visit! I knew your father in Gdansk, after the war – God rest his soul.'

She reached up to put her hands on his shoulders and examine him, then gave a single decisive nod.

'*Tak*. You have his good looks – and his character, too, I think.'

She waved him inside: 'You will have coffee? And *tort*. Of course! Who doesn't like cake?'

Janusz followed pani Tosik, her heels ticking on the lino, to the dimly lit, cinnamon-smelling interior.

The old lady settled Janusz on a velvet-covered banquette in the plushly decorated restaurant, its walls hung with oil paintings of Polish rural scenes. While she made coffee, Janusz retrieved a copy of *Gazeta Warszawa* from a nearby table. The front-page headline read: '"*Forget the past and move on"', Zamorski tells voters'*. Beneath it was a photo of a middle-aged man with a thoughtful yet purposeful expression: Edward Zamorski, presidential-hopeful and head of the Renaissance Party.

As pani Tosik returned, Janusz stood to take the tray of coffee and pastries from her. She nodded to the picture: 'What do you think of our next president?' she asked, pouring coffee into a hand-painted Opole porcelain cup and saucer.

'I saw him speak once, at a rally in Gdansk – it was before martial law, so I must have been about seventeen,' said Janusz, raising the coffee cup to his lips. His fingers felt gigantic, cumbersome, around its fragile handle. 'I remember at one point he spoke over our heads, directly to the ZOMO. He said, '*"When you raise a baton to a fellow Pole, the blow lands on your own soul."'*

He remembered something else, too. Zamorski had told the crowd that once they won their freedom, reconciliation and forgiveness – even of the hated riot police – would be more important than revenge if the country were to move forward. As a fiery teenager, Janusz had found himself bewildered, angered even, by these words, but after what happened a couple of years later he found himself revisiting them again and again.

Pani Tosik sighed, waving a hand in a gesture that combined regret and resignation. 'You young people got rid of the *Komunistow*,' she said, 'And got a country ruled by American multinationals instead. My friend's daughter is a teacher in Warsaw and what do you think she earns in a year?'

Janusz shook his head.

'*9000 euros!*' hissed pani Tosik. 'This is why young people have to come to London, although it is not a good place for a young girl.'

This was her cue to embark on the story of the missing waitress, interrupted only by the whines of the tiny Yorkshire terrier sitting beside her on the banquette begging for food.

'Weronika came to me six months ago, in November. No! Not November, darling, *October*' – as though he'd been the one to get it wrong – 'Such a pretty girl. Beautiful, even,' she widened her tiny blue eyes for emphasis. 'Like . . . Grace Kelly, but with modern outfits, you know. Yes, Tinka, you may have a little bit of *Napoleonka* because your mama loves you.'

She broke off a piece of the pink-iced *millefeuille* pastry and gave it to the dog, who wolfed it down, licking every scrap from her fingers. Then, using her still-moist hand, she picked up another slice and put it on Janusz's plate, appearing not to notice as the big man flinched.

'Proper Polish pastry,' she said, 'Not those things the English call cakes – "Mr Kipper" *etcetera*.' Reaching for a pink Sobranie cigarette she leaned forward to Janusz's lighter flame.

'Anyway, she was a good Catholic girl, very hard-working, very respectable – not like some of the English girls. With them, always a problem! One is a drunk, always arrives late, another gets a baby.'

Janusz sipped his coffee and nodded.

'So, now – only Polish girls. And with this girl, I know her mama, and I say to her, your Weronika is safe with me. And then one day: *pfouff!* She is gone.'

The old lady's eyes filled with tears. 'I feel terrible,

panie Kiszka. I cannot sleep at night, I can barely eat . . .'
A sharp glance down. 'You do not like your *Napoleonka*?'

Janusz broke off a piece with his fork, but only took another sip of coffee.

'Did she have a boyfriend?'

Pani Tosik's gripped Janusz's forearm with surprisingly strong fingers. 'No! I promised her Mama, no boyfriends. She is too young – only nineteen. She always sleeps here, upstairs, where I can keep her under my eyes. And I make sure she goes to confession every single week.

'Let me find a photograph for you.' As pani Tosik jingled off to the rear of the salon, Janusz took the chance to offload his toxic cake on Tinka. The dog took the *Napoleonka* in one messy gulp, then bit the hand that fed her. He stifled a cry – pani Tosik was returning.

'Here she is, my beautiful Weronika. She was making a portfolio – her dream was to be a model.'

Janusz examined the professional-looking black and white photograph, which pictured a striking girl with ice-blonde hair wearing a long fur coat, against a white backdrop. She struck a self-consciously model-like pose: legs planted apart, hands on hips, shoulder-length hair blown backwards by a wind machine. Her face was all sharply angled planes – cheekbones that could cut coal – but there was uncertainty in the eyes, and her lips were rounded, almost childlike . . . *like Iza's* – the thought surfaced before he could stop it.

'Nice coat,' he said, to cover his expression, waving at the pricey-looking fur. Pani Tosik laughed. 'Oh, darling! It's not *real*! The girls buy these *"fun furs"* from TK Maxx for pocket money!'

'Speaking of money, *pani* . . .'

'I cannot afford much,' she said, pressing a hand to her chest. 'I am not a wealthy woman. Maybe you want to help this poor girl as a Christian duty?' She gave him a hopeful smile.

He had to admire the old girl: everyone knew her restaurant was coining it in. London's Poles were desperate for a taste of home and these days Eastern European food was even getting a following among the English.

'We all have cash flow problems,' he said, opening his hands in apology.

The old lady's smile waned as her sharp little eyes sized him up.

'Okay. I give you £500 now, you report back in one week. If you have some information, maybe I pay more.'

'£1000 now.'

She puckered her mouth. '£800. This is a good price.'

He cocked his head in agreement, dropping his gaze to hide his surprise at how quickly she had caved in.

A key turned in the front door, admitting a girl with long dark hair, twenty-five or twenty-six, at a guess. Not as hot as Weronika, maybe, but still pretty, in an olive-skinned way. His mother – God rest her soul – would have said she had a touch of the Tartar. She wore a tan leather jacket and the ultra-tight jeans Polish girls liked, and carried bulging Lidl bags. On her way past their table, she greeted pani Tosik, nodded to Janusz, and took in the photograph of Weronika lying on the table, all in a couple of seconds.

Clever eyes, he thought. He would bet a truckful of Wyborowa that she knew the real story with Weronika – who she'd been sleeping with, whether she'd got herself knocked up, maybe even where she'd disappeared to.

When he asked to see Weronika's room, pani Tosik agreed readily enough and led the way up the narrow staircase. The small room with its single bed struck him as almost spookily spotless. The dressing table was empty, the bed made up and topped with a pink satin *pierzyna:* a traditional eiderdown he hadn't seen since his child-hood. Standing on the bedside cabinet was the sole trace of its previous occupant: an empty photo frame.

When he asked about it, pani Tosik shrugged. 'I don't remember, maybe a family photo?'

He could tell from the way the old dear hovered at his shoulder that there was no way she'd let him check inside the chest of drawers: a man rooting around in a girl's underwear was probably an occasion of sin.

Before leaving, he asked to use the toilet, and on his way back to the restaurant, took the opportunity to slip into the kitchen. He could always say he took a wrong turn.

He found the dark-haired girl standing just inside the doorway of a walk-in fridge, nodding her head to some discordant Polish rap on the radio. She was reaching up to stack vegetables onto a shelf, her shirt riding up to reveal the curve of her waist. Sensing someone behind her, she whipped around, hand flying to her throat. He grinned an apology and held out his card. She took it without speaking, a guarded look in her brown eyes.

'Call me,' he said over his shoulder, leaving her gazing after him, fingering the gold cross she wore around her neck.

Four

Kershaw was super-respectful to DS Bacon on her return to Tower Hamlets nick. Fair play to Streaky, he seemed to have forgotten the ruck they'd had that morning; in fact, he was surprisingly cheery as she drew a chair up to his desk, probably because she'd had the foresight to bring him a mug of tea and a chocolate Hobnob first.

'The PM is this afternoon, Sarge, down at Wapping mortuary. I've not got anything else on and I'd like to go, if it's okay with you.' She knew that it usually fell to Crime Scene Investigators to attend post mortems these days – but she couldn't bear to wait for the pathologist's report to find out if there were any signs of injury on DB16, the girl with the Titian hair.

Raising his eyebrows, Streaky leant back in his tatty swivel chair like it was a throne. 'Well, well. Keen to see a slab butcher at work, are you? My old Sarge used to call it a poor form of entertainment.' He paused, looking thoughtful. 'All right, I'll let you go this once, purely for educational purposes,' he said, pointing his biscuit at her. 'But try not to let the side down by chucking up on the Doc's shoes, there's a good girl.'

She gave him a big grin. 'Thanks, Sarge, I'll do my best. Can I tell you what else I've got on the floater?'

He checked his watch. 'Make it quick, I've got a pressing appointment at the Drunken Monkey at two o'clock. Crucial meeting with a CHIS.'

CHIS? It took her a moment to translate. Covert Human Intelligence Source – aka, criminal informer. *Yeah, right,* she thought, *more like three pints and a dodgy pie with your dinosaur mates.* All the same, she was beginning to realise she could learn a lot from an old-school throwback like Streaky. The other Detective Sergeants at Newham nick were younger, and mostly of the new breed. Smartly dressed and professional, they wouldn't dream of drinking while on duty, but they seemed to her more like bank managers than real cops. So what if Streaky liked a few jars at lunchtime? Everyone knew he had a better clear-up rate than any of them. Which was probably why he hadn't been shuffled off with a full pension years ago.

'Get on with it then,' he said, blowing steam off his tea.

Kershaw checked her notes.

'IC1 Female, I'm guessing in her twenties. Could have gone in the river anywhere up to Teddington Lock. No clothing or jewellery, but she's got a tattoo with her name, Ela, and a boyfriend's, Pa-wel,' she said, struggling with the unfamiliar name. 'Polish, according to the internet.'

'It's *Pavel,* like gravel,' said Streaky. 'Pawel Janas, played for Poland in the seventies – tidy left foot as I recall. I was only a tiny child at the time, of course. Any injuries?'

'Need the PM results for that, Sarge, body's all messed up.'

Streaky chewed his lower lip. 'So you're thinking lover's tiff, the boyfriend strangles her, stabs her – whatever ethnic tradition demands – strips her to get rid of any clues, dumps her in the river in the wee small hours, goes off to drown his sorrows in vodka?' That brought an appreciative ripple of laughter from the guys – her fellow DCs, Browning, Bonnick, Ben Crowther, all in their late twenties, plus Toby Brisley, a civilian officer, were all at their desks today.

'Something like that, Sarge.'

'Hmm. Well, I wouldn't usually be too optimistic about finding a perp in the circs, but having your prime suspect's name tattooed on the victim's arse does give you a major leg-up.' More chuckles from the audience. She could only see the back of Bonnick's PC screen but from his glazed look and half-open mouth she would bet he was watching Arsenal's top goals on YouTube.

'I'll be the first to congratulate you if the Doc says it's a murder,' said Streaky. 'And why is that, DC Kershaw?'

That threw her. 'Ah, because it's the most serious crime, Sarge?'

Browning made a two-tone comedy horn noise at the back of his throat, ie 'you lose', to more laughter, though there was sympathy in the look Ben Crowther threw her. Ben – the only other DC in the office who'd been to university – was the only one she'd really clicked with so far.

'Why do we like a murder, DC Browning?' asked Streaky.

'Two reasons, Sarge,' he said in that chirpy blokey

tone that got on her nerves. 'One, the job goes to Murder Squad but the body stays with us so we get the numbers if it's cleared up. Two, murder means *overtime*.'

'And what is overtime, Browning?'

'The only perk a hard-working detective gets these days, Sarge.'

'Co-rrect,' said Streaky.

She managed a grin, taking the stick. Did Streaky prefer Browning to her because he was a guy, or because he was a ranker, like Streaky, instead of a graduate entry cop like her?

'Any chance of a DNA test on the floater, Sarge?' she asked. 'She might be on the database.'

Streaky gazed at his half-eaten Hobnob.

'See what you get from the PM first – it's already costing us three grand. Got to watch the budget, the accountant-wallahs tell me. And get onto MPB – they'll want photos, dental work, you know the drill.'

As Kershaw searched her archived mails for the address of the Missing Persons Bureau, she considered her own reasons for wanting DB16's death to be chalked up as a murder. One, it would look good on her CV; two, she might get assigned to Murder Squad for the duration of the job and get a nice long break from these wankers.

Five

Pani Tosik had been insistent about one thing: once Janusz had discovered Weronika's whereabouts, he was not to contact her himself but simply to report back with the address. The old lady had decided that the best strategy was to forward the girl the 'heartbreaking' letter her mama had sent, begging her to return to the restaurant. But all he had to go on was a single crappy lead: a sticker on the back of the photo of Weronika, printed with the name of a photographer's in Leytonstone, a couple of miles east of Stratford.

Janusz took the Northern Line south from Angel to Bank, where he'd change for the eastbound Central Line. He hated the tube, refused to use it in rush hour, and if there was a crush on the platform he'd usually head straight back up the escalator. But today he was too pushed for time to do the three-bus Islington to Leytonstone safari.

Sitting in the half-full carriage, he caught the eye of a little girl, aged about eight or nine, sitting across from him with her mother. He pulled the cross-eyed gargoyle face that used to crack his boy, Bobek, up at that age. She grinned. Then he noticed the words picked out in sequins across her flat, pink-T-shirted chest – *FUTURE PORN STAR* – and the smile dropped from his face like a theatre curtain.

As the pair got up at the next stop, the girl sketching a shy wave goodbye, the mother shot him a searching look. *The cheek of it!* – he thought. You dress your little girl like a trainee whore, then treat me like a paedophile.

He emerged from the shelter of Leytonstone tube still wearing a thunderous frown, and headed for the high street, a raw wind wrapping the trench coat about his legs. Leytonstone reminded him of how Highbury had looked when he first arrived in London. The greengrocers' displays bloomed with strange foreign vegetables – the kind he'd only ever seen in a curry – and dark-skinned men wrapped in coats argued over glasses of coffee at pavement tables. He stepped into the road to let a young couple with a baby buggy pass, and they thanked him in broken English, their singsong lilt marking them out as fellow Poles. He found himself scanning the crowded pavements for Weronika's high cheekbones.

The photographs on display in the window of Parry's featured the usual suspects – wedding couples, aspiring models, obese children – but on closer examination, Janusz could see that the shots had a certain flair. Inside, a young man with a ginger goatee sat behind the counter reading *Photographer's Weekly*.

Janusz had decided his best strategy would be to act the dumb *Polak*, just off the plane from Lodz. He did a lot of smiling and nodding for openers, then showed the guy the photo. 'You make this picture . . . ?'

As the guy studied the photo, a look of professional pride came over his face.

'Yeah, I remember – she was very beautiful, this girl.'

Janusz tapped himself on the chest. 'My sister,' he said with a modest smile.

'Right,' said the guy, dropping his gaze. He handed the photo back, as though suddenly keen to get shot of it.

Janusz pretended not to notice. 'She came here with her boyfriend,' he said – a guess rewarded with a wary nod. 'This man is my good friend,' he explained, his jaw starting to ache from all the grinning. 'Today, he has to work, but he asks me to come because he likes to get more photos, to make her folio?'

'Her modelling portfolio,' the guy said, looking relieved. 'Yeah, I did the shots two or three weeks ago.' He started leafing through a tray of folders behind the counter.

Don't ask me for a name, prayed Janusz.

'What's his name again . . . ?'

Kurwa.

'Ah, here it is. Pawel Adamski,' his pronunciation suggesting he was used to Polish customers. He spread a series of black and white photos across the counter like a pack of cards, and examined them, frowning, before selecting one and turning it round to face Janusz.

'I think this is the best one,' he said.

It was a startling image. Shot from above, Weronika lay on her back, eyes half-closed and lips parted, naked beneath a white sheet that reached from her feet to her chest. The lighting had been arranged to capture the subtly different shades of white in the scene – the chalky pallor of her face, the marble-like arms, the ivory sheen of the silk shading into grey where it fell into folds. Her hands lay loosely cupped, one within the other, on her stomach, lacking only a bouquet to complete the portrait of a virgin bride. Or a dead one, thought Janusz.

He shuffled through the rest of the shots, but couldn't find anything that might explain the photographer's earlier discomfiture.

'They're good,' he said, then, taking a guess, leaned toward the guy. 'But I think he meant the other ones,' he hissed. 'How you call it? The "Page 3" stuff?'

The guy hesitated for a moment, then turned to open a filing cabinet.

'Your friend directed these ones,' he said, his tone guarded, pushing a folder across the counter with the tips of his fingers. 'All I did was set up the lights for him.'

Inside was a contact sheet of a couple of dozen shots, colour this time.

Wearing only a black G-string, Weronika struck a variety of unimaginative soft porn poses – sticking her butt out . . . pushing her smallish breasts together . . . reclining with legs spread. Not much *chiaroscuro* in this lot, thought Janusz. No wonder the photographer had panicked when Janusz announced himself as Weronika's brother – he'd probably thought he was in for a kicking.

The images offended and depressed him. The amateurish raunchiness of the girl's pose jarred with the innocence of those rounded lips, and her eyes looked glazed, as though she were drunk – or on drugs. In that moment, he decided he couldn't keep his promise simply to pass on the couple's address to pani Tosik. *No.* When he found them he'd do his best to persuade the girl to dump her lowlife boyfriend and come home, and then he'd give Pawel Adamski a short sharp lesson in gentlemanly conduct.

Janusz tapped the contact sheet. 'You can send him a copy in the post?' he asked the guy.

The guy checked the cover of the folder. 'Sure, but I'll need an address – he didn't leave one, or even a phone number.'

That was a blow. After promising to telephone with his friend's address, Janusz left.

Still, at least he had a name.

Six

Wapping Mortuary was housed in a low, grey brick building encircled by a high wall, which made it look more like an industrial unit than anything remotely medical, thought Kershaw, as she buzzed the battered entry phone beside the big steel double gates.

A few minutes later, a mortuary technician with spiky dyed black hair and a bolt through her eyebrow was helping her into a blue cotton gown, the type surgeons wore for operations.

'First time?' she asked, her tone neutral.

Kershaw nodded. 'I'm not squeamish, though,' she added, before realising she'd spoken with unnecessary forcefulness.

Goth girl ignored the comment. 'If you do start feeling a bit funny, just let us know before you keel over, okay?' She waited while Kershaw pulled on blue plastic over-shoes, then led the way through a tiled corridor and into the post mortem room.

Kershaw had seen the scene reconstructed a dozen

times in TV cop dramas – the low-ceilinged tiled room, the naked bodies laid out on steel gurneys, some still whole, others already dissected. But it was all a bit different when you knew you weren't looking at an artful arrangement of wax models and fake blood. And television couldn't prepare you for the smell – a terrible cocktail of chopped liver, body fluids, and bleach.

The Goth girl paused at the first gurney. 'DB16,' she said. Spread-eagled on the shallow stainless steel tray, under the unsparing fluorescent lights, lay the girl with the Titian hair – or what was left of her.

'I'll tell Doctor Waterhouse you're here,' she said, leaving Kershaw alone with the body.

The girl was opened like a book from collarbone to pubis, revealing a dark red cavern where her insides had been. A purplish pile of guts lay between her thighs, as though she'd just given birth to them. The skin and its accompanying layer of yellow fat had been flayed from her limbs and torso, and now lay beneath her like a discarded jacket, and her ribcage was cracked open, each rib separated and bent back. Water tinkled musically, incongruously, through a drain hole under the gurney.

The good news, reflected Kershaw, was that she looked more like the remains of some predator's meal on the Serengeti than a human being.

'DC Kershaw, I presume?'

Tearing her gaze away from the carcass, she saw a tall, silver-haired man in his sixties rinsing his gloved hands at a nearby sink. Shaking off the drops, he approached her, beaming.

'Welcome, welcome,' he said.

'Thanks for having me, Doctor,' she said.

'Not at all,' said Doctor Waterhouse. 'I'm always delighted to see a new detective braving the rigours of a PM.'

He handed Kershaw some latex gloves with a little flourish, like he was giving her a bunch of violets, then spread his arms to encompass the cadaver lying between them.

'Our lady,' he began, in a plummy voice, 'is an IC1 female who apparently enjoyed good health throughout her life, with no evidence of any chronic condition.' He spoke as though addressing a roomful of medical students.

'How old would you say she was?' asked Kershaw, wriggling her fingers into the second glove.

'Your guess is as good as mine,' he said with a tilt of his head. Then, seeing her enquiring look, 'I'm afraid it's no easier to estimate someone's age from the inside than it is from the outside.'

Over Doc Waterhouse's shoulder, Kershaw noticed the Goth girl at the next gurney along. Wielding a huge curved needle, she was sewing up the chest cavity of a big man with tattooed biceps. His face had such a healthy colour, that for a split second Kershaw expected him to sit up and rip the needle from the girl's hand.

Waterhouse was saying: 'She was certainly of child-bearing age.' He paused. 'I found a foetus *in utero* that, by my calculations, would put this lady in the late stages of the first trimester of pregnancy at the time of death.'

Kershaw's eyebrows shot up. If the girl's boyfriend didn't fancy being a daddy, the pregnancy might have sparked an argument that ended in the girl's death. She pulled pad and pencil from the pocket of her gown. 'How many weeks is that, Doctor?'

'Between nine and twelve, judging by the foetus,' Waterhouse mused. 'Perhaps you'd like to see it?'

'No, I'm fine, thanks,' said Kershaw, with a nervous smile. 'Have you found anything suspicious? Any signs of violence?'

Looking at her over the tops of his half-moon glasses, the smiling Waterhouse raised a latexed finger. *Patience.*

'Since the body was recovered from the river, let us first examine the evidence for drowning as the possible cause of death,' he said, with the air of someone proposing a picnic on a lake, and started to stroll up and down the gurney, hands clasped behind his back.

Kershaw groaned inwardly – she was clearly in for the full lecture theatre treatment. At that moment, she happened to catch the eye of the Goth technician. The girl responded with a fractionally raised eyebrow that said – yes, he was always like this.

'What evidence might we expect to find, post-mortem, in the case of a drowning, Detective?' Waterhouse went on.

'Water in the lungs?' said Kershaw, suppressing a note of bored sarcasm. She'd be here all day at this rate.

'But how do we know whether the water entered the lungs *post-* or *ante*-mortem?'

He stopped pacing and looked at Kershaw. She shrugged.

'You may be surprised to learn that we currently have *no means* of establishing the sequence of events,' said Waterhouse, as thought he'd only just discovered this extraordinary state of affairs himself. 'If we allow that our lady was in the water six, perhaps seven days, by my calculations, then it is entirely possible that the copious quantities of river water, weed and sand present in her lungs and stomach found its way there *after* her death.'

'So how do we find out if she drowned or not?'

'Well, we *could* run a raft of analyses, to find out whether any diatoms – a kind of river algae – have found their way into her organs.' He pulled a doubtful grimace. 'But since none of it is the least bit conclusive I consider it an egregious waste of public money.'

No way of telling if someone had drowned? So those TV shows where a brilliant pathologist solved tricky cases single-handed after the cops had failed were clearly a load of old bollocks, thought Kershaw. She realised that Waterhouse was looking at her like it was her turn to speak.

'So . . . if there's no such thing as conclusive proof of drowning,' she said. 'I guess all you can do is rule every-thing else out – a process of elimination?'

'Well done, Detective,' said Waterhouse with an approving nod.

'However, I must tell you I can find no evidence of foul play. The various injuries to the body are all *post*-mortem.'

Kershaw felt as though she'd been slapped. She wasn't ready to see the girl demoted from murder victim to just another bridge jumper.

'Are you sure?' she asked.

'Subcutaneous dissection reveals no deep bruising or other injury.' Waterhouse waved a hand over the flayed body. 'Nor could I find any sign of the pinpoint haemor-rhages in the conjunctivae or mucus membranes that would suggest asphyxiation.'

He beckoned her over to a deep stainless steel sink where he plunged a gloved hand into a pile of what looked like offal, spread out on a large plastic chopping board.

'Here we are,' he announced. 'The hyoid bone – from the lady's neck.' He brandished a pair of tiny bony horns with bits of tissue still attached – which, to Kershaw, looked a lot like a truncated chicken wishbone. 'When someone is strangled, more often than not, the hyoid gets broken. But this little fellow is intact.' With the air of a conjuror, he pressed his thumbs into the centre of the horns until they snapped. *'Voilà!'*

Kershaw stifled a grimace. 'So, in your view,' she said, pencil hovering over her notebook. 'She wasn't beaten, stabbed, strangled or suffocated.'

'Correct.'

'How did she die then?'

'Well, the chalky residue I found in the stomach does suggest she had ingested drugs a few hours before death,' said Waterhouse.

'Suicide?' Kershaw didn't try to disguise the disappointment in her voice.

'I'm afraid I must leave intent to you, Detective,' he said. He drummed gloved fingers on the board. 'But if I were to stick my neck out, I'd say it wasn't the common or garden bottle of paracetamol.'

Rummaging through the pile of entrails with the air of a man trying to find matching socks, he retrieved a glistening brown lobe the size of a fist and set it in front of her.

'Kidney?' she said. Disgusting stuff – wouldn't eat it as a kid, or now, come to that.

'Well done!' said Waterhouse, smoothing the organ

out on the board. 'Have a little poke around, tell me what you see.'

She took the proffered scalpel and used it to open up a series of incisions in the tissue. *What was she supposed to be looking for?* Then, bending closer, she saw something – a scatter of bright magenta dots across the pinky-brown surface.

'These spots,' she asked. 'Are they normal?'

'No, Detective, they are not.'

Waterhouse picked up the kidney and turned it to and fro in the light. 'These *petechiae* – haemorrhages – are suggestive of acute renal failure.'

Kershaw frowned at the constellation of dots. 'What could have caused it?' she asked.

'Half a dozen things.' He pursed his lips. 'But *off* the record, I'd put my money on rhabdomyolysis.' He smiled at the look on her face. 'Damage to muscle fibres releases a protein called myoglobin into the bloodstream, which can ultimately cause the kidneys to fail.'

'*Muscle* damage?'

'Yes, rhabdomyolysis is often seen in serious crush injuries, for example.' He paused, tilting his head. 'But I think the likeliest cause in this case is chemical. Drug-induced hyperthermia could have raised her body temperature so high that it started literally to cook her tissues.'

Kershaw remembered a news article someone had posted on the noticeboard at uni, about a student who took too many tabs of Ecstasy and nearly died from overheating. The 'alternative' types, the ones with facefuls of metalwork, had been routinely off their tits on the stuff, and even some of her fellow criminology students had dabbled, but she'd never been tempted. A few drinks was one thing, but the idea of losing control over her brain chemistry totally freaked her out.

'You think she OD-ed on Ecstasy?' she asked.

'I wouldn't dream of pre-judging the toxicology report, of course,' said Waterhouse. 'But it's *possible* that she died of renal failure brought about by an overdose of MDMA, yes.'

Kershaw tried to picture the scenario, how the girl might have ended up naked in the Thames. Maybe, after a night out clubbing with her boyfriend, they'd gone to bed, and he'd woken up next to a dead body. If he'd given her the drugs, or sold them to her, he could easily have panicked and dumped her in the river.

'What's she likely to have experienced, when she OD-ed?' she asked.

'A massive surge of serotonin in the brain would have caused a breakdown of the body's temperature control mechanisms, like a fire raging out of control through a house.' Waterhouse started scooping the girl's organs from the chopping board into a blue plastic bag in the sink. 'When her core temperature exceeded 39 degrees, there would be neuron damage; at 40 degrees, she was probably suffering seizures, followed by coma. When it reached 41, the organs would begin to shut down.'

He handed the bag to the Goth technician who took it without a word.

'Nasty way to die,' said Kershaw. 'Presumably she wouldn't be in a fit state to get down to the Thames and throw herself in?'

Waterhouse tipped his head. 'That depends at what stage of the overdose she did so – if indeed that's what happened.'

He started rinsing his hands under the tap. Over his shoulder, Kershaw could see the Goth girl inserting the bulging bag back into the dead girl's body cavity, pushing it this way and that, like someone trying to squeeze a last-minute item into an overstuffed suitcase.

Waterhouse snapped off his gloves and checked his watch. 'I'm afraid I must leave you, I have a court case at the Old Bailey.'

Kershaw said she'd walk with him to the tube. Five minutes later he emerged from the changing room, wearing a tweed jacket and carrying a briefcase.

He held the door open for her with a flourish. Out in the chilly air, she asked, 'So you reckon this is just a case of one too many tabs of E, do you?'

'Not necessarily,' he said. 'I attended a conference in Berlin last month where I met a very interesting toxicologist. He said they're seeing a rash of these deaths across Europe at the moment.'

They were out on the pavement now. Seeing Kershaw struggling to keep up with his long stride, Waterhouse slowed his pace.

'The toxicology shows the victims all ingested a counterfeit version of Ecstasy, called para-methoxyamphetamine.' He shot her a mischievous look. 'You'll be pleased to hear it's more commonly known as PMA.'

Kershaw wished she could take notes, she'd never remember all this. 'Does it have the same effect as Ecstasy?'

'It's similar, but much more dangerous. This chap told me that recently, three young women died in a single night.'

Kershaw raised her eyebrows. If the girl turned out

to be a victim of a dodgy drugs ring, it could still be a big case.

Waterhouse strode off the pavement and practically into the path of an oncoming truck – meeting the blare of the driver's horn with an urbane wave. Kershaw scurried after him.

'So why do people take this PMA, if it's so risky?' she asked.

'They often don't know that they are,' said Waterhouse. 'Apparently the dealers pass it off as Ecstasy. And although it's much more toxic, its effects take considerably longer to manifest themselves.' He shook his head. 'Consequently, the hapless user often takes *further* pills, believing that they have bought a weaker product.'

She could see the tube entrance only metres away, and she still had so much to ask him.

'But if these PMA deaths all happened in Europe,' she said. 'What's it got to do with DB16?'

'You said in your email that our lady might be Polish,' said Waterhouse, as if that made everything crystal.

Kershaw screwed her face up. 'I don't see the relevance.'

'Didn't I say?' he asked, turning to look at her. 'The three girls who died in one night – it happened in Poland. Gdansk, I think he said.'

Seven

Janusz raised his chin, and ran the razor from throat to jaw line, enjoying the rasping sound of the blade. As he rinsed it under the running tap he felt the prickle on the back of his neck that told him he was being watched.

He turned around to find Copernicus, the big grey tabby tomcat who had adopted him almost a decade ago, standing in the bathroom doorway. Although the cat's gaze was impassive, his message was crystal clear.

'Alright, Copetka. I know dinner is running a bit late at Hotel Kiszka,' said Janusz, towelling off the last suds. With fluid grace, the cat turned and led him to the kitchen cupboard.

After feeding him, Janusz opened the kitchen window to let the cat onto the fire escape and watched as he trotted down the half-dozen flights of stairs. Through the gathering dusk, he could make out the first daffodils under the plane trees that edged Highbury Fields.

These days, it was one of North London's most select areas. But back in the early eighties, when the latest wave of the Polish diaspora had washed him up on the shores of Islington, the locals – better-off English working-class types – couldn't get out fast enough. Taking their place were Paddies, Poles and blacks, and a few bohemian types who weren't fazed by the area's reputation as crime central. The flat had been a cheap place to flop once he'd split the rent with workmates from building sites. And he'd always liked the view.

By the time his Jewish landlord had decided to up sticks and start a new life in Israel, Janusz had earned enough for a deposit and got a mortgage to buy the place. Now, his only problem was the odd funny look from his newer neighbours, the City types and advertising executives who were taken aback to find a Polish immigrant living next door in a Highbury mansion block. Well, tough luck, he thought, he was here first.

Janusz went to the fridge to check he had everything he needed for supper – Kasia would be arriving in less than an hour. He was happy with the look of the beef, a good dark-coloured fat-marbled slab of braising steak he'd paid a crazy price for at the Islington farmer's market. It was always worth spending an extra pound or two when it came to meat.

He levered open the big bay window in the living room to get rid of the smell of stale cigars, and picked up a dirty glass and a pile of junk mail off the mantelpiece of the marble fireplace. Then he put them back, smiling to himself: Kasia would enjoy cleaning the place up later.

The evening started out well enough.

Sure, he and Kasia had been reserved with each other at first, an edge of awkwardness to their embrace at the door, but since this was their first date since they'd first slept together, it was to be expected. That night, a fort-night ago now, had been the culmination of weeks of assignations over coffee and cake snatched during her work breaks – encounters that couldn't have been more tantalisingly proper had they been chaperoned by a brace of *babcia*. It was just his luck, reflected Janusz, to be dating the world's most straitlaced stripper.

While Kasia tidied the living room, exclaiming at the mess, he cut the beef into three-centimetre chunks, and started to chop the onion and garlic.

After a few minutes she came and leant against the worktop, lighting a cigarette while he browned the beef. 'I never saw a Polish man cook before – not even a boiled egg!' she said, watching him slice a red pepper. He shrugged. 'I think it's good,' she added. 'I'm a *katastrofa* in the kitchen, and anyway, how would I cook with these?' She brandished her sinister talons at him.

'I always meant to ask: why do you paint your nails black?' he asked, quartering the chestnut mushrooms.

'I started doing it when I was a Goth,' she said surveying her outstretched hands. 'After that I never changed them.' She took a thoughtful drag on her cigarette. 'Maybe it's nice to be a bit different.

'So, how did you learn to cook? Do you watch the TV programmes from home?'

He shook his head. 'My mama taught me, right from when I was a little boy.' Using a wooden spoon, he scraped the onion and garlic into the hot oil of the pan, releasing an aromatic sizzle. 'When there was nothing in the shops we'd take a basket into the countryside to find treats for Tata's supper. In the summer, wild asparagus, lingonber-ries to make jam . . .'

Kasia smiled at the nostalgia in his voice. Janusz's childhood, with its visits to his grandmother's place, a crumbling farmhouse on the outskirts of Gdansk, was a million miles from her monochrome memories of a monolithic Soviet-built estate in industrial Rzewow. She loved to hear his boyhood tales of collecting warm eggs from the chicken house, or climbing up into the high branches of apple trees in the orchard. The funny thing was, even though his memories were so different from hers, they still made her feel homesick.

She tapped cigarette ash out of the kitchen window. 'How did your mama know what was safe to eat?'

'She came from a family of farmers, so she was a real country girl. She even knew how to make birch wine. In the spring, you cut through the bark', he used his wooden spoon to demonstrate the lateral cut, 'and drain off a few litres of sap. But you must be careful: if you make the wound too big the tree will die.'

Pouring a jugful of water over the meat and vegetables, he said over his shoulder, 'October, November, I take the tube to Epping and go into the forest to look for mushrooms. If you get lucky, you can find *boletas*. I could take you, if you like – show you which ones are good to eat.'

There was a moment of silence as they shared the unspoken thought . . . *if they were still seeing each other in six months' time*.

He threw a couple of roughly chopped red chilies in the pot. The dish's final ingredients, a little sour plum jam and a cup of buttermilk, wouldn't be added till the end.

He'd been sliding glances at her face while he cooked and was relieved to see that the old bruise on her cheekbone had faded completely, with no evidence of fresh ones. The warning he'd delivered to Steve had done the trick, at least for now. And according to Kasia, Steve had bought the story that Janusz was Kasia's cousin over from Poland, which was a relief – he didn't want to give that *chuj* another excuse to knock her about.

He opened the fridge and pulled out a jar filled with cream-coloured fat.

'What's that?' asked Kasia.

'Goose *smalec* for roasting the potatoes,' he said, doling some into a roasting tray.

'Ah, goose fat is good for you!' exclaimed Kasia, examining the jar, 'It helps you to lose weight.' Then, on seeing his sceptical look: 'It's *true* – I read it in a magazine.'

Kasia might be blade-sharp, reflected Janusz, but like all Polish women, she had a vast collection of cherished – and often crazy – dietary folklore: a rich brew of Catholic injunctions, old wives' tales from medieval Poland, and the crap peddled by glossy magazines.

Janusz brandished the jar in front of him and adopted a serious air: 'Top government scientists are warning: too much goose fat can cause dangerous weight loss – please use it sparingly.' Pretending to be insulted, she made to grab the jar back from him.

He caught her arm deftly, his big hand circling her slim wrist with ease. 'Can you stay tonight?' he asked. Best to get the question – and the phantom of Steve – out of the way early so that it didn't overshadow their evening. She looked along her eyes at him, then nodded. 'I'm staying at my sister's.' Breaking into a grin, he grabbed her by the waist and, ignoring her laughing protestations, danced her around the tiny kitchen.

Half an hour later, with a couple of glasses of a decent Czechoslovak pinot noir inside him, he settled into the big leather sofa and, wreathed in the aromas of the roasting potatoes and the peppery stew, let his gaze linger on Kasia, who stood examining the floor-to-ceiling bookshelves either side of the fireplace. He felt as relaxed and happy – the realisation rushed on him unawares – as he had with Iza, more than twenty-five years ago.

An image of her, sitting outside a harbourside cafe in Gdansk, flickered across his memory like an old home movie. One of her hands, wearing a red woollen glove, was curled around a steaming drink. She'd taken off her other glove and he was chafing the bare hand to warm it, laughing at how icy her fingers were.

He lit a cigar. To hell with the past, he thought.

'There's a Polanski movie on cable later, if you fancy it?'

His tone was careful – it wasn't the first time he'd tried to rekindle her passion for movies. Despite her first-class degree from the world-famous Lodz film school, the last time Kasia had visited the cinema was to see *GoodFellas*.

'Maybe,' she said lifting one shoulder, before bending to pick up a discarded envelope from under an armchair.

'It's *Knife in the Water*. The one with the couple on a boating trip on the Lakes?'

'The one with the *psychol*?' She made a comic grimace that turned her beautiful long mouth down at the corners. 'Too depressing!'

Oskar had once put forward a theory – which doubtless originated with his wife Gosia – regarding Kasia's lack of enthusiasm for films. Apparently, she regretted

68

abandoning her directing ambitions to marry Steve, and couldn't bear any reminder of her mistake. In this analysis, Kasia didn't stick with her marriage because of her Catholic faith, but because the alternative meant admitting she'd given up her youthful dreams for nothing.

Janusz was sceptical. To him, psychology was a slippery pseudoscience, without any empirical foundation. But now and again he found himself wondering if Oskar's theory mightn't contain a grain of truth.

'You like my new outfit?' she asked suddenly, doing a little catwalk sashay.

That put him on the spot: when she had arrived he'd noticed she was wearing a dress rather than her usual tight black jeans and T-shirt. But the longish black shift was the sort of thing a woman with a lousy figure might go for. Why would a looker like Kasia hide her body under a sack?

She sensed the hesitation. 'You don't like it?'

'It's . . . stylish, darling,' he managed, 'but I think you'd look good in something a bit more . . . figure-hugging.'

She cut her eyes away from him. 'You mean an exotic dancer should dress like a whore?'

Kurwa! This was dangerous ground – it wasn't the first time Kasia had gone all touchy over her job. It mystified him – if she didn't like stripping why did she do it? And if she did like it, why be so uptight?

'Of course not, darling. Anyway, you would look lady-like whatever you wore.'

She smiled at that, mollified, then came closer, wrinkling her nose at the cigar smoke – 'Smells like a bonfire,' she complained – before putting a Marlboro Light between her lips and leaning down for a light.

69

He took the opportunity, instead, to pull her face down to his and kiss her, properly this time. When she offered no resistance, he tumbled her onto the sofa and continued the clinch, pushing the dress, rustling, up her stockinged legs, desire humming between them. They had loads of time to make love before the oven timer started pinging, he calculated, and her tightly closed eyes signalled a green light.

Then the phone rang.

He cursed inwardly and for a moment was tempted to let it go to voicemail, but Kasia extricated herself and he caught her watchful look. He didn't want her to think he had anything to hide.

His abrupt *'Czesc?!'* was met with silence. Then a female voice, uncertain, said *'Pan Kiszka?'*

It was the dark-haired girl from pani Tosik's restaurant, the one he'd given his card to. She told him her name was Justyna, but didn't volunteer a surname. He apologised for his boorish manners, keeping half an eye on Kasia, who had returned to the kitchen. He could see her stirring the beef stew, ignoring the conversation, but something about the angle of her head suggested she was getting every word.

The trouble was, the girl was adamant that she had to meet him tonight, and when he suggested postponing, sounded like she might hang up. He was half-inclined to tell her no, but an undercurrent of urgency in her voice stopped him. Anyway, if he was to replenish his depleted cash reserves he needed to find the missing girl fast.

Thirty seconds later, he was jotting down the name of a Polish club in Stratford where the girl wanted to meet.

Janusz retrieved his cigar from the ashtray and joined

Kasia in the kitchen. With a stab at a nonchalant air, he said, 'Listen, darling. Something's come up – a job I'm doing for someone.'

'A woman?' she asked.

'Well, yes, the client is a woman, but an old lady – a *babcia*.'

'And the woman on the phone – she is an old lady, too?' Her green eyes had narrowed, and she would no longer meet his gaze.

'Well, yes, she *is* young, but she's just a contact. The thing is she insists on seeing me tonight, for some reason.'

Without a word, Kasia started to collect her things, her movements uncharacteristically jerky.

All his hopes for the evening teetered on a cliff edge. 'Listen, Kasia,' he said, aware of a cajoling note in his voice he didn't like, 'I can get there and still be back by ten, maybe half past, we can have a late supper.'

'So I sit here and watch Sky while you go out drinking with a woman?' She pulled a mirthless smile. 'All the lies I have to tell Steve, making excuses so I can stay all night, and now this.'

Janusz felt the anger bolt out of him like an unleashed dog.

'I have a job to do, money to earn! You are not my wife to tell me whom I can and cannot see!' His voice boomed around the flat.

'You are right – it's none of my business,' she said, her voice tight. 'How can I complain if you have other girlfriends? I am just some *dziwka* you are sleeping with who other men pay to see naked.'

He clutched his head, mute before this irrational torrent.

71

'And no, I'm not your wife,' she went on. 'I'm someone else's – and I shouldn't be here.'

Softening his voice with an effort of will, he said, 'Listen, Kasia. You are still young, you could *leave* Steve, start life over again,' but he knew it was hopeless – this was old ground, the argument well worn.

She pulled on her coat. 'You know I can't, Janek,' sounding weary now.

He caught her arm as she opened the flat door.

'Don't go off this way, *kotku*,' he said.

She smiled a sad smile at this big man calling her a little cat, touched her fingers to his lips, and left.

Thirty seconds later, the main door to the street boomed like a distant firing squad.

Janusz paced the flat, cursing; running the last hour's *dramat* through his head on a continuous loop. Half an hour later he still couldn't make any sense of it: what right did she have to be jealous when she was the one sleeping with another man? The fact that man was her husband didn't make it any easier. *No!* Being able to picture that rat-faced Cockney screwing her made it a thousand times worse.

With an effort of will, he pushed Kasia to the back of his mind, threw himself onto the sofa and drank a glass of red wine in a single draught. He took the snap of Weronika, the one of her in the fur coat, out of his wallet. Something about this girl, her innocent beauty, and yes, okay, the way she reminded him of Iza, had got under his skin, made him preoccupied with finding her. *Naprawde*, it was even worse than that, he realised with an embarrassed grimace: he wanted to *rescue* her.

He went to turn off the oven, and after a moment's

hesitation, scraped the roast potatoes into the bin: once cooled you could never recapture their crust.

Leaving the block's front door between the stone columns that flanked the entrance, Janusz noticed that a new 'For Sale' sign had sprouted overhead. Oskar said that if he sold up and bought a place further out he could pocket a couple of hundred grand, easy. But why would he want to live in some benighted suburb like Enfield?

When he left Highbury Mansions, it would be wearing an oak overcoat, as his father used to say – *God rest his soul*.

As usual, he took the shortest route to the tube, straight across the southern section of the darkened Fields, feeling the dew from the grass creeping into his shoes. Halfway across, without breaking his stride, he glanced backwards – there had been a spate of muggings here recently. All clear. But as his gaze swung forward again, he discovered that a big, heavyset man, almost as tall as him, had materialised on the pavement at the edge of the Fields, twenty-five, thirty metres ahead. He must have just stepped out of a parked car, but if so, why hadn't Janusz heard the distinctive clunk of a car door? He kept his gaze locked on the bulky figure, clad in an expensive-looking parka jacket, strolling through the pools of orange thrown by the street lights, until finally, the guy disappeared out of sight behind the Leisure Centre.

Janusz couldn't fathom what it was about the man that had caught his attention – he certainly didn't look like a mugger. All he could say was there was something about him that looked indefinably out of place.

FlashKlub, the place that Justyna had named for their

rendezvous, was located in a basement under a semi-derelict fifties factory building in an area called Maryland on Stratford's eastern fringe. The name might suggest rural romance, but the area was depressed and scruffy – no Olympic effect visible here. Lining up with a queue of youngsters chattering away in Polish he felt middle-aged, out of place, but the young bouncer showed no surprise, greeting him with a polite '*Dobry wieczor, panu.*' He did make an apologetic gesture at his cigar, though. Janusz ground it out on the pavement before heading down the rickety stairs toward the *klub* with all the enthusiasm of a man going to get his teeth drilled.

Justyna was sitting on a stool at the bar, fiddling with the straw in her drink. She was even more attractive than he remembered: glossy dark hair grazing her shoulders, eyes the colour of *conac*. She seemed relieved to see him – no doubt she'd been pestered non-stop by guys trying their luck. He ordered a Tyskie and another apple juice for her – she shook her head when he suggested a shot of bisongrass *wodka* to liven it up. Maybe she didn't want to let her tongue run away with her, he thought.

A huge screen on one wall playing pop promos dominated the basement. The current one had been shot in some semi-derelict Soviet housing estate and starred two skinny crew-cut boys. Dressed like gangsters from an American ghetto, they bobbed and grimaced through a Polski hip hop number, their faces deadpan. Maybe he was just a narrow-minded old fart, but it set Janusz's teeth on edge. The mindless beat and nihilistic lyrics struck him as an affront to the musical beauty of the language.

'You don't like it?' she asked with a half-smile at his tortured expression.

'No. Do you?' he said, raising an eyebrow.

She shrugged. 'Sure. I like all kinds of music.'

'When I was your age, studying physics in Krakow,' he said, 'there was a craze in the cellar bars, for traditional music, folk, I suppose you'd call it.'

Her expression was attentive, but detached. She had one of those faces that you felt compelled to keep scanning because her emotions were so hard to read.

He paused, remembering those nights, the frenetic violins, the thrilling sounds infused with the wildness of Gypsy music, often a haunting woman's voice in the mix, and felt the tug of nostalgia in his chest. He took a swallow of beer to cover his expression. 'The thing was, the dumbass . . . excuse me . . . stupid *Kommies* thought traditional music was wholesome, harmless stuff – but of course, all those old partisan songs about carrying your heart around in a knapsack were dynamite.

'The music had us stomping and cheering, climbing onto tables to sing along. After closing, all hyped up and full of *wodka*, me and my mates would dodge the police patrols and paint *Solidarnosc* graffiti all over town.'

'Did you ever get caught?' she asked. From the mild curiosity in her tone, she might have been asking about something that happened in the nineteenth century rather than two-and-a-half decades ago.

He hesitated. 'Just once. There were three of us – my mates had hung me by my legs over the side of a railway bridge so I could paint some slogan or other. *"THE TV LIES"*, I think it was. When the *milicja* arrived, the lads just about managed to drag me back up, but by the time I was on solid ground they'd legged it and I got nicked.'

'What happened to you?'

He looked away. 'Nothing much, spent a night in the cell, got a few slaps, got sent home in the morning.'

Bullshit. The *milicja* had thrown him in the back of a van and taken him to Montepulich, Krakow's notorious jail, where the Soviets had tortured and murdered hundreds of Polish nationalists after the war. It must have been a quiet night for them to commit so much time and effort to interrogating a seventeen-year-old boy over such a stupid thing – or maybe they just enjoyed their work. He'd been left with bruises and cuts that had taken weeks to fade, but they were nothing compared to the real legacy of that night, the thing that he carried inside him, like the shadow on an X-ray. He stamped the memories back down. *Forget the past.*

The girl and he gazed at the flickering video screen. The two boys were now in a car, lurching back and forward, zombie-like, to the beat. The camera cut to a shot of one of them, on his own, walking, before the camera pulled out to a wide aerial shot, revealing him as a tiny, lonely figure alone in a vast desolate wasteland.

She gestured with her chin. 'He is like you, when you were young.'

'Like *me*?'

'You and your friends, back then, under the *Komunistow* – life was bad, society didn't work for you. This music – for young people it says the same as your folk songs, it says fuck your society, we do our own thing.'

He knew that it was common for young women to swear these days, especially the ones who'd been in England a while, but it still shocked him in an almost physical way to hear it. When he had been her age it

76

would have been unthinkable to use such language in front of one's elders.

'Is that what you feel about Poland today?' he asked.

She sipped her apple juice, eyes cast down. 'I want to go back one day, I guess,' she said, choosing her words. 'But not yet. What is there for me, in Katowice? I would earn maybe half of what I get here – I'd have to save for years just to buy a five-year-old Polski Fiat.'

There was no anger, only a resigned pragmatism in her voice.

'Here, once I learn English, I can get a job in Marks and Spencer and earn good money, go to college part-time.'

'What will you study?'

Her eyes lit up, animating her whole face for the first time. 'Physiotherapy, or maybe chiropractic, I haven't decided yet.'

Janusz knew Katowice: a powerhouse of heavy industry under the Soviets, many of its residential districts were now half-empty, depressing places, peopled by the old, the sick, and by those who lacked either the resources or the courage to leave. The thought of living there made him shudder. Maybe his generation had been lucky, after all – at least fighting the *Kommies* gave them a sense of common purpose.

'Zamorski is a good guy,' he assured her. 'If anyone can put the country back on its feet, he will.'

His words hung there, shiny and shallow sounding, as she gazed at him with dark brown eyes.

'Politicians are all the same.' Her tone was polite but decisive. 'You and your friends thought that Walesa was superman, right?'

Janusz had to admit she was right about that. He had idolised Lech Walesa once, only to watch in horrified disbelief, after the *Solidarnosc* leader became Poland's first elected president, as he fell out with some of the revolution's brightest thinkers and surrounded himself with yes-men.

Zamorski shared Walesa's *Solidarnosc* credentials, but displayed none of his demagogic tendencies and had already pulled off an impressive political balancing act, drawing on Poles' instinctive conservatism while resisting the temptations of full-blooded nationalism. But spending the night arguing politics with the self-possessed Justyna wasn't going to help him find the lost girl, thought Janusz. He sensed he'd have to go gently – if he came out and asked where Weronika was, she might just clam up.

'Did you ever come here with Weronika?' he asked, taking a slug of beer.

'Yes, sometimes.'

'Was it here she met Pawel?' he asked.

The faintest frown creased her forehead, but she didn't ask how he knew about Weronika's secret boyfriend.

'No, he came into the restaurant one day and chatted her up as she served him *pierogi*.'

'Do you remember when he first came in?'

'Yes! It was February thirteenth – I remember because my Mama's called Katarzyna and it's her saint's day,' she said, with a shy smile. 'After that, he came back every single day, flattering her, slipping her little presents – *czekolatki*, perfume – till she finally agreed to go out with him.' Her voice became scornful as she talked about Adamski.

'You didn't like him.'

'He was bad news,' said Justyna, nodding her head for emphasis. 'Nika was only nineteen' – she used the affectionate diminutive of Weronika – 'and he was *thirty* – much too old for her.'

Janusz left a silence, letting her talk. 'He was always getting drunk,' she went on, after a pause, 'and then he'd get crazy. One time the three of us, we were in a pub and he threw a glass at the TV screen – just because they were talking about the election!' She widened her eyes at the memory. 'We used to come here, mostly – until he got barred.'

'What happened?' asked Janusz.

'He said it was for arguing with a bouncer,' she shrugged, sceptical. 'But he was such a liar, who knows.'

Since the girl's animosity toward Adamski appeared to outweigh her caginess, Janusz decided to play devil's advocate.

'Lots of Polish men like to drink,' he said with a grin. 'Maybe you were a bit jealous of your friend? Perhaps you would have liked Pawel for yourself?'

'No way!' she shot back, her face flushed, warming her olive complexion and making her even prettier, he noticed. 'I didn't say one word against him at the start – I'm not her mother. But then, one night, while Nika was in the *toaleta*, he put his hand up my skirt! Can you believe the guy?'

'Did you tell her?'

'I tried to, but she just shrugged it off, said he must have been joking. She was crazy about him, and anyway, you have to understand something about Nika: she's *bogu ducha winna*.' He smiled at the expression – innocent as a lamb – it was one his mother had often used.

'Where did he work?' If Justyna didn't know – or wouldn't tell him – where the pair were living, it would be his best hope of tracing the pair.

She fiddled with the straw in her drink, shrugged. 'It's a big mystery. At the beginning, Nika told me he's a builder, one of those who stands on the side of the road and waits for an Irish boss to hire him?' Janusz nodded – in the old days he'd sometimes had to tout himself out in that humiliating way. 'But then he started throwing big money around – taking her out for fancy meals, buying expensive hi-fi, flashy clothes, acting like a gangster.'

'Maybe he won some money – internet poker, betting on the football.'

'Enough to buy a new BMW?' she asked, her eyes wide. 'He *said* he was dealing in *antique furniture*.' Her words dripped with derision.

'So how do you think he made the *smalec*?'

At that, a cloak of inscrutability dropped over her face again, and she looked off into the bar area, which was filling up as the night progressed.

'I don't know,' she said after a pause. 'I just hope Nika isn't getting herself mixed up in any trouble.'

As Janusz waited at the bar to buy more drinks he let his eye roam over the club's clientele. In their teens and twenties, mostly Polish, but with a sprinkling of English faces, they appeared – for the most part – smartly turned-out and well behaved. His gaze fell on a group of youngsters sitting at the table nearest the bar. Two boys and two girls, deep in animated conversation, talking and laughing just a bit too loudly. And they were constantly touching each other, he noticed – a squeeze of the arm, a stroke of the cheek. Maybe it was just the buzz and bonhomie you'd expect between good friends enjoying the first rush of *alkohol*. Maybe not. The eldest, a boy, was 18, tops, and, under their make-up the two giggling girls looked barely old enough to drink legally.

He ordered the drinks and, leaving a twenty on the bar to pay for them, strolled to the toilets. After using the urinal, he lingered at the washbasin, combing his hair in the mirror and praying nobody took him for a *pedzio*. Just as he expected, a minute or two later, a shaven-headed, rail-thin guy in a hooded jacket slid up to the sink next to him, turned on the taps, and made a pretence of washing his hands.

'Wanna buy *Mitsubishi*?' he asked in Polish, without turning his head.

Janusz had a pretty good idea he wasn't being offered a used car. Pocketing the comb, he raised a non-committal eyebrow.

'It's good stuff,' the guy urged, 'double-stacked . . .' Suddenly, he found his sales pitch interrupted as his face was brought into violent and painful contact with the mirror.

'What the fu . . .?!' He gazed open-mouthed at his contorted reflection and scrabbled at the back of his neck where Janusz's rocklike fist gripped his balled-up hood.

Janusz shook his head, gave him another little push for the profanity.

'A word of advice, my friend. The undercover *policja* are all over this place. Apparently, some scumbag is selling drugs to youngsters.'

The guy tried to wipe snot and blood from his nose.

'Your best move would be to take your . . . business

up to the West End, and rethink your policy on selling to anyone under twenty-one.' Janusz bent his head down to the guy's level, locked eyes with him in the mirror. 'In fact, if I was you,' he said softly, 'I'd insist on seeing a driving licence.'

Straightening up, he released the guy, who bolted, and turning on the taps, gave his hands a thorough soaping. He frowned at his reflection. Had Adamski been dealing *Ekstasa* here? It could explain a lot: his bizarre and unpredictable behaviour, the glazed look Weronika wore in the dirty photos, his sudden acquisition of enough cash to buy a BMW. It might explain that fracas with the *klub* bouncer, too.

Rejoining Justyna, he told her he'd been offered drugs in the toilets. He hoped she might take the bait, confirm that Adamski was a dealer, but she just lifted a shoulder, non-committal.

'When I was a student,' he said, 'the only way to get high, apart from booze, was the occasional bit of grass. A guy I knew started growing it on his bedroom window-sill – in the summer the plants would get really huge. Anyway, one day, his *Babcia* was cooking the family dinner when she ran out of herbs,' he looked up, found her smiling in anticipation.

'The old lady decided that Tomek's plant was some kind of parsley, and chopped a whole bunch of the stuff into a bowl of potatoes. Luckily, it wasn't all that strong. All the same, he said that after dinner, when the state news came on – you know, the old *Kommie* stuff about tractor production targets being broken yet again – the whole family started cracking up, laughing their heads off, and found they just couldn't stop.'

Justyna met his gaze, a grin dimpling her cheeks.

'Anyway, Tomek said that the night went down in family history,' Janusz went on. 'And whenever his parents told the story, they always said the same thing: *"That batch of elderberry wine was the best that Babcia ever made!"*'

They laughed together, any remaining ice between them fully broken. He seized the moment to ask, 'But in London, you can get anything, of course. *Kokaina, Ekstasa,* so on . . .'

'Sure,' she agreed. 'If you are a fucking *idiota*.' She sucked some juice up through her straw. 'One of my friends died, back home, from sniffing glue. He was fifteen.' She shook her head. 'If I'd taken drugs I'd probably be dead like him, or even worse – still stuck in Katowice.' They shared a wry grin: the joke crossed the generational divide.

Seizing the moment, he asked, 'You think Pawel messes about with drugs, don't you?'

She hesitated, then met his eyes. 'I think so, yes. How else does someone like him make such money?'

Janusz made his move.

'You know that pani Tosik has hired me to find Weronika,' he said. Justyna gave a barely perceptible nod. 'I can see it's difficult for you – you are loyal to your friend. But I think you are right to be worried that this boyfriend of hers might put her in danger.'

She played with the straw in her glass, a frown creasing her forehead.

'I'm not asking you to betray her trust – just to give me a few pointers,' he went on. 'It would help if I knew how Adamski talked her into going off like that.'

The girl took a big breath, let it out slowly. Then, speaking in a low voice, she told him that two weeks earlier, while pani Tosik was out getting her hair done, Weronika had locked herself away in her bedroom above the restaurant. Suspecting that something was going on, Justyna kept knocking and calling her name through the door.

'In the end, she let me in,' she said. 'She was bouncing off the walls with excitement. Then I saw the half-packed suitcase on the bed. At first, she wouldn't tell me what was going on, said Pawel had sworn her to secrecy.' A line appeared between Justyna's dark eyebrows. 'But Nika couldn't keep a secret to save her own life. In the end she showed me the ring she was wearing on a chain round her neck.'

'They were *engaged*?' asked Janusz, incredulous. An image of Weronika in a G-string posing for the camera, her eyes unfocused, swam before him and he tensed his jaw. Some fiancé, he thought.

Justyna nodded. 'She was as excited as a little child on Christmas Eve,' she said, unable to suppress a smile at the memory.

'Did she say where she was going, where they would be living?'

She shook her head – but judging by the way her gaze slid away from his, he suspected she was lying.

'She said they'd be leaving London soon. Pawel had some business to finish up, and then they were going back home to get married.' She popped her eyes. 'All this, after she'd known him just a few weeks!'

Janusz was touched by Justyna's concern. She couldn't be more than five or six years older than Weronika, but it was clear the younger girl brought out the mother hen in her.

'I tried to talk her out of it,' she went on. 'I said, imagine how upset your mama will be when she hears her little girl has run off with some man she barely knows.'

'But it did no good?'

'She went a bit quiet,' recalled Justyna. 'But then she said Mama would be fine so long as no one cut off her supply of *cytrynowka*,' she shot him a look. The sickly lemon *wodka* was a notorious tipple of street drunks – and alcoholic housewives. 'Nika told me she would often come home from school and find her lying unconscious on the kitchen floor.'

Apparently, Mama had been little more than a child herself when she'd fallen pregnant with Weronika. The little girl had grown up without a father and the only family apart from her chaotic drunk of a mother had been a distant uncle who visited once in a blue moon.

Poor kid, thought Janusz. It was hardly surprising that after leaving home, she should fall head over heels in love with the first person who showed her any affection – like a baby bird imprinting on whoever feeds it, however ill-advised the love object.

By now, there was standing room only in the bar area, and the crowd was encroaching on the small table where Janusz and Justyna sat. The *thump thump* of the music, the shouted conversations and the bodies pressing in all around set up a fluttering in Janusz's stomach. So when the girl said she ought to go, she had an early start at the restaurant the next day, he felt a surge of relief.

He insisted on walking Justyna to her flat, which was

a mile away to the west, the other side of Stratford, beyond the River Lea. The route took them through the centre of town, where the music and strident chatter spilling from the lit doorways of pubs and clubs and the clusters of smokers outside suggested the place was just waking up, although it was gone eleven and only a Tuesday. As they passed the entrance to an alleyway beside one pub Janusz heard urgent voices and, through the gloom, saw two men pushing a smaller guy up against the wall. He froze, muscles bunching, but a second later the scene came into focus. The little guy was catatonic with drunkenness, head drooping and limbs floppy, and the other two, weaving erratically themselves, were simply trying to keep their mate upright.

Janusz and Justyna shared a look and walked on. No one would describe Poles as abstemious, but any serious drinking was done at home and public drunkenness was frowned upon. Janusz's mother, who'd visited London as a child before the war, had always spoken approvingly of the English as a decorous and reserved people, so it was fair to say that his first Friday night out with the guys from the building site had been something of an eye-opener. Still, the greatest compliment you could pay a man back then was to say he could carry his drink, and those who ended the night by falling over or picking a fight were viewed with pitying scorn.

Justyna shared a flat in a tidy-looking low-rise estate run by a housing association. Pausing on the pavement outside, she turned to him, drawing smoke from her cigarette deep into her lungs against the cold. 'Thanks for the drinks,' she said.

'You're welcome.' He took a draw on his cigar, then

exhaled, blowing his smoke downwind of her. She seemed in no hurry to go in.

'Look, I really shouldn't do this,' she said at last. 'I promised Nika . . .'

She pulled a folded slip of paper out of her pocket, and handed it to him.

'Pawel made her swear not to give their address to anyone. But she wanted me to look out for letters from her mama, forward them on. She knew she could trust me,' she stared off down the darkened street, '. . . *thought* she could trust me.'

He glanced at the paper, registering an address in Essex before pocketing it. 'Listen, Justyna. You are the best friend Weronika has.' He sought her gaze. 'She's probably found out by now that Pawel is no knight in shining armour – maybe she's wondering how to leave him without too much fuss,' he said, flexing his knuckles. 'If that's how it is, I'll make sure her wishes are respected.'

She took a step toward him. 'Be careful,' she said, in a low voice. 'I don't think Pawel is right in the head. Nika must have let slip that I warned her off him, because one day he followed me home, all the way from work,' her eyes widened. 'He grabbed me by the arm and went crazy.' Her lips trembled as she relived the shock of it. 'He told me if I didn't keep my fucking nose out, he'd kill me.'

The guy was clearly a *psychol*, thought Janusz. 'Don't worry,' he told the girl. 'Guys like him are usually all talk.'

She nodded, not entirely convinced. 'And Nika said she'd phone me, but I've heard nothing, not even a text.'

A child cried sharply somewhere in her block and she

shivered, then said in a rush: 'It's freezing – can I make you a coffee? Or maybe you'd like a *wodka*?'

That was unexpected. He sensed a fear of rejection in her averted face. Was she propositioning him? Compassion, good sense – and yes, temptation, too – wrestled briefly in his heart, and then a vision loomed up before him – the stern face of that old killjoy Father Pietruski.

He shook his head. 'Another time, darling, I've got a lot on tomorrow.'

'You'll let me know when you find out where Nika is?' said the girl, anxiety ridging her forehead.

'You'll be the first to hear,' he said.

He watched her walk into the block, and two or three minutes later a first-floor light came on in what he guessed was her flat. He lingered, thinking that she might appear in the window, but was then distracted by the screech of a big dark-coloured car pulling out from the estate. Gunning its engine, it tore off down the street. When he looked back up at the block, the curtains had been closed on the oblong of light. Feeling a pang of loneliness, he threw down his cigar stub and left.

Eight

For DC Kershaw, the following day would turn out to be what her Dad might have called a game of two halves.

As she stretched herself awake in the pre-dawn gloom, her triceps and calf muscles delivered a sharp reminder of how she'd spent the previous evening – scaling the toughest route on the indoor wall on Mile End Road, handhold by punishing handhold. It was worth it, though. Climbing demanded a level of concentration so focused and crystalline that it left no headspace for stressing about the job. And she was getting pretty good, too – last summer she'd ticked off her first grade 7a climb, up in the Peaks. She hadn't been tempted to mention her feat at work, obviously, because that would mean the entire nick calling her Spiderwoman . . . *like for ever.*

Still half-asleep, she stepped under the power shower, and found herself assaulted by jets of icy water. Gasping, she flattened her back against the cold glass and spun the knob right round to red, but it didn't make a blind bit of difference. A quick tour of the flat revealed all the radiators to be stone cold, too – the boiler must be up the spout. Cursing, she pulled on her clothes, then her winter coat, and hurrying into the minuscule galley kitchen, turned on all four gas rings.

While she was scaling K2 last night, the rest of the guys had gone out on a piss-up to celebrate Browning's birthday. She'd almost joined them, but luckily Ben Crowther tipped her off – with a look that said it *definitely* wasn't his thing – that the birthday boy wanted to hit a lap-dancing club in Shoreditch later. *No thanks.* Being 'one of the guys' in the office was one thing, but she could live without the sight of Browning getting his crotch polished by some single mum with 36DD implants and a Hollywood wax.

The milk she added to her brewed tea floated straight to the surface in yellowy curds. *Bugger.* After making a fresh cup, black this time, she took it into the living room. As she sat on the sofa in her coat drinking the tea – too astringent-tasting without the milk – she fretted about how she would find time today to hassle the letting agents, let alone wangle a half-day off for the boiler repairman. Life had been a lot less stressful when Mark had lived here. Not that he was some spanner-wielding DIY god – Mark drove a desk in a Docklands estate agents and the only gadgets he'd mastered were the remote controls for the telly and the Skyplusbox – but it was so much easier when there were two of you to sort out the tedious household stuff.

As she attacked her last surviving nail, unshakeable habit and source of much mickey-taking at the station, her gaze fell on the dusty surface of the TV cabinet and the darker rectangle where the plasma screen used to sit. She'd let Mark take it when they split up last month.

How did I get to be sitting alone in a rented flat that I can't afford, drinking black tea in my coat? she thought suddenly, and felt her eyes prickle.

She reminded herself how unbearable the atmosphere between her and Mark had become in those last few weeks, when their dead relationship lay in the flat like a decomposing body which they stepped over and around without ever acknowledging. By comparison, the previous phase had been preferable. The rows had started a couple of months ago, after she got the job at Newham CID and started coming home late and lagered-up two or three times a week. If she was in luck, he'd be asleep when she crawled into bed beside him, but if not, there'd be trouble. He'd complain she reeked of booze and fags, but they both knew that wasn't the real issue. Mark never really accepted her argument that she went drinking with the guys not because she fancied any of them, but because bonding was fundamental to the job. The argument would get more and more heated, and then he'd start in on her language. *Since you joined the cops, Nat, you talk more like a bloke than a bird.*

The last accusation hit home; but you couldn't spend all day holding your own with a bunch of macho guys, then come home and morph into Cheryl Cole. Sometimes she felt like she'd actually grown a Y-chromosome over the last few years.

Kershaw had always felt comfortable around men – probably because she'd been brought up by her father. The photos of her as a kid said it all – playing five-a-side with him and his mates in the park . . . holding up her first fish – a carp – caught at Walthamstow Reservoir . . . draped in a Hammers scarf on the way to the footie. Dad told her, more than once, that he never missed having a son, because with her he got the best of both worlds – a beautiful, clever little girl who could clear a pool table in under ten minutes.

Two years ago, when they told him the cancer was terminal, he confided, in a hoarse whisper that tore her heart out, that looking back, he had one regret: *I should have remarried after your Mum died*, he said, *so you had someone to teach you how to be a lady.*

Checking her watch, Kershaw gave a very unladylike sniff, wiped her face, and told herself to stop being such a wuss. Then, gulping the rest of the lukewarm tea down with a grimace, she picked up her bag.

As she closed the front door behind her, she heard her dad's voice.

Up and at 'em, girl, it said, *up and at 'em.*

Parking in the minuscule car park attached to Newham nick was the usual struggle, and it didn't improve Kershaw's mood to see Browning's car was already there. The little creep always got in early for his shift.

There was an email from Waterhouse in her inbox. The PM report had come back, and even better, the lab must have had a quiet week because they'd already done the tox report on DB16. It confirmed the cause of death as overdose by PMA – the dodgy drug Waterhouse had mentioned. *Yes!* She printed out the report, and surfing a wave of adrenaline, made a beeline for Streaky's desk.

Later on, she would reflect it might have been better to wait till Streaky had downed his first pint of brick-red tea *before* she started waving the report around.

He didn't lift his gaze from the racing pages. 'Sarge . . .' she tried, hovering over him, 'Sorry to . . .'

'Fuck off, I'm busy,' he replied, without looking up.

'The PM report on the floater . . .'

He lowered the paper, and fixed her with a bloodshot stare.

'Which part of the well-known Anglo-Saxon phrase, "fuck off" don't you understand? Go and wax your bikini line or something.'

With that he swivelled his chair to turn his back on her and circled a horse in the 2.30 p.m. at Newmarket. Face radiating heat, she slipped the report into his in-tray, and returned to her desk by the window. Browning, whose desk faced hers, caught her eye, his face a study in faux-sympathy.

'*Hangover,*' he hissed, leaning across the desk. 'It turned into a bit of bender last night.'

'Oh yes?' said Kershaw, opening her mailbox.

'You should have come,' he said. 'We had a good laugh at Obsessions – you know, the lap dance place?'

Suddenly, he started tapping on his keyboard. Glancing over her shoulder, Kershaw saw DI Bellwether standing behind them, deep in conversation with the Sarge.

Bellwether, a tall, fit-looking guy in his early thirties, was all matey smiles, although it was clear from his body language who was boss. Streaky had put on his jacket and adopted the glassy smile he employed with authority. Kershaw could tell he resented the Guv – not because the guy had ever done anything to him, but probably because Bellwether had joined the Met as a graduate on the now-defunct accelerated promotion programme, which meant he'd gained DI rank in five years, around half the time it would have taken him to work his way up in the old days. The very mention of accelerated promotion or, as he preferred to call it, *arse-elevated* promotion, would turn Streaky fire-tender red.

Kershaw thought his animosity toward Bellwether was all a bit daft, really, since Streaky was a self-declared career DS without the remotest interest in promotion. As he never tired of explaining, becoming an inspector meant kissing goodbye to paid overtime, spending more time on 'management bollocks' than proper police work, and having to count paperclips to keep the boss-wallahs upstairs happy. An absolute mug's game, in other words.

She could overhear the two of them discussing the latest initiative from the Justice Department.

'We'll make it top priority, Guv,' she heard Streaky say. He was always on his best behaviour with the bosses, and never uttered a word against any of them personally – a self-imposed discipline that no doubt dated from his stint as an NCO in the army.

As Bellwether breezed over, she and Browning got to their feet – Kershaw pleased that she'd chosen her good shoes and newest suit this morning.

'Morning Natalie, Tom. Are you early birds enjoying the dawn chorus this week?'

Ha-ha, thought Kershaw, while Browning cracked up at the non-witticism.

'What are you working on, Natalie?' Bellwether asked her, with what sounded like real interest, causing Browning's doggy grin to sag.

'I'm on a floater, Guv, Polish female taken out of the river near the Barrier.'

'Cause of death?'

'OD. Some dodgy pseudo-ecstasy called PMA – might be coming over from Europe.'

'PMA? That rings a bell . . .' mused Bellwether. 'Let me surf my inbox and give you a heads-up later today.'

Kershaw stifled a grin. Bellwether was alright, but attending too many management workshops had given him a nasty dose of jargonitis.

After he left, Streaky called her over.

'So let me guess,' he drawled, flipping through Waterhouse's PM report. 'The good doctor has got you all overexcited about a dodgy drugs racket. You do know he's a tenner short of the full cash register?'

'The tox report backs it up, though, Sarge,' said Kershaw, keeping her voice nice and low. He had once informed the whole office that women's voices were on the same frequency as the sound of nails scraped down a blackboard. *Scientific fact*, he said.

Streaky just grunted. 'So you've got an OD with this stuff, wassitcalled . . . *PMT* . . .' – no fucking way was she taking *that* bait – 'but even assuming you had a nice juicy lead to the lowlife who supplied the drugs, what's your possible charge?'

Keeping her voice nice and steady, Kershaw said, 'Well, Sarge, it could be manslaughter . . .'

Streaky whistled. '*Manslaughter.* We are thinking big, aren't we?'

'Supplying a class-A drug to someone which ends up killing them is surely a pretty clear-cut case, Sarge.' As soon as the words left her mouth she realised how up herself they made her sound.

Streaky leaned back in his swivel chair and put his arms behind his head.

'Ah yes,' he said, 'I remember my early days as a dewy-eyed young Detective Constable . . .'

Here we go, she thought.

'It was all so simple. Wielding the warrant card of truth and the truncheon of justice, I would catch all the nasty villains fair and square, put them in the dock, and Rumpole of the Bailey would send them away for a nice long stretch. End of.'

She resisted the urge to remind him that actually, Rumpole had been on the dark side, aka defence counsel.

'Then I woke up,' he yawned, 'and found myself back in CID.' He leaned forward and waved the PM report under her nose. 'Even if you *did* find the dealer – which you won't – and *prove* he supplied the gear – which you can't – I can assure you that our esteemed colleagues at CPS will trot out 101 cast-iron reasons why it is nigh-on impossible to get a manslaughter conviction in cases of OD. The main one being it's "too difficult to establish a chain of fucking causality", if memory serves.'

He scooted the report into his pending tray with a flourish.

'I'll tell those long-haired tossers in Drug Squad about it. They might be interested if there are some killer Smarties doing the rounds. You carry on trying to trace the floater, just don't spend all your time on it.'

'Yes, Sarge.' She hesitated, 'But I still think that whoever gave the female the PMA – maybe her boyfriend, this guy Pawel – panicked and dumped her in the river after she OD-ed. I mean why else would she be starkers?'

She tensed up, half-expecting him to go ballistic at that; instead, he sighed, and picking up the report again with exaggerated patience, flicked through to the page he was looking for and started reading out loud.

'*The levels of PMA found in the blood may have caused hallucinations*' – he shot her a meaningful look – '*. . . the subject's core temperature would have risen rapidly, causing extreme discomfort . . .*' – his voice was getting louder and angrier by the second – '*PMA overdose victims often try to cool off by removing clothing, wrapping themselves in wet towels and taking cold showers . . .*' He slapped the report shut. 'Or maybe, *Detective*, seeing as they are off their tits, by jumping in the fucking river!'

Kershaw noticed that Streaky's chin had gone the colour of raw steak, which was a bad sign. Now he picked a document out of his in-tray and shoved it at her.

'Here you go, Miss Marple, the perfect case for a detective with a special interest in pharmaceuticals – a suspected cannabis factory in Leyton. Enjoy!'

Three hours later, Kershaw was shivering in her car, outside the dope factory, with the engine running in a desperate bid to warm up, smoking a fag and trying to remember why she ever joined the cops.

Thank God that ponytailed, earring-wearing careers teacher from Poplar High School couldn't see her now. When she'd announced, aged sixteen, that she wanted to be a detective, he'd barely been able to hide his disapproval. He clearly had no time for the police, but could hardly say so. Instead, he adopted a caring face, and gave her a lecture on how 'challenging' she'd find police culture as a woman. She'd responded: 'But sir, isn't the only way to change sexist institutions from the inside?'

In truth, the police service hadn't been her first career choice. As a kid, when her friends came to play, she'd inveigle them into staging imaginary court cases, with the kitchen of the flat standing in for the Old Bailey. Turned on its side, the kitchen table made a convincing dock for the defendant, while the judge, wearing a red dressing gown and a tea towel for a wig, oversaw proceedings perched up on the worktop. But the real star of the show was Natalie, who, striding about in her Nan's best black velvet coat, conducted devastating cross-examinations and made impassioned speeches to the jury – aka Denzil, the family dog. As far as she could recall, she was always the prosecutor, never the defence. It wasn't till she reached her teens that it dawned on her: the barristers in TV dramas always had names like Rupert or Jocasta, and talked like someone had wired their jaws together. The Met might be a man's world, but at least coming from Canning Town didn't stop you reaching the top.

The dope factory was in an ordinary terraced house in Markham Road, a quiet street, despite its closeness to Leyton's scruffy and menacing main thoroughfare. Driving through, she had counted three lowlifes flaunting their gangsta dogs, vicious bundles of muscle, probable illegal breeds, trained to intimidate and attack. Obviously, she'd stopped to pull the owners over for a chat. *Yeah, right.*

The report said that the young Chinese men who had rented number 49 for four or five months hadn't aroused any suspicions among the neighbours. Kershaw suspected that in a nicer area, their comings and goings at all hours, never mind the blackout blinds and rivers of condensation running down the inside of the windows, might have got curtains twitching a lot sooner, but then round here, maybe you were grateful if the place next door wasn't actually a full-on crack house. In the end, number 49 had only got busted by accident, when a fire broke out on the ground floor.

As she pulled up, the fire tender was just driving off, leaving the three-storey house still smoking, the glass in the ground-floor windows blackened and cracked but otherwise intact. It looked like they'd caught the blaze early. Inside the stinking hallway, its elaborate cornice streaked with black, she picked her way around pools of sooty water, now regretting the decision to wear her favourite shoes. In the front room, once the cosy front parlour of some respectable Victorian family, she found a mini-rainforest of skunk plants, battered and sodden from the firemen's hoses. Overhead, there hung festoons of wiring that had powered the industrial fluorescent strip lights; on the floor, a tangle of rubber tubing that presumably supplied the plants with water and the skunk-equivalent of Baby Bio.

'Hello, beautiful, come to see what real cops do for a change?'

Frowning, she turned round, to find a familiar face – Gary, an old buddy from her time at Romford Road nick a few years back.

'Gaz! How's life on the frontline?'

Gary was a few years older than her – well into his thirties by now – and still a PC. He had been her minder when she had first gone on the beat as a probie, but they became proper mates after a memorable evening when they got called to a pub fight between football hoolies. West Ham had just thrashed old enemies Millwall at Upton Park, so it was the kind of ruck that could easily have become a riot. She and Gary could hardly nick them all: instead, they ID-ed the ringleaders and pulled them out, putting the lid on it without even getting their sticks out. Back at the station, Gary had told anyone who'd listen that Kershaw had thrown herself into the fray 'just like a geezer'.

'All the other rooms like this?' she asked, after they'd done a bit of catching up.

'Yep. Third one this month,' said Gary, shaking his head. 'You missed the best bit, though.'

Apparently, when he'd arrived on scene, he'd found a bunch of locals having an impromptu party outside the burning house.

'It was quite a sight – there was a boom box blaring, they were drinking beer, dancing around in the smoke, everyone getting off their face on the free *ganja*,' said Gary, shaking his head, grinning. 'It was like Notting Hill Carnival.'

Kershaw smiled but her eyes were uneasy. Gary was probably the least racist cop she'd ever met, but she hoped he watched himself in front of the Guvnors. That sort of chat could get you into big trouble these days.

'Down to us to do the clear-up, I suppose?' she asked.

'Got it in one, Detective,' he grinned.

Kershaw spent the next few hours cursing the Sarge for dumping this nightmare job in her lap. The cheeky slags who ran the factory had powered it for free, running a cable from the lamppost next to their garden wall, which meant she had to call out the Electricity Board. She took half a dozen statements from the neighbours – total waste of time, of course, but she'd still have to type them up – and the worst job was still to come. Kershaw, Gary, and a single probie would have to bag and label every single one of the 1000-plus plants and load them onto a lorry to go to the evidence store.

It was all a load of old bollocks, anyway. It was only ever the 'gardeners' at the bottom of the dope pyramid who got nicked – never the big fish.

As she sat in the car finishing her fag Gary came over and, leaning down to the open driver's door, handed her a clear plastic parcel – a Met-issue protective suit and gloves. 'Showtime,' he said, grinning.

'Sadist,' she muttered. Dropping her fag in the gutter, she ground it under her heel. Then the radio squawked into life.

'Go ahead, Charlie 1,' she said pressing the talk button.

'At the request of DS Bacon, please attend the Waveney Thameside Hotel, Wapping,' said the operator. 'Report of a Sus X11. He will join you at the scene.'

Sus X11 was control room code for a suspicious death.

Game on, thought Kershaw.

Nine

The engine of the Transit van shrieked as Oskar thrust it into second without any perceptible reduction in speed, and accelerated around a sharp bend. Janusz felt his right leg shoot out to slam on an imaginary brake – a movement that didn't escape Oskar, of course: 'It's like driving a *babcia* to church!' he chuckled. They screeched to a halt at a red light, and Oskar reached behind him, producing a six-pack of Tyskie, and popped the ring-pull on one with a hiss. 'Have a beer, mate, maybe it will help you grow a bigger pair of *jaja*!'

'Mother of God, Oskar! We can't turn up smelling of beer – I want the girl to *trust* us.'

Waving away the objection, Oskar took a heroic swallow.

'A man is not a cactus, he has to drink. Anyway,' he added, pulling a tube from his overall pocket with a flourish, 'I bought a packet of minty sweets.' He tapped his forehead, 'Always thinking one step ahead, Janek, always one step ahead.'

The two mates were in one of Oskar's rust buckets, heading northeast on the A12, bound for Adamski and Weronika's address deep in the Essex countryside. Janusz had never heard of Willowbridge, hadn't even realised how far out of town it was till he'd looked at a map.

He tried to suppress the niggle of guilt he was feeling for not calling pani Tosik with the news. The old girl had been emphatic that he was to do no more than discover Weronika's address so that she could forward her poor, frantic mama's letter. But the more Janusz learned about this lowlife Pawel Adamski, the more he felt some responsibility for the girl. Of course, he couldn't force her to come back, but he could give her some fatherly advice. And there was a good chance that she'd be having second thoughts about her engagement by now.

So he had talked Oskar – who was working night shifts – into giving him a lift, partly to avoid a marathon journey by train and taxi, but also because he might need reinforcements. Adamski was bound to cut up rough if Weronika did agree to come back to London, and women loved Oskar. He could put the girl at ease, get her into the van while Janusz dealt with the boyfriend.

There was the blast of a horn from the car behind them – the lights had changed. They lurched forward, Oskar steering with his left hand so he could use the right to make flamboyant gestures of abuse in the rear-view mirror. Janusz rolled his eyes. At this rate, they'd be lucky to reach Willowbridge without getting shot by some Essex gangster.

'*After one hundred metres, turn left,*' said a woman's voice from the box on the dashboard.

'No fucking way should we be going left!' complained Oskar. 'This satnav is dogshit!'

'Maybe you just don't like a woman telling you what to do,' said Janusz, grinning. He'd begun the day in a melancholic mood, returning over and over again to the row with Kasia, wondering if the affair really was finished. He kept visualising her: the aquiline nose and half-smile, that air of beguiling inscrutability. But ten minutes in Oskar's company had pushed her out of his thoughts, made him feel alive again. Who knew what women wanted – you could waste a lifetime trying to work it out.

'Anyway,' said Oskar. 'You said you had a photo of this chick we're looking for?' He waggled his bushy eyebrows like a pantomime villain.

Janusz dug out the shot of Weronika in her fur coat that pani Tosik had given him.

'*Ale laska!*' Oskar exclaimed, 'I'd like to rattle her bones.'

Five minutes later, they tore past a sign that said they were entering Willowbridge, and Janusz managed to persuade Oskar to slow down. The place had a thatched pub, a duck pond, and half-timbered cottages clustered round a green. Aside from the huge awning advertising Sky football, it was the kind of English village Janusz recognised from black and white movies shown in Poland when he was young. He was still half-expecting to find a grotty block of flats around the next corner, but instead, Adamski's address turned out to be a substantial cottage with a pretty garden bordered by a yew hedge and an oak porch silvered grey by the centuries.

As they pulled up a discreet distance away, Oskar whistled, rubbing his fingers together. 'Your boy is loaded, huh?'

There was no sign of Adamski's BMW outside, and after watching the house for ten minutes or so, Janusz concluded there was nobody at home.

'What now?' asked Oskar, an operatic yawn splitting his face – he'd come straight from a ten-hour shift. 'They could be gone all day.'

'That's why I wanted you to bring the overalls and the tools,' said Janusz. 'I'm going to get inside – check the place out.' He had some vague idea of finding evidence of drugs, using them as a lever against Adamski when he did turn up.

Oskar rubbed his hands with glee. '*Tak!* I always wanted to try some of this "James Bond" shit you get up to.'

'It's better if I do this on my own, Oskar. Gosia would never forgive me if I got you arrested.'

'*Kurwa mac!* Janek,' Oskar was already levering his stocky little frame out the driving seat, 'You're not gonna leave me sitting in the fucking van like a little kid.'

Sighing, Janusz started to pull on his overalls. A few minutes later, they were strolling up the front path, toting a toolbox and ladder, a pair of workmen on a routine job. Janusz rang the bell, which sounded horribly strident in the countryside hush, and waited. Nothing.

Leaving Oskar out front on guard duty, he headed round the back. The place had a huge garden – he couldn't even make out where it ended – and three big *kasztan* trees screened the rear of the house. At ground level, the windows and French doors were tightly closed, but on the first floor, Janusz found what he'd been looking for. A bathroom skylight, open a crack.

After collecting Oskar, Janusz leaned the ladder up

against the back wall. 'Just keep an eye out while I go in, okay?'

Oskar nodded. 'If anyone comes, I'll say I'm doing some work,' he produced a wood block wrapped in sanding paper, 'prepping the woodwork for painting.' He beamed at the brilliance of his ploy.

When Janusz reached the top of the ladder, he checked the lie of the land. Perfect: the chestnut trees, fifteen or twenty metres tall, protected the cottage from the gaze of any nosy neighbours. Thirty seconds later, he had the casement window open and was just extending his left leg onto the sill when a sudden cramp shot through his thigh. Cursing, he rubbed the ridge of muscle, waiting for the pain to subside before trusting his weight to it: *cat burglary was a young man's game*.

Once inside, Janusz undid the top button of his overall – the place was stifling hot – and glanced around. As well as a fancy roll-top bath, there was a shower that came straight out of the ceiling, and the polished limestone lining the walls must have cost fifty or sixty quid a metre.

Venturing downstairs, he entered the living room, ducking his head to avoid the blackened beams, and took in the elegant decoration, the two-metre wide state-of-the-art plasma screen and the pricey-looking furniture. Justyna had been right: Adamski must have deep pockets to rent a place like this. But it was a *chlew*, a pigsty. Magazines, papers and the cushions from the sofa were strewn about the place. The drawers of a sideboard were hanging open, the faint line of dirt on the wall behind suggesting it had been pulled out from its usual spot.

The dining room was in a similar state. An antique-looking bureau had been emptied and its contents piled on the floor, the wood on one of the drawers splintered as though it had been forced open. Janusz wiped his forehead with the back of his sleeve – the heat was coming off the radiators in waves, and a putrid stink hung in the air. He was starting to feel uneasy. It looked like a gang of burglars had been through the place – but how could they have overlooked the brand new iPad, still in its packaging, that stood against the wall? Leafing through the pile of papers on the floor, he found guarantees for the plasma screen and a Bose hi-fi, plus Ocado receipts, takeaway menus: the usual stuff. He sighed – what had he expected to find – invoices for *Ekstasa* shipments?

Turning to go, he knocked a London A to Z off the bureau, and a piece of paper fluttered from its pages onto the oak floorboards. It bore the words *'Bannister, 87 Porto Belo'*, scrawled in a childlike hand. Tucking it away, Janusz continued his tour.

In the L-shaped kitchen diner, the cupboard doors stood ajar, contents spread across the worktop, and the refrigerator door hung open. Janusz crooked his arm over his nose – the smell was overpowering, sickening in here. He made his way cautiously towards the dining area at the bottom of the L, which seemed to be the source of the stench. A trickle of sweat ran over his collarbone and he had to fight down a sudden gust of fear at what he might be about to find.

As he approached the dining table, on which there stood a bulging white carrier bag, the stink grew more intense. With his heart banging uncomfortably against his chest wall, he craned to peer inside the bag – and blew out a noisy breath. It held two bottles of lager and half a dozen tinfoil takeaway boxes, apparently unopened. As he peeled the lid from one, the foul stench made him gag. For a surreal moment, he thought the yellow noodles had come alive, before realising the food was seething with maggots.

He folded the carrier bag back over the horrible sight and returned to the open fridge. Clasping a hand round a bottle of milk on the top shelf, he found it cool to the touch and moist with condensation.

Janusz gulped some cold water straight from the tap and leaned against the worktop to think. The takeaway meal Pawel and Weronika had ordered but never got round to eating was clearly several days old. Whoever opened the fridge had been here much more recently, within the last few hours. There was one obvious conclusion. Unless Weronika was happy to leave rotting food lying around, the couple hadn't been back here for days. But earlier today, somebody had taken the place apart, clearly searching for something.

Catching a sudden movement out of the corner of his eye he whipped round, only to find Oskar's cherubic face at the window, grinning and making the all clear sign. Exasperated, he waved him away, and returned upstairs. In the couple's bedroom, the chest of drawers was half empty. All that remained was some underwear and a tube of contraceptive gel Weronika must have forgotten to take with her.

More surprising was the couple's choice of bedtime reading: on the bedside table lay a history of the Solidarity movement, a weighty, new-looking hardback, its cover emblazoned with a famous poster from the late eighties.

It showed a beaming Lech Walesa being borne aloft by triumphant supporters beneath the union's famous red banner – the word *Solidarnosc* daubed in that optimistic, almost childlike, lettering. It was a famous shot, taken at the end of the Round Table talks, which had wrung the promise of elections from General Jaruzelski's government.

Walesa was crudely rendered, but at least that ugly mug couldn't be anyone else. Of the faces clustered in the foreground Janusz recognised just two – Tadeusz Maziwiecki, later to become prime minister, and Edward Zamorski, the current presidential candidate. Compared to the portly middle-aged image of the election posters, the young Zamorski looked improbably young and fresh-faced.

Eccentric reading matter, thought Janusz, for Adamski the druggie, or Weronika, the immature teenager of Justyna's description. Realising he'd forgotten to ask Justyna what Adamski looked like, he made a mental note to call her later.

Then, still puzzling over the book, he strolled over to the built-in wardrobe that filled one wall, pulled open the door – and froze.

Inside, on a padded hanger, hung the fur coat Weronika had worn in the photo, the one pani Tosik had said was from TK Maxx. *Bullshit.* He stroked the pale soft fur. He might not be an expert on the discount chain's range but he was pretty sure it didn't include finest quality Russian sable.

If he needed any more evidence that Adamski was up to his chin in *gowno*, this was the clincher. Never mind the abandoned takeaway, whatever it was that made the lovebirds fly their coop a few days ago had been so urgent it had meant leaving behind a fur worth twenty grand. As for the people who ransacked the cottage, they'd shown a disturbing lack of interest in the valuables scattered about the place. It was Adamski they were after, and, finding him gone, they'd tossed the place – maybe for his drugs or money stash, maybe for a clue to where he was heading.

Janusz cursed under his breath. This job had seemed simple enough – find Weronika and try to persuade her to ditch the dodgy boyfriend. Now it looked like the couple was on the run from a bunch of *gangsterzy*, probably in some dispute over drugs, which meant she was in serious danger.

As he was closing the wardrobe door, he heard Oskar's voice outside, speaking at top volume – obviously trying to alert him. Peeking around the edge of the curtain, his stomach lurched. A well-built guy in a waxed jacket stood below, his body language radiating suspicion, while Oskar, gesturing at the house with his sanding block, trotted out his cover story.

It didn't look good.

Janusz ducked into the ensuite bathroom and stuck his head under the tap. Shivering and with his heart booming unpleasantly, he plastered down his wet hair, pulled on a bathrobe from a hook behind the door and crossed himself, twice. Here goes, he thought, throwing open the window.

'Can I help with anything?' he asked, in his best cut-glass accent, sending up fervent thanks for all those war movies his mama had made him sit through to learn English.

The guy looked up. 'Ah! There is somebody at home,'

he said in a confident voice. If he was flustered by this sudden appearance he didn't show it. 'I wanted to ensure this chap wasn't up to anything – I spotted him from the right-of-way footpath,' he waved a hand at the garden's boundary. Janusz cursed the inexplicable English laws that allowed any Tom, Dick or Harry free passage through a man's back garden.

'Well, that's very decent of you,' he drawled, baring his teeth in a grin. 'But as you can see, he's doing a spot of decorating for me. I do think it's important not to let things slide, don't you agree?' He almost chucked in a 'what ho', but stopped himself in time.

'Indeed,' said the man, starting to step backwards in the beginnings of a dignified retreat. 'Sorry to interrupt your shower. Can't be too careful, though.'

'Don't mention it,' Janusz beamed, 'have a nice day.'
Have a nice day?

The guy didn't appear to notice the bum note. Nodding to Oskar, who – thank Christ – had kept a straight face during this performance – he went on his way, raising his walking stick in farewell. When he was halfway across the lawn a rangy Alsatian emerged from the shrubbery and loped along at his heels.

Janusz towel-dried his hair roughly and pulled on his clothes. By the time he opened the front door, Oskar was already there.

'Fucking brilliant!' he said, eyes bright with excitement, barging in before Janusz could stop him. 'That guy was really grilling me till you turned up.'

'Let's just get the fuck out of here,' said Janusz as Oskar started nosing around the place. 'I'll grab the ladder, you get the tools.'

He had just stowed the ladder in the van and slammed the doors when Oskar came running up the garden path. His progress was slowed, partly by the toolbox, but also by the boxed iPad tucked under his other arm. Panting, he shouted: 'Drive! Drive! He's coming back!' A distant shout accompanied by deep barking rang out from the back garden.

Janusz kept up a breakneck speed all the way to the M11.

'What the fuck did you think you were doing back there? Playing Supermarket fucking Sweep?!'

Oskar cackled, still high on the excitement. 'Relax, Janek,' he said, throwing half a dozen mints into his mouth. 'The guy must have been sixty – he wasn't about to break into a sprint, was he?'

'Yeah? And what about his dog, *idiota*? It was the size of a donkey!'

Janusz recalled how, on exercises in the forest, often using live ammunition, the eighteen-year-old Oskar had been fearless to the point of recklessness. The instructors' reports routinely described him as 'not suitable for military service', which Oskar had, *naturalnie*, considered a badge of pride.

'And never mind the rabid fucking dog, what if the guy spotted the van, called the licence plate in to the cops? Imagine if you had to phone Gosia and tell her you were in a police cell?'

That wiped the grin off his chubby face, Janusz noted with satisfaction.

'Son of a whore!' said Janusz suddenly. 'I just realised why that guy rumbled us!'

'Why?'

'Your story about sanding the woodwork . . .'

'What's wrong with that?' Oskar protested. 'I decorated plenty of houses when I first came over.'

'Yeah. And you were probably crap at it,' said Janusz. 'But I bet even you never sanded down *UPVC windows*.'

For a beat, Oskar's face furrowed, then he erupted into peals of laughter.

After Oskar dropped him off at Stratford bus station, Janusz boarded a No. 25 bus for the West End, where he'd catch another bus to Notting Hill.

It didn't take a genius to work out that *Porto Belo* was Adamski's illiterate stab at Portobello Road. On the face of it, the scribbled address on the mile-long straggle of antique shops and market stalls in Notting Hill backed his antique dealing story, but Janusz didn't buy that for a minute.

Forty minutes later, he was changing buses at Oxford Circus, which meant crossing Argyll Street, his usual route to Kasia's club. In the middle of the pedestrianised road, his treacherous feet brought him scudding to a halt. As tourists streamed around him like water around a boulder, he struggled with a powerful desire to see Kasia, to drink coffee and eat pastries with her in the comforting old-world surroundings of Patisserie Valerie. Then, unbidden, came an image of Weronika at the mercy of a pursuing drug gang, getting knocked around – or worse – as a punishment for Adamski's sins. Resuming normal service, his feet took him to the bus stop.

Walking north up Portobello from the Gate, Janusz found the street barely recognisable from his occasional forays out here in the eighties on building jobs. Back then, it had been full of black men's clubs and the acrid tang of marijuana, but now tourists outnumbered the locals ten to one, thronging the upmarket antique shops and American-style chains that charged two pounds for a cup of coffee. As a chattering herd of Japanese forced him off the pavement for the second time, pushing up his blood pressure, he spotted the name *Bannister Antiques* painted in gold on a shop window.

A man Janusz assumed to be Bannister emerged from the rear of the shop before the sound of the doorbell had faded, his face wearing the good-natured expression of a man anticipating enrichment. The smile faded as Janusz handed over his card and delivered his *spiel*: he was acting for a firm of solicitors trying to trace Pawel Adamski in connection with a legacy. The legacy story nearly always got results: however passing their acquaintance with the supposed beneficiary, people tended to help on the off-chance they might get a cut for their trouble.

Not this time.

'Never heard of him, I'm afraid,' said Bannister, returning the card with a supercilious look. Janusz ignored it, leaving him to stand with his arm uncomfortably outstretched.

'I think perhaps your memory is at fault,' he suggested politely.

Bannister dropped the card on his leather-topped desk and pulled an insincere smile, revealing small, yellowish pointed teeth that gave him a predatory air.

'I don't buy from dealers,' he said, brushing a piece of invisible fluff from the sleeve of his jacket. 'All my stock comes from auction houses.'

Janusz didn't recall saying anything about Adamski being a dealer. He held Bannister's gaze until the foxy smile started to sag and started to stroll around the shop, hands deep in the pockets of his coat, examining the stock – a mix of bad Victorian paintings, genuinely valuable *objets* and heavy dark pieces of furniture. He stopped in front of an eight-foot tall *piec kaflowy* – a wood stove, decorated with beautiful blue and white tiles depicting a hunting scene. There had been a similar one in the parlour of his grandmother's house – as a child he'd loved toasting chestnuts on its iron lid.

Janusz strolled back towards Bannister.

'Nice stove,' he said, standing so close that the guy was effectively pinned against the desk. 'I suppose you're going to tell me you bought that from an English auction house?'

Bannister craned backwards, pursing his lips.

'I'm a very busy man,' said Janusz, his voice soft and reasonable. 'And it would be in your overwhelming interest not to play any more silly games with me.' He took a half-step forward, so his toes actually touched Bannister's. 'What was your business with Adamski?'

Still Bannister made no reply. Janusz tipped his head sideways to a corner of the shop where gilt gleamed dully from the shadows. 'Unless I am mistaken, that *ikona* is Russian, tenth or eleventh century,' he said. 'You know, friend, Putin and his FSB cronies take the illegal export of valuable artefacts from the Motherland very seriously.' He fixed Bannister with a meaningful look. 'As it happens, I have some very well-connected Russian clients. One word to them and you could soon find yourself entertaining far less civilised visitors than me.'

Seeing Bannister's expression grow thoughtful, Janusz rewarded him with an extra couple of centimetres' breathing space. The story had been a gamble: the idea of a Pole having anything to do with Russians, given their tendency to invade his country at the drop of a *czapka*, would make a cat laugh. Luckily for him, the average Englishman's grasp of European history got pretty hazy beyond Dover.

'I was simply observing professional confidentiality,' said Bannister with a failed bid at hauteur. He eyed Janusz warily, 'but since you clearly have . . . *pressing* business with Mr Adamski, I am willing to make an exception.'

Janusz stepped back – allowing Bannister to slide free. He stretched up to reach a bunch of keys hanging from a hook behind the desk and then, indicating that Janusz should follow, opened a door at the back of the shop. Bannister led the way across the cobbled yard to the double doors of a lock-up garage.

'Mr Adamski claimed that he could source high-quality pieces from Poland for me,' he said, assuming a confidential tone. 'Some of the nineteenth-century furniture is still remarkably good value compared to France.'

As he turned the key in a padlock hanging from the door, he bared pointy teeth at Janusz. 'But to be frank,' he said, 'the arrangement hasn't been an *undiluted* success.'

Inside, a fluorescent strip light fizzed into life, illuminating a room full of solid old Polish furniture. Janusz drew a sharp breath: the silent congregation of ornately carved wardrobes, massive dining tables and marble-topped washstands pitched him straight back to his childhood.

'We had talked solely in principle,' Bannister continued. 'And then this lot arrived in a great big pantechnicon, completely out of the blue.' Bannister flung an arm out. 'Not so much as a call from him! And apart from the woodstove you saw, most of it wasn't remotely commercial – poor quality, or just too large for all but the grandest houses.'

'What was he like to deal with?'

Bannister's weaselly little eyes scurried over Janusz's face. 'Mr Adamski isn't a *friend* of yours, I take it?'

Janusz smiled, shook his head.

'Well, speaking frankly, I found him somewhat volatile. When he did deign to turn up, a couple of days after the delivery, and I broke it to him – diplomatically – that there was barely anything here of any value, he became quite enraged.' He glanced at Janusz's big hands. 'I managed to calm him down, but this was weeks ago, and I've seen neither hide nor hair of him since.'

'Did he take anything away with him, from the shipment?'

'Yes,' Bannister trailed a finger across the dusty top of a washstand. 'A pretty walnut bureau, in the French style – more's the pity.' His voice took on a peevish edge. 'It was one of the few really saleable pieces.'

'Locked, was it?' asked Janusz, remembering the bureau with the forced drawer at the cottage.

Bannister nodded. Then, realising that the admission showed him in a less than flattering light, added, 'I was looking for anything that would help me contact him, so I could ask him to take all *this*,' he gave a dismissive wave, 'off my hands. He didn't leave a phone number, you see, always insisted on calling me, something about changing phones.'

Janusz opened one of the wardrobes and inhaled its

117

nostalgic brew of old furs, camphor, dust and sandal-wood. Closing it gently, he turned back to Bannister.

'What about the delivery docket?'

'He took that with him, too, I'm afraid.' Bannister started pulling one of the washstands out from the others. 'But there is one thing . . .'

Pointing to the rear of the stand, he said, 'Double-Dutch to me, but it might mean something to you.'

Plastered on the back edge of the marble top was a yellow sticky label with an address: *Woytek Magazyn, Gorodnik, Pomorskie 2577.* Adamski must have kept the furniture he bought in a storage facility until he had enough for a container load. Janusz knew the voivode-ship, or province of Pomerania, alright: the army camp where he and Oskar had first met had been located in its Kashubian Lakeland, an area of gentle hills peppered with tiny villages and lakes gouged out by some colossal ancient glacier. Its beauty had been wasted on him and his fellow conscripts, whose sole obsessions had been women, *wodka* and edible food – in that order. If his memory was correct, Gorodnik was the region's only major town.

Janusz tore off the sticker and pocketed it, then asked, 'May I borrow your phone?'

Bannister handed it over and Janusz accessed the address book. Having confirmed that there was no entry under either Pawel or Adamski, he punched in his own name and number.

'If he gets in touch, make sure I'm the first to know,' he said, putting the phone back into Bannister's jacket pocket, and grinned unexpectedly. 'I don't want to have to keep popping back to remind you.'

As he walked back down Portobello to Notting Hill

tube, frustration engulfed him. Okay, maybe Adamski was using old furniture imported from Poland as a means of smuggling drugs. But so what? None of it got him any closer to finding Weronika. Adamski might never contact Bannister again and anyway, with a bunch of gangsters after him, he'd be keeping a very low profile. All of which meant the trail was as cold as a witch's tit.

Forty minutes later, emerging from Angel tube into the chilly dusk air, he found his phone was showing a missed call from Father Pietruski.

'I was wondering if I could give pani Tosik any news regarding . . . our *zgubiona owieczka*?' asked the priest when he called him back. Janusz smiled at the phrase 'stray lamb' – obviously a reference to Weronika. The old guy had this habit of dropping into coded language when discussing anything delicate or confidential – a legacy, no doubt, of his youth. As a young curate in a mountain village, Father Pietruski had secretly aided the partisans in their campaign against the Nazi occupiers, acting as a postman for local resistance groups.

Janusz gave him the bare bones – the girl had run off with a man a good deal older than her, and a bad sort, to boot. But he admitted he'd hit a complete dead end in the search for them.

'Is there nothing at all you can do?' asked the priest, his voice strained with anxiety.

'Not really,' he said gently. 'They could be anywhere by now.' After a moment's hesitation, he went on to share his suspicions about Adamski's drug dealing and the *gangsterzy* on his tail. The priest didn't sound as shocked as Janusz anticipated – but then perhaps it hadn't sunk in yet.

'If I'm right, they're on the run,' Janusz went on, 'And that makes them almost impossible to find – unless you want to contact the police, see if you can persuade them to launch a full-scale manhunt.'

'No, no. I am sure that pani Tosik will not wish to involve the authorities,' said Father Pietruski after a moment. 'And from the sort of people you say we are talking about, it might do more harm than good.'

The old guy was probably right. Janusz had a sudden image of armed police surrounding the couple's hideout and shivered – the cops had a nasty habit of shooting the wrong people.

'You really believe there is nothing more you can do?' asked the priest, his voice leaden with disappointment. Janusz felt a knifepoint of guilt, but what was the point of giving pani Tosik, or the girl's mother, false hope?

'No, Father,' he said as gently as he could manage. 'All we can do is hope that our stray lamb realises the trouble she is in and comes home of her own accord.'

Ten

If you were looking for an image to put girls off drugs, the dead female in room 1313 ticked all the boxes.

That was Kershaw's first thought as she stared at the naked body splayed so humiliatingly across the snowy expanse of the super king-sized bed. The girl's long legs, knees bent so that the heels almost touched the buttocks, had fallen wide apart, in the position females adopted for a smear test, or to give birth.

The room was hot and thick with the animal smell of sweat and recent sex overlaid with stale cigarettes. The Crime Scene Investigator, a geeky civilian officer, encased, like her, in a white hooded suit and wearing latex gloves, was kneeling by the bed. She nodded to him. 'Alright, Dave?' He grunted a greeting, busy dusting an empty vodka bottle for prints.

She approached the body, treading carefully, her plastic overshoes slippery on the carpet. The girl's head was turned sideways, right cheek resting against the mattress, her face partially obscured by the hair fanned out across it. Her right arm was flexed, the hand lying beside the jaw, and her index finger lay crooked across the lips – as though urging someone to keep a secret. Together with the part-veiled face, the chance gesture gave the girl an enigmatic air.

Kershaw, who'd never seen anyone so recently dead, felt a sudden compulsion to touch the body. She looked around: Dave had his back to her, and the uniform who'd been first on scene was busy stringing tape across the doorway. She bent and put the back of her gloved hand to the girl's chest. The skin was still surprisingly warm, but it felt . . . *inert* – missing the sensation of physiological processes beneath, blood fizzing through the veins, cells renewing, electrical impulses firing.

The body had been discovered by the chambermaid, who'd let herself in thinking the guest had gone out and forgotten to take the 'do not disturb sign' off the doorknob. A police surgeon had attended, declaring life extinct at 1255 hours.

The twenty-storey Waveney Thameside was a brand new five-star hotel, a 'destination hotel' in corporate-speak, popular with wealthy tourists and business types. Squeezed onto what was surely the last remaining patch of waste ground between Wapping High Street and the river, it had shot up astonishingly fast, Kershaw recalled. When she got the job at Newham CID, Mark had treated her to a champagne breakfast in the restaurant here, overlooking the river.

Arriving at reception today, she'd found the manager, a middle-aged suit who introduced himself as Andrew Treneman, waiting to take her up to the room.

He had greeted her with a professional smile that didn't

quite hide his harassed air – a smile that dissolved when he turned to the young woman behind the check-in desk. 'You'll be sure to page me the minute Mr Nakamura's party arrives, yes?' The girl assured him that she would, but Kershaw detected a note of studied patience in her voice that suggested they'd had this conversation a dozen times already. Treneman was clearly a bit of a control freak.

He seemed to relax a bit once they were alone, travelling skyward in the empty lift. 'Finding people who've died in their room is more common than you might think,' he said with a grimace. 'Obviously we try to keep it as low-key as possible. Our guests are here for a break from the real world – the last thing they want is to be reminded of their own mortality.'

'Mmm. It must be awkward,' said Kershaw. 'But you do realise we'll need to interview some of the guests?'

'Of course,' he said, unleashing the smile. 'Anything we can do to help. I had the check-in record printed out for you.'

Kershaw scanned the computer printout Treneman handed her, which revealed that room 1313 had been assigned to a Steven Lampart, who had checked in just after 1 a.m., using a credit card, apparently alone. He'd requested a quiet room with no guests on either side.

'What about CCTV cameras?' she asked, looking up in time to catch Treneman's gaze sliding off her chest.

'There are two in the lobby, three back of house, and one in each lift.' He lifted his chin to indicate a camera above the doors. 'Although I'm afraid Security tells me these ones are out of order.' He threw Kershaw a look, inviting her to share his frustration at their incompetence, which she ignored.

As the lift doors opened onto the thirteenth floor, Treneman's pager went off. He examined it with a deepening frown and asked, 'Would you mind if I left you to it?' while fastening the top button of his suit over the beginnings of a paunch. 'I've got 140 Japanese businessmen arriving for a conference today, and I'm not convinced the banqueting department is going to have lunch ready on time.'

The scene that awaited Kershaw in Room 1313 presented a plausible explanation for the girl's death. Three tablets – thickish, chalky-pink imperfect discs – lay on the bedside table; next to them, on the satin smooth cover of the hotel brochure, two neat tramlines of white powder.

The uniform finished taping the doorway and came and stood next to her at the foot of the bed. An overweight guy with body odour, he was so close that she could hear him breathing through his mouth.

Folding his arms, he surveyed the tableau.

'Good party,' he said, shooting her a sideways glance – looking for a reaction.

'She'll have a terrible hangover,' Kershaw shot back, deadpan. 'Could you go and knock up all the rooms on this floor, see if anyone remembers anything?'

He departed, muttering under his breath.

CSI Dave hunkered down next to the bedside table and scooped the white lines off the brochure into a plastic evidence bag, before dusting the cover with silver developing powder.

'Are you getting anything?' asked Kershaw.

He frowned, 'Yeah, plenty. But how many people do you think have had their paws all over this in the last few weeks?' *Fair point*, she thought. 'I hate hotel rooms,' he muttered.

She started to examine the body properly, dredging up what she could remember from her pathology lectures. Finding a series of purplish patches along the underside of the girl's upper arms and legs, where the blood had pooled, she felt a little rush of satisfaction. From memory, the lividity was widespread enough to suggest that she had died at least six hours earlier, around 7 or 8 a.m., although it would take a calculation of the girl's rectal temperature and the room temperature to get a reliable time of death.

There was no clue to the identity of the girl, or her partner. 'Lampart' must have taken her clothes and personal effects with him, leaving only her empty patent leather handbag, which was probably too bulky for him to smuggle out unnoticed. From the grey tidemark she'd spotted in the bog, he'd even flushed their fag butts away.

'Can I check her bag?' she asked Dave, nodding at the handbag, lying on the floor in a plastic evidence bag.

'Yep, it's already dusted.'

Using her pen to open it up, Kershaw found the main compartment and the zippered side section empty. But when she took a closer look she discovered a tiny hidden pocket sewn into the lining, just big enough for a lipstick and easy to miss. Inside, she could see a pale pink tube ticket. She borrowed tweezers from Dave and pulled out a one-week Travelcard. It had been bought the previous day, and covered zones one to four, allowing travel right out to the burbs.

'Ah, if it isn't Miss Marple,' said Streaky as he breezed in, looking like a ginger-haired snowman in his protective suit. 'I take it the Department's pharmaceuticals specialist has already solved the case and completed the paper-work?'

She grinned – the wind-up was harmless enough and anyway, she was chuffed that Streaky had chosen her, and not Browning, for this job. Was the unreconstructed sexist routine just an act? Unless – *God forbid!* – he was getting the hots for her?

'Still a few loose ends, Sarge, but I did just find this,' showing him the ticket, 'tucked away in the handbag. The only lead on her ID.'

'You're hoping she used a debit card to buy it?'

'Or an Oystercard, Sarge. They're all registered to the holder's address these days.'

He nodded. 'Talk to my mate Terry at London Underground: he's as good as gold, he'll pull you a name and address off the system.'

Streaky folded his arms, and stood, scanning the girl's body intently as Kershaw filled him in.

'A male guest checked in alone at 0115 last night, Sarge. The desk clerk who swiped his credit card has gone off shift.'

'The credit card's probably nicked, but check it out anyway,' said Streaky, without taking his eyes off the body. 'And interview the desk clerk while his memory's fresh, get a description.'

She followed him as he moved up the side of the bed.

He bent over the girl. 'No obvious injuries,' he said, eyes flickering impassively over the splayed body.

Kershaw noticed a fuzz of underarm stubble beneath the girl's outflung left arm – a detail so personal it made her feel uncomfortably like a voyeur.

'The sex was probably consensual,' Streaky went on. Wetting his finger he dabbed up a trace of white powder left on the bedside table and rubbed it on his gums.

'Probable cause of death – one snort too many of the old Peruvian marching powder.' He hitched up his trousers. 'The late check-in . . . the drugs – I'd say we're dealing with a working girl and her client. When she OD-ed, the client took fright and legged it.'

Kershaw didn't reply. Bending to pick up a discarded black stocking that lay curled like a question mark on the carpet, between the head of the bed and the table, she turned it over in her hands. What were the stats? Sex workers were twelve times as likely as other women to die violently. She skirted round the bed.

'This is odd, Sarge,' she said, holding out a second stocking, retrieved from the same spot on the opposite side.

'What, the fact a sex worker wore black stockings?' he said, bugging his eyes at her.

'No, Sarge,' said Kershaw, ignoring the sarcasm. 'But when you take your stockings off, even in the throes of passion, they don't tend to end up so far apart and so . . .' she paused, struggling to put it into words, 'symmetrical.'

Streaky raised his eyebrows: 'I'll have to bow to your superior knowledge of stocking removal procedure,' he said, 'but what are you getting at exactly?'

She looped the stocking through the bed head's polished steel rungs and gave it a tug. 'He might have used the stockings to tie her up and rape her, then, when she started OD-ing, untied them to cover his tracks.' Freeing the stocking, she let it fall to the floor.

'Or the S&M could just have been part of the fun and games,' said Streaky.

He turned one of the girl's wrists and peered at it. 'No bruises or abrasions.' Replacing her arm on the bed, he stood silently for a moment. 'Still, it's not always obvious, post-mortem. Make sure the pathologist checks for bruising under the skin.'

Kershaw felt a ripple of excitement.

'But let's stick to the known knowns for now, shall we?' he said, fixing her with a look. 'What have we got here in terms of offences, detective?'

Kershaw checked her notebook, 'Leaving a body, administering and supplying Class A drugs. Maybe even manslaughter, if the girl was still alive when he legged it.'

Streaky sniffed his agreement. 'What's our best chance of finding him?'

'CCTV, Sarge,' she flipped open her notebook. 'Just two cameras in the lobby, the other three are all back of house: kitchens, store rooms and rear staff entrance.'

'More concerned about petty thievery than guest security, then,' said Streaky, frowning in disgust. 'No cams in the lifts?'

'Both out of order.' They shared a meaningful look. *Muppets.*

He picked up the vodka bottle, in an evidence bag now that Dave had finished with it. 'Spot anything, detective?'

She held her breath: was he thinking the same thing she was?

'It's Wyborowa, Sarge, a Polish brand,' she said, trying to keep the excitement out of her voice, 'and with the drugs, I'm thinking maybe there's a link to my floater?'

Streaky stared at her.

'Her tattoo – the name Ela – it's Polish, too . . . ?' she tried.

He shook his head slowly, tutting theatrically.

'What a load of old bollocks. You need to get out more, Kershaw. Any London offie worth its salt sells Polish vodka these days. Beats the Russian tackle hands down, the aficionados tell me.'

She bit her lip. He was right. There was sod all to link the two girls' deaths.

'What *I* see is a bottle – but no *glasses*,' Streaky went on. 'Of course they might have been drinking it by the neck, but our friend "Lampart" would hardly leave it behind if it was covered in his DNA . . .' His gaze swivelled to a coffee table near the foot of the bed. Giving her a chance to redeem herself.

Her suit crackled as she dropped to a squat – from this vantage point the light from the window struck the varnished surface at a more oblique angle – then took the bagged bottle and hovered it over the table.

'There's a ring, Sarge, too big for the bottle. Must be from a glass.'

'Well done, detective!' said Streaky, with only a trace of his usual sarcasm.

'But I haven't seen any glasses in here – or in the bathroom,' she said, frowning.

Seized by a sudden thought, she stood and crossed the room and opened the door to the room's minuscule balcony. From here, thirteen floors up, she could make out the half-built Olympic stadium, a few miles further east. Looking down, she saw a flat roof, five or six floors below.

'He might have taken the glass with him,' she said, re-entering the room, 'But it'd be easier just to chuck it out the window. I'll get a CSI up there to look for fragments.'

Geeky Dave, who was bagging the girl's hands, threw her an evil look. *Oops.* CSIs had honorary DC rank these days and any suggestion that they were the hired help was a total no-no, especially since they had a say in approving forensic tests.

'I'll leave you to sort that one out, shall I?' said Streaky with an acid smile.

Returning to the bedside he stood looking down at the girl's face, half hidden behind its curtain of hair. Taking a well-chewed biro from his inside pocket he handed it to Kershaw.

Gingerly, she scooped up the hair and hooked it behind the girl's left ear, a gesture that felt oddly intimate. Her mouth was reddened and slightly swollen, but other than that the face appeared unblemished, her long, mascara-blackened eyelashes standing out dramatically against skin as pale as candle wax. Kershaw bent closer, searching for a bruise, a scratch, anything, when suddenly, the mouth started to open, gaping slowly like a door in a horror movie, and the girl moaned softly.

Kershaw jerked her head back violently. *Jesus!*

Streaky chuckled. 'Never seen a stiff do that before, eh? Just a bit of air in the lungs.'

The girl lay, once again, utterly still.

'No bruising or ligature marks on the neck,' said Streaky peering over Kershaw's shoulder.

Kershaw shook her head and was about to stand up, when she caught a glint of something in the back of the girl's mouth, a flash of white up between the inside of her cheek and the gums.

'Sarge! She's got something in her mouth, at the back there.'

Streaky called Dave over. He bent over the girl, carefully manoeuvred a pair of long tweezers into her mouth, and drew out a whitish rectangle, tightly rolled into a cylinder. It was a business card, sodden and bloated with saliva, but still perfectly readable.

Eleven

Janusz was awoken by the insistent sound of a buzz saw, and the panicky feeling that he was suffocating. But it was only Copernicus, sitting on his chest and purring at top volume. Cursing, he pushed the cat off. Now he was awake, he knew that he wouldn't get back to sleep without addressing the urgent signals his brain was getting from his bladder.

Giving up on the search for Weronika yesterday had left Janusz feeling irritable and depressed, so when Oskar asked him over for a drink he'd leapt at the offer. His mate lived in a council house overlooking the A12 near the Olympics site, with a young couple and their two young kids, and three other guys who shared the two remaining bedrooms. Janusz had tried to persuade him to go down the pub, but Oskar insisted on drinking at home to save money.

Oskar's room-mate was working nights so at least they were able to retreat from the mayhem downstairs to his bedroom where they sank a case of Tyskie and watched

Legia Warszawa take *Wisla Krakow* apart on the Polish football channel.

Janusz swung his legs out of bed and stood up. Despite sticking to beer – it had been twenty-five or more years since he last touched *wodka* – he was already suffering the beginnings of a pounding headache, which would be even worse by the morning. Another fucking side effect of getting old, he thought.

He padded, naked and half asleep, down the hallway without reaching for the light switch: he knew from experience that even ten seconds' exposure to light would keep him tossing and turning till morning. Anyway, there was enough orange light coming through the living room doorway from the street lamps outside to allow him to navigate his way to the toilet. He kept his eyes half closed as he pissed, trying to remember a science lecture from his time at Jagiellonski about how different colour temperatures affect the visual cortex.

His eyes shot open. He might have been drunk last night but one memory was clear: before going to bed he'd shooed the cat out of the living room, and to stop it getting back in and scratching the furniture, he'd shut the door. For light to reach the hallway, *somebody must have opened it*.

The blow struck him heavily at the base of the neck. *You're getting slow, old man,* he thought, as he heard his cheekbone hit the ceramic tiles with a whang like a tuning fork. Floating up from the dusky region of semi-consciousness he wondered *what next?* in a weirdly detached way. The answer was a vicious kick in the kidneys that bent him double and made him spew up a quantity of beer mingled with stomach acid onto the floor.

Then he felt a cold sharpness pressed against his wind-pipe and a black man's face loomed close to his. No, not a black man, white skin gleamed around the edges of a black mask, like the ones ice hockey players wore. He got a flash of his eyes, full of malevolence, but before he saw anything else the guy shoved him face down into his own vomit so hard he felt his front tooth chip on the tiled floor. The blade pressed harder into his neck, breaking the skin.

'Stay away from me and the girl, you dirty old fucker,' hissed the man, in Polish. 'If you fuck up my business with all your poking around I'll come back and cut your balls off. Then I'll watch you bleed to death.'

The guy had a powerful grip, but Janusz managed to crane his head around enough to see the edge of the masked face over his shoulder. He croaked out two words: 'Fuck you.' Then came a mighty crack as the man whacked his head onto the floor again, plunging him into darkness.

The sky outside the bathroom window was almost light when Janusz opened his eyes and saw grey floor tiles. He flinched reflexively – for a split second he was back in a cell in Montepulich, after getting worked over by *milicja* thugs. Using the edge of the bath to lever himself up, he rose cautiously to his feet, his head a pulsing balloon of pain. Propping himself against the sink, he risked a look in the mirror.

From his left cheekbone to his eyebrow the swollen flesh was the colour of stewed red cabbage, and the cut on his temple where the fucker had cracked it on the floor had spun a spider's web of dried blood across his face. At the base of his skull, a bruise the size of his palm was already beetroot purple, and just to round it all off, blood from the wound in his throat had run down in rivulets and clotted obscenely in his chest hair. He looked like the hands-down loser of an illegal cage fight.

Straightening up with exaggerated care, he gasped with pain and fingered his side. *Kurwa mac!* The fucking bastard had broken, or at least cracked, a rib as well. Seized with a paroxysm of rage, Janusz grabbed the ceramic tooth-brush holder off the sink and smashed it into the mirror. It made a satisfying racket. He pulled a savage grin at his reflection, broken and distorted by the cracked glass. 'Just wait till I find you, *skurwysyn*,' he said out loud.

A minute or two later he heard an urgent knocking. Holding a wad of bloodied bog roll to staunch the fresh cuts on his hand, Janusz threw open the front door to his flat so hard it hit the wall, sending up a puff of plaster dust. It was his next-door neighbour, a weedy type with trendy thick-rimmed glasses, worked in an art gallery or something, almost certainly gay.

At the sight of Janusz, the guy's mouth fell slackly open.

'I was . . . I just . . .'

He couldn't get the words out.

'I heard . . . or, I *think* I heard . . .'

'I broke a cup,' said Janusz, deadpan. 'You want to come in and check maybe?' he swept an arm into the flat, 'Be my guest.'

'No! No.' The guy – Sebastian, that was his name – now had both hands out in front of him, palms flat, and started backing away down the hall.

It was only then that Janusz remembered he was stark naked.

'Sorry!' he called out after his neighbour.

He cranked the shower up to its hottest setting and let the jets batter his bruised flesh while he digested the meaning of his night-time visitation.

It seemed that Adamski – who else? – had heard that Janusz was on his tail and tracked him down to the flat. The *chuj* could have no idea, of course, that he'd already quit the job.

He had just finished soaping himself all over when the landline started chirping. Cursing, he was tempted to ignore it, but then a thought struck him: it could be Kasia, calling before her shift. Maybe she regretted the stupid row two days before and wanted to meet up. He strode into the living room, towelling off the suds roughly.

'*Czesc?*' he said into the cracked receiver.

'Am I interrupting anything?' It was Marta, and straight onto the attack, as usual.

'No, Marta, I was just in the shower,' he said.

'*Naprawde*, Janusz, I can never get hold of you – haven't you got a new mobile phone yet?'

He glanced at the black oblong winking in its charger on the mantelpiece.

'I'm still looking for a good deal – shopping around,' he growled, pulling the towel round his shoulders. 'What is it you want, Marta?'

She adopted her understanding tone, the one that always made him grind his teeth.

'I know you are busy, Janek, but Bobek is thirteen next month – and it's over six weeks since you telephoned him.'

Christ. Was it really fourteen years since that stupid drunken night when they nearly got back together? He recalled waking the next morning, gradually focusing on the watercolour landscapes hung on the grey walls – Marta had a modest talent as a painter, and they were her touching, pathetic attempt to enliven the tower block hutch in the Warsaw suburbs that had once been their marital home. Then the sensing of the body next to him and the jab of fear as he remembered her whispered 'Don't use anything.'

'I sent him cash at Christmas,' protested Janusz, hunkering down in his towel by the radiator, suppressing a gasp as his rib sent out shards of pain.

'Oh, the cheque was fantastic,' said Marta, lapsing into her usual sarcasm. 'Let me see. It took him out to play football, it helped him with his homework, it gave him a beating for taking a knife to school . . .'

'He took a blade to *school*? Mother of God, Marta!' He was gripped by the sudden, irrational fear that Bobek would grow up like Adamski. 'You've got to be tougher with him!'

'Oh! And now *Londynek Tata* tells me I don't bring my son up properly!' When Marta raised her voice it became thin and grating, like a drill going through steel. Anger clawed at his throat.

'Marta . . .'

'But no doubt you are busy having a great time with some new girlfriend while I get teenage dirty looks and non-stop *hip hop*.' She was on a roll now.

He fought down his rage and guilt.

'Listen Marta, I swear on the Virgin that I will telephone him for a chat – soon.' Ignoring her enraged response he continued: 'I have to go – there is someone at the door.'

Crashing the receiver into its battered cradle, he leaned

against the radiator, and fingered his swollen and aching face. All this *dramat*, from a single drunken shag – and that after they had been apart for seven years!

Copetka was giving him the silent treatment from the kitchen doorway.

'Don't you start on me!' he burst out, causing the startled cat to flee, claws scrabbling on the floorboards. Then he realised he hadn't fed him since the previous morning. Going to the kitchen, he clattered out a double portion of dried food onto a plate and stroked him, murmuring endearments as he ate.

Janusz filled a pint glass from the tap and stood drinking it, looking out of the kitchen window. In all his twenty-odd years living here, he'd never been burgled, but now he noticed for the first time how easy it would be to break in. Any reasonably fit guy could scale the two-metre fence at the rear of the block, and from there it was three flights up the handy cast-iron fire escape to the kitchen's sash window, usually left open so the cat could go to and fro.

'No more Hotel Kiszka for you, Copetka,' he said to the cat as he closed the window and fastened the catch. 'You go out in the morning and don't get back in till I come home, like a homeless hostel.'

The idea that someone had simply strolled in while he slept filled him with impotent rage. Worse, it also made him feel vulnerable, an emotion he hadn't permitted himself for many years.

Getting dressed was a slow and painful process. Then he propped the medicine chest on the bathroom sink and, using the shattered mirror as a guide, dressed his wounds with antiseptic salve, stuck a small plaster over the cut on his temple, which wouldn't stop bleeding, and wound a bandage round his cut hand.

Marta's call had dredged up the past like silt in a storm drain. He found himself reflecting that marrying her had been his life's biggest mistake – no, make that the second biggest. He couldn't even remember the marriage service: he had been as drunk as a log. Back then, in the weeks after Iza's death, he had been smashed from the time he opened his eyes in the morning till the moment he fell asleep – lost consciousness, more like – in the early hours.

When he'd finally sobered up, weeks later, he found that somehow, amid all the craziness, he really had married Marta, even though friends like Oskar, and his mother, God rest her soul, had apparently tried repeatedly to talk him out of it. Well they'd been proved right. He and Marta were a disaster: the only thing that bound them was Iza, his lover and her best friend. When Marta found out she couldn't compete with a ghost, she soured faster than a pail of milk in August – and who could blame her?

As for Bobek, he loved the boy – would kill for him, no question – but he wasn't cut out for parenthood. Whenever he remembered with a jolt that he was a father, he had the sensation of something reaching up from the depths of a murky lake to drag him under.

He decided to make some *kompot*, defrosting his last precious kilo of damsons, retrieved from the back of the freezer. As always, the simple pleasures of cooking – weighing out the sugar, juicing a lemon, the sharp autumnal fragrance as he stirred the simmering berries – helped to settle and focus his thoughts. Until the harsh electronic tone of the doorbell made him drop the wooden spoon.

Pressing the entry phone speaker, he heard the voice

of a girl saying she was from the police. He froze for a moment, then buzzed her up – what else could he do? He spun through all his recent deals, racking his brains for what the visit might be about. The Smeg appliances he'd got for Slawek? Okay, he hadn't *stolen* them, but the payment method – a wad of cash handed over in a pub to someone called John – probably wouldn't go down well with the cops. And there was the escapade at Adamski's cottage: what if someone had got the van's plate and traced it to Oskar?

Then he opened the flat door – and almost laughed out loud. The girl looked about twenty, for Christ's sake, she barely came up to his chest, and she was much too pretty to be a policewoman. Okay, she had a Met ID card, but from her smart trouser suit, he guessed she was a civilian officer – maybe working in community liaison or some such crap. If it were anything important they would hardly have sent a girl.

Kershaw accepted Kiszka's offer of coffee and took a chair at the kitchen table. From the moment she set eyes on him, adrenaline had started coursing through her veins. Two metres tall and powerfully built, the guy was the size of a wardrobe, and from the state of his face, he'd been in a major ruck in the last few hours. As he reached up to get some cups off a shelf, she noticed his hand shooting to his side. *Broken rib, too.* Janusz Kiszka was clearly no stranger to violence.

While he was spooning ground coffee into an old-style steel percolator, Kershaw checked the place out. The scruffy, orange pine kitchen units hadn't been replaced since the eighties, and the piles of junk mail and dirty crockery on the worktop screamed 'man living alone', but a rack of pricey-looking copper-bottomed pans, and the hot fruity smell emanating from the hob suggested a girlfriend, or wife, in residence.

'That smells good,' she said. 'Does your partner enjoy cooking?'

'Partner?' He laughed. 'I live alone.' He waved a self-deprecating hand. 'Anyway, it's not really cooking – just some conserve.'

Go figure, she thought, *Eastern European thugs make their own jam.*

When the percolator finished burbling, Janusz served the coffee in proper cups and saucers, and offered the girl milk in a china jug – she was a guest, after all. Then he sat down opposite her and leaned both forearms on the table. 'Let me guess,' he said, with an apologetic grin. 'One of my neighbours called to complain about some noise this morning?'

Kershaw just smiled and took a sip of the insanely strong coffee. The guy's condescending look, his relaxed body language, suggested he thought a female was nothing to worry about. Well, if it meant he was off his guard that suited her just fine. While he gave her some old bollocks about how he'd slipped getting out of the shower and smashed the bathroom mirror, she gave him the discreet once-over.

Fortyish, with dark brown hair, longish – a style that went out of fashion in the nineties – and peppered with grey. Not bad looking, if you went in for the caveman look.

'Was that how you hurt your face, sir, the accident with the mirror?' she asked, scrunching up her forehead in sympathy.

141

He hesitated, then nodded, touching the swollen flesh over his cheekbone. *Shit*, he'd almost forgotten how he must look.

She lifted the coffee to her lips, 'And the bruise on the back of your neck?' meeting his eyes over the rim of her cup. He was about to agree when he realised that wouldn't wash.

'Actually, I was involved in a car crash last night. Nothing serious but, well, I must confess I wasn't wearing a seatbelt,' he said with an apologetic grin. 'I've learned my lesson now.'

Bullshit. 'Was this your car, Mr Kizz-ka, or a friend's car?'

He looked up at the ceiling.

'It was a hackney cab, actually.'

'You mean a *black cab*?' Aside from the odd prehistoric phrase, his English was surprisingly fluent. In fact, if it wasn't for the accent and something indefinably foreign about his look, his clothes, she might almost describe him, as well, *posh*.

'Yes. I missed the last tube, so I hailed one in the street.'

Making it untraceable, of course, should she want to check his story.

'A broken mirror *and* a car crash!' she said. 'Would you describe yourself as accident-prone, Mr Kizz-ka?' she asked, a hint of sarcasm entering her voice.

'It's *Kish-ka*,' he corrected her, stretching his lips into a smile, '*Yan-ush Kish-ka*.' His head had started booming like a timpani, but he knew he had to keep his cool. *What the hell was this girl doing here*?

'Can I ask what you do for a living, Mr Kish-ka?'

'I am a businessman,' he said, cradling his coffee – the

cup almost disappearing in his hands, she noticed. 'Import and export, mostly.'

Kershaw nodded at a pile of *New Scientist* magazines lying on the table.

'Is your line of work scientific?'

'Not really, I just have a inquiring mind.' He smiled again, to soften any rudeness in the remark.

She drank her coffee. Streaky had told her once that silence was the most underrated weapon in interrogation.

Janusz resisted filling it, felt the strain begin to tell in his smile muscles. He noticed her bitten nails: an ugly habit, especially in a woman.

'Can I ask if you're married, Mr Kiszka?'

'Yes, my wife lives in Poland, we have a son.'

'But you choose to live here?' She raised an eyebrow – deliberately needling him now.

'Poland's economy isn't in good shape at the moment – many people work somewhere else,' he said, his perfect English coming a bit unstuck, Kershaw noted. 'Listen, darling, I don't want to be rude, but what is this all about?'

She flashed him a sweet smile. 'Oh, it's probably nothing,' and rummaging in her handbag, pulled out a plastic evidence bag, which she put on the table between them, 'Do you recognise this?'

He leant closer, earning a jab of pain from his rib. *Kurwa mac!* It looked like it had been through a washing machine, but he recognised it alright. How in the fuck had she got hold of his business card? If he'd dropped it in the cottage, he was in big trouble.

'Sure, it's my card,' he said, leaning back, and pulled out his box of cigars. 'Is there a problem?'

'Yes Mr Kiszka, I'm afraid there is. I have to inform you that it was found in the possession of a female found dead of a suspected drug overdose yesterday. We are investigating the circumstances leading up to her death.'

Janusz loathed this kind of police-speak, its opaque menace reminded him of the language the *milicja* had used under Communism. It was clear this slip of a girl was a detective, if only a junior one, he realised, cursing his stupidity. Lighting a cigar, he took a drag to compose himself.

'I'm sorry to hear that, but I've given my card to hundreds of people,' he said, describing an arc with his cigar to indicate how widely they might now be scattered.

'You don't seem particularly interested in who has died,' said the girl. Her grey-blue eyes were steely now, boring into his, and her flat Cockney vowels were starting to irritate him. He recalled a proverb his grandfather had been fond of quoting: *Where the devil can't go, he sends a woman.*

'Maybe I'm in shock,' he said, staring back at her. 'But since you are obviously dying to tell me, go ahead.'

The charm was slipping, thought Kershaw. Keeping her eyes pinned to his face she said: 'Justyna Koz-low-ska.'

Janusz's breath clotted in his lungs like soft snow and a high ringing sound filled his ears. He was engulfed by an extraordinary sensation, as if his body were physically unravelling from the back of his throat down to the pit of his stomach, while his mind floated up and watched the scene from above, a disinterested observer. One section of his brain noted that the cigar was burning his fingers, but was somehow unable to issue the order to act.

144

He just sits there, thought Kershaw, *cool as a fucking cucumber*.

With an enormous effort, Janusz reassembled himself, and transferring the cigar to his left hand, put it to his lips.

'Did you know Ms Koz-low-ska?' asked Kershaw, rhyming the middle syllable with 'cow'.

'The name rings a bell, but I can't place her.' He let a cloud of smoke drift between them to obscure his expression, making Kershaw wrinkle her nose, despite herself.

'So when I view the Waveney Thameside's security camera tapes from the early hours of yesterday morning, I won't find you on them, right?' *A stab in the dark*.

He gave one shake of his head, his lips pressed into a line.

'When did you last see Ms Koz-low-ska?' she persisted.

Janusz exploded out of his seat: 'It's *Koz-loff-ska*. You could at least get her fucking name right!'

Kershaw counted to five, then spoke in a level and calm tone.

'I think you *were* with Justyna. Maybe she was your girlfriend or maybe a working girl. Either way, when she overdosed, you got scared.'

Janusz was barely listening. He was staring into space, seeing Justyna's face light up when she talked about the future, her plans to train as an physiotherapist, the motherly concern in her brown eyes when she spoke of Weronika . . . Finished. Over. How could a girl who was so . . . *alive*, two days ago now be lying on a shelf in a mortuary fridge?

The guy was looking agitated now, thought Kershaw

145

– probably wondering how he'd managed to overlook his card when he'd cleared the hotel room.

'Listen, Mr Kiszka,' she said, putting warmth into her voice. 'I promise you this will turn out a lot better if you tell me about it now.'

Janusz didn't respond. He just wanted this manipulative little *dziwka* to go, so he could think. Then he realised that he'd gone straight home after leaving Justyna on Tuesday night, which meant he didn't have an alibi. *Play for time.*

Taking a deep breath, he sat down again. 'I remember the name,' he said, speaking slowly, not quite trusting his voice. 'We went out for a drink once.' He paused to relight his cigar. 'But it went no further, and I can assure you I never went to any hotel with her.'

'Can anyone account for your movements in the early hours of Wednesday?'

'Yes, I was drinking with a friend in Stratford on Tuesday, till about three in the morning.' Shifting last night's session back by a day was the simplest thing to do – Oskar would back him up.

3 a.m. – the girl's estimated time of death, thought Kershaw – *how very convenient.*

Janusz started clearing the empty coffee cups from the table.

'I can tell you one thing,' he said over his shoulder as he carried them to the sink. 'She was no whore.'

'Okay, but did you have sex with her in the last few days?' the girl persisted. 'We might need a DNA sample.'

Janusz resisted a powerful urge to smash the cups to the floor. To be asked such questions by a girl young enough to be his daughter! Setting them on the worktop with care, he said, in as casual a tone as he could manage:

146

'I should be more than happy to make a statement, or provide a sample should you deem it necessary, but right now I'm afraid I'm late for an appointment.'

Then he turned, but his big frame was backlit by the window, making it impossible for Kershaw to read his expression. 'Unless, of course, you are going to arrest me now.'

She hesitated: all her instincts told her to drag Janusz Kiszka down the station and give him the third degree. Everything about him screamed involvement in Justyna Kozlowska's death, and just maybe, in Ela's, too. Despite the educated way of speaking, she could almost *hear* the static crackle of suppressed violence in the air around him.

In the end, it wasn't the prospect of trying to get the cuffs on the big bastard single-handed that stopped her reading him his rights; it was picturing herself explaining to Streaky why she'd arrested him before checking out his alibi.

She stood up. *Take control.* Pushed her card across the table to him.

'We'll let you know about the DNA sample, Mr Kiszka. For now, since you are a person of interest to the investigation, I would ask that you let us know if you make any plans to leave London.' He made a tiny bow of acknowledgement.

'And I'll need contact details for your friend – the one who you say can account for your movements Tuesday night?'

He gave her Oskar's number and accompanied her to the door. At the last moment, she turned and tilted her serious little face up to him – funnily enough, he reflected, she didn't look quite so cute anymore.

'One last thing, Mr Kiszka,' said Kershaw, remembering the tattoo on her floater's buttock. 'Do you happen to know anyone called Pawel?'

He gave a dismissive laugh. 'I know about a dozen guys called Pawel, darling.'

Which sounded reasonable enough, thought Kershaw, as she descended the staircase of the block, but then why had those big mitts of his clenched into fists at the mention of the name?

Janusz paced his living room, cigar clenched between his teeth, replaying the evening at the FlashKlub with Justyna over and over. According to the girl *detektyw*, just after he walked Justyna home, she had decided to head to some posh hotel in Wapping for a sex and drugs session. That just didn't sound like the girl he'd met.

Had she lied about her relationship with Pawel Adamski? Perhaps she really had been his girlfriend first, before he took up with Weronika. Maybe he still had her on a chain that he pulled whenever he felt like it.

Janusz stood staring out over Highbury Fields. He knew that a scorned woman could be ruthless, but the more he went over his encounter with Justyna, the harder he found it to make her fit the role. Recalling her steady gaze, the way she called the younger girl by her pet name, he could find no hint of duplicity or deviousness – her concern for Nika seemed as genuine as her contempt for Adamski.

No. She had been tricked into going to the hotel, perhaps on the pretext of meeting Weronika, he was sure of it, and forced to take the drugs – and everything pointed to Adamski being her killer.

Then Janusz remembered her asking him in for coffee

148

that night. He stopped his restless pacing, and closed his eyes. *Mother of God!* What he'd seen in Justyna's expression hadn't been fear *of rejection*, it had been *fear*, plain and simple. He gripped the mantelpiece to steady himself. Justyna had been so frightened of Adamski that she had asked him in – would perhaps even have slept with him, a man old enough to be her father – rather than spend the night alone. And he had turned her down.

Guilt reached out to Janusz like an old friend: for the sake of some pious fucking hang-up about what he would say to Father Pietruski at his next confession, he had signed the girl's death warrant.

Just then, Janusz's mobile rang.

'It's me, sisterfucker,' bellowed a familiar voice. Oskar had never quite accepted the idea that mobile phones could carry the human voice unaided.

'*Kolego!*' said Janusz, with heartfelt warmth. 'I've been trying to call you.'

'*Kurwa!* What's with you? Does hearing my voice give you a hard-on?'

Janusz grinned. Oskar had always had this knack of lightening the gloomiest moments.

'Anyway, gayboy, your dick's not big enough for me. So pull up your panties and tell me this – why are the fucking cops on your case?'

'The girl *detektyw*? Did she ask you about Tuesday night?'

'Yeah, she did, but here's a funny thing, the signal was so bad I couldn't hear a word,' said Oskar with elaborate regret, 'In the middle of central London, too! I said I'd call her back later.'

Janusz grinned. '*Brawo.* When you do, tell her we

149

were drinking at your place till late – I didn't leave till 3 a.m., okay?'

'*Tak*, leave it to me, Janek – I'll talk to her, give her the old Oskar magic with both barrels. After five, maximum ten minutes, she'll be begging me for a date.'

Janusz arranged to meet his mate later in the day.

After hanging up, he pulled the photo of Weronika out of his wallet. She looked like a little girl playing at dressing up in her mama's fur coat. There was no point going over and over how he'd let Justyna down – that would be to indulge in self-pity. His storm of emotion had passed, but it had left a sense of resolve as hard as tempered steel: he would do everything within his power to rescue Weronika from Pawel Adamski.

Then his phone rang again. According to the display, the caller was Father Piotr Pietruski.

Twelve

Kershaw gave the stubs of her nails a bit of a savaging as she drove away, worrying about how far she'd pushed Janusz Kiszka. Not that she gave a flying fuck about upsetting him – whatever alibi he and his Polish mate might dream up, she was convinced that Kiszka was mixed up in Justyna's death – but because she was uncomfortably aware that Streaky might blow an artery if he found out.

Right from the off, the Sarge had been sceptical about the significance of Kiszka's card being found in the girl's mouth. According to him, it didn't even put Kiszka at the scene. Maybe she'd used it to snort coke, he said, which would explain how it came to be rolled up.

Kershaw hadn't risked arguing the toss, but inside she was fizzing with excitement, convinced that the card changed what looked like a random OD into manslaughter – or even murder. A gorilla like Kiszka could easily have overpowered Justyna, tying her up and forcing drugs down her throat before raping her. Maybe the poor girl had a flash of intuition about her fate and, in desperation, managed to hide his card in her mouth – pointing the finger straight at her killer.

Streaky had trusted her to check out the lead alone. Well, to be strictly accurate, by the time Terry had coaxed the girl's name and address out of London Underground's computer system, he was running late for his usual appointment at the boozer – but he had made it crystal that she treat Kiszka solely as a potential contact of the girl.

'We'll send a uniform to her address to find a next of kin, and you pay this Mr Kiszka a visit. But don't get carried away, Miss Marple,' he had warned as they left the Waveney Hotel together, the revolving doors spitting them out into a wintry dusk. He paused to light a fag and continued, apparently oblivious to the bitter wind coming off the river.

'We've got nothing concrete to put him at the scene. If it turns out he's got no alibi *and* you ID him on the CCTV, that's a whole different kettle of fish.' Jabbing the fag at her, he continued, 'But if you start going hard at him now, he'll just put the shutters up, or worse, fuck off back to Poland. Last thing we want.'

Now she was back at the Waveney to check out the CCTV footage – grimly aware just how much was riding on it. The credit card used by the man checking into the hotel, had, predictably enough, turned out to be a clone. The real Steven Lampart was a blameless dentist from Guildford who'd been tucked up in bed with his wife while the sex and drugs party had been kicking off in room 1313, so that was a dead end. But as she locked the motor, she felt a sudden conviction that she would find Kiszka's Neanderthal mug on the tapes.

After collecting her from reception, Derek, the hotel's head of security, wasted no time telling her he was a retired cop – which couldn't hurt, cooperation-wise. At the end of a corridor behind front desk he unlocked a door marked security, and ushered her into a world a million miles from the front of house luxury. Here the monogrammed carpets, modern sculpture and £100-a-roll wallpaper gave way to imitation pine laminate flooring and painted breezeblock walls.

The drop in temperature as she stepped over the threshold made her shudder. 'Air con,' said Derek. 'Got to keep that lot cool,' nodding at the bank of CCTV screens and winking recorders.

Surveying the Stone Age technology she felt a sinking sensation. 'VHS recorders?' she asked, incredulous. 'Five-star hotel and they don't have hard drive recording?'

He fiddled with his keys, embarrassed. 'Not yet. The system came from some hotel the owners closed down.' He shrugged. 'They say it's only temporary.'

It was a pocket version of the M25 control room she'd once visited, except here the ebb and flow of traffic on the screens was of the human variety. 'Are those the lift cams?' asked Kershaw, indicating two blank screens.

'Yes, on the fritz, I'm afraid,' said Derek. 'But I've pulled out the tapes for the check-in and the lobby.' He ushered her into a smaller, much warmer, room – his 'cubbyhole' – so she could watch the footage from a comfy armchair, then went off to make her a cup of tea.

She felt a tingle of anticipation as she pressed play on the first VHS, which was from the security camera trained on the check-in desk, but that soon gave way to disap-pointment when she saw the footage. The guests trailed ghostly auras and the picture quality was so grainy you could barely make out faces – the tapes must be endlessly recycled. To cap it all, the numpty who'd positioned the camera had angled it to favour the *check-in clerk,* rather than the guests. She pressed fast forward, looking for the section that would cover 'Lampart' – aka Kiszka – checking in, her sense of gloom mounting as she spooled through indistinct rear-view shots of hotel guests, catching not much more than an occasional glimpse of profile.

Fast-forwarding produced a kind of fascinating time-lapsed loop of hotel life: people checking in and out, picking up messages, having arguments. One couple looked like illicit lovers checking in for a quickie, a girl in a revealing shoulderless dress – her hair too fair to be Justyna – who couldn't keep her hands off a guy in a suit. But something about them sparked Kershaw's interest, and rerunning the tape she detected a mechanical quality to the girl's attentions that made her re-categorise the pair as sex worker and client.

She reached 0100 hours by the 24-hour clock in the corner of the screen, but the only people checking in at that time were an overweight couple, American tourists, she guessed, judging by their matching tartan jackets and trousers.

Checking back on her notes she confirmed that the suspect had checked in at 0115, when Mr and Mrs Tartan were still at the desk. Returning next door, she quizzed Derek, the security guy, making a real effort to conceal her impatience.

'Ah, you know what's happened there, don't you, sweetheart,' said Derek, chuckling. 'I bet they never changed the time setting when the clocks went back. I'd check an hour earlier, if I was you.'

Resisting the temptation to ask who else would be responsible for resetting security cameras, *if not the head of effing security*, Kershaw returned to the sofa. As the numbers on the clock spun backwards to reach 00.08, eight minutes past midnight, she pressed play – and felt the hairs on her forearms prickle.

A wide-shouldered guy wearing a three-quarter-length leather coat and one of those trendy retro hats – a pork pie hat, they called it – strolled up to the desk, alone. As he went through the check-in procedure, she literally held her breath, praying that he would glance behind him, or at least turn his head enough to reveal his right profile. But the guy kept the back of his head resolutely turned to the camera. She kept the breath bottled up right to the last moment when the desk clerk handed him his room card. *Turn right*, she urged silently. After viewing a stream of check-ins, she knew that if he turned right now, she'd get a look at his face, just for a second. If he went left, the camera would lose him straight away.

Turn right, you bastard.

He turned left. Kershaw let her breath out, exasperated. *Fucking typical.* She ran the footage back and forward a dozen or so times, concentrating in particular on the few seconds when the guy was walking up to, and away from, the desk. When she compared the image with her memory of Kiszka, she had to concede it wasn't a brilliant match. The man in the hat carried as much muscle as the big Pole, but he was a good half-head shorter, and his swagger suggested a much younger man, in his early thirties, tops.

She turned her attention to footage from the camera trained on the hotel's revolving doors and lobby – her last chance of getting a good look at the guy. But after pressing play she wanted to scream with frustration: the camera was mounted so high that by the time guests emerged from the revolving doors all you got was a superb view of the tops of their heads. Cursing, she spun through to 0100 hours. At 0106, a lively group of youngish people – office workers out on a beano, from the look of them – came barrelling through the revolving door in a scrum, the boys fooling around and yanking each other's jackets.

Behind this group and partly obscured by them, came the man in the hat and a girl who, from the long dark hair, was almost certainly Justyna Kozlowska. The top shot gave little away: he appeared to be holding her by the elbow, but her body language betrayed no fear – their pace was brisk and purposeful, and they were out of shot within three seconds.

Having replayed it several times, Kershaw came to two conclusions. The pair's businesslike demeanor confirmed her suspicion that Justyna was a working girl, but as much she hated to admit it, the man in the hat definitely wasn't Janusz Kiszka.

Which left her with a puzzle – what was his business card doing in the dead girl's mouth?

Thirteen

Two flags flapped and rattled on their poles outside the four-storey Georgian terrace, one red and white, surmounted by the implacable profile of the Polish eagle, the other the banal circle of stars on a blue background denoting membership of the EU. As Janusz passed through the stuccoed arch of the Polish Embassy, he reflected that he was hardly dressed for a reception at such an august institution, but Father Pietruski had insisted they meet there to discuss the 'terrible news'.

The priest said he couldn't miss the event: it was to raise money for *Do Domu* Foundation, which helped Poles sleeping rough in London to return home. Janusz had seen Polish down-and-outs around Stratford, usually guys from the poorest backgrounds, who – despite having no skills to sell – thought they'd get off the coach at Victoria and walk into well-paid jobs. Stranded and broke, they were often too ashamed to admit their predicament, even to their families back home.

Janusz was trying to explain to a flunky with a

superior air why his name was absent from the guest list when Father Pietruski rescued him. He waved away the old man's horrified enquiries about his injured face with the cab crash story he'd given the girl detective – no point worrying the old guy – and the pair entered the embassy's main salon. The tall-ceilinged room echoed with well-bred chatter and the expensive chink of champagne glasses, and a flock of black-tied waiters wove their way, trays aloft, through the throng. Before one of the tall windows, a girl in a long gown, red hair swept up in a chignon, sat at a grand piano playing a lively *Polonaise*.

Many of the guests greeted Father Pietruski or bowed as he bustled through the crowd, but their eyes widened at the sight of his bruised and dangerous-looking companion. Janusz stopped a waiter to scoop up a few elegant canapés – he hadn't eaten all day – earning a disapproving look from an elderly woman with some long-dead animal, complete with glassy little eyes, draped round her neck. As he passed, he couldn't resist reaching out to pat the furry head, making the old girl start back, eyes popping. Once they were out of earshot, Father Pietruski hissed, 'Behave yourself! That was the Countess Jagielska.'

It was certainly an upmarket gathering. Alongside the frayed elegance and confident hauteur of the old nobility, Janusz noticed several expensively cut suits of the *klasa biznes*, made rich by Poland's free market reforms. The priest paused to exchange pleasantries with one of them, a man with the face of a crafty peasant. On one arm, he wore a watch with too many dials, on the other, a perfect-bodied but bored looking girl of about nineteen.

'He owns Europe's third largest haulage business,' said

Father Pietruski, looking up at Janusz with an expression at once sheepish and excited. 'He's pledged a million *zlotych*.'

'Well, I hope he's paying through the nose for this little shindig,' growled Janusz as they pressed on through the throng.

Like a tugboat with a battered warship in tow, Father Pietruski piloted Janusz into the relative quiet of a private alcove, which held two carved and gilded antique armchairs and a low table, and watched, face creased in pained sympathy as the younger man lowered himself with care into one of the frail-looking chairs.

After ordering him a Tyskie from a passing waiter, Father Pietruski leaned in and spoke in hushed tones. 'You can imagine the state that poor pani Tosik was in after she heard the news. The policeman told her it was an overdose – *narkotyki*!'

His lips trembled. 'I would never have imagined it of Justyna, such a sensible girl, she never gave any hint of that kind of thing in confession!' A champagne cork popped in the salon, making him jump. Janusz had never seen the old guy so shaken up. Reaching out a bandaged hand he gave the bony shoulder a clumsy pat.

It appeared the uniformed cop had told pani Tosik about Justyna's death at precisely the same time he'd heard of it from the discourteous girl detective: the timing clearly coordinated so that she could spring the news on him before he received any prior warning.

'The policeman also asked about you – implied that you knew Justyna . . .' said the priest, a question in his darting eyes, anxiety showing itself in the repeated clasping and unclasping of his hands.

'Don't worry, Father,' said Janusz, touched by the old guy's concern. 'If the *policja* had any real evidence against me I'd be in a cell by now.'

But the priest's hands continued their mime of anxiety. He gazed past Janusz's shoulder to the crowd beyond. 'The loss of Justyna . . . it's a tragedy,' he said. A note of resolve entered his voice, 'But it makes finding Weronika and Adamski all the more urgent.'

'Listen, Father, I know I told you I'd hit a dead end—' Janusz stopped, and the parquet floor of the salon seemed suddenly to tilt beneath his feet. He gripped the chair's delicate arms. 'How do you know about Adamski?' he demanded. 'Pani Tosik said Weronika was as pure as a tear – that she didn't *have* a boyfriend.'

The priest's hands were still now. His watery blue gaze met the younger man's fierce, questioning gaze.

'Janusz, my boy. For once, it is I who must make a confession. I was unable to be completely honest with you about the . . . business with Weronika. Please don't blame pani Tosik: she was only following my request for . . . *dyskrecja*.'

'Discretion?!' burst out Janusz, causing a couple of highly-coiffed heads nearby to turn. The priest raised his hand to quiet Janusz, a look in his eyes that was part apology, part entreaty.

'You call it discretion, lying to me, who you have known for twenty years and more?' Janusz continued in an angry whisper. 'You send me off on a job half blind – and an innocent girl ends up dead. What the devil is going on?'

'We knew that Weronika was in danger, it's true,' said the priest, his face distorted with anguish, 'but we *never* expected Justyna to become involved – how could we know you would talk to her?'

'She was Weronika's only friend! How the hell else did you expect me to do my job? Visit a fucking sooth-sayer?'

The waiter arrived with the beer, and when Janusz failed to take it from his outstretched hand, set it on the side table atop a circle of felt, his gaze darting warily between the priest and his ruffian companion.

After he'd left, the priest continued. 'We see that now, of course, but at the time, I just thought, you seem to know everyone in the community, that you would find some other way . . .' His voice trailed off. 'I realise now that was naïve.'

'Who is this "we" you keep talking about, anyway?' Janusz shot a suspicious glance into the crowded salon. 'It's sure as hell not just you and pani Tosik.'

The priest hesitated, fiddling with the sleeve of his robe. 'There is someone you need to meet who can explain it better than I.' He looked at Janusz with a plaintive expression. 'Then you'll understand why I was unable to be entirely truthful with you.'

Janusz followed Father Pietruski back through the salon, feeling his grip on reality slipping. The scene seemed surreal now: the crowd's chatter had become shrill, piercing, the women's make-up looked garish and cruel, and he imagined himself the subject of mocking glances. Gazing down at the familiar balding head in front of him, he grappled with disbelief that his old friend – his *confessor* – could have lied to him this way.

The girl at the piano had started to play Nocturne No. 1, her slim fingers gliding over the keys. Janusz had a sudden image of himself, aged about three, sitting on his mama's lap while she played it at Grandmother's house. One of the most beautiful nocturnes, the piece, which combined an almost painful poignancy with a sense that in the end all would be well, calmed him a little.

The priest led Janusz down an oak-lined hallway heading to the embassy's rear. Behind one final old panelled door a second, modern swing door opened into the cacophony of the embassy kitchen. At the threshold, they passed a man coming out who, on seeing the priest, made a deep bow. Janusz caught a whiff of his aniseedy cologne as they passed.

Inside, chefs in tall white hats were arranging canapés on trays like checkers pieces, shouting for waiters, but after passing through a second swing door, the pair entered an oasis of peace. From the odd empty plate and some kitchen whites discarded on a long table, Janusz guessed it was the staff eating area.

In the far corner sat a bald man in his sixties, drinking a glass of lemon tea. He was dressed in a freshly ironed open-necked shirt and a windcheater type jacket: the uniform of a working-class Polish man of a certain age. He stood up to meet them, and clasping the priest in a hug, kissed him on both cheeks. He stood almost a head shorter than Janusz but had the solid, compact build of a man with a lifetime of physical labour behind him. He hesitated, before holding out a hand to Janusz in the English manner.

'Konstanty Nowak.' Janusz shook it, making no effort to conceal his reluctance.

'Would you both like some tea?' asked Nowak. 'One of the lads in the kitchen was so kind as to make me a pot.'

'Not for me, Konstanty,' said the priest. 'I must get back to the reception – I want to talk to Monsignor Zielinski.'

'Quite right, Piotr. And make sure you get a fat cheque out of Dubrowy, he can afford it.'

Janusz recognised the name from the papers – Dubrowy had made millions, billions even, from telecoms back home.

Father Pietruski, who had regained a little of his composure, laid a hesitant hand on Janusz's shoulder. 'Come and find me after your chat?' he said. He got a half-nod in response.

Janusz guessed Nowak's age to be around sixty-five. His head was as smooth as a hen's egg, with the telltale bluish shadow that betrayed daily shaving. These days, many men preferred total baldness to the tonsured look of a medieval monk. He resisted the narcissistic urge to run a hand over his own head of hair: still thick, thanks be to God, if greying fast.

Nowak invited Janusz to sit, and once again offered tea, which he declined. Pouring himself a cup from a white china teapot, he asked: 'What did you think of the reception? Father Pietruski certainly manages to get some fancy types along to these fundraising dos, doesn't he?' The guy's accent had the rough edge of those who hailed from Poland's eastern fringes.

'I didn't come for the *szampan* and canapés,' said Janusz, sticking his chin out. 'A girl is dead because of this job Father Pietruski got me into, and now I find out I don't even know who I was working for. What the fuck is all this about?'

He was aware that such bluntness, especially toward a man of Nowak's age, was rank bad manners, but he didn't care – Justyna's death and the lies he had been told gave him the right to be impolite.

Nowak appeared not to take offence. 'I can see that you are a man who doesn't – how do the English put it? – "*mince his words*",' he said. He took a gulp of his tea and his clear hazel gaze met Janusz's eyes.

'I am an old friend of Edward Zamorski,' he said.

Janusz sat in stunned silence. *Zamorski?* Mother of a whore!

'Edward Zamorski the *presidential candidate*?'

Nowak gave a single nod, his expression sombre.

'What the hell does Zamorski have to do with a runaway waitress in London?' asked Janusz with a disbelieving gesture.

'It's a long story.' Tipping his head sideways, Nowak set his glass of tea back in its saucer. 'But it's probably helpful if I explain, first of all, how Edward and I know each other.'

Janusz shrugged.

'We first met in 1972,' said Nowak. 'On an early morning train, heading to new jobs at the Nowa Huta steel works.' He chuckled. 'Edward hadn't brought any food – he didn't know the journey would take eleven hours – so we shared my bread and *kielbasa*.'

Janusz knew Nowa Huta – a sprawling industrial city built from scratch on the edge of Krakow, and named 'The New Steel Mill' with typical Communist flair.

'Tens of thousands of lucky peasants like me and Edward got drafted in.' Nowak's tone was one of amused cynicism. 'You can imagine the sales pitch – flats for all, holidays on the Black Sea, a workers' paradise. All the usual Soviet garbage.' He waved a weary hand.

164

The harsh clatter of plates being thrown into a dish-washer reached them from the kitchen next door.

'Anyway,' Nowak continued 'it was a crazy place for a steel plant – no coal, no iron ore for hundreds of miles. The whole thing was just a *Kommie* tactic.'

Janusz shifted in his chair. 'I don't see what any of this has to do with Weronika.'

'Young people are always in a hurry,' said Nowak in a tone of gentle reproof. 'Please permit me to tell you the story in my own way.'

Janusz leaned back and folded his arms.

Nowak took a sip of tea. 'The *Kommies* thought that bringing in a couple of hundred thousand thick-headed proles would keep all those dangerous Krakow intellectuals in check.' He chuckled. 'As we know, it didn't quite work out like that.'

Janusz couldn't help but grin. By the time he'd arrived in Krakow to study physics, Huta had become a hotbed of resistance second only to the Gdansk shipyards, and a smouldering coal in the lap of the regime.

'I often wonder what happened to the civil servant who dreamt up Huta,' Nowak said, pouring tea into his glass. 'He probably got a nine-millimetre bullet from a Makarov in the back of the head for that bright idea.'

'So that's where Zamorski got involved with *Solidarnosc*?' asked Janusz, interested in spite of himself.

The older man nodded. 'We were workers' repre-sentatives, taking grievances to management, organising strikes and sit-ins, generally making trouble for the bastards.' He smiled at the memory. 'You know Father Pietruski was there, too, for a while?'

Janusz shook his head.

'He was quite the firebrand,' said Nowak, eyes twinkling. 'During one strike he even held a mass inside the steelworks – which drove the *Kommies* mad, of course.'

Janusz tried, without success, to find a position on his hard chair that would ease the pressure on his throbbing rib. 'And now – you're something in *Partia Renasans*?', he said, his tone grudgingly respectful now he knew the guy's history. 'An adviser to Zamorski, maybe?'

Nowak opened his eyes in mock horror. 'Mother of God, no. I did my time on the barricades in the old days, even saw the inside of a few cells at Montepulich. But after Walesa got elected,' he shrugged, 'I decided I'd had enough of politics. I just wanted to get on with my life.'

Janusz found himself nodding. 'What have you been doing for the last twenty years?' he asked.

'I set up a small construction business, refurbishing flats – in Huta, as it happens. After a few years, I'd made all the money I could ever need, enough for a little fishing boat and a place in Krakow.' He smiled. 'Now I'm retired I can play the *dyletant:* I go fishing with old friends like Edward, do a little charity work, try to keep out of trouble.'

He drained his glass of tea and met Janusz's gaze. 'So that's how I know Edward.'

Janusz folded his arms. 'Okay. So you're telling me that when pani Tosik hired me to look for Weronika, I was really working for Edward Zamorski?' He tried to keep his voice level.

Nowak raised a hand, let it fall. 'Please understand, I was just as much in the dark as you are, until Edward called me yesterday.' Looking suddenly old, he worked the bridge of his nose with the tips of his fingers. 'He told me about this . . . mess he'd got himself into and asked me to help.' He shrugged his shoulders. 'He's a dear friend, so of course, I said yes.'

Janusz thought of Oskar, who he had extracted from various scrapes over the years.

'When Father Pietruski recommended you for the job, it seems Edward insisted on keeping his name out of it,' Nowak went on. 'But then this terrible business with the girl, Justyna, changed everything. After Edward took me into his confidence, Father Pietruski and I talked, and we managed to persuade him that you should be told about the situation.'

Janusz felt another flare of anger – and hurt – at the way the priest had put his support for Zamorski and the Renaissance Party above their friendship.

'Since I was already in London on charity business, Edward asked me to talk to you,' said Nowak. 'So here we both are.' He scanned Janusz's face, perhaps still undecided as to whether he could be trusted with Zamorski's great secret.

'I'll bet you're a smoking man,' he said suddenly, a mischievous grin animating his face.

Janusz shrugged, '*Naturalnie*, but you know it's forbidden inside?'

Waving the objection away, Nowak stood up and went over to a nearby window. 'Who will ever know?' he hissed in a stage whisper as he opened it.

They pushed their chairs closer to the window. Nowak pulled out a battered packet of *Mocne*, a brand of ultra-cheap cigarettes Janusz hadn't seen since he left Poland. The innocent directness of the brand name – *Mocne* meant Strong – had always amused him.

'Even the greatest of heroes has a secret, some foolish weakness or other. Usually – no, *always* – to do with sex.' His eyes met Janusz's and they shared a wry grin.

Janusz lit Nowak's cigarette, then his own cigar, and there was a companionable silence as each man savoured the first glorious lungful.

'This Adamski has been blackmailing Edward about a . . . private affair, a matter of the heart,' said Nowak, his voice becoming serious. 'He is threatening to sell the story to a newspaper just before the election.'

Janusz recoiled. Blackmail was a distasteful crime, a cowardly, hole-in-the-corner business. But blackmailing the president-to-be? That took some balls. Zamorski had certainly never struck him as a playboy type – he was a family man, married for thirty years, children . . . every inch the upright – detractors might even say up*tight* – citizen. He wasn't a secret *homoseksual*, surely to God? At one time the newspapers here had been filled with such revelations about politicians, but this was England, after all: their boarding schools bred queers like mushrooms in a damp cupboard.

Janusz waited for Nowak to go on, to reveal Zamorski's secret, but the stocky figure had fallen silent, his expression brooding behind a curl of smoke. Was this all he was going to be told – a few hints about sexual misbehaviour?

'Listen,' said Janusz. 'Zamorski obviously wants me to carry on looking for Adamski, or I wouldn't be here, so I've got a right to know what this big secret is.'

But Nowak was in no hurry. 'Blackmail is one thing, but after what happened to this other girl, Edward is worried that Adamski is a *psychopata*,' he said with the

168

air of someone thinking aloud, 'He's convinced he might kill Weronika – and I think he might be right.' He looked at Janusz, frowning.

Janusz was struggling to keep up. Adamski had a motive for killing Justyna, for giving away his address, but Nowak was talking as though Weronika, too, was in danger.

'Is all this business something to do with Adamski dealing drugs?' he asked. 'Did he maybe sell Zamorski some *kokaina*?'

Nowak chuckled. 'Adamski might be a drug pusher, but I can tell you, the most I ever saw Edward indulge in was a little too much *Zubrowka*.'

Janusz stubbed out his cigar. 'I'm a busy man,' he said. 'I don't have all afternoon to play Twenty Questions,' and setting his hands flat on the table, made to stand. Nowak reached out, and laying a hand on his forearm propelled him with gentle pressure back into his seat. Then, pinching out his cigarette with a decisive gesture, he pulled his chair so close to Janusz that their knees almost touched.

'When Edward asked me to meet you today I made it clear that if I decided you could be trusted, you should be told everything,' he said. 'He wasn't happy about it, but I told him he was being foolish. How could you retrieve what Adamski is using to blackmail Edward if you don't know what you are looking for?'

He tapped Janusz on the knee. 'But first, you'll have to put up with a bit more history from an old man.

'Edward is a few years younger than me, so I suppose I looked out for him back at Huta, tried to make sure he didn't go too far and get himself disappeared. But in

169

1980, when everything kicked off, the union leadership heard about this gift he had, his ability to inspire people, and pretty soon they had him speaking at all sorts of events.' Janusz recalled Zamorski's speech at the rally in Gdansk at the height of the uprising – his quiet charisma, the way his words could stir the emotions.

'I went along to watch him speak once, in the Rynek in Krakow,' said Nowak, 'and from that moment, I knew politics was going to be his life.'

According to Nowak, before Zamorski turned thirty he had become practically a full-time activist for the movement, travelling all over Poland, giving speeches calling for democracy at union meetings and demos.

'Edward was in his element,' said Nowak, with a smile. 'Okay, it was life out of a suitcase, and you'd think it could get lonely once the crowds had gone home, but he used to say that in all his years of travelling, he never spent the night alone except by choice.' He looked at Janusz and raised an eyebrow, torn between amusement and disapproval.

'You might not be old enough to remember, but those big *Solidarnosc* names, they were like rock stars,' he went on, all his former reticence gone. 'Edward would get up and do the big rousing speech and by the time he'd finished he said the ladies would practically be throwing their underwear at him.'

So this was the great secret? thought Janusz. *Edward's gift for speaking got him laid a lot in the days before he grew a paunch?* He frowned.

'Zamorski's supporters, they might be conservative,' he said. 'But they're not going to turn their back on him just because he was a ladies' man thirty years ago.'

'No, no, of course not,' said Nowak. He picked up his pack of cigarettes. 'But there was one particular lady who he met at a rally in Poznan, in 1989 – one of the last before Jaruzelski threw in the towel. A very beautiful blonde, apparently, if a little wild.' He sighed at the glorious imprudence of youth. 'Anyway, they go back to the room where he was staying, they do what comes naturally to young people, and the next day he's off on the train to his next destination.'

He passed a hand from the nape of his neck up over his shaven head; they were sitting so close that Janusz could hear the crackle of the bristles. 'When you are young, it is easy to think that actions have no consequences, but a few months later, he discovered that the girl was what the English call *"economical with the truth"*.' Smiling at the phrase, he lit his cigarette from Janusz's proffered lighter. 'She was not, as she had told Edward, eighteen years old – but had, in truth, just turned *fifteen*.'

Janusz gave a low whistle: now that *was* dynamite. If news got out that the solid, honourable Zamorski, *Solidarnosc* hero and would-be saviour of Poland, had shagged a schoolgirl, even as an honest mistake, it would have the Party's elderly female vote foaming at the mouth – probably in sufficient numbers to lose him the election.

'But the girl obviously kept quiet about it all these years, so how did a *chuj* like Adamski manage to unearth the story?' Janusz stopped, struck by a sudden thought: what if Zamorski *still* had a penchant for young blonde girls? 'Did Adamski find out that Zamorski had an affair with Weronika?' he asked, his face creased with distaste.

Nowak shook his head. 'Worse than that, I'm afraid.'

He paused and picked a shred of tobacco off his tongue. 'He discovered that Weronika is Edward Zamorski's *daughter*.'

That jack-knifed Janusz out of his seat. Turning his back on Nowak he stared out of the open window, which gave onto a brick wall a metre away, and dug blindly in his pocket for his cigars. Zamorski, Weronika's *father*?! Damn Father Pietruski for keeping him in the dark!

Mastering his confusion, he turned back to Nowak.

'So, the hot fifteen-year-old was Weronika's Mama,' he said. 'Did the girl tell Adamski the big family secret, then, when they started going out together?'

'No, no,' said Nowak. 'Edward says Weronika doesn't know the truth: she grew up thinking her father had died. He always looked after the two of them, sent money and visited regularly, became very fond of the child it seems. As for Mama, she kept her side of the bargain and to the little girl he was always just Uncle Edek.

'Then, as Nika got older, she saw him popping up on television, and started boasting to her friends about her famous uncle. With the election coming up, Edward decided it would be safer if she came to London – at least for a while – in case the press should get wind of the story and put two and two together. Pani Tosik is an old friend and was happy to give the girl a job and a place to stay.'

Janusz was finding it hard to process all this new information, partly because his head had started pulsing again. Pressing both hands to his temples he asked, 'Does Father Pietruski know all this, about Zamorski having an illegitimate daughter?'

Nowak nodded. 'You know, I think the church is more

forgiving than we give it credit for. Edward made his peace with his own confessor about his . . . love child, I think they call it these days, many years ago.

'Excuse me a moment, would you?' he said, raising his stocky frame up on muscular forearms – steel worker's arms. He left his cigarette burning in the ashtray.

Janusz recalled the empty photo frame in Weronika's bedroom – maybe it had held a snap of Uncle Edek that she'd been loath to leave behind – and felt a stab of pity. Poor naïve little Nika, who believed she had found the love of her life in Adamski, had actually fallen victim to a vicious scam. He didn't allow himself to doubt that he would find her and bring her home, but what then? Would she ever get over such a callous betrayal?

He was still lost in thought when Nowak returned and set a tumbler of water and a couple of pills down in front of him. 'Aspirin,' he said, letting himself down into the chair again with the wary movements of someone no longer young.

'*Dziekuje bardzo*,' said Janusz, sluicing the pills down his throat. 'One thing I don't understand,' he asked, as he set down the empty glass. 'If Weronika didn't know that she's Zamorski's daughter, how did Adamski work it out?'

'Edward has no idea,' shrugged Nowak. 'But somehow Adamski got hold of a birth certificate naming him as the father – and sent him a photocopy, along with a blackmail demand. At first, he paid up, sent him a few thousand, hoping he would just go away.'

Janusz and he exchanged a dry look. 'Of course, the demands just got bigger. And then, the bombshell: a dirty photograph of Weronika,' Nowak's lips thinned to a line, the first sign he'd shown of anger.

173

Janusz eyes narrowed – remembering the pornographic photos, he'd half-guessed that was coming.

'Edward read the letter out to me on the phone,' Nowak went on. 'It said that Adamski was "enjoying fucking his little girl" – and if he didn't send half a million euros, he would kill her.'

'And by this time, Adamski had run off with Weronika?'

Nodding, Nowak waved a hand. 'Gone without a trace.'

A thought struck Janusz. 'Does Zamorski have anyone else out looking for them?'

Nowak shook his head. 'Good God, no – as far as Edward's concerned, the fewer people who know about the whole ugly business, the better.'

Janusz decided not to share his hunch about the gangsters on Adamski's tail: he wanted time to digest all this, decide if any of it changed the plans he'd already made.

'So what are you asking me to do?' he asked. 'Get the girl away from Adamski, obviously.' Nowak nodded. 'And destroy the birth certificate, I assume. But what's to stop him getting another one issued?'

'Edward tells me that the original no longer exists,' Nowak raised a sardonic eyebrow. 'You know politicians – they always have a friend in the right department.' A grimace of distaste crossed his face. 'It's all a shabby business. But whatever mistakes Edward has made, he doesn't deserve to have his future destroyed by someone like Adamski.'

'So Adamski gets to walk away? After what he did to Justyna?' said Janusz, anger roughening his voice.

Nowak struck the table with the flat of his hand: 'Absolutely not,' his voice hard. 'That must not happen.

Apparently, there's a warrant out for Adamski's arrest back home – he tried to force an old man to sell him some antique furniture, and when he said no, he knocked him about quite badly.'

He raised a finger. 'When you find him, Edward will make sure the scumbag gets extradited – and he'll get a prison sentence. Even if the English police can prove Adamski was with Justyna when she died, they would probably only charge him with supplying drugs.' He shrugged. 'What do you get for that here? Probation and a few weeks picking up dog shit in the park.'

He was right, thought Janusz. Adamski would be handed down a much tougher sentence in Poland, and his jail wouldn't resemble a university campus. He shivered at a sudden memory: Montepulich's interrogation room. He could barely remember what it looked like, but the smell of the place, a ferrous reek of blood and sweat overlaid with cleaning fluids, would stay with him for ever.

Nowak sought his gaze. 'You're an honourable man, and I know that your decision won't be based on financial considerations.' He hesitated. 'But Edward is anxious that you have sufficient funds to continue your investigation.' Reaching into the pocket of his windcheater jacket, he pulled out a manila envelope, and held it out to Janusz, looking embarrassed. 'He has doubled the instalment pani Tosik paid you, and he will pay the same amount again when everything is settled. You don't need to make your mind up right away – if you should decide against continuing, just return the money to Father Pietruski.'

Janusz paused a moment, then took the envelope with a nod.

Nowak walked with him to the door. 'I doubt either of us are particularly fond of politicians,' he said, looking searchingly into Janusz's eyes, 'And Edward is my friend, so perhaps I am biased, but I am sure of one thing. He has always chosen the hard road when he could have taken the easy road, and I think you are the same kind of man.'

Downstairs, Janusz craned his head around the main salon's doorway, looking for Father Pietruski. The guests had become rowdier, their chatter and laughter louder and higher pitched. He saw the Countess Jagielska leaning on the arm of a smirking businessman, regaling him, no doubt, with some three-centuries-old family anecdote.

The priest stood in a corner, talking to a tall guy in a long black robe with a pink sash who looked surprisingly young to be a Monsignor. Noticing Janusz, the Monsignor put a hand on Father Pietruski's shoulder, and bent to whisper into his ear. Following his pointing finger, the priest saw Janusz and, dipping his head in a respectful farewell, made his way over.

They stepped out into the street and he looked up into Janusz's eyes, his gaze full of almost comic penitence. Janusz looked down at his friend and confessor, the strands of white hair falling across his forehead. He was a long way from forgiving the lying old bastard, he realised. Pulling out the brown envelope, he leafed through the notes and extracted about a third – the amount he'd need for the next few days. The rest he handed to the priest, who looked up at him in surprise.

'I'll do it,' he growled. 'Send this to Justyna's people.' And he left, without a word of farewell.

He walked on autopilot for a good ten, fifteen minutes,

as though in a bubble. Across bus-choked Oxford Circus, all the way down Carnaby Street, through drifting shoals of tourists and laser-guided office workers on their lunch break, till he hit Beak Street – at which point he realised he was heading straight for Kasia's club.

He slowed his pace, and took a detour through Berwick Street. The sun was out, the fruit and veg market was in full swing, and the cacophony of the market traders' calls, like a flock of raucous magpies, pushed the clamour of thoughts from his head. *Fuck it*. He decided to take a peace offering to Kasia. He wouldn't be seeing her for a few days and he had to know if there was anything to be salvaged between them.

He browsed the best of the produce stalls, at the market's southernmost end, near the junction with Peter Street. These guys supplied the finest produce to £100-a-head restaurants where the chefs, according to Oskar, for some unfathomable reason, turned good honest food into *foam*. He spotted the perfect thing: a basket of fresh, wavy-edge chanterelles which, fried in butter and garlic and finished with a spoonful of crème fraîche and some chopped dill, would make a delicious breakfast.

Holding the brown paper bag of fragile mushrooms carefully in his big fist, Janusz left the market's almost-rural scene and ducked into the darkened piss-smelling alley that served as the gateway to Soho's warren of sex aid shops, strip joints and lap dancing clubs. Here, pretty girls with tired faces leaned from doorways, touting for business from punters, but on seeing him, their sales pitch gave way to a smile of recognition, and, from the occasional Polish or Ukrainian girl, a *Dzien dobry, panu*.

He was pleased to find Kasia fully dressed behind the

bar of the club today. 'Pale chickens!' she exclaimed when she saw his face – a saying he hadn't heard since he was a child. 'Just a little bump in a car,' he said. She lifted a sceptical eyebrow.

'I'm brewing a cold,' she said, when he asked why she wasn't dancing today. 'So Ray promoted me to club manager while he goes to Costco.' She seemed pleased to be given the responsibility, however temporary.

The bag of chanterelles earned him a sexy lopsided smile, which made him absurdly happy, and after making them both a lemon tea, Kasia sat on a bar stool beside him to drink it. Fifteen metres away, through an archway, a girl in a G-string and feather boa gyrated to a thumping pop track, watched with dog-like concentration by a handful of motionless punters. It was hardly a romantic backdrop but after a few moments Janusz had completely blanked it out.

There was warmth in Kasia's half-smile, but also a wariness around those long, lovely eyes that didn't bode well for their future. He tried to formulate the words that might repair this breach between them, but the prospect of another trudge around the topic of her jealousy, and the everlasting nature of her marriage to Steve depressed him. And there was something else nagging at him, a question that she, too, was doubtless aware of. Even if she were to leave Steve, did he really have the stomach to set up home with a woman again?

They sipped their tea and said nothing for perhaps a minute. Shifting on his bar stool, he felt a blade-thrust of pain from his damaged rib so fierce that it made sweat prickle coldly on his upper lip.

'I've never told you about Iza, my first real girlfriend,

the one before Marta,' he said, his hand cradling the hot glass. Kasia became stock-still: she'd often wondered how Janusz had ended up married to Marta, but he had never volunteered any details about his love life before meeting her. 'She died . . . or rather, she was killed,' he went on, almost as though to himself, 'when I took her to a demonstration in Gdansk. In '82.'

He shivered suddenly, violently, at the force of the memories. *A bitterly cold dusk, snow blizzarding down.*

As Janusz told Kasia the story, the words seemed to fall from his mouth without him being aware of his lips forming them.

He had taken Iza to his home city at Christmas, to meet his mother, but once he'd heard whispers of an illegal march to commemorate four people who'd been killed in a protest over food shortages, he was determined to go. His mama had tried to talk him out of it, and even Iza wasn't that keen, but he wouldn't be dissuaded. It was a matter of national duty, he said, with the certainty of youth. His real reason for going was more shameful – and more compelling – but he could say nothing of that – either then, or now, to Kasia.

It had begun as a peaceful march to a Catholic shrine to lay flowers for the dead. But as the sun set, and the snow started to fall, the helmeted ranks of ZOMO riot police started pressing in, shoving the demonstrators with their shields. The familiar chant of 'Ge-sta-po! Ge-sta-po!' rose from the crowd, and the snatch squads went in, pulling out young men at random, beating them unconscious and throwing them into the back of the pale blue *milicja* vans like sacks of turnips. Then the unmistakable crack of an AK47 sent the crowd into a panic. Helicopters wheeled overhead, their loudhailers ordering the crowd to disperse, but there was nowhere to go: the ZOMO had everyone hemmed into one corner of the square, trampling their red and white banners into the slush underfoot. The crowd, old and young, workers and students, were cornered and panic-stricken, all the earlier wild elation of resistance gone.

At the crowd's back stood the famous Gdansk Post Office, its windows boarded up. Still the visored police pushed them back. Above the screams and curses and the clattering of horses' hooves, the sound he would never forget – the obscene *thump thump* of lead-filled rubber truncheons striking human flesh.

He sucked in a breath, remembering the sensation of being crushed: the weight of humanity like a massive door closing inexorably on his chest.

He'd still got Iza's hand in a tight grip but he couldn't always see her, she was so tiny and so far beneath him in that crush. He felt a wave of relief when he caught sight of her. Her face, jammed sideways against a man's chest, was papery-white, set, every ounce of will bent on getting air into her compacted lungs.

'I shouted to her "I'll get you out!"' he told Kasia. 'But really, I wasn't too sure about getting either of us out by then.'

His stomach had been jumping with fear. Taller than anyone else in the heaving mob, he had at least been able to turn his head, and realised they were only a couple of metres from a wide ledge, shoulder height, behind them on the Post Office facade. A scream rang out as another surge of the human tide felled two, three people. Their heads disappeared beneath the surface, which closed above them in an instant. He tightened his grip on Iza's gloved hand and flexing the big muscles in his legs started to carve a path through the wall of flesh towards the ledge. He trod on something soft, felt bone snap beneath his boots. As he forced his way on, a girl in a red wool hat sank beneath his elbow without a sound.

With a last heave he managed to drag Iza to the ledge, and used it to brace himself against the press. With no breath left for words of reassurance, he sent her a look that said he would get them up there but first he'd have to let go of her hand for a moment. Panting, he levered himself up and drew his legs up behind him. Grasping a window bar to brace himself with one hand he reached down with the other and gripped Iza's hand. Between the freckles her face had a bluish tinge now like skimmed milk, but she rested her gaze on him and smiled, and his heart opened.

He started to pull her upwards, like a stubborn cork from a bottle. Her shoulders emerged above the wedged morass of people, but then the crowd surged again. He saw something go out of her face at that and felt her grip on his hand loosen. He made a desperate grab for her wrists. But as he did so, her section of crowd lurched sideways, then started to topple. Half a dozen went down as one, dragging her from his grasp.

Some of his mates found him, later, amid the wreckage of the demo, as paramedics tended to the injured and checked bodies for signs of life.

He was slumped against the wall under the ledge, among torn banners, hats, shoes – shell-shocked and mute, but uninjured, still clutching one of Iza's gloves.

181

He found the lemon tea still in his curled fist, tepid now, and Kasia's shocked gaze locked on his face.

'They all thought it strange that I never asked what happened to her,' he shrugged, 'as if I needed to.'

'And Marta?' asked Kasia after a moment.

'She was Iza's best friend. We clung together to survive, I suppose. The wedding was six weeks later. Madness.'

Just then, Kasia's boss, Ray returned.

'What's all this then, a Polish tea party?' he said, in his flat London accent, seemingly oblivious to the sombre moment he was interrupting. He grinned in that unpleasant way he had, as though enjoying a private joke at someone else's expense. 'You keeping my staff from their duties, Janek?'

Janusz hated the over-familiar way Ray used the diminutive of his name, but he could hardly pull him up on it – not because he was a good customer for the booze, but because he was Kasia's boss. The truth was, Janusz didn't like Ray. He told himself it was because he couldn't respect any man who lived off women, but now and again it occurred to him that maybe his dislike was rooted in the fact that it was Ray who had talked Kasia into showing strange men her *pizda* for money.

Kasia rose from her bar stool with dignity and spoke to Ray in English: 'I already finish stock take, call the Rentokil for get rid of the mice, and throw out one drunk,' she said. 'Tell me other things you like me to do, and I do it.' With that she clip-clopped in her high heels out the back, Janusz gazing after her in admiration.

Grinning, Ray took Kasia's stool at the bar, slinging his leather jacket over the seatback. 'Did you two have a falling-out?' he said, nodding at Janusz's injured face.

'I've always thought that one would have a good right hook on her.' Janusz shot him a look, but deciding he was just taking the piss, let it ride.

'I had a crash in a cab,' he said, in a voice that discouraged further enquiry, and drained the dregs of his cold tea.

Ray started cleaning his fingernails with a business card. 'By the way,' he said. 'You wouldn't know anything about some bloke hanging around, scaring off the punters, would you?'

Janusz raised his eyebrows with polite interest. 'No, why?' he asked, meeting Ray's penetrating gaze.

'I had some bloke's lawyer on the phone yesterday. Turns out some idiot has been going round telling people that we film them in the booths – y'know, bashing the bishop,' he chuckled, 'and put it on fucking YouTube or YouWank or something.' He hadn't taken his eyes off Janusz, who started laughing, too.

'You're kidding!' he said, shaking his head. 'London is full of crazy people.'

Ray seemed to accept the performance. 'Yeah, well, business is already shit without losing any more punters,' he said. 'Especially since I hear I might be losing Kasia.' He raised a questioning eyebrow at Janusz, who frowned.

'I thought you'd know all about it,' he said. 'I heard her on the phone yesterday to that girlfriend of hers in Poland – you know, the one with the funny name . . .'

'Basia?' offered Janusz: the diminutive of Barbara always amused Londoners.

'Yeah, *Basher*,' said Ray, shaking his head at the hilariousness of foreign names. 'So I'm down in the cellar putting a new barrel on – you can hear everything down there – and from what I can make out, they're chattering away about setting up a *nail bar*. In Warsaw, believe it or not.'

Janusz denied any knowledge of the plan, but as the news sank in he felt a horrible sense of inevitability. He recalled Kasia enthusing, a few weeks back, about Basia's *fantastyczny* business plan to set up some beauty clinic in the capital. Several big multinationals, banks and so on, had relocated there, and it seemed the business district was awash with well-off women.

Kasia had never hinted that she might be part of the venture, but he knew that *chuj* Steve had been trying to persuade her that they should leave London and start afresh in Poland, where it was cheaper to set up a business. Typical of Steve that the business in question would be one in which his wife did all the graft.

Having dropped his bombshell, Ray disappeared into the office to do some paperwork and Janusz called out a goodbye to Kasia. She came out and they kissed farewell in the Polish way. 'I'm going to be away for a few days on business,' Janusz told her, examining the toe of one boot. 'Maybe I will see you when I come back?'

She hesitated, then inclined her head and smiled that crooked half-smile of hers. 'Of course. We are friends, no?' she said, which only deepened his gloom. He must have looked depressed, because she leaned close to him. 'Listen, Janek, maybe you will tell me it is none of my business, but . . . Iza's death, I think maybe you still need to forgive yourself for what happened,' she paused and gazed into his eyes. 'Maybe she just didn't have the will to live.'

Great, he thought, she was off to Poland with her

worthless husband, but at least he got some free psycho-analysis as a parting gift. He pounded the pavement, head down, his whole body aching and his head befuddled by the day's revelations. As for the last hour, he had no clue what made him spill his guts to Kasia about Iza, the demo, all that ancient history. Maybe to make her see that staying with Steve was a criminal waste of her life.

In his heart of hearts, though, he knew she was *uparta* – stubborn. No, more than stubborn, she was obdurate. There was nothing in Polish to match the stony finality of the English word.

Fourteen

Since the Waveney Thameside's security cameras had clearly been rigged by a total cretin, Kershaw was going to have to rely on the observational powers of the desk clerk who'd been on duty the night of Justyna Kozlowska's death.

His name was Alex Hurley, a young, smartish guy, living in a new, smartish studio flat on the outskirts of Stratford – and Kershaw took a dislike to him from the word go, though to tell the truth she was in a pretty foul mood after spending half an hour locked in the one-way system eating diesel fumes.

The place was the size of a postage stamp – hardly enough room to swing a hotel desk clerk, she thought – but it was stacked full of shiny appliances and 'look at me' gadgets. As he made coffee, using a proper Italian stainless steel machine, she said over the hiss of steam, 'Nice place you've got: the Waveney pays its desk staff well, then?'

'Actually, I'm a management trainee, so I pull down a

pretty good package,' he said with patently false modesty. 'Mr Treneman reckons I'll be running my own hotel in a few years.' Typical corporate ladder climber, she thought, smiling encouragement at him. As he topped their coffee with foamed milk, she let her eyes drift to a pile of paperwork on the polished stone kitchen worktop. The headings of one, two, three different credit card statements were visible. *Not* that *good a package then, Boy Wonder.*

As they drank their coffees on his cow-sized leather sofa, he was all helpful smiles and body language, and examined the computer printout recording the check-in of the man in the hat, with a studious frown. But in answer to all her questions – 'Would you describe him as tall?' 'Well-dressed?' 'Slim or well-built?' 'Did he have an East European accent?' – he just shook his head.

'I'm really sorry, officer, I just don't remember him at all,' he said, opening up his hands in that 'nothing to hide' gesture that always made her suspicious. Even when she got out the DVD onto which she'd had the CCTV footage recorded and played him the section that showed the guy checking in – and Alex chatting and grinning away on the other side of the desk – he *still* shook his head and looked blank.

'What about these two?' she tried, rewinding the DVD to the American couple. On his huge TV screen their backsides looked like twin baby hippos wrapped in tartan.

He grinned the superior grin of the young and toned, making her dislike him even more, and said, in a comedy American accent: '*Mr and Mrs Waldenheim the Third, from Plastic, Colorado!*' Then, realising his feat of memory had pissed her off, he shrugged apologetically. 'Unusual names – easier to remember, I suppose.'

Kershaw pressed fast forward till she reached the girl in the shoulderless dress, the sex worker groping her male companion so enthusiastically she was practically giving him an intimate body search. 'Remember this pair?'

Alex creased his forehead in concentration, then shook his head. 'Um, no not really.'

'How many of your guests at the Waveney are there to have sex with prostitutes would you say?' she asked sweetly. 'Just a rough estimate.'

Apparently unfazed by the question, he showed her his palms again.

'The hotel has a very strict policy preventing sex workers touting for business in the public areas, but if a couple arrive and check in together, there's really no way of knowing if it's a . . . professional arrangement.'

He looked well pleased at this little sample of hotel-management-speak bollocks, but it did nothing to allay Kershaw's suspicions. She had a hunch that, alongside the usual rich tourists and business-wallahs, the hotel was doing a roaring trade among working girls and their clients. A suspicious death on the premises was one thing, but if it turned out Justyna was a sex worker who got murdered on the job then it could put a nasty dent in the hotel's upmarket reputation. Maybe Alex really did have early onset dementia, or maybe Andrew Treneman had put the word out to the hotel's staff: keep *schtum* in the hope the cops get bored and go away.

When she got back to the office, Kershaw had to run to catch the phone ringing on her desk.

'You sound a little out of breath, Detective Constable,' came a plummy voice. 'Chasing down ne'er-do-wells, I hope?'

'Oh, hi, Dr Waterhouse. Anything for me on Justyna Kozlowska?'

The PM had taken place that morning, about the same time she'd been grilling Janusz Kiszka. She held her breath, on tenterhooks for his response, but Waterhouse was in playful mood.

'May I congratulate you on your Polish pronunciation, Detective. At this rate, we'll have *paramethoxyamphetamine* tripping off your tongue in no time!'

She forced herself to join in Waterhouse's peals of laughter, venting her feelings by pulling a crazed serial killer face down the phone.

'Did you find those . . . dots on her kidneys?' asked Kershaw.

'*Petechiae*? Yes, I did. And since I know how keen you are to get the results, I had a little word with the toxicologist,' he said. 'And strictly *off* the record, his initial tests *do* suggest the presence of PMA in the young lady's bloodstream.'

'What about any signs that she'd been tied up, like I said in the email?'

'Nothing conclusive, I'm afraid, Detective. And there were no vaginal tears, bruising or abrasions to suggest she was anything other than a *willing* partner in the encounter.'

Yeah, thought Kershaw – with the shed load of drugs and booze Kozlowska had on board, consent became a somewhat fluid concept. Waterhouse hadn't found any semen on the body either, so the man in the hat must have used a condom. But the Doc saved his best bit of news till last.

'I did find a single pubic hair – which I'm delighted to

say appears to have an intact follicle attached. If your DS signs off the request I'll have it sent it for DNA profiling.'

After she hung up, Kershaw punched the air. Streaky would surely approve DNA-testing the hair: if hat man had previous, he'd be on the national database. At the very least she'd have cast-iron forensic evidence to put the bastard at the scene – when she found him.

She ploughed through the twenty-three emails waiting in her inbox, hitting delete on most of them – another community policing initiative from the Justice Department, a clampdown on overtime, a warning for the person leaving tea bags in the sink ('you know who you are'), a leaving do in the Drunken Monkey that evening – someone from Traffic she didn't know – and several mails aimed at the long-suffering uniforms. One reminded them of the regulation sock colour, ie black or navy, to be worn on duty, the correct shade of sock presumably being a critical factor when poor plod had to insert himself between some drunken lowlife and the girlfriend he was using as a punch bag outside the kebab shop in Leyton High Road on a Friday night.

That left only one mail worth reading. DI Bellwether had come good on his promise to dig out the PMA info he'd mentioned, and had attached an EU-commissioned report called 'Europe: Global Centre of Synthetic Drug Production'. It was 250 pages long, and she was just thinking she was glad to have the office to herself for half an hour so she could have a proper read of it when Streaky and Tom Browning barrelled in, talking about some announcement by Scotland Yard, or as Streaky preferred to call it, 'The Dream Factory'.

'It's what we used to call LOB, in the bad old days

before detectives learned to watch their Ps and Qs,' said Streaky, resting one considerable buttock on the edge of Kershaw's desk. 'Load of old bollocks,' he added, seemingly for her benefit, although she'd heard the phrase a hundred times before, mostly from him.

'What's that then Sarge?' she asked as Browning fired up his computer opposite her. He looked as smug as ever, but he'd had to stick a bit of bog roll on his chin to staunch a shaving cut, she noticed.

'They've announced they're taking rape cases off CID now, handing it over to "specialist units"' said Streaky, picking at a piece of crusted food on his tie. 'Apparently, nasty old-school detectives don't take rape seriously, which is why the conviction rate is a piss-poor six percent, according to the boss-wallahs and their feminist pals in the univer-shitties.'

She managed an interested smile.

'What's your view, Browning?' asked Streaky, craning round.

'Waste of resources, Sarge,' said Browning, leaning back in his chair. 'Rape convictions are always going to be hard to get because, well, it's one person's word against another, isn't it.' He gave a man of the world shrug.

'Do you agree, DC Kershaw?' asked Streaky.

'Up to a point, Sarge,' she said. 'But it's also because some jury members think if a girl goes off on her own with a bloke then she's asking for it.'

To her surprise, Streaky nodded. 'I think you'll find DC Kershaw brings a useful perspective to the issue,' he said to Browning. 'Unlike you, she's probably had to deal with many a nasty little nonce trying to get into her knickers.'

Streaky stood up and stretched, giving Kershaw a scary glimpse of coppery belly hairs through his gaping shirt buttons.

'Call me old-fashioned,' he said. 'But in my book, there's only one way to put more of the dirty fuckers behind bars – don't give 'em a jury trial.' And with that searing judicial insight, Streaky ambled off to his desk.

Browning, who had been giving Kershaw the evils since Streaky sided with her, now flashed an insincere smile across their desks. 'What's happening with that floater you're on, the Polish girl?' he asked.

'Sarge has her down as a suicide, jumped in the river when she was off her head,' said Kershaw, trying to get back into the PMA report.

'Sounds about right,' said Browning, checking his text messages. 'Tattoos, drugs, East European: it all says sex worker, doesn't it? Probably trafficked.'

Kershaw gave Browning a sweet smile: 'Do you ever read that bit at the front of the paper – it's called the news section? Poland's been in the EU for, like, years. She probably flew in on Ryanair.'

He just grinned. 'Whatever. If I was you I'd try and bosh that job, you've got no chance of ID-ing her.'

What made his smug assurance so exasperating was that he was probably right. If Ela, like Justyna, was a sex worker, and a foreign one at that, identifying her would be a total nightmare. Kershaw's gaze fell on the image of Ela that Missing Persons Bureau had created from the post-mortem photographs. Like digital undertakers, they had erased her injuries, photoshopped eyes back into the empty sockets, and restored her Titian hair to frame her face. At least it gave her something half-decent to put on the system, but what if no one had reported her missing? A working girl could slip beneath the murky waters of her life without leaving a ripple.

Suddenly angry, Kershaw leaned across the desk and nodded at the shaving cut on Browning's chin.

'You want to be careful with that,' she said, concern in her voice. 'All the arse-kissing you do, it could go septic.'

Juvenile, yes, but it wiped the smirk off his face.

She pressed print on her PC and while the machine chugged out the PMA report, made herself a really strong mug of Tetley's. Then, grabbing the still-warm printout and her coat, she headed for the door – and ran straight into Ben Crowther, spilling tea onto his shoes.

'Sorry, Ben – my fault,' she said, digging out a tissue from her coat pocket.

He just laughed, and taking the tissue, crouched to wipe his shoes clean.

'Where are you racing off to?' he asked, looking up at her with an expression of amused tolerance.

'Oh, just trying to find some peace and quiet to read this,' waving the report, Kershaw rolled her eyes in the direction of Browning's desk.

Ben just pulled his slow grin. 'Have you been letting Tom wind you up again?' he asked, getting to his feet.

'Yeah, probably,' she said. 'He does know how to press my buttons.' She cringed at the *double entendre*, but Ben didn't seem to notice.

'Listen,' he said, looking over her shoulder. 'Do you fancy a drink after work on Saturday?'

Aye, aye, she thought – *is Ben Crowther asking me out on a date?!*

'I'm meeting some guys from uni, up in town,' he went on. 'I think you might like them.'

Right – not a date, then. It was just as well really, she thought. She'd slept with a fellow cop in Romford Rd once, and it had gone round the nick like wildfire. It was much too soon to be dating, anyway – Mark was barely out of the door.

'Yeah, sure,' she said. 'Sounds good.'

She took the lift to the top floor and after checking there was no-one around, pushed open a heavy door labelled 'Fire Exit Only' – wedging a bit of folded cardboard underneath so she could get back in. She'd discovered the nick's flat roof a few weeks earlier and made it her own private spot, somewhere to have a think or read in peace.

She lit a cig and spread out the copy of *Metro* she'd brought to sit on. On a mild, sunny day like today, the view over London was like something out of a movie: the glittering curve of the river and the great squished 'O' of the London Eye in the distance.

After thirty minutes of speed-reading, a technique that had got her through every exam she'd ever sat, she reckoned she was an expert, if only of the armchair variety, on PMA. It seemed that the world supply of synthetic drugs, aka Ecstasy and the like, used to come from – *where else* – the Netherlands, but in the last ten years, under pressure from the Yanks, Dutch police had clamped down, closing dozens of drug factories. Of course, that did nothing to reduce the demand for E; it just meant the drug gangs packed up their chemistry sets, and re-opened in countries where the authorities had fewer resources: Estonia, Lithuania – and Poland, which with the longest border in Europe was a smuggler's wet dream.

But the villains had another problem: European governments had enacted tough new controls on the starter chemicals needed to make the E – and that was where PMA came in. Although its effects were similar to E, its basic constituent was a harmless compound called anethole – cheap, widely used in the perfume and food industries, and impossible to regulate.

She shifted position, the newspaper rustling beneath her, trying to ease the creeping numbness in her bum. The equation for the drug gangs was brutally simple: why buy expensive illegal chemicals on the black market to make E, when you could use dirt-cheap anethole and pass off tabs of PMA as the real thing? And if people took too many tabs because it took longer to come on than E – well, that was their problem. It was just like the fake handbag business, Kershaw reflected, except a Gucci bag from Korea didn't leave your organs cooked medium rare.

She lit another cigarette – the third of the five a day she allowed herself – and re-ran what she knew about Justyna Kozlowska's death. The man in the hat caught on CCTV was clearly the prime suspect, but she still felt sure Janusz Kiszka was involved – why else would Justyna hide his card in her mouth? Maybe he was part of a drugs ring, manufacturing PMA and smuggling into the UK? But why had Justyna, and maybe Ela, too, been killed?

An idea pinged into her head. Could the girls have been caught in the middle of some drug gang stand-off? She recalled Kiszka balling his fists at the mention of Pawel, the mystery man whose name was tattooed on

Ela's buttock. If there was a vendetta raging between the two men, then maybe, just maybe, the man in the hat was the mysterious Pawel, and he had lured Kiszka's girlfriend to the hotel to murder her.

A gust of wind rattled the pages of the report, making Kershaw shiver. Something occurred to her. Maybe it wasn't Justyna but her *killer* who put Kiszka's card in her mouth – to incriminate his enemy, or to taunt him.

After leaving Kasia's club, Janusz went straight to an internet café that he sometimes used in St Anne's Court, a tiny Georgian passageway off Wardour Street. Kris, the Bulgarian who ran the place, took one look at his face and disappeared out the back. He returned a few minutes later with a lemon tea, setting it down beside Janusz's workstation with a graceful nod that said it was on the house.

Janusz was surprised to find that Nowak rated a Wikipedia mention on a page dedicated to Polish industrialists; there was even a shot of him, taken maybe ten years earlier, balding and energetic-looking in shirt sleeves, before he'd shaved off his remaining hair. The biog said he was born in 1945, the same year his father had been taken away to a Soviet prison camp along with the hundreds of thousands of Poles designated enemies of Socialism in Stalin's post-war purge. His father's crime: he had fought alongside Britain and American forces during the invasion of France. Five years later, he had died, supposedly of TB.

The write-up noted Nowak's sixteen years as a *Solidarnosc* official in the Vladimir Lenin Steel Works in Nowa Huta, and mentioned his second career in the construction business, setting up *Nowak Budowa*, two years after the *Kommie* regime fell in 1989. He hadn't done badly out of it, selling up for two million zloty, just under half a million sterling, in 2003.

But it was Nowak's later activities that earned him the Wikipedia entry. The guy's 'bit of charity work' was clearly a full-time job – he was the founder or patron of half a dozen charities, mostly connected with social housing and urban regeneration. There was a Nowak quote from *Gazeta Wyborcza*, March 2007: 'The older generation can exhort the young to come back to Poland and help the country's revival, but these are empty words unless we guarantee them well paid jobs and decent places to live.'

Edward Zamorski – naturally enough – got a more detailed biog and a gallery of photographs spanning his thirty years in politics. Here was a black and white shot from the eighties that captured the young Zamorski, moustachioed and wearing a workman's jacket, in the front line of some demo or other, right arm raised to fend off a wedge of helmeted ZOMO. Beside him a young, stocky priest, semi-crouched beneath the blur of a white rubber truncheon on a trajectory aimed at his head.

Janusz instantly recognised the priest Zamorski had been trying to protect: *Marek Kuba.*

Although Kuba had been just twenty-six at the height of the uprising, not much older than Janusz, he'd been a fearless critic of Communist repression from the pulpit of the Church of the Holy Ark in Gdansk, his courage making him a much-loved figure in the campaign for democracy. Until May 1986, that is, when those *skurw-ysyny* from the SB, the secret police, decided to make an example of this turbulent priest. They kidnapped the young Kuba, tortured him, murdered him, and dumped his broken body in one of the rivers that criss-crossed the Kashubian Lakeland. And yet, as Janusz recalled, instead of intimidating the people, Kuba's murder caused a nationwide upsurge of defiance that was the beginning of the end for the regime.

The final image of Zamorski, the one Janusz had seen on presidential election posters, showed a portly man in his late fifties, wearing a sober suit, with kindly but serious light blue eyes – a million miles away from the soulful-looking young activist who'd apparently been such a ladies' man. This older Zamorski looked like a bank manager whose darkest secret was a weakness for plums in chocolate.

Peering more closely at the screen, Janusz could just make out an indentation on his left cheekbone – memento of a severe beating by the SB after the *milicja* broke up a rally he had led in Warsaw. Janusz had only been about fourteen, but he could still remember his burning sense of outrage on seeing the grainy photo of Zamorski's battered, barely recognisable face in the *samizdat* that had travelled furtively from hand to hand beneath the school desks.

After logging off, Janusz dialled Oskar's number on his mobile.

'*Czesc, kolego,*' he said. 'How do you fancy a little trip home?'

Fifteen

A little after 7 a.m. on Friday, two days after Justyna's body was discovered, Oskar's battered Transit van hurtled off the Stratford roundabout and entered the stream of traffic heading north on the A12 without any recourse to the brakes.

'When you said you'd take me to Poland you didn't mention anything about *him*,' grumbled Janusz, jerking his thumb to the van's rear.

'What's the big problem, Janek? What have you got against my friend Olek?' said Oskar pulling an innocent face. 'Is it because he is such a chatterbox?'

Olek didn't join in the exchange, which was hardly surprising, since he had been dead for six days.

When Oskar had picked Janusz up from his flat and he'd gone to throw his bag in the back of the van, he'd found half the floor space taken up by a white metal box, roughly strapped down with bungee cords. He soon learned that it was a double-skinned, lead-lined coffin holding the body of some guy Oskar was delivering home to Poland.

Janusz sighed. 'What did the poor bastard die of, anyway?' he asked.

'An I-beam fell on him, over at one of those apartment block sites. They had to use a shovel to scrape him off the concrete.' Oskar shook his head mournfully. 'The site was a fucking shambles, a real death-trap. I never met him, but apparently he's got three kids. The day after it happened, we had a whip round for the widow.'

Both men crossed themselves and fell silent.

'I still don't understand how come you're an undertaker now,' said Janusz, finally.

'Business, Janek! What else?' Oskar rubbed finger and thumb together. 'The contractor Olek worked for heard I was taking a trip home, and offered me *two thousand euros* to repatriate the body!' He drummed a jaunty tattoo on the steering wheel. 'It's the least they could do after they killed the guy.'

'That's all *fantastycznie*, Oskar, but did you forget what I told you? The whole point of going by sea was to keep a low profile, in case that girl *detektyw* has put my name on some airport blacklist.' Janusz could feel his voice rising with exasperation. 'So maybe you can explain to me how smuggling a stiff on board a car ferry counts as low fucking profile!'

'Relax, Janek, you'll grow an ulcer!' said Oskar. 'I told you, everything's above board. The guy at the contractors arranged it all with the undertaker, gave me all the official paperwork.' He reached a hand across to the glove box in front of Janusz and fumbled through a small drift of sweet papers and parking tickets, swerving

200

into another lane in the process and drawing a barrage of car horns.

Cursing, Janusz bent to pick up the sheaf of papers that fell out, and leafed through them. At least his mate seemed to have all the right documents – death certificate, forms from the coroner and so on. In any event, he could hardly complain. Oskar had agreed without hesitation to change his planned booze-buying trip to Calais in order to drive Janusz to Poland. It was an epic trip, too – eighteen hours on a ferry to Denmark and then a straight twelve-hour drive hugging the Baltic coast across Germany. If Oskar were grabbing an opportunity to turn a profit from the trip – who could blame him?

'So I *export* Olek, and *import* booze – cooking two roasts on one fire,' Oskar was explaining. 'I've got to deliver our friend to a funeral home in . . .' he squinted at an address written in felt tip on the palm of his hand, '. . . Elblag before they close tomorrow evening. But it's only twenty *kilometrow* outside Gdansk, so we can spend the day in town. You can take me on a trip around your boyhood haunts and we'll have a few beers in the harbour.'

Janusz didn't have the heart to pour cold water on Oskar's plans, but Gdansk, with all its painful memories, was the last place on earth he wanted to play tour guide. He had only been back once since Iza died, to attend his mother's funeral – what, sixteen, seventeen years ago – and even then, he'd managed to avoid the centre of Gdansk, taking cabs between the airport and Lostowicki cemetery, which, lucky for him, stood on the outskirts of town.

'So where did you say you were heading, after I leave you in Gdansk?' asked Oskar with a sidelong glance.

'I didn't,' growled Janusz. Oskar's grasp of abstract

concepts like confidentiality was tenuous at best, so he had decided to reveal as little as possible about his trip. The single, fragile lead he had on Adamski was the storage depot in Gorodnik. A bit of digging around might turn up someone who knew him, or some other lead.

'Are you sure you don't want me to come with you?' asked Oskar, for about the third time. 'I could go round the bars, make a few discreet enquiries, while you play *Sherlock Holm-es*,' he said, giving the English name an extra syllable. 'You could have got in a lot of trouble at that cottage, you know, if I hadn't been there to watch your back.'

Janusz turned to give him a look.

But Oskar just whistled admiringly. '*Kurwa mac*. That's the worst bruise I've ever seen, and I've seen some pretty bad shit on the site. So, you reckon it was this guy you're after who whacked you?'

'Well, it wasn't the Man from Milk Tray,' said Janusz, already regretting telling Oskar about his night-time visitor.

'You were lucky, *kolego*,' said Oskar. 'At least he didn't kill you when you told him to fuck off.' Janusz frowned – he was still puzzling over that himself. 'You know the best thing about this trip?' Oskar went on. 'It's only three hours from Elblag to home, so I get a whole eight hours with Gosia. She's roasting goose with sour cherries, and' – he turned to give his mate a big wink – 'I'm getting something special for afters.' Janusz felt a rush of affection, mixed with a little envy, at the smile of lustful happiness on Oskar's face.

Remembering what Ray had told him about Kasia's plans, he lit a cigar, and asked, 'What do women do in a *nail bar*?' using the English phrase.

Oskar hooted with delight. 'Where were you living the last ten years – in a cave with the *Talibowie*? I never did understand how you pulled such a good-looking girlfriend when you know fuck-all about women.' Shaking his head, he folded two sticks of gum into his mouth.

'Okay, lady boy,' said Janusz. 'Since you're so in touch with your feminine side, why don't you enlighten me?'

'It's . . . a place where women go to have things done to their nails, of course,' said Oskar.

'What things?'

'You know . . . having them filed, painted different colours, stuff like that,' said Oskar, waving a hand.

'It's possible to make a business out of *that*?' asked Janusz.

'Sure,' said Oskar. 'You know, Janek, there's no limit to the shit women can waste a man's money on,' he grinned up at the rear-view mirror. 'Isn't that right, Olek?'

Suddenly, a jarring noise filled the van – *ding di ding ding* – a high-pitched voice imitating a motorbike engine. Janusz massaged his sore head: Oskar had been among the first to put the Crazy Frog ring tone on his mobile and he'd probably only replace it if something even more irritating came along, which seemed pretty unlikely.

'*Czesc* . . .' said Oskar. 'No. We're not even at Dover yet. Should be at Elblag by tomorrow evening, about six, like I already said. Yes, okay.' Hanging up, Oskar sighed, 'The guy from Olek's firm who gave me the job. He's a right old woman.'

A little over an hour later, as Janusz and Oskar were pulling into the customs lane at the Harwich ferry

203

terminal on the Essex Coast, Kershaw was easing her Ford Ka into a parking space in Lambeth, just south of the river. She locked the car and looked around: that minging pile of seventies concrete must be it, she thought. Sure enough, as she got closer she could make out the name of the building's sheer grey side spelled out in large steel letters: *Cavendish College*.

Kershaw thought the excursion was a load of old bollocks, frankly. It was hardly likely that her drug OD-ed floater had been a student at a Catholic theology college, for crying out loud – but Streaky had insisted she follow it up, gave her the old 'leave no lead unturned' routine, so she'd sat in traffic all the way through the City and over to the wrong side of the river. Still, she'd cut easily half an hour off the journey by taking the little-known route over Southwark Bridge which her Dad had shown her when she was learning to drive – a secret passed on by successive generations of Kershaws he used to say to her, only half-joking.

She had arranged to meet Timothy Lethbridge in the student refectory, and as the drinks machine dribbled straw-coloured tea into her plastic cup, she scanned the tables for the likeliest candidate. None of them looked like any students she'd ever seen: instead of the usual arse-skimming skirts, tatts and piercings, there was a high incidence of cable knit pullovers, an epidemic of facial hair, and she even spotted one guy wearing Birkenstock sandals *with socks*. The atmosphere was relaxed though, everyone having nice smiley chats rather than the screeching interchanges she remembered from her uni's refectory.

As she looked around for the sugar, she spotted a

blond-haired guy hovering nearby. He was in his twenties, wearing jeans and a pale blue Ben Sherman shirt, and carried a satchel-type bag. He met her gaze. 'I'm guessing you're probably DC Kershaw?' he asked – a faint accent, some kind of Northern. Introducing himself as Timothy Lethbridge, he offered his hand. For a beat she just stared at it, such old-school niceties not being part of an East End cop's daily routine. His handshake was as limp as a damp tea towel.

After finding an empty table, she pulled out her notebook and cut to the chase, keen to get this over with and back to the nick.

'So you contacted the Missing Persons Bureau yesterday?' He nodded.

'And this was how long after Ela . . . *Wronska* went missing?' She looked at him for confirmation of the name.

'It's pronounced *Vronska*,' he said, smiling to lay off the correction. 'She was known as Elzbieta, here, although I think it can be abbreviated to Ela.' He had a bashful smile, which, together with his pale, heart-shaped face and longish fair hair, gave him an androgynous air.

Pulling an iPhone out of his pocket, he tapped the keypad. 'The last time I saw Elzbieta was here in refectory, on March the thirteenth.' He showed her his calendar. 'I know because I remember telling her about a brilliant lecture by a visiting professor I'd just been to.'

He turned the phone over and over in his hands, anxiety ridging the pale skin around his eyes. 'After that I didn't see her around for a while, and nobody seemed to know where she was, so that's when I phoned the Missing Persons Bureau.'

Kershaw scribbled down the dates.

'Sorry, Timothy, my Sergeant took the message so I don't know all the details, but what exactly was it Elzbieta was studying?'

'She was reading for a PhD on the relationship between Church and State in Medieval Europe.'

'The Catholic Church?'

'There wasn't really any other kind, at the time,' he said gently.

She flushed at her slip – *great*, now he'd have her down as a dumb-arse cop.

'How would you describe her social life?'

He pulled at his lip. 'Well, she didn't drink and she was quite shy. She'd occasionally came along to a meal at a restaurant – you know, end of term celebrations, that kind of thing, and after lectures she and I would sometimes have coffee together. But she spent most of the time in her room, reading, or writing in her journal.'

'Did Elzbieta have any boyfriends, as far as you knew?'

He stared at the tabletop and shrugged. 'I've been here a year and I never heard her mention anyone.'

Kershaw could tell the subject made him uncomfortable, but then, he was a theology student.

'She didn't ever mention the name Pawel, or someone called Janusz Kiszka?' tried Kershaw.

He shook his head.

She took a despairing swig of her cold tea, wishing it was gin. This was *such* a dead end. Elzbieta Wronska: teetotal wallflower studying medieval sodding theology was on a different *planet* from Ela the druggy floater with a lover's name tattooed on her arse. She was starting to suspect that it was all an elaborate wind-up on Streaky's part.

Stifling a sigh, she retrieved the photoshopped image of Ela from her bag and pushed it across the table to Timothy. He sat motionless for several seconds, studying it intently, and when he looked back up at her, she was startled to see that his lips were trembling.

'This is a picture of a . . . *dead person*, isn't it?' he asked in a whisper.

Fuck. Of course, Missing Persons wouldn't have told him they had an unidentified floater – they would have left that for the cops to handle face to face, *with all due sensitivity*.

'Um. Yes, Timothy, I'm afraid it is,' she said. 'We found this lady in the river a few days ago.'

To her horror, she saw tears gathering in his eyes. He reached out and touched the photo.

'This is Elzbieta.'

Double fuck. 'Are you absolutely sure?' asked Kershaw, trying to keep the incredulity from her voice. Nodding, he wiped his eyes, and drew a shuddering breath.

'She looks different here . . .' he said, indicating the picture, 'Older. More . . . *serious* than in real life. She was always smiling, you see . . .'

He broke off, shading his eyes with one hand.

Jesus Christ, thought Kershaw.

She reached out and rested an awkward hand on his arm. 'There, there,' she said. *There, there?*

'Listen, Timothy, I'm *so* sorry. I've made a total arse of myself,' she said, dropping the police-speak. 'I should have realised you weren't expecting to see Ela – Elzbieta – this way – it must be a terrible shock.'

He nodded rapidly, trying to compose himself.

Kershaw stared at Ela's picture, mortification at her

screw-up giving way to a surge of excitement: she had identified DB16 – the girl with the Titian hair! She didn't have the faintest idea how Elzbieta Wronska had ended up in the Thames with her veins full of counterfeit Ecstasy, but maybe the discovery that she wasn't another dead sex worker would boot the case up the priority ladder. Officially, it made no difference, but in her view the shockingly low clear-up rate for murders of working girls spoke volumes.

She went to the machine to get Timothy another cuppa and by the time she returned he seemed calmer.

'Listen, Timothy,' she said as she sat down again. 'I hate to ask this, but do you know if Elzbieta ever took drugs – the softer stuff, like Ecstasy?'

'What? Are you saying she died of an overdose?' he asked, his eyes wide.

'Yes, I'm afraid so.'

He stared into his plastic cup. 'Elzbieta is the *last* person I could imagine taking drugs,' he said. 'She used to say that more than one glass of wine gave her hiccups.' The ghost of a smile played at the corners of his mouth.

Timothy said that Elzbieta had turned thirty a few months earlier – an occasion marked by a rare night out with a couple of other students at a nearby curry house. She had lived in England since she was about eleven or twelve, brought up by an aunt who adopted her after both her parents died in a car accident.

'This aunt would be the next of kin, then?' asked Kershaw.

'No, I'm afraid she died a few months ago. Elzbieta went straight home, somewhere in Kent, and didn't come back till after the funeral. She was devastated actually.' He shook his head, eyes lost in the memory.

'You seem a bit surprised by her reaction,' said Kershaw.

'I suppose I'd never seen her like that before. She was usually so happy, and so . . .' – he looked around, hunting for the word – 'sorted. She told me once that after her parents died she had a terrible time, but, in the end, it made her a survivor.' He nursed his tea, gazing at the tabletop.

Kershaw nibbled discreetly at the remains of the nail on her little finger. From the way Timothy talked about Elzbieta, and his reaction to her picture, she sensed they'd been more than just friends.

She leaned towards him. 'You were really fond of Elzbieta, weren't you?' He nodded. 'Did you two have . . . a romantic thing going on?' She couldn't bring herself to use more matter-of-fact terminology.

'No, we were just good friends.' But he cut his eyes away from her.

'Are you sure?' she pressed. 'You never wanted more than friendship?'

'Alright!' The word burst out, his face reddening. 'I did ask her out, once or twice, but she . . . she turned me down.'

With his pink cheeks and shock of blond hair, he looked like an angry choirboy.

'She said she didn't do the boyfriend thing,' he said, trying – without success – to iron the resentment out of his voice.

She sipped her tea, studying Timothy Lethbridge over the lip of the cup. He wasn't unattractive, exactly, but there was a fatal girliness about him that, to women, would always say 'friend' more than 'lover'. Elzbieta had obviously been letting him down gently. All that 'reading in her room' could simply have been cover for her secret affair with the mysterious Pawel, his name etched on her buttock where no-one could see it.

Kershaw knocked back the dregs of her tea and stowed the notebook in her bag. 'I'm going to have to talk to the principal, Timothy,' she said. 'I assume he knows Elzbieta's gone missing?'

He fell silent, fiddling with his watchstrap. 'I haven't mentioned it to any of the college staff yet,' he said finally.

'Can I ask why not?' she asked, keeping her eyes on his face.

He shrugged. 'Well, she's a PhD student – she can come and go as she pleases. I didn't want to cause a fuss when she might simply have gone off to Poland on a research trip or something.'

Kershaw did a quick calculation. Your best friend goes AWOL for nearly two weeks and you don't say a dicky-bird to any of the lecturers? That was weird. Maybe he was still embarrassed by his unrequited pash for Elzbieta and didn't want to face awkward questions.

'Right. Well, I need to see this Monsignor Zielinski straight away,' she said, pushing back her chair. 'Can you show me where his office is?'

The middle-aged female guarding the portal to the principal's office was dismissive: the Monsignor was tied up in a staff meeting and would then be going straight on to an appointment with the Bishop. From the secretary's lofty manner and disdainful gaze, Kershaw was left in no doubt that, in her world, a Monsignor easily out-trumped a pushy police girl with a Cockney accent.

'Perhaps you'd like to leave a card, officer,' breezed the battle-axe, like the matter was closed. 'And I will ask the Principal when he is able to grant you an appointment?'.

Bring it on, thought Kershaw. 'It's a real shame he can't spare me the time now,' she said, moving to stand beside the secretary's desk, invading her personal space and eyeballing her paperwork. 'I was hoping to let him know, just as a matter of courtesy, really, that I'm about to cordon off the halls of residence and bring in a CSI team to start a search of the student accommodation.'

The secretary gave a gasp of outrage.

Just at that moment, six or seven men started spilling out of the principal's office, some in the penguin outfits advertising their hotline to God, some in ordinary suits. Talking in loud, self-important tones, they passed the two women without a glance. The secretary grabbed her chance, leapt up and bolted through the open door, closing it behind her.

Thirty seconds later, Kershaw had penetrated the inner sanctum. But instead of the grizzled old cleric she'd expected to find there, the man who emerged from behind his desk to greet her was fresh-faced, in his late thirties. As they shook hands – *blimey, twice in a day*, thought Kershaw – she took in Monsignor Zielinski's get-up: a dog collar under a closely fitting long black gown with fuchsia buttons that showed off his tall slim figure. As the door closed, he ushered Kershaw over to a seating area by the window that held a boxy orange sofa, a black leather chair and a coffee table shaped like a kidney bean – the kind of understated retro-chic that cost a small fortune.

'Mrs Beauregard said something about a death?' asked

Monsignor Zielinski, his voice becoming serious. His English was perfect – second generation Polish, Kershaw decided.

Leaning forward, she placed the post-mortem image of Elzbieta on the coffee table between them. He put on some trendy wire-rimmed glasses and, drawing the picture closer, studied it, blinking once, twice.

'Do you recognise her, sir?' she prompted. He knew the girl, she was sure of it, but he seemed reluctant to say so.

'Well, I can't be certain, officer, but yes, this lady does look like one of our students. I'm sorry, but I just can't recall her name.' He made a self-deprecating face: 'Old age, I'm afraid.' He removed his specs, sadness defocusing his eyes.

'One of your students, Timothy Lethbridge, has identified her as Elzbieta Wronska,' said Kershaw. 'I'm afraid it appears that Ms Wronska died following a drug overdose: her body was recovered from the Thames five days ago.'

'That's dreadful news,' he said, slumping back in his chair. 'Yes, of course, Elzbieta was one of our PhD students. She was blessed with a rather brilliant mind.'

The Monsignor stared out of the window into the tree-lined courtyard one storey below. Students sat reading, or chatting with friends on the sunlit benches between silver birch trees, their branches dusted with the pale green of still-furled leaves. 'The great adventure of life before her, snuffed out like that,' he said, as though to himself.

Kershaw's gaze fell on a solitary red-haired girl sitting directly beneath the window, eating an apple. The sight pitched her back to the riverside at Wapping and Ela's white hand lying upturned on the stainless steel.

'I'm going to need all the information you have about Elzbieta to help us pursue our enquiries.'

He got to his feet. 'I can certainly help you there. We keep administrative files on all the students, although, of course, I've never had to consult them in such terrible circumstances.' On the other side of the room stood three filing cabinets: crossing to the furthest of them, he opened the bottom drawer and returned with a slim blue loose-leaf file.

Inside was a photograph of a girl paper-clipped to a sheaf of papers. Kershaw scanned the image. There was no doubt that Elzbieta Wronska was the girl in Wapping mortuary. The snap showed her standing with one foot resting on a stile in a country lane – an unmistakably English scene – the tawny hedgerow echoing the backlit spun copper of her hair. Elzbieta hadn't been conventionally beautiful, but she had a trusting smile and a country-girl freshness that suggested pails of creamy milk and sunny meadows.

'Isn't her hair a pretty colour?' said Kershaw.

The Monsignor flushed at the observation. *Oops*, she thought, maybe that wasn't the sort of thing you said to a Catholic priest, but he just said, 'Yes, I suppose it is', and smoothed the black robe over his knees. The shoes poking out beneath his robe were beautifully stitched and shiny as a conker, she noticed, and his socks were the same shade of dark pink as his buttons. *A nice bit of schmutter*, she heard her dad saying with a wink. Kershaw suddenly wondered if the Monsignor might be gay.

Leafing through the file, she came across a foreign newspaper article carrying a black and white photograph of what she took to be the college orchestra. Elzbieta sat to the left of frame, upright and serious-looking, a violin tucked under her chin; her bow hand a blur of motion and her gaze bent on the conductor, whose back was to the camera. And there, almost opposite her, sat Timothy Lethbridge, a cello between his legs and bow hanging limply from his hand, awaiting his cue. At the moment the shutter had clicked he'd been looking straight at Ela and the snap had captured his expression: *lovesick puppy*. Looking on, from beyond the orchestra's back row, was the Monsignor himself.

The file held half a dozen other cuttings, too – Kershaw didn't recognise the language but she could take a guess.

'So Elzbieta went to Poland with the College Orchestra?' she asked, showing him the article.

He peered at it: 'Yes, Elzbieta was an accomplished violinist – could have gone professional had she chosen that path,' he said. 'We toured central Europe last year, and the Polish concerts were a particular success: we made several thousand pounds for church charities. As you probably know, the Poles are a very musical people – as well as being very devout, of course.'

'I see Timothy Lethbridge was on the tour, too?' she enquired.

'Yes, yes indeed,' he said. 'Not in the same league as Elzbieta, but a very decent cellist, nonetheless.'

Kershaw closed the file, and before she could ask, he said, 'Please feel free to take that away with you.'

'Thanks. I understand Ms Wronska's adoptive mother has passed away, so I'm hoping to find something in here to give us a next of kin.'

'You will keep us informed?' he asked, his eyes

anxious. 'We'd consider it an honour to hold the funeral service – if Elzbieta's family agrees, of course.'

Kershaw nodded and stood up to go.

'I'd like to take a quick look at Elzbieta's room, before I go. But I'll be in touch later, once I know whether we want to send a CSI to check it out.' He looked mystified. 'Forensics people,' she clarified.

The Monsignor sketched a map of the campus on a piece of paper to show the way to the halls of residence and wrote down the access code. As they walked to the door, he said, 'I'll telephone the janitor and ask him to meet you there so he can let you into the room.'

On the way to the halls, Kershaw went over her encounter with the Monsignor. Why had he appeared shifty, at first, about knowing Ela? Was it the prospect of bad publicity? A student dying of a drugs overdose OD was hardly an ideal calling card for a theology college.

She certainly needed the map – the route wound confusingly through a sprawling private housing estate, and soon she had completely lost her bearings. Ten or fifteen minutes later, she emerged from a walkway into a low-rise development made of the same rain-stained concrete as the main college building, and immediately spotted a sign for 'Francis House', Elzbieta's block.

Room 209 was on the second floor, easily identified by the elderly caretaker who waited outside, jangling his keys. He opened up and acknowledged her thanks with a wordless nod, before making himself scarce. That was a relief. She was desperate to discover the real Elzbieta, the girl behind the theology PhD, and she couldn't do that with some caretaker lurking in the background.

When her eyes had adjusted to the darkness, she made

out floor-length curtains covering the windows through the gloom. Then, pulling on the latex gloves she always carried in her bag, she groped for the light switch, feeling a frisson of anticipation. For a moment, nothing, before the dim glow of a low-energy bulb sprang to life.

The greenish light revealed the pale wood utility furniture she recalled from her own college halls – a desk by the window, though oddly, no computer, a chest of drawers, and a four-foot bed, large enough for a quickie, if not ideal for overnight stays. *Well, you wouldn't want to encourage any mortal sins*, she thought.

The room was tidy, the bed linen freshly laundered, and the only smell was the synthetic sweetness of furniture polish. The only clue that anyone had ever lived here was a handful of personal knick-knacks lined up on the chest of drawers – a white plastic 'Make Poverty History' bracelet, a framed photo of a middle-aged woman with salt and pepper hair, presumably the dead aunt, and a gingerbread heart with Polish writing on it, no doubt bought on the orchestra tour. A scoot through the drawers revealed nothing interesting – hippyish clothes in muted colours, which gave off a faint smell of lily of the valley – a bit of an old lady fragrance, thought Kershaw, for a girl of thirty. A trawl of her bedside cabinet produced only a Bible, a rosary and a well-thumbed Mills and Boon novel.

Kershaw sat on the bed. The only sound was the intermittent buzz of a fly hurling itself against the window. Either she was being paranoid or the room was impersonal to the point of creepiness. No sign of the journal Timothy had mentioned, no contraceptives, none of the *clutter* of modern life – let alone any illegal drugs.

Who are you, Elzbieta?

Her gaze wandered to the wall facing the foot of the bed and she jumped, hand flying to her mouth. Lit by the sullen glow of the low-energy bulb was a lurid medieval picture of Jesus, parting his robes with a coy gesture to reveal a heart, bleeding and entwined with thorns. She pushed away a sudden, vivid memory of Elzbieta's post mortem, her chest cracked open like an animal carcass.

Until now, she'd always imagined her floater dying in a hotel, like Justyna. But now the total absence of any personal effects in her room was making the hair stand up on her arms. Someone had cleared this place to remove anything incriminating, she could feel it in her bones. And the river couldn't be more than a five-minute drive away – if that.

Three strides took her to the curtained window. A pull cord opened the heavy curtains with a deep swoosh and light surged into the room. For a split second the in-rush of daylight whited everything out. Kershaw blinked four or five times – and not just because of the glare. Elzbieta Wronska's room wasn't a short drive from the Thames: it was as close to the river as you could get without actually having to do backstroke.

Feeling a cold excitement, and with her heartbeat going *boo-boof boo-boof* in her ears, she opened the balcony door, taking care not to smudge any prints, and stepped out onto the tiny overhang. As a lone gull keened overhead, Kershaw hefted an imaginary body from her shoulder onto the rail, then pitched it into the dark water ten metres below.

Sixteen

The waters of the North Sea roiled and foamed along the ferry's side, the light from a platinum moon tumbling on the choppy black swell. Janusz flicked his spent cigar into the waves and buttoned his trench coat against the wind. Where the fuck was Oskar? He'd gone to the bar over half an hour ago to buy a Coke, just so they'd have some plastic glasses for the beers awaiting them back in the van. He wondered if he'd got into any bother. Earlier, they'd noticed knots of hard-eyed Englishmen on board, presumably on their way to the Brondby vs Liverpool game in Copenhagen. They looked like they'd be in the market for a ruck at some point, but surely not before they'd put away another seven or eight pints.

Just then, the door from the bar to the deck area opened, releasing a blast of raucous noise from the bar, and Oskar's barrel-shaped outline appeared in the lit doorway. He held the door open with one foot and then, moving carefully so as not to drop the armfuls of stuff he was carrying, he made his way, chinking, over to where Janusz stood at the rail. He had a Liverpool scarf wound round his throat and he was humming a song, though it wasn't till he got closer, that Janusz recognised it as 'You'll Never Walk Alone'.

'Oskar, what the hell have you been up to?' said Janusz as he rescued a bottle of premium vodka from under his mate's right arm and a giant Toblerone wedged beneath his chin. 'I thought you were just getting some glasses?'

Oskar raised an eyebrow and tried to look mysterious: 'Maybe you aren't the only smartass around here.' As Janusz gave a dismissive snort, he reached into the pocket of his jacket and drew out a wad of notes with a flourish.

'*Five hundred quid* jackpot!' he crowed, waving the notes under his mate's nose and doing a little jig of triumph. 'You should have seen it, Janek! I had three bars and then I got a lucky nudge. There were so many tokens the barman had to get the purser down to change it all into cash!'

Janusz picked up one end of the red and white scarf. 'And this? I thought you supported West Ham.'

Oskar gave a sheepish shrug. 'One of the Scousers gave it to me, after I bought the lads a round.'

'Yeah? I bet that put a hole in your winnings,' growled Janusz.

'Ah what the fuck, it was free money!' Oskar hopped from foot to foot. 'Anyway this wind is blowing my balls off. Let's go and celebrate.'

An hour later, the mates were sitting cross-legged in the back of the van on folded bubble wrap, drinking from plastic cups: Oskar on the premium vodka and Janusz on bottled Budwar. Opening a Tupperware box, Janusz started laying out the snacks that he'd prepared the night before on top of Olek's coffin. He and Oskar had debated whether using it as their dinner table would be disrespectful, but they soon agreed that Olek wouldn't mind – it was all good Polish food after all.

'Anyway, the Egyptians used to put food and drink inside the tombs of their kings,' said Oskar, adopting a knowledgeable air. 'To give them something to eat and drink when they got to heaven. I saw a programme about it on Discovery Channel.'

Janusz arranged slices of *wiejska* and gherkins on a slice of buttered light rye, then paused to watch Oskar take his first bite of the homemade minced veal *kotlety* stuffed with goats' cheese and herbs. Janusz had found it hard to sleep at the flat after what had happened the previous night, so he'd stayed up cooking with all the lights blazing, before falling asleep on the sofa just before dawn.

'This is good shit,' mumbled Oskar, although Janusz noticed that before finishing his mouthful of *kotlety*, he absent-mindedly threw in a triangle of Toblerone.

After they'd finished the food and swept the debris off the top of Olek's coffin, the serious drinking started.

'Do you ever wonder what the fuck we're doing with our lives?' asked Oskar suddenly.

'What do you mean?'

'You know, working away from home, living among strangers, maybe even *dying* among strangers,' he said and nodding to the coffin, crossed himself. 'All that shit.' He stretched out for the vodka bottle, bringing a chorus of pops from the bubble wrap beneath him. 'When we were kids doing military service I thought if I could get a flat, get married, and find a job paying enough to live on, I'd be happy. At least under the Kommies everyone had jobs. What would we earn back home now? Peanuts.'

'Bullshit,' said Janusz. 'I'm sick of all this *"The Kommies looked after people, gave everyone a job"*. Most of the jobs back then didn't pay shit either – unless you were one of those Party bastards pulling in the backhanders.' He pulled on his cigar. 'You should know – you were always the one dreaming up crazy money-making ideas.'

Oskar sighed in agreement, then grinned: 'Remember that time we smuggled the Levis from Yugoslavia to Moscow?'

'Yeah, I remember,' said Janusz, with a rueful grin. 'I can't believe I let you talk me into it. We were lucky not to end up in some fucking gulag living on cabbage soup and watching frostbite turn our dicks black.'

They'd been fresh out of the military, sharing a room in a grotty Warsaw hostel. Even then, Oskar had been quick to spot ways to make cash. Communism had killed all normal commerce: the only stuff in the shops was the crap from 'fraternal countries' that nobody wanted. But since Poles could travel more or less freely there was a thriving trade in smuggled goods. Janusz had taken a lot of persuading, but Oskar finally wore him down: after all, apart from the promise of riches, getting one over on the *Kommies* was practically a national duty.

'And you made me swear on a fucking Bible that if you went with me, I had to find you a copy of that song you were crazy about.' Oskar's brow furrowed. 'You know, the one by that poofter with the high voice.'

'Bohemian Rhapsody'. From the thrilling moment when Janusz had first heard it played on a mate's transistor radio on Radio Luxembourg when he'd been what

– fifteen, sixteen? – getting his hands on a copy had become an obsession.

'I don't remember,' he said.

'You remember taking the night train to Belgrade, though,' said Oskar, waggling his eyebrows mockingly.

The pair had travelled with every *zloty* they and their mates could scrape together, and the address of a back-street dealer scribbled on a scrap of paper.

Oskar knocked back another shot of vodka and his face split into a grin. 'Every time you heard the *milicja* coming down the corridor to check passports you'd go "Look casual! Look casual!"' said Oskar, mimicking a squeaky voice. 'And you kept threatening to swallow the piece of paper . . .' – he started to crack up – 'to . . . to . . . stop it falling into enemy hands!' He bellowed with laughter, slapping his thigh, tears brimming in his eyes.

All Janusz could remember was the cold fear of what it would do to his mother if he was caught: something that hadn't occurred to him till the moment he'd met the steady stare of the official checking his passport. Thankfully, they got away with it, selling two dozen pairs of Levis to eager punters in Moscow for three times what they'd paid the dealer. Oskar had duly produced a shiny copy of 'Bohemian Rhapsody', bought from the *Pewex* dollar shop – but Janusz vowed never to put himself at risk again. Then, within three months, he had won a place to do physics at Jagiellonski, got involved in the protests, and all such resolutions flew out of the window.

'Anyway, *kolego*,' said Oskar, clearing his throat. 'I was thinking, when you've finished playing detective, why don't you go down to Warsaw, spend a few hours with Bobek?'

Janusz picked at the label of his beer bottle. The idea had occurred to him, too. In his imagination, he'd even got as far as the yellow door of the apartment, but the thought of Marta opening it, and her disapproving expression at the sight of his bruised face had been enough to dissuade him. No matter what he said, she'd be convinced he was back on the booze and had got himself into a fight.

'I'm here to work, not to play happy families,' said Janusz. His tone was level but Oskar detected a warning note.

He hesitated, then decided to have one last go. 'It's only a couple of hours on the train from Gdansk.'

'Don't start nagging me, Oskar, you're not my fucking wife,' Janusz growled.

Oskar decided not to press the issue. Janusz could be touchy on the subject of his family, which, according to Gosia, was because he felt guilty about being an absent father. Women's heads were nine-tenths full of garbage, of course, but any reasonable man had to admit they were usually right about shit like that.

An hour or so later, after a string of formal toasts to Olek, the pair were bedded down for the night under a couple of rugs, and Janusz was drawing a sigh of relief at the sound of snoring from his mate. Just before they turned in, he'd had to spend several minutes talking Oskar out of his plan for a final valedictory gesture: prising open Olek's coffin to give him a packet of crisps for the afterlife.

Seventeen

'What do you mean, he's gone to Poland?'

As soon as the words were out of her mouth Kershaw realised it was a silly question: the nerdy guy in the retro glasses could hardly have been clearer. His neighbour, Janusz Kiszka, had left the country yesterday, just hours after she'd questioned him about Justyna Kozlowska.

'Another Polish guy, in a white van, came and picked him up,' said the neighbour, 'at about five in the morning.' He raised his eyebrows to show what he thought of that.

'How d'you know the other man was Polish?'

'Because after he got in the van there was a lot of shouting,' said the guy with a scowl, waving at his window. 'I could hear everything.'

'Did it sound like a falling-out?'

He nodded. 'Janusz was having a go at the other guy, I think.'

'Did he say when he was coming back?' she asked,

aware of a note of panic entering her voice. If Kiszka had done a bunk, Streaky would kick her arse all over the office for scaring him off and he'd be right: she'd gone too far and too fast with him.

The neighbour looked worried now. 'I certainly hope so – the night before he left he asked me to feed his cat for a few days.'

Phew. He hadn't left for good then. Another thought occurred to Kershaw – if he *was* part of some drugs ring, maybe he'd gone to Poland to pick up PMA from one of those illegal factories the report talked about.

'I have quite a bad allergy to animal hair, actually,' the guy was saying.

He didn't strike Kershaw as the old-fashioned neighbourly type, but then she couldn't quite see Kiszka as a cat lover either.

'You and Mr Kiszka must be good friends.'

'No, no,' the bottom half of his face twisted into a grin, but behind the trendy glasses, his eyes looked nervous. 'Not at all. I just . . . he said it was an emergency.'

Yeah. She imagined Janusz Kiszka would be a hard man to say no to.

The savaging Streaky gave her when she got back to the office was as bad as she'd anticipated and then some, but at least Browning and Bonnick were on lates, so Ben Crowther was the only other person to overhear the roasting. The worst thing about Kiszka's disappearance was that Streaky now seemed to have a downer on every other bit of progress she'd made on the two dead Polish girls.

'Tell me if I'm missing something,' he asked, all

innocence. 'But on the Waveney Thameside case, you've got some CCTV footage of one suspect that's about as useful as a chocolate fireguard, right?'

'Yes, Sarge,' she muttered.

'And, you've put the wind up a second suspect so bad that he's legged it to Poland?'

'Sarge, I . . .'

'Now some stude who saw a picture on the missing persons website has conveniently handed you a name for the dead female in Wapping mortuary. And your latest devastating insight', he shook his head, 'if I'm not actually *dreaming* this, is that since this Ela Wronska had a room with a *river view*, she can't have jumped in of her own accord – she must have been pushed!' Streaky jumped out of his chair. His face was so close to hers she could trace the tube map of broken blood vessels in his cheeks. 'Just remind me – am I training you to be a detective, or a fucking clairvoyant?!'

'That's not quite what I said, Sarge,' said Kershaw keeping her voice reasonable. 'It's just that I can't see Elzbieta Wronska doing drugs. She was a total wallflower, she didn't drink, and her idea of a fun night was curling up with a book on twelfth-century theology.'

Streaky sat down, still breathing heavily. 'So what? Maybe she was experimenting, seeing if a bit of Dr Feelgood would give her confidence, then got the heebie jeebies and topped herself.' But she could tell he was considering her point.

Kershaw put her hands behind her back and picked at a ragged nail. If the Sarge didn't buy the possibility of foul play there was no way he'd approve forensic checks on the room.

'What makes you think her room's a scene, anyway?' he asked. 'Any sign of forced entry?'

'No, Sarge. But the place looks like it's been cleared out,' she said. 'If she suicided, where's her phone, her handbag, her laptop?'

'And no trace of the drugs she took?'

She shook her head. 'I checked with the cleaner – she found nothing out of the ordinary in the room when she went in last week.'

'This vicar, or whatever you call him, who runs the place, what makes you think he's a shifty character?'

She checked her notebook. 'He couldn't ID Elzbieta from the post mortem composite, but when I checked back with this friend of hers, Timothy Lethbridge, he told me Monsignor Zielinski was her personal tutor up till a year ago.'

Streaky cracked open a can of Lilt and took a slurp. 'Hardly a hanging offence – he's probably tutored hundreds of studes.'

He tapped his fingers on the can. 'If the girl *was* murdered' – he shot her a warning look – 'and I'm not saying you've got an ounce of evidence for it, I'd put this Timothy bloke top of the list. He fancied her but got the knockback, you say?'

'Yeah, but he fessed up to it pretty quick.'

'Still sounds like your best motive to me,' said Streaky. '*If* anyone else was even involved in her death.' He picked up his half-eaten sausage sandwich from the desk, then used a wetted finger to wipe a smear of brown sauce off the arrest warrant he'd been using as a plate.

Kershaw held her breath.

'Go on then,' said Streaky. 'Get the CSI boys over

there to check out her room. I've already had two bollockings for going over budget this month, I might as well make it the hat trick.'

'Brilliant, thanks Sarge.'

'Now piss off – before I find another wacky baccy factory for you to add to your collection.'

Eighteen

When Janusz first noticed the guy in the hat, he and Oskar were just tucking into two platefuls of brined Baltic herring aboard an old fishing boat moored on the Gdansk waterfront.

The boat had been converted into a floating restaurant by the addition of a few makeshift benches and tables. In Janusz's childhood, the quayside had been thronged with working vessels of all shapes and sizes, their shore ropes a cat's cradle apparently designed to trip up small boys. Now this one, which had hauled its last cargo of herring long ago, was the lone survivor.

Rather than *wodka*, the traditional accompaniment to *sledz*, they'd ordered steaming glasses of spiced wine, because – as Oskar had complained about a hundred times since they'd got here – it was bitterly cold, a good five degrees colder than London, in spite of the spring sunshine and clear cobalt skies.

The boat deck gave them a good overview of the harbour front. It was teeming with tourists, bundled up against the cold in fleecy jackets and woolly hats, mostly Polish and German from the snatches of conversation Janusz had overheard. They lounged on café terraces, or drifted along the cobbled quayside, admiring the tall, slender facades of the Hanseatic merchants' houses, their wedding cake parapets reflected in the petrol blue surface of the Motlawa River.

Janusz tried to work out what it was about the man that made him stand out from the crowd. He walked at the same unhurried pace, but the way he held himself was more purposeful somehow, and his leather coat and hat jarred among that parade of leisure wear. He moved like a shark cruising through a shoal of ornamental carp.

'Oskar,' said Janusz, with a tilt of his head, 'don't be obvious about it, but check out the guy in the hat who just went past.' Oskar craned his head over the boat's gunwale, forcing Janusz to kick him in the shins. By the time he thought it safe to look over his shoulder, the guy had disappeared, probably up one of the turnings leading off the waterfront.

'Forget it,' said Janusz, taking a warming mouthful of wine. But he couldn't shake the uneasy feeling he'd seen the man before. 'Do you remember a guy wearing a hat on the ferry?'

Oskar put his fork down and tightly screwed up his eyes, a look which meant he was utilising all his powers of memory. 'One of the Scousers was wearing a striped red and white top hat,' he offered finally, spearing his last chunk of herring. He wagged the loaded fork at Janusz. 'You're just jumpy,' he said, popping the fish in his mouth. 'Because of the kicking that guy gave you.'

'Maybe,' said Janusz.

Oskar drank his remaining *grzaniec* in one draught and leaned back, slapping his stomach. 'So, lady boy, what are we doing now? If your bus isn't till four, we've got a couple of hours – although if the roads east of here are as crap as they were this morning I'll probably be driving all night.' Janusz grunted agreement. After Germany's autobahns, crossing the border had been like going back in time – mile after mile of potholed country roads, relieved only by the occasional stretch of dual carriageway.

'Let's go to the Post Office!' said Oskar, eyes widening. The building had been the site of a famous siege in '39, when the Nazis reached Gdansk. In a suicidally heroic act of resistance, a band of postmen and boy scouts armed with a few grenades and assorted firearms fought off repeated assaults by SS units with armoured cars and artillery for fifteen hours. It only ended when the Germans used flamethrowers to rain burning gasoline on the men inside.

Janusz avoided Oskar's eyes. He didn't want to remind him that the square the Post Office stood on had witnessed another futile act of resistance, four decades later – the protest rally where Iza had taken her dying breath.

'Nah, I don't fancy it,' he said, counting out enough *zloty* bills to pay for their food. 'I've got a better idea. Let's see if you've got the balls to make it to the top of the cathedral tower.'

Janusz had been fearful that his home town would stir up dangerous memories. Instead, as he and Oskar made their way to St Mary's, he was aware of an inexplicable sense of unfamiliarity. The feel of the cobbles underfoot and the screams of the gulls were just as he remembered, the layout was unchanged, yet it all felt strangely surreal.

Then he caught sight of a little boy clutching a yellow balloon, and realised what was bothering him. The street scene of his childhood had been drab, almost completely monochrome, the only relief the red flags of occupation flying outside government buildings. Now, Dluga, the town's central promenade, looked almost gaudy in the bright sunshine, strung with the bright awnings of outdoor cafés, its ancient houses freshly painted. He welcomed the air of unreality: it put a layer of gauze between him and the past, making him feel as though he were just another tourist.

As they meandered through the crowds in the pedestrianised old quarter, Oskar elbowed Janusz. 'Where did you pick up your first leg over then?' His booming voice drew a few shocked glances from passers-by.

'Hold your muzzle, Oskar,' hissed Janusz. 'You're not in England now.'

On nearby Mariacka, the sombre Gothic facades, with the stone animal-head gargoyles that had frightened and fascinated Janusz as a little boy, were obscured now by a flock of white canvas parasols that sheltered jewellery and gingerbread stalls.

'I'm going to get some amber for Gosia,' said Oskar, stopping at one.

Janusz waited, arms folded, as Oskar held pieces up to the light, squinting critically, weighed them in his hands, and tapped the stones against his teeth. Finally, he settled on a big uneven chunk set into an oval-shaped silver brooch.

'Why don't you get Kasia something?' he said, as he exchanged his notes for a box tied with yellow ribbon.

Janusz shrugged uncomfortably, 'I don't know if she likes amber.' Maybe he didn't know anything about her, he thought gloomily, remembering the nail bar.

'She's a woman, isn't she?' said Oskar, as though to an idiot child. 'I'd like someone to show me a woman who doesn't like jewellery. Isn't that right, sweetheart?' he said to the girl running the stall, whose only response was an embarrassed smile.

Janusz's eye fell on a chain strung with tiny nuggets of green amber, the colour of seaweed waving in a rock pool, and he asked the girl to wrap it up, suddenly confident that Kasia would approve.

As they left the tourist quarter, the streets grew quieter and shabbier and yellowing 'To Let' signs started to appear in shop windows. Oskar paused to peer through the grimy window of a derelict government grocery store. 'Look at this, Janek,' he said chuckling. 'It's just like the old days.'

Reluctantly, Janusz bent down and, shading the glass with his hand, peered inside. The ancient chiller cabinet spotted with rust and old fan-shaped scales on the dusty counter pitched him back to the seventies.

'I know this place,' he exclaimed. 'I used to come here after school, join the queue.' He shook his head. 'Half the time I didn't even know what they were queuing for, but if I went home with toilet rolls, or flour, Mama would give me a bar of *Princepolo*.' He straightened. The place stirred an uncomfortable mix of nostalgia and disquiet.

'Remember the jokes people used to tell in the queue?'

asked Oskar. He punched Janusz lightly on the arm. *'What would happen if communists took over the desert?'*

'Nothing for a while, and then they'd run out of sand,' Janusz supplied.

They grinned at one another. Then the infuriating *di-ding ding ding* of Oskar's mobile rang out.

'*Czesc* . . . Yes, I'm in Gdansk now,' shouted Oskar, rolling his eyes at Janusz.

He squinted at a street sign. 'On Szeroka with my mate . . . Yeah, like I said, I'll be at Elblag before the undertaker shuts tonight . . . Okay . . . Cheerio.'

Oskar snapped the phone shut. 'That guy nags me so much we might as well get married. Maybe he's keen to get Olek into the ground so he doesn't come back and haunt him.' He drew a windy sigh. 'I'd better get going, though, what with the Stone Age roads in this country.'

The two men embraced. When Oskar had gone twenty metres he turned, and cupping his hands into a megaphone shouted, 'And stay away from the rent boys – I'm not bailing you out again!'

Ten minutes later, as Janusz emerged from a tobacconist, he suppressed a shiver – the temperature had dropped sharply. Overhead, a bank of leaden cloud pressed down on the slate roofs, and the damp chill in the air signalled a sea mist rolling in off the Baltic. Buttoning up his coat, he checked his watch and set out for the bus station, but he'd barely gone a dozen steps, when he felt a prickle at the top of his spine.

A casual backward glance caught a rapid movement, a split-second impression of a dark figure outside the tobacconist he'd just left. Wheeling round, he scanned the pavement behind him. Clear. He strode back to the shop. Empty. The man – if the figure were more than just a phantom of his paranoid imaginings – must have ducked down neighbouring Mariacka, where he and Oskar had bought amber earlier.

Around the corner, he was startled to find the lively street mysteriously restored to how it had looked in his youth – the tall medieval facades dark, shuttered and silent. The stallholders had closed up for the day, taking their parasols with them, he realised, leaving the narrow cobbled street empty but for a group of seagulls pecking at the ground halfway down.

He scoped the only side turning at the top of the street, finding it empty. And only an Olympic sprinter could have covered the hundred metres or more to the Gothic archway at the far end that led to the waterfront. Which meant that if someone had been following him, he must still be on Mariacka. The flights of ancient stone steps that ran from every front door down to street level offered plenty of hiding places – as a child he remembered running ahead to duck behind them, then jumping out to surprise his mother.

Janusz advanced cautiously, eyes flicking left and right, every sense cocked, tensed for a crouching figure to spring out. The age-pitted gargoyles perched at the top of each stairway – a crocodile, a lion, a monstrous fish – seemed to stare at him sardonically as he passed, his footsteps echoing. Mist had started to creep up from the river, softening outlines and making him mistrust his eyes. Then his eye fell on the stone head of a dragon, jaws ajar, three houses down to his right, and it came to him – he couldn't say why – *That's where the son of a bitch is hiding*. At that moment, the heel of one of his

235

shoes skidded on the cobbles, made slippery by the mist. He cursed and a man bolted from behind the dragon's head stairway, heading for the waterfront, scattering the scavenging gulls screeching into the air.

By the time Janusz regained his footing, the guy had almost reached the archway at the foot of the street, leather coat flying out behind him.

Janusz raced after him, his heart thudding.

Leather coat, hat . . . He wasn't going crazy – it *was* the guy he'd spotted that morning on the quayside.

On the waterfront the wall-to-wall crowds had thinned, but Janusz couldn't see any trace of him. Bands of sulphurous mist rising off the Motlawa pawed at the legs of the remaining sightseers. Right or left? He gambled on left, making for where the quayside was busiest and where the guy could more easily hide.

For the next couple of minutes, he ducked and jinked through the idling throng, getting his feet tangled in the wheels of a baby buggy, knocking a *hausfrau's* handbag off her shoulder, scattering apologies like confetti – *przepraszam, przepraszam*. He didn't spot anyone wearing a hat, except of the woollen variety. Until a middle-aged couple, walking hand in hand thirty metres ahead, drifted momentarily apart as the lady paused to study a restaurant menu. Through the gap, Janusz revealed a glimpse of broad leather back moving with stealthy speed. The man's crew-cut head was hatless now. *Of course*.

Janusz slowed his pace, half-bending his knees to stay hidden by the crowd, snatching the occasional flash of his quarry. He realised his rib had stopped hurting and remembered reading something about the powerful analgesic effect of adrenaline.

With the river to the right and no further left turns back into the old town, the guy was stuck on the quay-side, and would soon reach the last of the shops and cafes. The path continued alongside the river but since most of the sightseers turned back at that point, he'd find himself out in the open.

Recognising the sprawling Soviet-era housing estate looming up ahead, Janusz discovered that he still possessed a surprisingly good mental map of Gdansk. If the guy headed inland through the estate, he'd enter a labyrinth with a dozen choices of routes, and Janusz would almost certainly lose him. If, on the other hand, he continued along the river, he would have missed his last chance of escape. Janusz could picture the riverside route with pin-sharp recall. Unless something had rad-ically altered, the towpath narrowed rapidly and, on the landward side, the high perimeter fence of the old Gdansk shipyard reared up to close off all other routes. Five hundred metres on, the path simply dead-ended – and the guy would be caught like a rat in a trap.

Janusz saw him reach the end of the busy section of quayside some thirty metres ahead and shoot a single look over his shoulder as he emerged into the open. Janusz only got a fleeting glimpse of the guy but he was left with a vivid impression – *a face like a clenched fist.*

Reaching the spot where the crowds thinned, Janusz took cover behind a notice board, and peeked around its edge. The man's pace was swift but unhurried – perhaps he thought he'd shaken his pursuer by now – and his rolling gait, together with shoulders unnaturally broad for his height, reminded Janusz of a security guard he knew at home who was a body-building nut.

A couple of minutes later, the guy reached the river-side entrance to the housing estate. Janusz held his breath. Would he escape into that warren of walkways? But he didn't even pause, continuing on the riverside path. *Brawo*! muttered Janusz grimly.

Once he was sure the guy had reached the point of no return, he counted to three. Then he exploded from his hiding place at a run. Pounding down the riverside footpath, ignoring the gasps of passers-by, he kept his gaze fixed on that distant mist-veiled figure. He heard the rumble of diesel engines and the tinny strains of a sea shanty as a converted fishing boat, taking sightseers out to the seafront at Westerplatte, passed him, its passengers gawping at the sight of a big middle-aged man racing flat out along the towpath.

Beyond the housing estate, the paved path gave way to dirt and gravel underfoot, and the high fence of the extinct shipyard rose to his left, just as he remembered. The fog rolled off the river like dry ice now and his breathing grew ragged as he sucked in great draughts of the chilly air. He tore past one of the old shipyard buildings, its walls scarred with graffiti – the *Solidarnosc* slogans of his youth long replaced by gang tags – stumbling badly when one of his feet snagged on a rusted coil of steel cable hidden by the increasingly overgrown path.

Through a window in the mist, Janusz spotted the leather-coated figure, less than fifty metres ahead now, approaching a sharp leftward bend in the river. Just before the bend, the man glanced over his shoulder for the first time and seeing his pursuer, broke into a fast barrelling run.

Janusz grinned savagely as he disappeared from view,

dying to see the look on the *skurwysyn*'s face when he hit the dead end, where the shipyard fence curved down to meet the riverfront. It must be seconds away now. Fingering the scabbed knife wound on his throat from two nights ago, Janusz slowed to search the bushes beside the path for something to even the odds. Finding a rusted but sturdy length of two by four, he hefted it in his hand, then loped cautiously around the bend, panting, the blood roaring in his ears.

It took a moment to compute the scene that confronted him there.

Seventy metres ahead, just as he remembered, the sheer wire cliff of the shipyard fence veered rightward to bar the path – but the towpath ahead was empty. Then he worked it out. The tourist boat that had passed him a few minutes ago was steaming at a sharp angle away from the riverbank. At the stern handrail, above the burbling foam and smoke thrown up by the diesel engines, stood the guy in the leather coat. He was tucking something into the inside pocket of his coat. Behind him stood a crewman, coiling a shore rope.

Janusz clenched his jaw – the son of a whore had obviously waved a wad of *zlotych* to persuade the crew to pull over and pick him up. Now the guy pulled something out of the leather coat. He settled the hat back on his head and spread his arms wide on the stern rail, just another sightseer enjoying the view. The boat was too far away for Janusz to make out the guy's expression, but his body language radiated arrogant triumph.

Half an hour later, Janusz trailed back along the fog-shrouded quayside in the failing light, totally drained from his exertions. His rib throbbed insistently as the adrenaline rush faded and his brain buzzed with questions. Was the guy in the leather coat Pawel Adamski? He certainly shared the powerful build of the masked intruder who'd held a knife to his throat, and Janusz couldn't think of anyone else with a reason to be shadowing him. It seemed that Adamski's promise to kill him if he continued looking for Weronika had been no empty threat.

Suddenly remembering his bus to Gorodnik, Janusz checked his watch – and groaned. It had left three minutes ago. Now he'd have to stay in town for the night. He tried to look on the bright side – at least leather coat's unscheduled trip to Westerplatte had got him off Janusz's back.

He passed one of the waterfront cafes, its lights blazing against the intense blue of the Baltic dusk. He didn't notice the brightly lit windows, nor register the outline of a man silhouetted in one of them, coffee cup in hand – a heavy-set man wearing a fur-lined parka, who got to his feet the moment Janusz went out of view.

Nineteen

Kershaw felt in a mood to celebrate. She'd identified her floater and persuaded Streaky to authorise forensics on Elzbieta's college room, and in CID, celebration meant one thing – a proper drinking session. It was the evening of her 'non-date' with Ben, so she left her car at work and they took the tube to Tottenham Court Road together.

His mates turned out to be cool guys, graduate entry cops like her and Ben, and the four of them had a good old session putting the criminal justice system to rights over beers in a trendy bar on Dean Street.

The other two peeled off before closing time, pleading earlies, and Kershaw realised she was really enjoying Ben's company, and not just in a matey way. She'd always had a laugh with him, but now she found herself thinking – *How did I miss those sleepy brown eyes?* – and she was pretty sure it wasn't just beer goggles. As fellow cops they had a lot in common – how tough it was dating civilians, for starters. Ben told her that when he went to

241

train at Hendon, he had a girlfriend he'd been going out with for ever, like since he was fifteen or something.

'I was ready to get married, save up for a house, have babies, barbeques on the patio *blah blah* . . . the whole package,' said Ben, nice eyes crinkling, having a laugh at himself. 'But then she got accepted to do Fine Art at St Martin's.'

'That's the big-deal art college, right?' asked Kershaw.

'Yeah, so I was over the moon for her,' said Ben. 'But by the end of the first term she'd put green streaks in her hair and was dragging me along to every demo and action going' – he counted them off on his fingers – 'Stop the War, Stop the City, Reclaim the Streets . . . we even went Guerrilla Gardening.'

Kershaw frowned her incomprehension.

'Planting pansies on a roundabout on the A12 at three in the morning.'

She spluttered as a mouthful of Pinot Grigio went the wrong way.

'Yeah, *I know*,' he gave her a rueful look. 'I was paranoid that I'd be caught on camera and get the sack, so I wore wraparound shades 24/7.' He took a gulp of beer. 'Waste of time, anyway – by the end of the second term she decided I was an unthinking cog in a fascist machine, said I had to choose: her or the job.' He shrugged, but there was a sadness in his eyes before he dropped his gaze.

'At least she took you seriously,' said Kershaw, 'Most men get their image of a female cop from watching porn, so they just want you to put on your uniform and get out the handcuffs.'

'Do you have to read them their rights first?' asked Ben,

raising an eyebrow. She gave him a pretend-stern look, then told him about the time during her detective training, when she'd gone on a date with a George Clooney look-alike – leaving out the Clooney ref, obviously.

'So he takes me to this really expensive sushi bar and while we're talking about him and his Really Important Job in the City – which is most of the night.' – they shared a grin – 'it all goes pretty well. But then he asks me about the training.'

Ben raised an eyebrow, wondering what was coming. 'We were actually in the middle of this fascinating pathology module at the time,' she said, meeting his gaze. He winced. 'And I just kind of forget who I'm talking to, and start telling him about this broken baby case.'

'Good move.'

'I know, I know, what was I thinking?' she shook her head. 'So there I was trapping off about how a baby's brain tissue is so soft that the lab had to spend weeks hardening it in fixative before taking samples, when the guy suddenly jumps up, knocking his wine all over the table, and legs it for the loo.' She cupped both hands over her face, half laughing, half mortified at the memory. Ben shook his head, grinning at her screw-up. She shrugged. 'He never did come back, but at least he paid the bill on his way out.'

After another couple of drinks, Ben asked if she fancied a Chinese. The look in his eyes before he cut them away was pretty easy to decipher – the invite had no strings attached, but when it came to dessert, the ball would be in her court. She escaped to the bogs, where she splashed her face in the sink and pulled in her cheeks, staring self-critically in the mirror. A bit red-eyed, but still passable, she thought, if you went for the dishevelled look. She did really like Ben. In fact, this was the first time she'd even *noticed* a guy since Mark left, she realised.

But. The big fat 'but' that came with the job, she thought, letting her shoulders slump. The catch-22 of police life. The only guys you ever met – apart from villains – were your fellow cops: but sleeping with fellow cops was a total no-no; for a woman, anyway.

Leaning across the sink, she gave her reflection a stern talking-to. 'Remember what happened last time you slept with a cop? It went through the nick like a dose of ExLax. Fancy facing the schoolboy sniggers and snide comments again? No, I didn't think so.'

The speech was the first thing that popped into her mind as she surfaced in the semi-gloom just after dawn, and she basked in the memory of her good sense, until she turned over and saw window blinds – *her flat had curtains* – and the profile of a man's face outlined against them – *Ben's* – and the rest of the night rushed across her retina like a movie on fast forward. *Crispy duck with pancakes and more wine in Chinatown . . . throwing random shapes on the dance floor to Human League at some eighties retro night . . . snogging in the taxi back to Ben's gaff . . . fumbled sex on the sofa, then again – MUCH better this time – in his bed.*

She cringed, remembering that they'd even come perilously close to getting jiggy in the lift on the way up to his high-rise flat – thank Christ she'd spotted the security camera in time.

A sudden overwhelming desire to escape before Ben woke up seized her. She extracted herself, limb by cautious limb, from under the duvet and retrieved her clothes and handbag from the crime scene in the lounge. After a last check to ensure she hadn't left anything incriminating, she got herself dressed – all bar her shoes, which she put on in the lift – and reached the safety of the pavement, all in six minutes flat.

Only then did she feel a sharp little stab of regret at the thought of Ben's nice brown eyes opening to find an empty bed. *Get a grip*, she thought, the whole thing had been an epic mistake. Ben was lovely but the idea of having a relationship with someone in the same CID office was lunacy. It would leak out, and then the piss-taking and gossip would never end.

It took another ten minutes to discover she was in Wanstead, a leafy burb full of twee shops selling vintage crapola, but at last she found a caff which made her a passable triple shot latte for the tube journey home – four stops west on the Central line to Mile End. Before going underground she hesitated, then decided to text Ben. If he sent her some lovey-dovey text first, she might weaken. *Way 2 much 2 drink last night!!!* she tapped out. *Had a fab time but prolly not a great idea! Nx.* She pressed send, hoping that it spelled out where she stood, but in a friendly way that should head off any risk of revenge gossip – not that Ben was the type. *You hope.*

As Kershaw hung off the handrail in the packed tube carriage, she realised that last night had been her first evening out, not counting work piss-ups, for weeks. It might have left her with scratchy eyes and a dull thudding at the back of her head – never mind the cringe-making prospect of facing Ben in the office – but it had also left her feeling strangely energised. And her hang-over had pulled another weird trick: it had made her realise that there was something about the Waveney Hotel, or at least its CCTV system, that didn't add up.

As Kershaw battled the rush hour crush, Janusz was riding a two-thirds empty bus to Gorodnik through bright morning sunshine. As the suburbs of Gdansk thinned, giving way to fields of earth newly-greened by spring crops and birch forest, he felt the gloom that had seized him since Justyna's death begin to lighten.

The previous evening, he'd checked into a tiny hotel in a back street near the bus station and ordered pizza – the only takeaway option – he wasn't taking any chances on running into leather coat man again. When he awoke at dawn, he felt guilt lying on him like a too-heavy duvet, and realised there was something he had to do before he could leave town.

At Lostowicki Cemetery, he made his way to the Kiszka family plot, where he laid flowers on the graves of his Mama and Tata. After his escape to the UK, he'd seen them, what? Half a dozen times in twenty years? Father had died first, his mother following within months. No chance now to make it up to them. Standing there, picturing their old worn faces, in which he'd never seen a trace of accusation or censure, he felt a wave of regret so powerful it made him momentarily dizzy.

As the bus left the fields and scattered farms behind and the forest became unbroken on either side, he caught a glimpse of Prussian blue between tree trunks – the Lakes! – and felt a flutter of childish excitement.

The bus disgorged its passengers in the midst of Gorodnik's market day. The stalls nearest the bus station were indistinguishable from a London market, piled with mass-produced trainers, lurid sweets and cheap socks, except the stallholders were almond-eyed, their hair blue black – members of Poland's Tartar population. But as Janusz neared the town square, he was reminded of market day outings with his grandmother. At one stall, a man was sealing a bargain to buy a protesting chicken, its scrawny-looking legs and wings tied with string. At another, a beady-eyed old *Babcia* in a bright print dress and gardener's apron was selling wild garlic, potted chives and tomato plants, doubtless from her own allotment. As he lingered at her stall, she asked, 'Are you buying today, *panie*?' It took him a moment to make out her broad Kashubian accent, but her no-nonsense tone was as clear as the sun, so he handed over some coins for a cone of radishes and walked on, munching them like sweets.

Gorodnik's cobbled market square stood in the shadow of an impressive brick-built Gothic church, a smaller version of St Mary's in Gdansk, hung with a large banner advertising a forthcoming concert of works by Paderewski. Beyond the bustle of the market, the town became dusty and lifeless, and many of the shuttered shops looked as though they would never re-open. The *Hotel Pomorski* – which the *Babcia* told him was the only inn open outside the holiday season – turned out to be a bit of a dive, although admittedly a dirt-cheap one at sixty *zloty* a night, basically a working man's restaurant with a handful of rooms and a shared bathroom. The taciturn landlady doled out a towel and told him breakfast was between 7 and 8 a.m. In the room, he paused only to drop his bag and pick up a map of the town from the chest of drawers, its peeling veneer striped with dozens of fag burns, before heading out.

Away from the market square the traditional architecture quickly gave way to the inevitable Soviet-built apartment blocks, fifties vintage, many pitted with craters where the render had fallen off, giving them a leprous air. It took Janusz ten minutes to find the Woytek storage depot, a corrugated iron warehouse on the outskirts of town, with a portakabin out front acting as an office – not the sort of place he'd trust with his family heirlooms. Behind a counter inside the portakabin sat a guy in a huge puffa jacket, reading the local paper. When he looked up, Janusz saw he had a wall-eye.

'*Dzien dobry, panu,*' he said, his good eye flickering over Janusz.

Janusz returned the greeting with a smile, then quickly straightened his face. He'd already earned a few confused – and suspicious – looks in Gdansk, beaming unthinkingly at shopkeepers and passers-by. It was a habit he'd picked up in England, where a smile was the smallest and commonest coin of social currency.

'My business partner and I store antique furniture here, from time to time,' he said. 'In fact, he came out a few days ago on a trip to buy more, and we're meant to be meeting up, but now . . . ' – he waggled his mobile – 'I can't get through to him on his phone.'

'Maybe it got stolen,' said the guy, setting his newspaper aside.

'Exactly,' said Janusz. 'The trouble is, I've got no other way of contacting him.' He shrugged, trying to look helpless. 'So I'm asking around, to see if anyone has another number for him, or an address – anything to help me find him.'

The guy's expression suggested no more than a polite

interest in this fairy story. Janusz's gaze fell on a calendar tacked to the wall behind him. Miss April was a buxom blonde, pretty beneath her carapace of make-up, but the amount of cleavage and fake-tanned thigh revealed by her cowgirl outfit struck him as touchingly modest by UK standards.

'His name's Pawel Adamski?' tried Janusz, returning his gaze to the guy.

He shook his head, his left eye fixed disconcertingly on a point somewhere over Janusz's shoulder. 'Sorry – I've never heard of him,' he said. 'I'm new, you see, and the boss is in Budapest this week.'

'Perhaps you might have something on file that might help me find him?' Janusz shivered inside his coat – it couldn't be more than twelve degrees in here.

The guy dipped his head sideways in apology. 'Regretfully, *prosze pana*, we are not permitted to share customers' confidential details,' he said, but his good eye held a speculative gleam that suggested he was nothing if not a reasonable man.

A few minutes later, and fifty zloty poorer, Janusz emerged from the portakabin. Once around the corner, he pulled out the photocopy of Pawel Adamski's sole invoice, anticipation making him breathe a little faster.

Woytek Storage had received one container's worth of goods, on February 1, which had been collected by a shipping company on February 16. The billing address matched the rented cottage in Willowbridge, but aside from Adamski's name, there was no phone number, no credit card info, and no contact details of any kind in Poland.

He struck the wall with the flat of his hand. *Kurwa mac!* Travelling a thousand miles to Gorodnik had always been a long shot, but he'd convinced himself the depot would produce another lead – *something*, no matter how small, to help him track down Adamski. He was on the point of screwing the piece of paper up in a rage, but managed to stop himself. Adamski must have some local connection to use the storage depot here. Why else would he choose a backwoods place like Gorodnik rather than one of the dozens of facilities in Gdansk? Folding the invoice away carefully, he lit a cigar and set off in the direction of town.

It always cracked Kershaw up, the way people behaved when they thought they were alone. She was back at the Waveney Thameside Hotel, observing a guy who'd just entered the North lift on the CCTV feed. The minute the doors shut, leaving him as the sole occupant, he'd started scratching his balls, and now, looking comically furtive, he plunged his hand right down inside the waistband of his suit trousers and had a proper old juggle. *Pocket billiards*, her dad would have called it.

The camera, positioned to one side of the lift doors, captured the guy's face as clear as day. If it had been working the night Justyna Kozlowska and hat man checked in, it would have provided a perfect shot of her suspect.

Derek, the security guy, came into the office, carrying two brimming mugs of tea, 'Let's go into my cubbyhole, it's warmer,' he said.

She tore her gaze from the lift feed and followed him. 'Don't you have to keep an eye on the screens?'

'No, darling, they're only there in case of an incident,' he said, chuckling, 'We're not a Swiss bank, y'know!'

After turning on an electric fan heater at her feet, Derek started reminiscing about his twenty-five years in the cops. 'We didn't have all these piles of paperwork you poor sods have to wade through nowadays,' he said, settling back into his armchair with his cuppa and a Garibaldi. 'Or all this human rights bollocks – excuse my French.' He dropped his voice confidentially, 'And if a villain sometimes picked up a black eye in the cells, was that the end of the world? Our clear-up rate was a sight better than it is now.'

Kershaw sipped her tea, nodding. 'Yeah, it's a nightmare these days,' she said. 'You can't imagine the grief my DI is giving me about that girl who died in room 1313. *You and I* know how much time police work takes, but all *he* cares about is targets and budgets.'

'One of these cops who came straight out of college and into management is he?' asked Derek.

'Got it in one,' she said with a rueful grimace. 'Anyway, I thought I'd pop back and check a few things out, earn some brownie points.'

'I'll help in any way I can, sweetheart.'

'You mentioned there was something wrong with the CCTV in the lifts at the time the girl was going up to the room?' she asked. 'Do you remember how long it was down for?'

'I can't say I recall offhand, sweetheart, but I'll get you the logbook,' he said, hauling himself out of the armchair.

Security was clearly something of an afterthought at the Waveney, thought Kershaw, as she opened the tatty A3 book and examined its handwritten entries. There were separate sections for the cameras and recording systems in the guest areas – check-in desk, foyer entrance, the north lift and south lift. In the section headed 'North Lift Cam', an entry dated March 23, the day before hat man checked in, recorded: 'Cam out of order: Viztek called.' The next entry, dated three days later, read: 'Cam repaired by Viztek'. She flipped through to the page for South Lift Cam, and found exactly the same entries and dates.

Suddenly aware of the thump of her own heartbeat, she said, 'Sorry, Derek, I'm a bit rubbish at technical stuff, but I've been thinking – each lift cam is obviously separate, with its own recorder, right? So how could they both go wrong at the same time?'

Derek looked at both entries and scratched his grey-stubbled cheek, 'Dunno – I can't say I'm particularly up on technology myself.'

'It wasn't you who called this . . . Viztek in to check the cams?' she asked. Angling the book into the light, he squinted at it and shook his head. 'No, I haven't spoken to them for ages. It must have been Milo.'

Derek went off to see if he could raise Milo, who worked the night shift, on the phone, and left Kershaw looking through the filing system – a series of metal cabinets with deep drawers holding hundreds of tape cassettes, arranged in date order – for the CCTV tapes. The tapes from both lift cams were filed together in one drawer and, sure enough, there was a tape for March 22 but then nothing until March 27. Picking out a few for a closer look she noticed that they all bore the label 'LIFT CAM', with no indication which lift they came from.

Just then, Derek came back, looking troubled. 'I spoke to Milo – he says he remembers a note taped to the recorders a few days back saying the cams were up the spout, but he thought it was me who put it there.'

'And you didn't?'

'No, and neither of us took the note off and put in new tapes, either.'

Derek seemed reluctant to look her in the eye during this exchange.

'But surely it must have come up, when you and Milo handed over between shifts that morning?' She checked her notebook, 'Milo starts at eight in the evening and clocks off when you start, at six in the morning, right?'

Derek's mouth worked silently for a moment, then he burst out: 'To tell you the truth, sweetheart, we don't see each other most mornings'. He finally met her gaze. 'Milo has to leave at six to get his train, and my first bus doesn't get me here till at least quarter past.'

Kershaw left a pause – they both knew that he and Milo could be handed their P45s for leaving the hotel without security cover, even for ten minutes.

'Could you do me a favour, Derek?' she asked. 'Could you give Viztek a call for me, see what they've got to say?'

As she suspected, the guys at Viztek had no record of any callout to the hotel in the last week – in fact, the last engineer visit had been to carry out the routine annual service, the previous November.

Her hunch had been right: both lift cameras going wrong at the same time was just too big a coincidence. As she absorbed the significance of this discovery she felt her breath coming fast and shallow. *Somebody had got into security and waltzed off with the video tape – the very tape that must show Kozlowska and hat man going up in the lift*. The thief had to take the tapes for *both* lifts, north and south, because the failure to label them meant there was no way to distinguish one from the other. Was it hat man, destroying the evidence? *Don't be thick, Nat.* Even if he'd managed to get into security to steal the tapes, why would he cook up a cover story about broken cameras? The thief was clearly someone who needed to cover his tracks, in the frankly fucking unlikely event of Milo or Derek actually noticing that any tape cassettes had gone missing.

Kershaw's eye fell on Derek, who sat bolt upright, both hands gripping the armrests of his chair. 'You were a cop, Derek,' said Kershaw, her grey eyes serious. 'I don't need to tell you what a big deal it is, those tapes going missing.'

She felt a rush of pity at how terrified he looked: a job like this wouldn't pay much more than minimum wage, but the poor bastard probably relied on it to supplement his pension. She ought to keep turning the screws on him to get maximum leverage, but instead she found herself saying, 'Listen, I'll do everything I can to keep you out of trouble, but you've got to help me find out who could have got in here and stolen those tapes.'

His whole face lifted at the prospect of a reprieve.

Kershaw stood and started walking back and forth – she always thought better on her feet. 'So nobody else, not even the manager, has another key?'

'No, I've always kept the spare locked in a drawer at home.'

'Right. So if the office is never left unlocked – how does Milo get the key to you at the end of his shift, since he doesn't see you?'

Derek admitted that, at the end of the night shift, Milo would lock up and put the key into a jiffy bag. On his way out, he'd slip it into the pigeonhole behind front desk where post for security was left, for Derek to pick up when he got in. Kershaw did a quick mental calculation. The arrangement left the key unattended for at least fifteen minutes – plenty of time for the thief to get into security, nick the tapes and alter the logbook, before returning it to the pigeonhole in time for Derek's arrival.

'And no-one else knew anything about this key hand-over business?'

He shook his head. 'Just me and Milo.'

Kershaw paced around, chewing at her thumbnail, Derek's anxious eyes following her. Then she took another Garibaldi, and offering the open packet to Derek, said, 'When you picked up the key from the pigeonhole that morning, was Alex Hurley still on front desk?'

Twenty

Gorodnik nightlife was enough to make a man pine for the bright lights of Stratford, thought Janusz as he paced the town's deserted streets with a growing sense of desperation.

It was only 7 p.m., and he had already eaten a solid and almost completely tasteless dinner alone in the *Pomorski's* dimly lit dining room, under the suspicious eye of the landlady. She'd served him a bowl of watery *zurek*, unmistakably out of a packet and minus the essential boiled egg, followed by *pierogi* that seemed to be filled with nothing more than sauerkraut over-seasoned with black pepper. He said it was delicious, of course, but declared himself too full for dessert.

The market square stood deserted, except for a gaggle of kids who were taking turns to rattle across the cobbles on a skateboard. Two cafés that had been busy earlier in the day were now tightly shuttered. Pulling his great-coat tight against the chill wind coming off the lake, which according to his tourist map lay a kilometre to the east, he set out in search of a drink, cursing Adamski for bringing him to this provincial shit-hole.

A half-hour later, he was taking a deep, cold draft of Tyskie and thanking all the saints: if he hadn't spotted the wink of light at the end of the narrow alley, he'd have walked straight past, and *Pod Kotkiem* turned out to be the only bar open in the evening. The place wasn't half bad, either – the worn tables and chairs and faded prints of Lakeland scenes on the walls suggested the place hadn't been decorated since the fall of Communism, but the cigarettes of the dozen or so middle-aged punters created a comforting fug, and a tape of lively Gypsy music played in the background.

The barman seemed the chatty type, so after standing him a drink, Janusz unfolded the storage depot invoice and spinning it round on the bar, tapped Adamski's name. 'I'm trying to get back in touch with this guy,' he said, lighting a cigar. 'He's someone I sometimes do a little business with in the UK.' The barman scanned the invoice, then let his eyes flicker over Janusz's battered face with frank curiosity. Nothing interesting ever happened in here, unless you counted that time the buck rabbit Kaminski brought in on market day escaped from its sack and bit the lunch waitress. He handed the invoice back to him without a word.

'I don't suppose you recognise the name?' asked Janusz. 'Or maybe you might have heard of somebody looking to buy antiques round here?'

Wringing out a cloth, the barman started to wipe down the crazed Formica surface of the bar. 'Did this guy do a flit and leave you to pay the bills?' he asked.

Janusz gave an embarrassed shrug, 'Something like that, yeah.'

He shot Janusz a look. 'Sounds like Adamski, alright,' he said.

Janusz involuntarily inhaled a mouthful of cigar smoke, sending him into a fit of violent coughing. As he wiped his eyes, the barman, lips pressed together to keep from laughing, poured him a glass of water. 'Everybody knows Pawel Adamski. Until a few months ago he was always in here – when he wasn't barred, that is,' he added, raising a meaningful eyebrow. 'But that guy over there,' he said gesturing to a man with a greying thatch of moustache who sat upright and alone in a banquette, 'Tadeusz Krajewski. He's the one you should talk to.' As Janusz thanked him and stood up, the barman tapped him on the forearm. 'He drinks *Zubrowka*.'

Janusz took a drink over to Tadeusz, and introduced himself, somewhat warily, as a friend and sometime business associate of Adamski. He needn't have worried – the older man's face visibly brightened on hearing the name and he waved Janusz into the banquette opposite.

'So you're another one of those who's gone off to London, are you?' he asked in his soft country burr. Janusz spread his palms in apologetic assent. 'You must have been over there a while – your Polish is shocking,' said Tadeusz with a smile. His eyes played over Janusz's bruised face, but he made no comment, perhaps accepting violence as a routine feature of London life. 'In my day, if you were born in Gorodnik, you died in Gorodnik,' he mused. 'And we were all a lot happier for it, I can tell you.' Janusz nodded, hoping his expression didn't betray what he thought of such a prospect.

It turned out that Adamski had worked for Tadeusz as a mechanic in the little backstreet garage that he used to run, before the recession bit and the bank called in the loan.

'It was a good little business, too,' he told Janusz, with sudden vehemence. 'But do you know what the bank told me?' Janusz shook his head. 'They had to be stricter with loan conditions in the light of *the economic climate*.' He enunciated the phrase with disbelieving contempt. 'I told them, don't talk to me about economic climate – you're the ones who made it snow!'

There was hurt in his eyes behind the anger – he had clearly taken the loss of the business hard. Janusz tried to work out his age and came up with early sixties – not *that* old, but too old to start again, especially in times like these. He studied Tadeusz discreetly. His jaws were clean-shaven and his shirt, although fraying at the cuffs, was freshly pressed. A man keeping up appearances, in spite of everything.

'So how long did Adam . . . Pawel work for you?' asked Janusz, lighting a cigar.

'A year or more – right up to the end,' said Tadeusz, taking a decorous sip of the *Zubrowka*. 'He wasn't bad around engines, once I showed him the ropes.' He smiled to himself.

'Was his timekeeping any better when he worked for you?' asked Janusz with a grin, taking an educated guess at Adamski's work ethic.

Tadeusz lifted a shoulder. 'I won't pretend there weren't problems. Turning up late, sometimes still drunk from the night before.' He waved a hand. 'And now and again he would lose his temper with customers.'

Janusz nodded. It certainly fit with the picture Justyna had painted of Adamski – and yet the old guy spoke protectively, even affectionately, of his former employee. 'Everyone told me to sack him,' he said, sticking his chin out. 'But I said, after the start the boy had in life, he deserved a second chance.'

Tadeusz told him the Adamski clan was notorious in Gorodnik – the father a falling-down drunk who supplemented his meagre income from agricultural work with petty thieving, the mother forever pregnant, and not always by her husband. 'With such parents, is it any wonder that Pawel grew up wild?' Tadeusz asked. 'Anyway, when he was just a little kid, he set fire to an outhouse at Jabonski's place – they said it was a miracle the farmhouse didn't catch – and that was that,' he said dusting his hands. 'They took him away and put him in a children's home.'

'Terrible,' said Janusz, shaking his head. It sounded like Adamski's career as a *psychol* had started early. He took a slug of beer and decided to risk a bit more digging. He sensed that Tadeusz was keen to discuss Adamski with someone less censorious than the locals.

'When he was working for you, do you think Pawel ever messed around with *narkotyki*?' he asked.

'Drugs?' exclaimed Tadeusz, setting his glass down. 'No, no, not to my knowledge, only the drinking.' He scanned Janusz's face with eyes the colour of stone-washed denim. 'What makes you ask such a thing?'

'Just something I heard somebody say about him,' said Janusz. *The girl he killed, actually.*

Dropping his gaze, Tadeusz traced an ancient glass ring on the tabletop with a finger, his expression troubled. Janusz went to order more drinks.

'Getting anywhere?' asked the barman as he pulled a small beer for Janusz.

Janusz tilted his head, non-committal.

'Tadeusz is a good sort,' said the barman, his voice low. 'But when it comes to Adamski, he puts on rose-tinted spectacles.' Janusz raised his eyebrows enquiringly. The barman set the beer in front of Janusz, and leaned toward him, one elbow on the bar. 'He lost his son a couple of years ago – some kind of cancer,' he said, with a sympathetic grimace. 'Everyone knows Adamski is a bad lot, but maybe for Tadeusz, he filled the hole, if you know what I mean.' Janusz nodded – it explained a lot.

He returned to the table carrying his beer and a bottle of Tadeusz's tipple.

'You know,' said Tadeusz, taking slightly bigger sips of the *wodka*, Janusz noticed, now its supply was assured, 'If the business hadn't folded, I think Pawel would have been alright.' His fingers tapped and stroked the table. 'I could have got him on the straight and narrow, I know I could.'

Janusz nodded his encouragement.

'You know, I took him pike fishing on the river a few times – he was a different lad, out there in the fresh air,' Tadeusz smiled, revealing a flash of unnaturally white dentures. 'Once, he caught a big one, two kilos easily.' His grin broadened. 'It had such an ugly mug, we called it Vladimir, after Putin.'

Both men chuckled.

'Listen,' said Janusz, becoming serious. 'We both know

261

Pawel is . . . a good guy at heart' – he examined the end of his cigar, avoiding Tadeusz's hopeful gaze – 'but do you think it's possible he fell in with some bad characters – around here, or maybe in Gdansk?'

The old man looked at Janusz for a long moment. 'After the garage went bust, he told me about this idea he had. He was going to buy up old furniture and ship it to England, to sell to rich folk,' he said, hesitantly. 'I think that was what got him into trouble.'

Janusz adopted a sympathetic expression, feeling like a heel. Tadeusz clearly trusted him, perhaps even thought this stranger might be able to help his wayward young friend.

'The last time I saw Pawel,' Tadeusz pointed at Janusz, 'he was sitting right there, in that very chair. It was about six weeks ago, the middle of February. I remember because it was the last time we had proper snow, yet the crazy boy came in wearing nothing but a T-shirt.' He plucked at his shirt, his expression a mixture of exasperation and affection.

Janusz stayed silent, let Tadeusz do the talking.

'He was all nerves, jumpy as a young deer. He drank four, five shots.' Tadeusz tipped his hand, mimicking how fast they'd gone down. 'At first, he wouldn't say a word. Finally, he grabbed hold of me,' he said, gripping Janusz by the forearm. 'And he said, "*Tadeusz – all my life, people have been fucking me around. Now it's my turn*".'

'What did he mean by that?' asked Janusz.

'No idea,' said Tadeusz. 'He wouldn't say any more. Next thing I hear, someone's spotted him on the bus to Gdansk. He tells them he's off to live in London – and if he ever comes back it will be driving a BMW.'

Janusz relit his cigar, hoping that Tadeusz would never find out that Adamski's scheme to get rich ran to blackmail and drug dealing.

'A week later, there's a story in the *Baltic Daily*,' said Tadeusz, his voice so low Janusz had to lean close to hear him. 'An old man called Witold Struk who lived outside town, has been found lying at the bottom of his own cellar steps – dead.' He spoke haltingly. 'The front door was open, but there's nothing missing, so the *policja* decide it was an accident.'

Janusz struggled to take in what Tadeusz was telling him. Mystification must have been written all over his face, because the older man tapped a finger on the table between them and said slowly, as though to a child, 'The week before Struk died, everyone saw the advertisement he put in the local paper. He was looking for a buyer for some antique furniture.' He watched the light dawn on Janusz's face. He leaned forward and continued in a whisper. 'Struk died the *very same night* that Pawel came in here talking like a crazy person.'

Janusz froze. Did Adamski *murder* the old guy? He remembered what Nowak had told him – that Adamski roughed up someone who'd refused to sell his antique furniture. He glanced over his shoulder, to check no-one was listening, but found the place nearly empty now, and the barman leaning on the counter reading a paper, yawning.

'You think Pawel killed him,' he said in a murmur.

'Not deliberately, no,' said Tadeusz shaking his head. 'Pawel wouldn't do such a thing.' He sighed. 'But maybe he lost his temper and somehow it . . . led to Struk's accident.'

Or maybe, thought Janusz, he hit the old man over the head with a baseball bat and shoved him down the stairs.

'Did you tell the police?'

'I couldn't do that to Pawel,' said Tadeusz, in a whisper. 'In any case, it's not as if I had any proof.'

The two men fell silent for a moment, then Tadeusz leaned forward. 'The thing is,' he said in a meaningful whisper, 'the police weren't really interested – everyone round here was glad to see the back of Struk.'

'Why, what did he do that made him so unpopular?'

'Witold Struk was an *esbek*.'

Janusz eyebrows shot up. So this Struk character had worked for *Sluzba Bezpieczenstwa*, Communist Poland's hated secret police, the equivalent of the East German Stasi. If you were considered an enemy of the regime, it was the SB who tapped your phone and read your mail, who bribed or bullied friends, neighbours, land-ladies, to turn informer against you. And the knock at the door in the middle of the night that every Pole dreaded back then invariably came on the orders of the local *Sluzba Bezpieczenstwa* office.

Janusz became aware of an eager expression in Tadeusz's faded blue eyes.

'So when you see Pawel, will you let him know that the police have officially declared Struk's death an acci-dent?' he asked. Janusz stared at him. 'And tell him it's safe to come home?'

Just in time, Janusz remembered his role as Adamski's supposed friend. 'Of course,' he said. 'The trouble is, I seem to have lost touch with him. Do you know anyone who might have his new phone number, or address?'

The older man sunk back into his seat. 'No, nobody at all,' he said. 'As far as I know, I was his only friend.'

Twenty-One

Streaky agreed with Kershaw that Hurley might prove more cooperative if the interview took place in the nick, outside his comfort zone.

Kershaw had played it down when she called to ask him to come in. 'We're just crossing the t's and dotting the i's,' she said, putting on a singsong bored voice. 'You know, routine police paperwork . . .'

'Should I be calling my solicitor?' he asked with a nervous laugh, and she chuckled along.

'Listen, Alex, obviously you're *completely entitled* to legal representation.' She paused, letting a note of doubt creep into her voice. 'But, to be honest, I didn't have you down as the kind of guy who'd even *have* a solicitor.' If he got the impression that bringing a brief along might put him under some sort of suspicion, well, that would be unfortunate, but it was absolutely not her intention.

Streaky told Kershaw he'd be sitting in on the interview.

'I'm not going to say a word,' he said as they walked

down to the basement of the nick, 'But after half an hour the little fucker will be so spooked he'll be spilling his guts just to get away from me.'

'The time is 11.30 a.m. on March 30th. I am Detective Constable Natalie Kershaw and I am interviewing – Alex, please give your full name and date of birth.'

'Uh, Alex Richard Hurley, 21.3.82.'

'Alex, can you confirm for the purposes of the tape that you do not want a solicitor present for the interview?' She spoke flatly, with the air of someone going through the bureaucratic motions.

'That's right,' he said in a faint voice.

Kershaw consulted her notebook. 'Also present is – Detective Sergeant, er, Alvin Bacon.' *Alvin?* she thought, *who knew?*

Streaky, sitting to Kershaw's left and slightly back from the table, produced a paperclip from his pocket and keeping his eyes levelled on Alex Hurley, started to straighten it out. Hurley stared at him nervously, his expression turning to one of horror as Streaky proceeded to use the length of wire methodically to clean his teeth, somehow managing to imbue this simple, if disgusting, procedure with a brooding menace.

Hurley had expected a friendly chat and a chocolate biscuit. Instead, he found himself in a real police interview room stinking of Dettol, facing the girl detective, who'd suddenly gone all cold and serious, and a red-faced gorilla who was coming on like a scary cop out of some movie set in Mississippi – the kind that ended with the camera panning away as the victim is gang-raped in the cellblock showers by whooping Hells Angels.

Not bringing a solicitor had been a big mistake.

'So, Alex,' said Kershaw, giving him a bright and transparently insincere smile, 'when would you say you first noticed that Derek and Milo were leaving the key to security behind front desk for each other to pick up?'

'I . . . I didn't know they were doing that,' he said, showing her his palms. She left a pause, while Streaky gazed at something on the point of the paperclip he had dug out from between his rear molars, before once again locking his malevolent glare on Alex.

'According to the rosters, you're usually on night shift twelve days every month, right?'

'Ye-es.'

'And you've worked at the Waveney for three and a half years?'

He nodded, keeping his eyes fixed on hers, trying not to look at the scary ginger bloke.

'And how far from where you sit at front desk is the security pigeonhole, would you say?'

'Four or five metres?'

'Actually, it's only *one and a half* metres!' she said in a *'fancy that!'* tone of voice. 'I measured it.'

Streaky made a noise between a sigh and growl, like someone who couldn't wait for the talking to end so he could get his rubber truncheon out.

'By my calculations, there were more than 500 occasions when you were on front desk and Milo or Derek toddled past carrying a jiffy bag and popped it into the security pigeonhole,' she said fixing him with a curious look. 'But you say you never noticed what was going on? Would you describe yourself as *visually impaired*, Alex?'

He shook his head, then a look of cunning flashed

across his face. 'Here's the thing,' he said, a little of his previous self-importance returning. 'The security pigeon-hole is behind me,' he gestured over his shoulder, 'and, anyway, I'm always really busy with people checking out around that time.'

Gotcha, fuckwit. 'What time would that be, Alex?' asked Kershaw. He opened his mouth and then, realising he had dropped a bollock, closed it again.

'So you *have* noticed Milo and Derek going to and from the pigeonhole at 6 a.m.,' she said. 'Do you really expect me to believe you never noticed what they were doing? Never said, "What's with the jiffy bag, guys?"' She heard Streaky emit a derisive snort. 'Never once been tempted – in *three and a half years* – to check out what was inside?' Her voice dripped with polite incredulity. Alex just shrugged.

She sat back again, dropped her eyes to her notes, exchanging a little look with Streaky out of the corner of her eye. *Yeah, yeah, I know: catch him out in a provable lie.*

'Tell me, Alex, have you ever entered the security office?'

'Er, yes . . . now and again. It's part of my management training to monitor all areas front and back of house.'

'But that wouldn't include rifling through the filing cabinet that holds the CCTV tapes?'

'No, of course not,' he said, with a firm shake of the head.

God, he was properly thick, thought Kershaw.

'You see, we're running forensic tests on the cabinet and the tapes themselves, and if you *had* touched them,

269

the CSI team are going to find your fingerprints all over the place.'

At the mention of fingerprints, his face froze for a moment, and then crumpled, like a seven-year-old who'd just lost the egg-and-spoon race.

'We know for a fact, Alex, that *somebody* went into that cabinet and stole some VHS tapes. Not just any old tapes, either – the ones that showed the girl going up to the room with the suspect just before she died.' She left a beat. 'So if we find prints on that cabinet that have no business being there, we're going to assume they belong to the man who tied her up, raped and killed her.' Okay, the last bit was her own scenario, but judging by Alex's sudden sweaty pallor it did the job.

Kershaw could feel her pulse ticking in her throat. She didn't think for a nanosecond that Alex was the killer, but it was crystal clear that the little creep had *something* to hide. She looked down at her notes, giving him time to work out the horrible catch-22 he was in. The only way he could prove he *hadn't* been in the lift with the girl would be to hand over the tapes, but that would mean admitting it was him who nicked them.

She leaned forward, elbows on the table, hands loosely clasped. 'Listen, Alex,' she said, with something of the old mateyness in her voice. 'You strike me as someone who's never been in any sort of trouble' – he nodded rapidly – 'so I'm wondering if what's happened here is that someone has talked you into doing something, without you having *any idea* what you were getting yourself into.'

Alex's eyes flickered round the interview room – clearly thinking it over.

Finally, in a small voice, he said, 'I don't want to lose my job.'

Kershaw smelled blood in the water.

'I don't see why you *should* lose your job, Alex, so long as you're totally honest with us now,' she said, crossing her ankles beneath the desk. 'Did you take the key from the pigeonhole after Milo left it there that morning?'

He nodded miserably.

'For the benefit of the tape, Alex Hurley is nodding his head,' she said. 'Then you used it to get into security, where you pulled out the VHS tapes for the lift CCTV, and made the logbook entries saying the cameras were out of order.'

'Yes.'

'So where are those tapes now?'

'I haven't got them,' he burst out desperately, 'But I swear, it wasn't me in the lift with the girl.'

'So what did you do with them?' She felt a needle of panic – if the silly little twat had destroyed them, they'd be mullered.

Alex seemed to clam up again, but at that moment Streaky threw his paperclip on the floor and stood up, breathing hard through his mouth.

Alex looked up at him, and emitted a single whimper.

'I gave them to Andrew Treneman,' he said.

Twenty-Two

The Waveney Thameside's manager proved to be rather more slippery a customer than Hurley. When Kershaw phoned the hotel, she couldn't even get past Treneman's secretary to talk to the guy, let alone get him down the nick for a chat. She left three messages for him throughout the morning, and was starting to wonder whether she should just drive down there and doorstep him, when his solicitor phoned. Treneman clearly wasn't short of a bob or two: Dearbourne, Bunch and Hassock was a blue-chip firm known for its unstinting work on behalf of the deserving rich: if Godfrey Dearbourne had ever come across the phrase *pro bono* he probably thought it was something to do with the gazillionaire rock star.

'I simply won't have my client hounded in this way, Detective *Constable*,' said Dearbourne, putting a none-too-subtle emphasis on her rank, 'I really must insist on talking to your Inspector to discuss whatever it is you've been calling Mr Treneman about.' She let the silly old buffer go on like this for a bit, his approach a familiar combo of bluster, bullying and legalese designed to frighten her, before deciding it was time to get a word in.

'It's unfortunate that your client has decided not to cooperate with a very serious police inquiry, Mr Dearbourne,' she said. 'He is well aware of the suspicious death of a young woman in his hotel five days ago – a case which might very well evolve into a murder investigation – and I'm afraid that we now have reason to believe he is deliberately concealing a crucial piece of evidence.'

'*Concealing crucial evidence?* I hardly think so, Constable,' said Dearbourne, with a condescending chortle. 'Mr Treneman runs one of London's top hotels, he's invited to the Queen's Garden Party, for goodness' sake – he's hardly a gangster!'

'No, of course not,' said Kershaw, chuckling along. 'But if the press get wind of the latest development on the case, I'm afraid his days of patting corgis will be a distant memory.' Dearbourne fell silent. She continued, 'I've just taken a statement from a hotel employee who will swear in court that your client, his boss, instructed him to steal CCTV footage from hotel security – footage that we believe shows the victim with our prime suspect.'

Dearbourne had suddenly gone very quiet, and she couldn't resist adding, '"*Five Star Hotel Chief Steals Murder Tape*" is quite a grabby headline, don't you think?' When he spoke again his tone was businesslike, but a whole lot more respectful: 'I'll get back to you within the hour.'

Janusz was awoken by the pealing of Gorodnik's church bells calling the faithful to morning Mass. *Da dong da da dong* ting . . . *Da dong da da dong* ting . . . the final tinny note the telltale sign of a cracked bell.

He told the landlady he'd skip breakfast, and asked for directions to Kosyk, the hamlet the other side of the lake where Witold Struk had lived. After buying an apple pastry from a baker's shop, he sat at a bench on the sunny side of the square to eat it. A trio of squabbling kids trailed by, on their way to school judging by the dark blue uniforms and their dawdling pace. They looked about twelve or thirteen – *Bobek's age*, he thought suddenly.

As he ate, he looked over the landlady's hand-drawn map showing the three-kilometre walk to Struk's place. Tadeusz had told him that the house was up for sale and the agent, patently surprised and delighted to hear from a potential buyer, had agreed to show him around that morning. Janusz wasn't entirely sure what he might gain from visiting the house – but he had some idea of getting to the bottom of Adamski's supposed career as an antique dealer.

He balled the paper bag and rose to post it in a litter bin. *Come on*, he told himself, *you think you can unearth some dazzling piece of evidence to prove that Adamski murdered Struk* – a fantasy that ended with the bastard doing life in a Polish jail.

The footpath cut through ancient broadleaf woodland, and emerged half an hour later onto the sandy shore of a lake. Its surface quivered like mercury in the morning light, reflecting the chalk stripes of young birch trees on the opposite bank. Janusz paused for a moment, listening to the water whisper and chuckle in the reeds. Then a terrific *Bang!* reverberated off the water, making him drop instinctively to his knees. His gaze scanned the opposite bank wildly. *Was some fucker shooting at him?* The second bang, further away this time, sent a flock of birds flapping out of the trees in the distance. He straightened and dusted the grit from his palms, grinning sheepishly – it was just some farmer, out shooting crows or foxes. If he didn't want a backside full of buckshot, he'd better keep his eyes peeled.

Struk's house stood up above the lake, surrounded by run-to-seed farmland, a good half-hour walk from the nearest house. Old SB men probably didn't do a lot of socialising with the neighbours, Janusz reflected. Under communism, the *nomenklatura*, the chosen few who worked for the regime, were considered traitors to Poland, and the SB had been the most hated of all, despised more even than the *milicja* or the gorillas of ZOMO.

Long and low with a steeply pitched roof, Struk's house was the sort of place a rich farmer might have built a couple of hundred years ago. Now it looked neglected and melancholy, its carved and painted wooden shutters split and down to the bare wood in places, the traditional gabled porch sagging between classical pillars. As Janusz mounted the steps he saw that one of the double doors stood ajar – the agent must have already arrived.

In the pentagonal lobby, three panelled doors led into the rest of the house, and as Janusz hesitated, wondering which to choose, one of them swung open, and the agent appeared, dusting his hands off on a handkerchief.

'I've been opening a few windows, trying to get some fresh air into the place,' he said, offering his hand in

275

greeting. 'No one's been in here since the owner passed away, so the place is a bit musty.'

His eyes slid over Janusz's bruises. 'You said you were over from London – is it a holiday home you're looking for?' he asked, showing him into the main salon.

'A holiday home, yes,' agreed Janusz. 'I did my national service in a camp not far from here, and I always hoped to buy a place in the Lakes one day.'

The agent, who looked to be about the same age as Janusz, grinned and raised an eyebrow. 'Reckon you could still re-assemble a stripped Kalashnikov?' Both men started miming the procedure that a thousand repetitions had burned into their memory, each bringing his imaginary AK47 up to the shoulder, ready to fire, at almost the same instant. After sharing a sheepish grin, they resumed their roles.

The high ceilings and long windows of the main salon reminded Janusz of his grandmother's house, but that was where the similarity ended. Struk had wallpapered the room decades ago with chocolate- and tan-striped wallpaper, faded now and peeling along the seams, and replaced the traditional woodstove with a garish seventies-era fireplace made of yellow stone with a beaten copper surround. In spite of the open window, the smell of boiled cabbage and the liniment old men rub on arthritic joints lingered in the room.

'There are four good-sized bedrooms and a converted loft,' said the agent. 'It's a pretty good price for one of these old manor houses – an hour closer to Gdansk and you'd be looking at twice as much.'

Janusz picked up an expensive-looking ashtray sawn out of a heavy lump of multicoloured glass. 'I heard some gossip that the guy who lived here used to be an SB man?'

The agent nodded, 'I heard the same. But that's no bad thing: people round here will be so grateful to get a new neighbour I'm sure they won't object to any renovations or extensions.'

He was probably right: many people, especially those old enough to remember life under Communism, still reviled those who had done the regime's dirty work, feeling that they had gone unpunished. Janusz had felt that way, too, once, but these days he found himself agreeing with the Renaissance Party: the priority was the economy, the future – not endlessly raking over the past.

'I like it so far,' he told the agent. 'Would you mind if I took a look round on my own? You're probably busy, and I'd like to spend some time getting a feel of the place.'

The agent handed over the key without hesitation. 'No problem, just hand it in at the office when you get back to town, and give me a bell to let me know what you think?' He made the irritating and unnecessary hand-to-ear gesture that Oskar was so fond of.

As the sound of his car faded away, Janusz stood with his hands in his coat pockets gazing around the living room, trying to picture the old man's life. When Struk had worked for the SB, back in the seventies and eighties, the revolving chair and sofa upholstered in beige PVC, along with that hideous fireplace, would have been the height of fashion, and the huge television cutting-edge technology. Janusz's eye fell on something he hadn't seen in twenty-five years: a music centre – turntable, radio and cassette deck combined in a metre-long case. Under its dusty Perspex lid a record lay on the turntable, and beside it, an empty album sleeve – 'Beach Party' by James Last.

Janusz could imagine the parties Struk would have hosted here for his fellow *apparatchiks*, back in the good old days, while everyone else queued to buy flour. Caspian caviar on *blini*, ice clinking in the Cinzano as they danced.

But the path trodden into the carpet between the swivel chair and the TV bore witness to Struk's friendless and solitary final years. His wire-rimmed spectacles lay where he'd left them on a coffee table, the lenses sticky-looking and furred with dust, one of the arms held on with Sellotape. Janusz couldn't help but feel a whisper of pity for the old man.

So where was the antique furniture Struk had advertised in the local paper? After a quick survey of the ground floor revealed nothing, Janusz tried upstairs. But after working his way through every room in the house, he couldn't find a single piece that pre-dated the seventies. Then he remembered the agent saying something about a loft. At the rear of the first floor hallway a modern-style fire door opened onto a narrow staircase made of varnished pine. At the top, he emerged, not into the dark junk-filled space he'd expected, but into a room so bright it made him squint.

Two huge windows set between the rafters of the sloping roof flooded the long room with light. The reason was plain – the whitewashed walls were lined with dozens, no, *scores* of framed paintings. They all appeared to be landscapes, painted in watercolour, and on closer

278

examination he found that each bore the tiny, neat initials 'WS' in the bottom right-hand corner. They weren't bad, Janusz decided – the work of a mildly gifted amateur. But as he went from picture to picture, he felt a growing murmur of disquiet.

Witold Struk had painted *exactly the same scene*, over and over again – a green-painted wooden *dacza*, like a house in a fairy tale, encircled by birch trees, on the bank of a lake. There were never any people in sight, and the *dacza*'s curtains were always drawn. The only variations were the weather conditions, and slight changes in the artist's vantage point.

Janusz stood staring at one, eyes screwed up as though trying to work out a difficult quadratic equation. It had been painted in high summer, with the birch trees in full shimmering leaf, the surface of the lake a milky blue. As in all the others, the composition drew the eye to the *dacza*, its windows curtained, showing not a glimmer of life. He couldn't explain why, but the pictures seemed to radiate a brooding menace. The house itself was unremarkable but there was something in the fixity of the artist's gaze – the way he always placed the *dacza* dead centre, in its tunnel of trees – almost as though viewing it down the barrel of a gun.

Janusz turned away, defeated. Trying to decipher Struk's artistic obsession wasn't going to help him discover why Adamski killed the old man.

Returning to the ground floor, he found another modern-style door set into the wall of the kitchen. It looked like it might lead to the cellar – where Tadeusz said Struk's body had been found. The door was locked, but its wooden frame, dotted with woodworm, was freshly splintered – perhaps the police had forced it to gain access. He inserted the blade of his penknife between door and frame, and the honeycombed timber easily gave way with a puff of dust. Inside, an old ironwork staircase led down into the darkness.

As the door swung closed behind him, Janusz found the light switch on the wall and flicked it up and down. Nothing. He sparked a flame from his lighter and, feeling his heart bumping against his chest wall, descended cautiously into the subterranean gloom.

At the foot of the stairs, he dropped to a crouch and started to sweep the lighter flame in an arc across the concrete floor. A metre and a half out from the bottom step, he found what he was looking for – a dark brown stain the size of his spread hand, soaked indelibly into the concrete. The last remaining trace of Witold Struk. Looking back at the staircase he calculated the trajectory of a falling body, and decided that the position of the bloodstain fitted exactly with Struk falling – or being pushed – from the top of the stairs.

In the centre of the cellar, the massive outline of a desk loomed out of the darkness. Making out an anglepoise lamp craned over its surface Janusz fumbled along the cord and flipped the switch.

Using the lamp as a torch, he tracked it over the desk's grey metal surface. To his surprise, the pool of light revealed wire trays filled with papers, and a desk-tidy bristling with freshly sharpened pencils. A fountain pen lying across an old-fashioned blotter looked as though it had been left there moments before, and sitting beside it was an early digital calculator the size of a house brick. It was clear from the lack of dust that the desk and its contents were in regular use – but why would Struk set up his study in the cellar when he had rooms to spare upstairs?

He picked up a black plastic nameplate from the desk's front edge. The gold letters spelled out '*Lieutenant Witold Struk, Sluzba Bezpieczenstwa – Dzial Trzy.*' So, Struk had worked in the SB's infamous Department Three, which had spearheaded the surveillance, imprisonment and torture of those who campaigned for democracy. Janusz felt his pulse jumping unpleasantly in his throat. Righting a photo frame that lay face down on the desk, he examined the two age-bleached photographs it held under the light. One was a black and white shot of the young Struk dressed in Army uniform, striking a Stakhanovite pose in Moscow's Red Square, no doubt taken during his SB training. The other, colour this time, showed him upright behind his desk in a high-ceilinged office, while a woman, out of focus, typed in the background. By this time, he wore spectacles and his hair had turned steely grey.

Thirty years or more separated the portraits, but one thing remained unchanged: Struk's piercing gaze, which burned out at the viewer untainted by any trace of humour or self-doubt.

Swinging the light around to the wall behind the desk, Janusz found it lined with damp-mottled propaganda posters he recognised from his youth. The nearest one showed a girl in the green shirt and red tie of the Union of Polish Youth, driving a combine harvester, her face a rictus of near-manic socialist resolve. Next to her, atop a battered oak filing cabinet, a brass bust of Vladimir Ilyich Lenin cast a monstrous shadow up across the wall and ceiling.

Janusz wiped a line of sweat from his hairline. When the regime had finally crumbled, leaving its lackeys scrambling to dump, burn or shred the evidence of their crimes, this bastard had *rescued* every possible memento of his traitorous career to create a shrine to Communist rule.

He pulled out the swivel chair from beneath the desk and lowered himself into it, shivering a little now, despite his greatcoat. The bizarre tableau had erased at a stroke any trace of sympathy he might have felt for the old man. It was clear that Struk entertained not a single regret about a life spent persecuting his fellow Poles.

The contents of Struk's desk were a disturbing snapshot of a busy SB office in the early eighties. In one drawer, Janusz found copies of confiscated pro-democracy *samizdat*, together with a file of arrest warrants for the group of students who'd been caught printing them. He couldn't bring himself to read the transcripts of their interrogations, but a black and white photograph of a skinny young man pinned to one of them drew his unwilling gaze like a magnet. One of the boy's eyes was darkened and ballooned to a slit, but what hit Janusz like a gut punch was the expression of scared defiance that shone out of his other eye.

He slammed the drawer shut, breathing hard, fighting down the clamour of unwanted images – seeing once again his interrogators in Montepulich, their jeering faces far worse than the kicks and punches. There were certainly plenty of people with good cause to kill Struk, but revenge was unlikely to have been Pawel Adamski's motive – he could only have been a kid back then, after all.

The desk's filing drawer opened with a metallic shriek.

Inside, hanging wallets carried a collection of dreary reports from communist symposia. But as Janusz went to close it, something niggled at him. There appeared to be a mismatch between the depth of the drawer and that of the desk. Pulling the drawer out as far as it would go, he aimed the anglepoise lamp inside. Fitted either side of the drawer back he noticed two small metal brackets with no apparent purpose – except to prevent the drawer opening fully. He fiddled around with them, trying to work out the mechanism, and after a few seconds, they retracted with a dull ping, allowing him to slide the drawer right out.

Cradled in a hidden compartment at the back lay a grey box file. Inside, Janusz found a sheaf of photocopied documents hole-punched and held together with old-fashioned green file ties. Beneath the *Sluzba Bezpieczenstwa* insignia, the front page bore the stamp '*Scisle tajne*' – Most Secret. With a mixture of excitement and foreboding, he started to leaf through the file.

Suddenly, he cocked his head. Was that the squeak of a door, opening overhead? He held his breath. A second or two later, heavy footsteps and the murmur of cautious voices. *Mother of a whore!* He remembered the open windows in the salon. Or maybe the agent had returned with more clients? One thing was certain – he wasn't going to risk finding out.

Janusz took a last look at Comrade Struk's desk. He'd have liked to spend hours going through it, but he'd have to make do with the file that the old bastard had taken such trouble to hide. Folding it in two, he shoved it inside his coat pocket and levered himself carefully upright.

He padded deeper into the shadowed recesses of the cellar, using an outstretched hand to navigate his way, crablike, along the damp walls, praying that there was another way out. The crazed farm girl grinned malevolently from her poster as he passed. As he left the pool of feeble light cast by the desk lamp, the darkness closed around him. Then his boot met something with a tinny clunk.

The voices above fell silent, then one piped up cautiously, interrogatively. Janusz's groping hand found cold metal – an old bedstead. Peering desperately into the gloom, he felt his pupils stretching to maximise the light. He heard the footsteps overhead leave the salon and re-enter the hall. *If they cornered him down here* . . . As he groped his way around the bedstead, he thought he glimpsed a chink of light. And started praying in earnest.

Hail Mary, full of grace, the Lord is with thee . . .

Shuffling forward, eyes stretched wide, he saw it again – a narrow crack of daylight ahead. He made out a pair of rough timber doors. Was it a timber store? That would mean a trapdoor to the outside – if Struk hadn't nailed it permanently shut.

Blessed art thou amongst women . . .

Reaching the doors, he opened them with infinite care, and felt his stomach swoop at the sight of the trapdoor overhead. He reached up to his full height, and holding his breath, used the flats of his hands to push gently at the lid.

Blessed is the fruit of thy womb, Jesus.

It opened as sweetly and silently as if it had been used yesterday, blinding him with an inrush of daylight.

He heard muffled shouts and footsteps hurrying

towards the rear of the house, to the kitchen. Any minute now they'd find the cellar door. Gripping the trapdoor frame with both hands, Janusz put the toe of his boot into a loose bit of brickwork and started to lever himself up.

Holy Mary, Mother of God . . .

A trickle of mortar spilled out of the hole. He straightened his knees, and gripped the edges of the frame firmly.

Pray for us sinners now and at the hour of our death . . .

A strident chirruping shattered the silence – and nearly gave him a heart attack. His mobile phone. He heard shouts – louder than before. They were through the cellar door and had seen the light below. Abandoning all attempts at stealth, he flexed every muscle in his upper body, braced his foot against the wall and heaved. He just managed to get his backside onto the edge of the trapdoor frame, which creaked ominously.

Feet were clattering down the iron stairs at the cellar's far end. Janusz swung his legs out onto some long grass, and scrambled upright. He sprinted for a line of trees that seemed to mark the boundary of the back garden, hurdling a low thicket in his path.

His mobile was still chirping but he dared not stop to shut it off, concentrating on putting as much ground between himself and his pursuers as humanly possible – *or as possible for an old man of forty-five with a cracked rib*, he thought grimly. Beyond the boundary the land sloped sharply down into forest. He barely slowed his pace, running headlong through thickening trees and scrub, praying he wouldn't trip.

Judging by the shouts coming from his rear, the men were outside, and gaining on him. He threw a look behind him, but could see nothing through the trees. Skidding on a thick mulch of last year's leaves he reached the bottom of the slope, and stopped, panting noisily.

He found himself in a densely wooded valley, with his path barred by a stream – a deep one, fast flowing. He looked up and downstream, trying to work out the best way to go. Then he saw a movement through the leaves, some fifty metres away. A middle-aged man wearing old-fashioned hunting garb strolled out of the woods, a bulging game bag slung over his shoulder. He possessed two things that Janusz prized above all else at that moment: a trustworthy face and, crooked over his arm, a great big double-barrelled shotgun.

Janusz shouted, and as the guy turned, loped to meet him, holding his side. '*Prosze pana*, there are two men chasing me,' he panted. 'I think they're gangsters,' he waved back at the hill, 'up there.' The gunman's seamed face grew stern. Without a word, he broke his weapon and slipped two fat red cartridges into its gaping nostrils.

Suddenly, the silhouette of a man appeared up on the crest of the slope, about seventy metres away. Without a word, Janusz's companion swung his gun up, narrowed his eye along the barrel and loosed off a mighty bang. As the smoke cleared, they could make out the figure stumbling back through the trees. Even at this distance, Janusz could see that the man wore a hat.

'I think I winged the bastard,' said the gunman with modest satisfaction, pulling out two fresh cartridges.

Janusz grinned nervously. 'Maybe you'd better not,' he said, putting a hand on his arm, as the guy made to reload the shotgun. 'You know what the police are like these days about citizens defending themselves.'

The man frowned, but returned the cartridges to their pouch, shaking his head. 'You're probably right,' he grumbled, 'nothing is sacred any more.'

Janusz scanned the crest of the hill again, but all was still. Seconds later came the distant screech of a car burning rubber on the road above. His breathing was almost back to normal when the mobile started chirping again.

He flicked it open. '*Czesc*?' he said wearily.

'It's me, sisterfucker,' a voice boomed. 'Why aren't you answering your phone?'

Twenty-Three

Kershaw had to hand it to Godfrey Dearbourne. Once she'd told him that a member of Andrew Treneman's own staff had fingered him as the tape thief, he moved with impressive speed. Less than an hour after their chat, the nick's Uniform Skipper was calling up to let her know that Dearbourne was at the desk, asking for Detective Constable Kershaw – no demand to *'speak to your DI'* this time, she noted.

Now she sat across the table from him in the interview room, arms folded. Dearbourne opened his briefcase and extracting a bulky package, placed it delicately on the table between them, like it might contain a very large stool sample. Then he flashed a set of perfect veneers, the exact same shade as his creamy Oxford-weave shirt, and unleashed a tsunami of the famous Dearbourne charm. Kershaw was so keen to get her hands on the contents of the envelope that she didn't pay much attention, but she got the gist. *Mr Treneman wishes to convey his sincere apologies . . . moment of madness . . . understand-able fear of blackmail . . . etc etc.*

'I don't need to tell *you* how seriously the CPS takes conspiracy to pervert the course of justice,' said Kershaw. 'I'm not a legal expert, but I seem to recall there's no maximum sentence – it's entirely up to the judge?'

Dearbourne twinkled at her. 'I am sure that any judge would take into account my client's desire to cooperate fully with the police, once he realised the seriousness of the investigation,' he said clasping his hands in front of him. 'It is our sincere hope, Detective Constable, that now Mr Treneman has provided the items in question, you might be minded to show some consideration of the, uh . . . *awkward* position he found himself in *vis-a-vis* the tapes.'

Yeah, I can imagine what that position might be, thought Kershaw, seeing an image of herself and Ben Crowther snog-ging in the lift – *I nearly ended up in it myself the other night.*

She was suddenly sick to death of Dearbourne's oily charm, the Philippe Patek watch that probably cost what she earned in a year. Unfolding her arms, she picked up the envelope.

'You had better advise your client to take some urgent personal leave from the hotel while we pursue our inves-tigation,' she said, standing up and fixing him with a look. 'And at the risk of stating the obvious, if Mr Treneman has any contact whatsoever with the witness Alex Hurley, he'll find himself in even more serious trouble than he is already.'

As porn videos went, thought Kershaw, it wasn't exactly a fine example of the form – apart from the crap tape quality, there was very little plot and zero character development.

At 11.38 p.m., according to the time code, a man in a suit – aka the Waveney Thameside's manager, Andrew Treneman – followed a short blonde girl wearing a clinging animal-print dress – unidentified sex worker – into the North Lift. He leaned against the rear wall, and she stood to one side, each ignoring the other. But soon after the lift started moving, Treneman reached out to hit a button, bringing it to a sudden halt. The girl turned, and without any preliminaries, dropped to her knees, unzipped his fly and started giving him a BJ. *Eeeow!* Kershaw watched the bobbing blonde head and Treneman's gurning face, one hand planted on the sidewall to steady himself, with a kind of queasy fascination.

According to Alex, it had long been rumoured among the hotel's staff that Treneman got freebies from working girls in return for letting them tout for trade in the hotel bar. But Kershaw still couldn't work out why the manager of a five-star hotel would take the insane risk of getting blown *in the lift*? The advice 'get a room' had never seemed more appropriate. Derek and Milo might not be the brightest stars in the security firmament, but they could easily have been watching their screens at this moment, as could anyone passing through security. Then, as Treneman reached climax, he looked straight up into the camera lens – and Kershaw understood. The lift was the one place where control freak Treneman let himself off the leash – and the risk of getting caught was part and parcel of the thrill.

Kershaw sped through the rest of the tape from the North Lift camera. When the time code reached 1.10

p.m., just after hat man had checked in, she pressed play, aware of a pulse starting to quiver in her throat. What if, after all the graft she'd done to recover the tape, it turned out he'd snuck Kozlowska up the back stairs?

The first people into the lift were the pissed-up office types she'd seen on the lobby cam. A second later, one of the guys reached out to hit the button for their floor. But a split second later, it became clear he'd been pressing the 'doors open' button, because in walked someone else: a girl with long dark hair. *Justyna Kozlowska*. She stood there alone for what seemed like an age while Kershaw stared at the screen, worrying at the nail on her forefinger. Then the guy in the hat sauntered in. But as he turned to hit the button, Kershaw groaned out loud – between the positioning of the camera high on the wall, and the fact that he was stood right next to the doors, the shot was ninety percent fucking hat.

Until he glanced up for a split-second, probably to check the floor indicator. She rewound, and hit pause. *Gotcha!*

Twenty-Four

After their little woodland *dramat*, Janusz's shotgun-toting saviour introduced himself as Krzyzstof Bielski.

A farmer with arable land on the other side of the lake, pan Bielski had been out shooting rabbits for the pot when their paths crossed. He showed a refreshing lack of curiosity as to why Janusz should find himself being chased by gangsters, but as they parted, Janusz couldn't resist asking, 'What made you trust me, *panie kolego*?'

The farmer furrowed his leathery face. 'It's true you speak Polish like a foreigner,' he said at last. 'But you've got an old-fashioned face.'

As he headed back through the woodland, Janusz felt strangely calm for a man who'd just had such a narrow escape. Without being quite aware how it got there, he found himself phone in hand, ringing Marta's number. The long, lazy Polish ring tone sounded half a dozen times before he heard his wife's voice. The answer machine. He left a message saying that he was in Poland unexpectedly on business, and if he took the train down to Warsaw tomorrow, could he spend some time with Bobek? Remembering that he'd put the phone down on her the last time they spoke, he made a big effort to sound friendly.

As rain started to patter softly on the leaves, Janusz turned up his collar and tried to make sense of what had happened up at Struk's house.

Maybe Adamski had somehow followed him from Gdansk, or perhaps one of the locals had alerted him, told him someone was sniffing around in Gorodnik. Either way, Adamski appeared to be deadly serious. God only knew where Weronika was – safe in London, Janusz fervently hoped.

As Janusz arrived on Gorodnik's outskirts he remembered that the Hotel Pomorski's main entrance opened directly onto the town square. If Adamski and his cronies had found out where he was staying, the square offered them a dozen vantage points from which to watch the front door. He stopped to pull out his tourist map.

The old wooden door he found set in a high wall at the back of the hotel looked like it hadn't been used in a hundred years. At first, it wouldn't budge but a couple of good shoulder shoves opened a gap wide enough for him to squeeze through. He picked his way past a discarded plastic table and a pile of broken chairs, eyes fixed on a solid-looking double door at the rear of the hotel. As he got closer, he grinned – its single lock was an old Yale. A minute later he was creeping up the stairs to his room having stowed the homemade bump key he always carried back in his wallet.

After making himself comfortable on the bed, Janusz

started examining the file of SB documents recovered from Struk's hiding place. They all dated from the early 1980s and each document carried the heading '*Operational File number 37909/07*', suggesting they'd all been extracted from the same SB dossier.

It took him a while to decipher the documents, which were couched in the opaque language beloved of the secret services. Opponents of the Communist regime whom Struk and his comrades had under clandestine surveillance were described as 'targets'. Aside from the inevitable phone taps, most of the information on these unwitting victims appeared to come from people designated by the initials *TW*, followed by a codename. Trying to decode the mysterious yet familiar initials sent Janusz half mad with frustration, until his middle-aged brain suddenly relented, delivering the answer. After democracy came to Poland, the media had been full of stories about newly opened secret files, and in them, TW had stood for *Tajny Wspolpracownik* – 'Secret Collaborator'. These were ordinary people, recruited – whether by bribery or coercion – as informers, freelance spies able to move unsuspected among their fellow Poles.

The documents all appeared to relate to a single SB informer, recruited in 1981, referred to throughout only as *TW Sroka* – Secret Collaborator 'Magpie'. His case officer had been Lieutenant Witold Struk. From what Janusz could glean, Magpie had been a regular source of high-level information regarding pro-democracy activists: their clandestine meetings, planned strikes and demos, as well as their mistresses, drinking problems and gambling habits.

Magpie's job clearly brought him into frequent contact

with dissidents in both *Solidarnosc* and the church, but Janusz could find no clue to his identity or even his occupation. The informer might have been anybody – a male prostitute, a piano tuner, even a priest . . . the SB had been an equal opportunities employer. Magpie's targets, too, were only ever called by their cryptonyms; names such as 'hunter' and 'redhair' clearly referred to personal traits, while 'cutter' and 'blackboard' appeared to hint at the victim's occupation.

One of Magpie's victims, a target called *Papiezek*, earned more entries than all the rest put together. The intelligence on him was invariably cross-referenced to several other files, and several entries recorded Struk's persistent demands that Magpie produce more detailed information on Target *Papiezek*'s activities. He was clearly a well-connected figure, but once again Janusz could glean no clues as to his true identity. *Papiezek* could be a surname, but that was hardly likely. The name could also be taken to mean 'little pope'. Perhaps he was a union leader or intellectual given to long speeches – the codename a mocking reference to his 'preaching'.

Towards the end of the sheaf, Janusz found a series of entries, beginning in May 1985, which recorded Struk's weekly meetings with Magpie and the delivery of his *'wyplata'* – his wages. The SB often paid their informers sweeteners, usually in foreign currency, to reward them for the risk they were running and to make them financially dependent. Struk, however, appeared to find his role as Magpie's paymaster beneath him. *'Lieutenant Struk once again requests that the delivery of TW Magpie's wage packets be handled by a more junior officer'* was a typical entry.

Several entries in similar vein followed, and then, on 19 August 1985, Janusz came across a new twist in the story.

'Lieutenant Struk wishes to record his respectful recommendation that in the light of Magpie's character and unsocialist attitudes, the Service should consider discontinuing his wage packets and ending its relationship with him.'

Lieutenant Struk evidently nurtured a dislike of the Magpie so strong he was willing to risk his own position to attack him. Perhaps he had even been the one to name him after the greedy bird, infamous in folklore for stealing shiny baubles.

The final act of the drama came on 11 September 1985. The entry said simply: *'Lieutenant Struk will henceforth relinquish his duties as case officer and take over the reorganisation of filing systems for SB Office 371. Lieutenant Grazyc will assume responsibility for Lt Struk's contacts, and for future delivery of TW Magpie's wage packets.'*

Janusz sat back on the bed frowning. He was no expert on the SB hierarchy, but it was pretty obvious that Comrade Struk would have viewed his transfer – from managing an important informant to tinkering with filing systems back at the office – as a big fat kick in the teeth for a loyal servant of the struggle. Magpie appeared to be more important to the SB top brass than one of its own senior officers.

He closed the file and rubbed his eyes. What had he learned from it all, anyway? He still couldn't discern any possible link between Adamski and Struk.

As he fiddled restlessly with the file ties that held the sheaf of documents together, his eye fell on something he hadn't noticed before. A tiny fragment of paper, clinging to the green string of the file tie. No, not paper, he realised, holding it under the bedside light – thin card. Pale and buff-coloured, the type that medical files used to be written on. There had been a further page, perhaps a cover page, at the front of the bundle, which had been removed. Feeling suddenly bone weary after the day's drama, Janusz leaned against the pillow to mull it over. Within seconds, sleep reached up and grappled him down like a great bear.

When he awoke, the room was almost dark, and according to the phosphorescent hands of his watch, he had slept for more than three hours. A fierce gurgle from his gut reminded him that his last meal had been a breakfast pastry. Gathering the documents together, he stared at them again, willing them to surrender their mysteries. Something stirred in the back of his mind – but in his befuddled state he couldn't quite join the dots. It would have to wait till he'd filled his belly and had a good night's sleep. He scanned the room, looking for somewhere to hide them, but decided to take them with him – he wouldn't put it past the hotel landlady to nose around his room while he was out.

At *Pod Kotkiem*, he burned his tongue forking down a *bigos* that the barman warmed up for him in the microwave, with half a dozen gherkins and the best part of a loaf of light rye on the side.

Once his plate was cleared away, the barman leaned across the counter. 'You chose an exciting time to be in town,' he said, eyes bright with intrigue. 'There's been a *shooting*.'

Taking a cigar out of his tin, Janusz raised his eyebrows politely. 'Really? Hunting accident?'

'No!' said the barman. 'An old woman up at Kosyk was out collecting kindling on the roadside, when she hears a shotgun blast. She thinks nothing of it – but a minute later a man comes running out of the forest, shirt soaked in blood!'

Kurwa! So the shot *had* hit Adamski.

'You're kidding! Where did he go?' he asked, feigning gossipy interest.

'She says he and another man jumped into a car and drove off! The police were in here at lunchtime, asking if any strangers had been in.'

Janusz didn't like the sound of that.

'Did the old girl recognise the guy who got shot?' he asked.

The barman shook his head. 'No, her eyes aren't too good. Everyone's saying it must be gangsters from Gdansk – you know, a drug deal gone wrong.'

After another half hour listening to the barman retell the tale from every possible angle, Janusz asked to borrow the local newspaper and took himself off into a corner. He was half inclined to beat a retreat back to the hotel, but that could look suspicious, and anyway, he was hoping Tadeusz might turn up. He wanted to find out why Struk would spend good money advertising antique furniture when he didn't appear to own any. Three hours and three small beers later, Janusz concluded that the old man was having a night off the sauce. Giving the barman a wave goodnight, he headed out into the darkened alleyway.

Janusz was no more than five metres from the archway leading to the street when two dark-clad figures wearing baseball caps suddenly filled the passageway.

He froze. Then, as one of the men reached inside his jacket, he dropped into a fighter's crouch, throwing a wild uppercut at the one nearest him. A split second later, he found himself lying face down on the ground, half-conscious, with his skull still singing from the impact of a blunt object, and the press of cold steel on his wrists.

Do gangsters use handcuffs? he remembered thinking, before the unmistakable crackle of a radio made him realise that he'd just punched a cop.

Kershaw had experienced her first ever taste of public praise from Streaky in the weekly meeting that afternoon. Okay, it *was* only seven words – 'Good work on the Waveney Thameside case' – but the queasy look on Browning's face was proof, like she needed it, of their rarity value. She'd drawn a big sigh of relief to see that Ben Crowther wasn't in the meeting – the more time that passed before she had to face him, the easier it would be, although every time she checked her phone and saw there was no new message from him, she had to confess to feeling a bit, well, *miffed*. She had no desire to go out with Ben, she told herself – lovely as he was; it would be way too awkward working alongside him. Still, it would have been nice to be asked.

After the meeting, she went to the kitchen to make a brew and bumped into Browning, who was pouring boiling water onto a Chow Mein flavour Pot Noodle. No wonder he was such a pasty little fucker, all the garbage he ate. Remembering their last exchange, when she'd basically called him a brown nose, Kershaw pulled an insincere smile – she really should learn to keep her gob shut – and took a mug off the shelf.

Stirring the evil-smelling Pot Noodle with a knife, Browning asked: 'Want some?'

'Er, no. Thanks, all the same,' she said, suppressing a look of disgust, as she refilled the kettle under the tap.

'Really?' he smirked, 'The word is you can't get enough . . . Chinese,' – she looked up sharply, but his expression was bland. He picked up the steaming carton. 'You have to be careful with Chinese food, though,' he said. 'We were down the pub a couple of nights back, and guess who came in, looking a right state?' He slid her a look. 'Ben Crowther.'

What the f . . . 'Oh yeah?' she said, pulling the teabag tin off the shelf.

'Yeah,' said Browning. 'Apparently he had a crispy duck with all the trimmings the night before . . . but he was *really* regretting it.'

He picked up his steaming Pot Noodle, looked pointedly at her chest, then straight in the face, eyes twinkling with malice. 'Yeah. He said it was minging – if he hadn't been completely wankered he would have sent it back.' With that he sauntered off, leaving her standing there like a dick, a teabag dangling from her fingers.

That dirty fucking . . . She pulled out her phone to check what Ben had said in his text back to her yesterday morning. '*Yeah had fab time 2, c u @office Bxx*'. She couldn't detect any hidden hostility, unless '*see you at office*' could be interpreted as some sort of a veiled threat? She tore a strip of skin from the side of her thumbnail, making it bleed. What next? – '*I screwed Natalie Kershaw*' scrawled on the bog wall?

She told herself to calm down: Browning's jibe about Ben calling her a minger was obviously just spite, but that aside, she had to face facts – the only way the nasty little pervert could have any idea she'd shagged Ben Crowther was if lover boy had let it slip in a moment of bar-room bragging.

Janusz fingered the spongy lump on the top of his skull and watched the police car's headlights illuminate the road ahead through half-closed eyes. His head was pounding after the blow from the cop's baton. The two *policja* had said barely a word to him since they bundled him into the back of the car, but then he could hardly expect friendly chit-chat after the smack in the jaw he'd given the shorter, pudgier one, who was now doing the driving.

What a fucking *idiota* he'd been, lashing out like that. If only he'd remembered that cops wore those stupid bloody baseball caps these days. His mind raced at the prospect of what faced him for assaulting a cop: a prison stretch was surely inevitable.

When they drove straight out of Gorodnik, he thought nothing of it – maybe the town didn't have a proper police station – but what happened next made his stomach turn over. The taller, more senior cop, a bony-faced guy in his fifties, muttered something to the driver, and they turned off the road, taking a narrow dirt track into the birch forest. Janusz's mind started doing somersaults: what the fuck was going on? Were they gonna work him over for the punch he threw – or worse?

After a few minutes, they drew up in a clearing, and the tall cop opened the back door, gestured for Janusz to get out. He obeyed, keeping his cuffed hands visible in front of his body, his eyes glued to the nine millimetre holstered at the cop's hip. Once upright, he said, 'Listen, there's been a big misunderstanding,' spreading his hands as wide as the cuffs would allow. The wind in the trees roared like distant surf, and he wondered wildly if it would be the last sound he heard. The cop dropped his right hand to his side – and took a pack of cigarettes from his pocket.

'Smoke?' he asked. Blinking at the turn of events, Janusz took one, and a light from the cop's brass Zippo.

After taking a leisurely drag on his own fag, the cop produced a dog-eared Polish passport and started flicking through it. Janusz didn't need to see the face on the final page to know it was his; they must have picked it up from the hotel before coming to find him at the bar.

'Listen,' said the cop conversationally, 'We know you took a little tour of Witold Struk's house, pretending to be a buyer.' The guy was surprisingly well spoken, thought Janusz.

He shrugged. 'Well, it's true I'm not looking to buy right now,' he admitted. 'But I am thinking of buying a holiday home round here at some point, so I was curious to see what I might get for my money.'

'*Naprawde*?' said the cop, head on one side. 'I heard it was because Tadeusz Krajewski was bending your ear with some crazy theory about Witold Struk being murdered.'

Shit. That barman must have ears like a bat. Janusz took a drag on his cigarette – no easy manoeuvre with both wrists cuffed – pressing his right forearm into his chest at the same time. He felt the reassuring crackle of the SB documents, still safe in the inside pocket of his coat.

'And the shooting near the Struk place, right after you met the agent there,' said the cop. 'I suppose that was just an unfortunate coincidence?'

'Yeah, I heard about that,' said Janusz, shaking his head, 'but I didn't see anyone running round with a gun while I was at the house, I swear.'

The cop took a drag on his cigarette and blew the smoke out with a sigh. 'How old are you?' he asked, finally.

'Forty-five?' said Janusz, puzzled.

'Old enough to remember the SB, the ZOMO – that whole bunch of bastards, then?'

'Yeah, I remember them.'

The cop tapped ash off his cigarette, 'My father lost his job at Gdansk University for refusing to inform on his students,' he said. 'When the time came for me to apply to university, I found my family was designated undesirable, so I was refused a place.'

Janusz gave a sympathetic nod: it wasn't an uncommon story.

'So, it's like this, *kolego*,' said the cop looking him straight in the eyes. 'Struk was just an old man who fell down the stairs: it happens all the time. We conducted extensive enquiries but found no evidence of foul play.' He threw his spent cigarette down. 'Of course, it's possible somebody *did* give the old bastard a shove.' He ground the butt underfoot. 'But you know what? Maybe the world's a better place with one less *esbek* in it.'

Pulling open the lapel of Janusz's coat, he tucked the passport into his shirt pocket. 'Your little holiday in the Lakes is over. We're taking you to the airport – if you want any of your stuff from the hotel we'll get it sent on to you.'

303

Suddenly remembering his plan to go and see Bobek tomorrow, Janusz felt a blast of disappointment, followed by a back draft of guilt. He'd have to call Marta from the airport and make a grovelling apology.

When they were back in the car, the boss cop craned around and locked his gaze on Janusz. 'My colleague, Osip here, has agreed not to bring charges against you for assaulting a police officer,' he said. 'But if he should change his mind, you're looking at ten years in Mokotow Prison.'

Osip turned and gave Janusz a murderous look, revealing a jaw line that was swollen and already turning an impressive shade of purple.

'So when you do decide to look for that holiday home, it had better not be anywhere round here,' added boss cop. 'I'd try Bulgaria,' he advised, turning to face forward as Osip started up the engine. 'Everyone says it's the next big thing.'

Twenty-Five

The morning after Janusz slugged a Gorodnik cop, Kershaw was standing in her kitchen watching an over-alled engineer fix the boiler, when her mobile rang.

It was her cousin Jason, calling to tell her that Janusz Kiszka's name had popped up on the passenger list of a flight in-bound for Stansted, scheduled to arrive in twenty minutes. Getting Jason, who worked in Special Branch, to slip Kiszka's name onto a watch list after his dawn flit to Poland had probably been the riskiest thing Kershaw had ever done, but she'd told herself that she didn't have the time for the snowstorm of paperwork an official request would involve.

Now, tearing up the M11 in her five-year-old Ford Ka, her eyes kept flicking to the clock on the dashboard. She had no chance of reaching the airport before the plane was due to land, but she was hoping that the watch list mention would get Kiszka a proper grilling, long enough for her to get there before he cleared customs and disappeared. Of course, he *might* simply be heading home to his gaff in Highbury, but after losing him once she wasn't taking any chances.

By the time she reached the terminal, it was fifteen minutes past the flight's scheduled arrival time, so she dumped the car right outside arrivals, hazard lights flashing, threw her Met logbook on the dashboard and raced inside.

Trying to get her breath back – how long had it been since she'd been for a proper run, four, five weeks? – she lurked at the end of the cordon of people waiting outside customs, excited friends and family interspersed with somnolent minicab drivers holding up name placards.

Twenty-five minutes later, she was starting to think she might have missed him, when his craggy mug appeared, towering above the crowd. He wore an old military greatcoat and his only baggage was a pair of carrier bags bulging with booze and cigarette cartons. Although the bruises to his face appeared to be fading, he seemed to have acquired a new lump the size of a crème egg on his right temple.

She scurried alongside him, uninvited, as he made for the exit.

'Welcome back, Mr Kiszka,' she said – a greeting he met with a grunt. 'Listen,' she said to him, scampering to keep up as he lengthened his stride. 'The way I see it you've got two options: come down the station and get stuck in an interview room for hours on end, or, I drive you back to town and we clear up all my questions on the way.' He slowed a little. 'It's a good offer,' she said reasonably. 'An off-the-record chat and a lift home has got to beat a day wasted down the nick.' He came to a halt, sending her a look of hostility tinged with resignation.

She opened the boot for his clinking bags of booze, 'Been stocking up on the vodka, have you?' she asked, smiling, trying to break the ice. 'I don't drink *wodka*,' he growled. 'I don't like the taste.'

She rolled her eyes at his cliff-like back. *Fuck me. This is going to be hard work.*

Kurwa! thought Janusz as he climbed into the tiny car, forty minutes with a stupid little *dziwka* who probably thinks Chopin was French.

Kershaw decided to keep her gob shut till they were off the airport perimeter and on the M11. She kept to the inside lane – if she could just keep her speed down, she'd have more time to grill him.

'There's been a breakthrough on the dead girl found in the Waveney Thameside,' she said. 'Your friend, *Yu-steena Kosh-lov-ska.*' She framed her lips carefully around the unfamiliar sounds to get the pronunciation right this time. She cut her eyes across to Kiszka to see if there was any reaction. *Nada.* 'We've got footage of her in the hotel lift with a man that night.'

Janusz grunted derisively: 'Finally got round to checking the CCTV, did you?' he said, looking out of the window.

Don't rise to the bait, she thought. 'It was harder to get than you might imagine,' she said mildly. 'Anyway, the good news is that we have a clear image of the guy, and it isn't you.'

'No shit,' he said, still looking at the view of Essex. 'I told you that last week.'

He put a cigar to his lips, remembering just in time to ask, 'It's okay if I . . . ?' English people were real health freaks about smoking.

'No problem,' she said, wondering with irritation how

long it would take for the upholstery to lose the pungent smell of cigar smoke.

Even if Kiszka had nothing to do with Justyna's death, Kershaw still had a powerful feeling that he had *something* to hide – and she only had about half an hour to find out what.

'Do you know if Justyna did drugs?' she asked, fiddling with her rear view mirror. 'You know, just the soft stuff, like Ecstasy, that kind of thing?' In its new position, the mirror let her keep an eye on Kiszka's face.

'*Soft* stuff?' Janusz snorted. 'Do you know what psycho-active drugs do to serotonin production in the long term?' Pretending not to notice her mirror gambit, he resolved to stay on his guard and, above all, to keep his temper this time.

Kershaw gripped the steering wheel. 'Well, as a *police officer,* I am fully aware of the dangers of synthetic drugs,' she said. 'But you certainly seem to know a lot about Ecstasy.'

As she accelerated hard to pass a dawdling car, he shot out a hand to grab the strap above his door. *Kurwa!* The girl drove worse than Oskar!

'I read physics and chemistry at university in Poland before I came over here,' he replied, speaking to his window.

Kershaw recalled the pile of *New Scientist* mags in his kitchen. A chemistry degree would certainly come in handy for producing drugs, but then why volunteer the information?

'You see, Justyna died from an overdose of something called PMA,' she said, 'a nasty little drug cooked up by backstreet amateurs.'

'I've never heard of it,' he said, shifting around, trying to make himself comfortable in the tiny seat.

'It's made out of a compound called anethole – ring any bells?'

He shook his head.

'Did Justyna ever talk about taking drugs?' she persisted.

He turned to look at her. 'I would bet my apartment that Justyna never in her life took anything stronger than aspirin,' he said.

My apartment, Kershaw noted – he *owned* that place on Highbury Fields? It had to be worth getting on for a million. All the same, going by his expression, he appeared untroubled by her questions. So what the hell *was* his connection to hat man – and to Justyna's death?

A white van veered in from the outside lane, cutting her up so badly she had to slam the anchors on, before it sped away.

'What about the people she hung out with?' she persisted.

Feeling the car accelerate as the girl pulled into the fast lane, Janusz tightened his grip on the door strap. He didn't answer for a moment, preoccupied with her mention of anethole. It made him think of children's sweets, of all things. *Sherbet? No. Liquorice, for some reason.*

'She didn't strike me as the type to hang out with druggies,' he said finally, which was more or less true – her contact with Adamski had been solely a result of her friendship with Weronika, certainly not a matter of choice.

Already formulating her next line of attack, Kershaw didn't clock the hesitation. When she'd found Kiszka's card in Justyna's mouth, she thought the girl was pointing the finger at her killer. Now she believed that hat man had left it there – either to incriminate his enemy or to send him a twisted message. Either way, it suggested Justyna had been more than just a one-night stand to Kiszka.

'I have to ask you again if Justyna was your girlfriend, Mr Kiszka,' she said, her voice tense with determination. 'It's important to the investigation.'

'I told you before, I only went out with her once, and I never even kissed her.' He turned to face her. 'She was young enough to be my daughter!'

Kershaw had a nasty feeling he was telling the truth.

A moment later, they drew alongside the van that had cut them up. The driver was a grinning Neanderthal, holding what looked like a can of lager. When he saw that it was a girl overtaking him, he started to mime a blowjob, causing the van to weave out of lane. Then he accelerated and the van roared away again, trailing clouds of burnt oil.

Her expression icy calm, Kershaw dropped the car into fourth, making the engine scream. The G-force pressed Janusz back in his seat. *Mother of God!* Had he escaped Adamski just to get killed by a psychotic girl cop?

As the speedo needle crept past ninety, they started to draw level with the van driver. Keeping an eye on the road ahead, Kershaw dipped into the side pocket next to her seat and extracted something. The driver came into view, face gurning with hatred as he mouthed a stream of abuse, before shooting out a hand to give Kershaw the finger. Keeping her expression deadpan, she extended her left hand and dangled her Met issue handcuffs at him. Janusz watched, fascinated, as the guy's mouth fell slackly open, like a broken puppet, before he suddenly disappeared from view. Soon he was no more than a dot in the wing mirror, crawling along in the inside lane.

'Sorry about that,' said Kershaw with an apologetic smile. 'I've got zero tolerance for bad manners.' She put the car back into fifth and pulled over to get into lane for the A406 westbound.

Even if Kiszka hadn't been Justyna's boyfriend, one thing came across loud and clear: he cared about her, and seemed to want to defend her good name.

'If you weren't going out with Justyna, can you really be sure that she wasn't a sex worker?' asked Kershaw, her tone reasonable. 'I mean, she did check into a hotel at midnight with this guy.'

'She was a good girl, she had a degree – she wanted to be a physiotherapist, for Christ's sake,' said Janusz, his voice tense with restrained anger.

'Do you want to see a picture of the guy who checked in with her?' asked Kershaw, as if the idea had just occurred to her.

'Sure,' he said, mastering himself.

She leaned over, and opening the glove box, pulled out the photocopy of the image grab from the videotape. *What harm could it do?* If Kiszka realised the guy had killed Justyna, he might just grass him up. She stared ahead into the traffic, keeping half an eye on his face in the mirror.

Janusz instantly recognised the guy he'd chased along the towpath in Gdansk. So, this was Pawel Adamski: features crowded into the centre of his face, a pursed

311

mouth, and beneath the hat brim, close-set eyes which radiated the arrogant contempt of a man convinced he'd always come out on top.

'Well?' asked Kershaw, unable to read his expression.

Shaking his head, Janusz opened his window a couple of inches and threw out his cigar stub. 'No, I don't know the guy.' If the cops started a hunt for Adamski, it would cause untold complications, and very likely risk Weronika's life, too.

Something in his voice, a hint of strained indifference, told Kershaw he was lying. 'Are you absolutely sure about that?' she asked.

He nodded, then pointed to the guy's head, playing for time. 'What do you call this kind of hat?'

'A "pork pie" hat, I think,' said Kershaw. 'They're supposed to be trendy.'

'*Pork pie?*' said Janusz staring at her in mystification. 'Like those . . .' he searched for a word adequate to describe the cardboard-like pastry horrors with their unnaturally pink contents '. . . *things* they sell in petrol stations?'

'Yeah. I think it's 'cos of the shape,' she said, indicating left to turn into Lea Bridge Road.

'Someone who wears a hat like that, when he should be keeping a low profile,' said Janusz, tapping the photo. 'This bastard thinks he's untouchable.' Visualising his fist smashing into that face, he filed the image away in his head.

The venom in Kiszka's voice made Kershaw glance up at the mirror, but his face was calm as he returned the picture to the glove box. He was stonewalling her, she could smell it.

'You're right. He's a dangerous man.' She paused, re-adjusted the mirror a fraction. 'I think he killed Justyna to send you a message.'

He frowned. 'What do you mean?'

'He left your business card in her mouth.'

He whipped round to stare at her. 'In her *mouth*?'

She nodded. Now she had his attention.

Mother of God! Rage and impotence battled inside him as the sense of responsibility for Justyna's death came rushing back.

'Do you want him to get away with killing her?' she asked, watching his jaw muscles working.

He didn't answer for a moment, then raised one shoulder, let it drop.

'Even if you catch . . . this guy who fed her the drugs, you can't prove for sure that it's murder.'

'Not *yet*, I can't,' she said, and Janusz picked up the steely note in her voice.

'What if I told you he was probably involved in the death of someone else, another Polish girl?'

He waited for her to say more.

'A girl by the name of Elzbieta – Ela – Wronska,' she said, 'reported as a misper.' He frowned in incomprehension. 'A missing person. She was found floating in the Thames. Her stomach was full of PMA – just like Justyna.' She could read him better now, and sensed that beneath his veneer of indifference, he was hanging on her every word.

'She didn't do drugs, either,' she went on. 'In fact, she was a Catholic, studying theology at Cavendish College, so her worst vice was probably the occasional sip of communion wine.'

A man like Adamski probably wouldn't even know what theology was, thought Janusz, a grim smile tugging at the corner of his mouth.

'What's the joke?' she asked, changing down to turn off Balls Pond Road into Highbury Fields.

'Nothing,' he said. *The girl had eyes like a hawk.* 'Where in Poland did she come from?' If she said Gorodnik, he might get interested.

Kershaw shook her head. 'I don't recall off the top of my head, but I've got her college file – it's bound to be in there.' Together with all those Polish newspaper articles about the orchestra tour, she remembered.

She did some quick thinking. Streaky would have her attending Friday night domestics for a year if he found out she was sharing sensitive information with this guy, but *fuck it*, she needed a break. If Kiszka could help with the Polish angle, where was the harm? And maybe she could gain his trust, even get him to reveal hat man's identity, if she spent a little time with him.

Pulling into a parking bay outside his flat, she put the hand brake on and levelled unblinking grey eyes at him.

'If I show you Ela Wronska's file – would you talk me through the Polish stuff? It might help me nail the guy who killed her – and Justyna.'

Janusz put his hand on the door handle. 'I'm a very busy man, darling,' He wanted to help the girl – she might be a bit of a *psychol*, but he respected the way she seemed to take the murders of these girls personally.

Kershaw felt a rush of determination not to let him walk away. Staring down at her white hand gripping the steering wheel, she suddenly visualised a heart, drawn in indigo ink, on lifeless waxy skin.

'I shouldn't be telling you this,' she said. 'But I'm pretty sure that Ela Wronska had a boyfriend called Pawel.'

He didn't take his hand off the handle, but from the way his eyes narrowed she could tell that the name meant something to him.

Janusz remembered her mentioning the name Pawel before. If she really could connect Adamski with a second death, prove he was a murderer – no, worse, a serial killer – then that would change everything. A murder charge would get Adamski a proper jail sentence, even in the UK courts. Maybe if he helped her with the girl's college file, she might let something slip, some detail that would help him find Adamski. Then, once he'd got Weronika away safely – and retrieved the birth certificate – he could hand over the murdering bastard.

'Yes, okay,' he said finally.

'You'll look at the file, help me nail this guy?' Kershaw confirmed, trying to keep her voice neutral.

He nodded. *As long as I get to him first, darling. As long as I get to him first.*

When Kershaw got back to the office she found that DI Bellwether had just called Streaky with some news. *Crimewatch* was running the CCTV image of hat man on tomorrow's show, saying the police were seeking him in connection with the Kozlowska case. Trouble was, they also wanted to interview an officer on the case – and had specifically requested a female. She'd never thought of herself as a wuss, but the thought of performing on live TV – and having her performance rated by every cop in the land – sent her stomach into an aerobics routine.

'Congratulations, Miss Marple!' said Streaky, brushing fragments of sausage roll from his ample lap. 'Not many detectives get their *Crimewatch* debut at such a tender age.'

'But Sarge,' she said urgently, leaning over his desk, head bent and voice low. 'You'd be loads better at it, I'd be scared I'd freeze up at the wrong moment.' She was trying to keep their conversation private – she could practically *hear* Bonnick and Browning earwigging from their desks. She'd also spotted Ben's jacket slung on the back of his chair, so there was the toe-curling prospect of their post-shag encounter to look forward to as well.

Streaky tossed his crumpled paper bag into a bin two metres away – prompting an 'And he scores!' from arch-creep Browning. Leaning back and putting both hands behind his head, he addressed the room. 'What do we do when the TV-wallahs offer to broadcast a mug shot of one of our favourite scrotes to a couple of million curtain-twitchers?'

'Bite their arm off, Sarge,' said Bonnick.

'*Correcto*,' said Streaky. 'So can anyone explain to me why Miss Marple here has suddenly gone all camera-shy?' Grins and shrugs all round. She gave him a pleading look. '*Sarge* . . .'

'It's not *Britain's Got Talent*,' said Streaky, warming to his theme. 'They're not asking you to do a Madonna tribute act.' Over her shoulder she could hear Browning and Bonnick start singing the lyrics to 'Like a Virgin'. She swung round to give them the Kershaw Death Stare – and met the deep brown gaze of Ben Crowther, who had just walked in carrying a mug of tea. *Shit!*

As the tuneless duo reached the chorus, Browning stood up, ran his hands down his body and raised his eyebrows suggestively at her. Ben made a half-arsed attempt to look sympathetic but she could tell he was about to crack up.

Surfing a wave of murderous hatred, Kershaw swung back to Streaky, 'Why don't you get Crowther to do it, Sarge? He's got the biggest fucking gob in the whole nick!' and stormed out of the office.

By the time she'd reached her rooftop hideaway she was mortified. Not because she'd slagged Ben Crowther – he had it coming, after blabbing to Browning about their night together – but because she'd broken Rule Number One. She had *let them see they'd got to her.* Cigarette in hand, she slumped against the wall.

Two minutes later, who should emerge onto the roof, blinking like a pit pony in the hazy sunshine, but the Sarge. *What the f . . . ?* He leaned against the wall next to her and lit a Rothmans, then blew out a stream of smoke with a sigh.

'Have you and Crowther had a falling-out?'

'No, Sarge,' she muttered, head down.

'You could have fooled me,' he said. 'Anyway, your private life is your own affair. But remember what I'm always telling you – never jump straight to the obvious conclusion, however tempting.'

She shot him a curious look.

'Brisley's pal from Traffic was in the office the other day,' said Streaky, flicking ash off his cig. 'And I happened to overhear him saying he'd seen you and Crowther, well lagered-up, in a Chinky in Soho the other night.'

He absent-mindedly adjusted his genitals through his trousers.

'Now, personally, I couldn't give a flying fuck if you and Crowther are playing hide the sausage,' he said. Her face flamed a deep, shaming red. 'But I'll tell you one thing: Ben Crowther's not the sort of bloke to kiss and tell.'

Streaky threw down his half-finished fag and hitched up his trousers. 'Anyway, Ms M, I've an urgent meeting at the Drunken Monkey in half an hour. So when you're over your hissy fit, get your arse back inside and we'll work out what you're going to say unto the nation on *Crimewatch*.'

Twenty-Six

'I present myself before the Holy Confession, for I have offended God,' said Janusz.

'Back so soon?' enquired Father Pietruski drily. 'Nothing serious, I hope?'

Janusz shifted around on the hard bench, triggering a battery of creaks and squeaks. When the shutter had opened, he'd been relieved to see Father Pietruski's familiar profile through the wire grille rather than some spotty young stand-in just arrived from Poznan. He wasn't here to observe his religious duty, but to ask for the priest's guidance about the decision he'd made: a decision that had kept him awake half the night and dredged up some memories he'd hoped were irretrievably buried.

Keeping his deep voice low in case any nosy old dears arrived outside to await their turn in the box, Janusz laid out everything he'd discovered on his trip to Poland: Adamski's likely involvement in Struk's mysterious death, the old man's basement shrine to Communism, and the puzzling contents of the SB documents. The priest listened in silence, only commenting when Janusz told him of his lucky encounter with the shotgun-toting farmer in Kosyk.

'God watches over fools and children,' said the old man, folding his hands in his lap.

Janusz ignored the implied insult. 'Ever since I got back yesterday, I've been going over it all in my head,' he said. 'And I think I've worked it out.'

He had pored over the documents and methodically revisited every step of his investigation late into the night, trying to identify a link between the blackmailer Adamski and the old *esbek* Struk.

'Right after Adamski visits Struk's house, the old man is found dead,' said Janusz. 'The next day Adamski leaves for London, and a few days later he turns up at Weronika's café and launches his dirty little blackmail plot.'

The priest waited, head cocked.

'I realised that ever since I laid eyes on those documents, I've been ignoring what's in front of my nose.' Janusz bent closer to the grille. 'The link between Adamski and Struk is Edward Zamorski.'

He gave the priest time to digest the idea.

'You think that the SB was aware of Zamorski's . . . liaison with the underage girl,' said the old man after a moment, 'and the subsequent birth of Weronika.' Janusz tipped his head in assent – it was common knowledge that the regime had spied on all the key people in *Solidarnosc*. 'So the birth certificate Adamski is using to blackmail Zamorski came from Struk's files?' The priest raised his eyebrows.

'I think the birth certificate is the least of his problems,' growled Janusz.

He pulled the cellophane off a new tin of cigars, then, remembering where he was, slipped them reluctantly back in his pocket. 'If the SB had proof, back in the eighties, that an opposition figure like Zamorski had fathered a baby with a fifteen-year-old girl, then why on earth didn't they release it, to discredit Solidarity?'

The priest pulled at his earlobe. 'Perhaps they planned to use the information in some other way?'

'Precisely,' said Janusz. 'If I were the SB, I know what I'd do. Use it as a lever.'

The priest turned to face him, and even through the grille Janusz could see the old guy's face had suddenly paled.

Janusz tried to think of a way to soften the blow – and failed. 'I've gone over and over it in my head, Father, and I keep coming to the same conclusion. The informant who the SB called Magpie, is almost certainly Edward Zamorski.'

'No, no,' Father Pietruski shook his head fiercely. 'Zamorski was a *hero*!' he protested. 'The SB imprisoned him, beat him up – *countless* times. It's beyond belief that he could have been a traitor!'

'Is it?' asked Janusz. 'When the SB's files were opened, didn't it come out that all sorts of people passed on information – even priests?'

'And what about the priests who defied the authorities every week from the pulpit? What about Marek Kuba, murdered for daring to speak out?' demanded the old man. 'If it hadn't been for them, and the tireless work of the Holy Father, we could never have beaten the Communists!'

'It's true,' said Janusz shrugging. 'But they were

dreadful times, and even good people did dreadful things.' He rubbed the heel of his hand across his brow. 'Is it really so hard to believe? All the time Zamorski spent in jail, getting beaten up, humiliated, threatened . . .' Janusz's voice cracked with emotion, making the priest squint through the grille. 'Maybe they made threats against his family, who knows?' He lifted a hand, then let it fall. 'Sure, he took the SB's money, but what difference does that make, once he'd sold his soul?'

The two men fell silent.

'Do you have any proof of this?' asked the priest finally.

'No, but I think Adamski does.' Janusz leaned so far forward his nose brushed the grille and dropped his voice to a murmur. 'I think what he's holding over Zamorski is much worse than the birth certificate.' He pictured the fragment of card clinging to the file ties, traces of a missing page. 'Struk was Magpie's case officer. I think Adamski got his hands on something at Struk's house – something that proves Magpie and Zamorski are the same person.'

Janusz could see the old man's hands working together on his lap.

'The SB *fabricated* documents in order to frame Walesa,' said the old man suddenly, hope brightening his voice. 'Perhaps this is the same thing.'

In the early nineties, stories circulating in the media claimed that Lech Walesa, then Poland's president, had once worked secretly for the SB under the codename Bolek, informing against his *Solidarnosc* colleagues. Walesa denied it and the whole business was almost universally dismissed as a clumsy smear attempt by former SB officers. Had the story been proven, however, it would have ended his career in a heartbeat – just as

322

this affair, should it become public, would end Zamorski's. In modern-day Poland, communism might seem like a dark and distant fairytale, Janusz reflected, but there was no statute of limitation when it came to betraying one's fellow Poles.

'If it's a pack of lies,' said Janusz, 'then why didn't Zamorski come out fighting, like Walesa, instead of handing over tens of thousands to Adamski to hush the story up?'

Father Pietruski drew a shaky sigh. Janusz felt a stab of pity – it was a hard thing to see one's heroes fall from grace.

The priest managed one final objection. 'If you're right, I don't see where Weronika comes into it,' he said, folding his arms. 'If Adamski had such damaging information against Zamorski then why not simply blackmail him? Why did he need to . . . elope with his daughter?'

Janusz couldn't help but smile at the old-fashioned gallantry. 'I'm not sure. Maybe she was an insurance policy, in case Zamorski told him to fu . . . get lost.' In truth, he had no answer to this mystery – what *did* Adamski stand to gain, other than a world of trouble, by luring Zamorski's daughter away?

The old man subsided against the wall of the confession box. 'If this story comes out, it will finish him,' he said. 'And throw away the best chance Poland has had for a generation.' His voice had dropped to a hoarse whisper.

'I know,' said Janusz, fingering the lump on his forehead. 'And I'm not sure I can face doing that.'

The priest stared at him.

'When I find Adamski,' Janusz went on, 'I'm going

to destroy these SB documents about Zamorski he's got his hands on.'

The priest hesitated, one hand plucking at his robe. 'And Nowak? Will you tell him your suspicions?'

'No,' said Janusz wearily. 'Why burden him with such knowledge?' He shrugged his big shoulders. 'I'm only telling you about it because it is something I've been wrestling with. But do *you* think I'm doing the right thing – keeping this secret of Zamorski's under wraps?'

The priest put his head on one side, considering the matter.

'Why are you doing it?' he asked.

'Because it's time to forget the past,' said Janusz, his voice a low murmur. 'And because . . . I'm the last person to stand judgement on a man who was guilty of cowardice.' A sudden detail of his night in Montepulich Prison bubbled to the surface of his memory – the sobbing cries of some poor bastard getting worked over in the next cell.

'First of all, the question of his punishment and his forgiveness are not your responsibility,' said the old man, seeking Janusz's gaze. 'It is possible that pan Zamorski confessed to these crimes against his country long ago and has done proper penance for them.'

Janusz nodded, waiting for the priest's final pronouncement.

'As a Polish patriot, my instincts tell me that a man guilty of betraying his country should be exposed and punished,' said Pietruski. He took a breath and let it go in a heartfelt sigh. 'But as a *priest*, I believe that the path you have chosen is the Christian one.'

Janusz bent his head. 'Thank you, Father.'

He knelt for the priest's blessing, letting the sonorous

Latin wash over him. When he got to his feet, he felt somehow purified – as though the ancient sins he had confessed were not Edward Zamorski's, but his own.

That afternoon, Janusz settled himself in an armchair in his living room with the big central sash open – in one of England's bizarre weather swings, spring had suddenly arrived – and started flicking through his old address book. He was hoping that since Adamski was on the run he could be running out of cash by now – leaving him just one thing to fall back on: his experience as a builder. Although it had been a decade or more since Janusz had worked on site, he stayed in touch with the bigger outfits that acted as an informal employment exchange for thousands of young Polish men.

After putting the word out among his contacts, he sat stroking Copernicus, who lay draped along the arm of the chair, and watching the Polish news channel. The second item covered Zamorski's opening of a new children's hospital in Lublin: the presidential candidate looked confident and assured, joking with the crowd when the curtains covering the commemorative plaque didn't open properly. As he left the stage, though, and was ushered away by aides, Janusz thought he could discern something else, a certain tension in his body language, a fixity to the smile. It couldn't be easy, waiting for the axe to fall.

Minutes later, his phone rang and the name Konstanty Nowak appeared on the display.

'*Czesc,*' said the sprightly voice. 'I thought I'd give you a call to see if you've made any progress on finding our friend?' The drone of traffic in the background meant Janusz had to strain to hear him.

Janusz played for time. 'Father Pietruski said you were out looking for homeless people today,' he said. Apparently, Nowak was spending the week in London with an outreach team from the charity that helped down-and-out Poles to return home.

'*Tak*, I was. But after three hours of drunken Poles telling me how much I enjoy sexual relations with my mother – God rest her soul – I thought I deserved a break.' Nowak sounded cheerful. 'I'm leaving it to the youngsters for a bit. So, is there any news to report back to Edward?'

'Well,' said Janusz. 'I've checked out several avenues, and I'm doing a big trawl of my London contacts right now.'

'Anything I can do to help? You have the necessary to cover your expenses?'

'Yes, plenty thanks,' said Janusz. 'Has our friend been in touch with . . . Edward again?'

'No, not a word for over a week,' said Nowak, sounding puzzled. 'You'd think that would come as something of a relief, but it just seems to be making him more nervous.'

'There's a lot at stake, I guess,' said Janusz, checking the date on his watch. *Kurwa!* – the election was only three days away.

'Yes, of course, you're right,' Nowak said. He spoke to someone at the other end. 'I have to go – someone's just thrown up on one of the volunteers.' Janusz could hear a drunken voice in the background. 'Let me know if you hear anything.'

Janusz had barely hung up when his mobile started chirping again. This time the display read *Girl Detective*.

Twenty-Seven

Kershaw checked her mobile for about the tenth time. Where the hell was Kiszka? Arranging to meet him like this, in a pub, did feel a bit weird, but bringing him down the station would have meant a load of awkward questions. Streaky had no idea she was sharing information with a possible suspect – as far as he was concerned she was spending the day with the CSI team who were going over Ela Wronska's room at Cavendish College.

She'd chosen The Founders Arms, a pub on the south bank of the Thames, because it was only ten minutes' drive from the college, but all the tables inside were taken, so she'd been forced to sit out on the terrace, packed with lunching tourists and overlooked by anyone crossing Blackfriars Bridge. If a fellow cop spotted her and reported her meeting to Streaky, she'd be in a world of pain.

Ah, sod it, she thought – after her toe-curling public denunciation of Ben Crowther yesterday, it was worth the risk just to stay out of the office.

After thinking over what Streaky had told her on the roof, she had decided that he was probably right. Browning's jibe about her and Ben had been no more than a lucky guess – and by her behaviour yesterday she'd simply gone and confirmed it. Trouble was, the knowledge that she owed Ben a monster-sized apology made the prospect of facing him even harder.

At last Kiszka appeared, strolling unhurriedly across the pub's decked area. He gave her a little bow. 'Please accept my apologies for being so late,' he said, his deep voice making people look round at them. 'I got lost – I don't often come south of the river.' He sat down next to her, facing the river. 'Nice view,' he said, getting out his tin of stinky little cigars.

After she'd bought him a lager, Kershaw pulled Ela's file out of her shoulder bag and placed it on the table with the gesture of someone making an opening bid.

'This is strictly off the record, okay?' she said. He inclined his head sideways. 'Is that a yes?'

He opened his hands. 'Sure.'

Kershaw shunted the file sideways towards him, and he started to leaf through it, holding his cigar at a safe distance from the paper. 'If you see anything unusual in here,' she said, 'anything at all, you might help us stop this guy from killing someone else.' All she received in reply was another non-committal gesture.

She crossed her legs and waited. After a moment he shot her a look beneath his eyebrows and nodded towards her foot. Realising it had been jigging impatiently, she stilled it.

'Pretty girl,' he said when he reached Ela's photograph. Then he found the Polish newspaper articles that had covered the college orchestra tour. 'Ah, a violinist,' he said, respect warming his voice.

'Yes, the college orchestra toured Poland last year.' Kershaw leaned forward and indicated one of the articles. 'I think she gets a mention in this one.'

'"The highlight of the evening was Ela Wronska's performance of Samuel Barber's Violin Concerto,"' Janusz translated, '"during which her naive delight in the music was never outweighed by her undoubted virtuosity."'

They shared an amused look.

'Can you see any link between the towns she played in?' she asked. He went through the cuttings again, screwing up his eyes to make out the newspaper titles printed on the edge of the cuttings. She thought he lingered a second or two longer over one of them, but in the end he just shook his head.

'Lodz . . . Szczecin . . . Zakopane . . . they're all over the place, from right up north down to the Czech border.' He took his time reading the final page, which detailed Ela's personal info – her date of birth, educational background, and so on. 'An orphan,' he muttered, as though to himself.

'Yes. Adopted by an English aunt when she was about twelve, so she did most of her growing up in Kent. The aunt's dead though.'

Janusz wasn't listening. Something had just clicked in his head, like a set of points shifting a train onto a new track.

'Can you see anything at all, any Polish angle I might be missing?' Kershaw asked. He shook his head slowly. 'Where she grew up, in Kent – Tunbridge Wells,' she tried, aware of an edge of desperation in her voice, 'Do you know if it has a big Polish population?'

'I've never heard of it.'

Remembering that she had a prospectus for Cavendish College, Kershaw retrieved it from her bag and flipped to the title page, which carried photos of the faculty. Kiszka's gaze skipped over most of them, but snagged on the photo of Monsignor Zielinski.

'You know this guy?' she asked.

'Not really.' He shook his head. 'I was at a reception at the Polish Embassy the other day and I saw him talking to my priest.'

Kershaw stared at him. *The Polish Embassy? His priest?* The more time she spent with this guy the harder she found it to get a handle on him.

He shrugged his shoulders. 'It's just a coincidence – my priest knows a lot of important church people.'

As Janusz closed the file and pushed it back to her, he saw disappointment crease the girl's face. She might be a pushy little creature but at least she gave a damn about catching the killer. 'Have you got any forensics that might nail the guy you're after?' he asked.

It couldn't hurt to tell him. 'A single hair from Justyna's body,' she said, noting the angry scowl that crossed Janusz's face. 'And I've got people crawling all over Ela Wronska's room today, to see if we can place him there.' She pulled a tight smile. 'One "girlfriend" dying of an accidental overdose a jury might buy, but not two.'

'You mentioned the name Pawel,' he said, studying the tip of his cigar. 'How did that come up?'

In for a penny . . . thought Kershaw. 'Ela had a heart tattoo on her right buttock, with the name Pawel inside.'

He turned away toward the river to blow his cigar smoke downwind of her. 'Amateur sort of thing, was it?' he asked.

'Yeah, it looked homemade,' she said, 'Why?'

There was a second satisfying click in Janusz's head. He was pretty sure now how Pawel Adamski and Elzbieta Wronska had first met.

'Just a good guess,' he said, covering his tracks. 'I can't see a theology student baring her backside in a tattoo parlour.'

She stowed the file back in her bag. 'I'd better get down the college,' she said, 'see if the CSIs have found anything.'

Janusz walked her to her car, pausing under Blackfriars Bridge to light a fresh cigar. Then he turned to her.

'Apart from the fact they both died from an overdose of this . . . PMA?' – she nodded – 'what makes you think that the same person killed Justyna and this girl Ela?' he asked, picking a flake of tobacco off the tip of his tongue.

'It's difficult to explain,' she said after a moment, staring out at the dark water lapping at the stanchions of the bridge. 'But these two cases, they just *smell* the same.'

On reaching her car, she whipped out the file and returned to the cutting that Kiszka had appeared to linger over when she'd asked him where the orchestra had gone on tour. It appeared no different from any of the others – a headline and a picture of the orchestra above a few lines of story. The edge of the cutting bore the dateline, September 13th of the previous year, and what she presumed was the name of the newspaper – *Kurier Gorodnik*.

Kershaw started the car, aware of a niggling sensation that Janusz Kiszka had got more out of the meeting than she had.

'Zilch, so far,' said Dave, the CSI, glancing up at Kershaw. He scowled at the doorknob to Ela Wronska's balcony, which he'd just dusted with silver fingerprint powder. 'I reckon the cleaner must have OCD.'

Kershaw gazed around the room, which looked just as eerily impersonal as on her first visit. The white-clad feet and ankles of a second CSI protruded from the doorway of the ensuite bathroom.

'You haven't found a journal tucked away anywhere, I suppose?' she asked.

Dave stood up and stretched his spine, making his white forensic suit rustle. 'That's it, I'm afraid.' He gestured to the bed, with its pitifully small pile of belongings.

Kershaw checked her notes. 'Her friends say she definitely owned a mobile phone, as well. I've got the mobile company digging out the records for me.'

Dave tipped his head toward the Thames. 'If she jumped, maybe it went with her over the balcony.'

'What, with her laptop under her arm, too?' she asked, raising a sceptical eyebrow.

He just shrugged and, hunkering down again, started stroking the brush along the surface of the windowsill. Sensing a chill in the air, she remembered that the last time they'd met, at the Waveney Thameside, she'd rubbed Dave up the wrong way. She bit her lip, wondering if it would stop him going the extra mile for her now.

Kershaw suddenly saw her Dad, squatting to talk to her in the corner of some kids' party. His eyes were kind, but the voice firm: if she didn't apologise, they were going straight home. The details of her offence were long forgotten, but the memory of his disappointed silence as they drove back to the flat was as sharp today as it had been twenty years ago.

'Look, Dave,' she said. 'I might have been . . . a bit out of order last time we met.' Frowning, he bent closer to his work. She grimaced, bunching her shoulders. 'Scratch that – I was *properly* out of order. So, I just wanted to say, sorry for being such an arse.'

Dave shot her a surprised look. 'Apology accepted,' he said.

'When Streaky told me you were down to do this scene, I was over the moon,' Kershaw went on. 'He said, "If someone farted in that room, Dave'll get you a sample".'

Dave just grunted, but she could tell from the way his cheeks pinked up that he was chuffed at the compliment.

As Kershaw left Ela's block, heading for Monsignor Zielinski's office, she caught sight of a man's back and a flash of fair hair disappearing round the corner ahead of her. She jogged after him, but by the time she got there, there was no sign of him. The guy had looked an awful lot like Timothy Lethbridge – which struck her as odd, because when she'd left a message on his phone earlier, hoping to fix up another chat, he'd texted her to say sorry, he was at the British Museum all day, doing research.

Monsignor Zielinski wore a dark grey suit today, a dog collar the only sign of his calling. The shoes poking out from beneath his trousers were the deep sheeny colour of a chestnut racehorse, almost exactly the same shade as his curly hair. He shook hands with his usual confident charm, but his eyes looked a little bloodshot – having the police crawling all over his campus was evidently proving an uncomfortable experience. Kershaw asked if he knew whether Timothy Lethbridge was in college today.

'Yes, I saw him in the refectory at lunchtime,' said Zielinski. 'Would you like me to find out whether he has any lectures this afternoon?'

'If you could,' said Kershaw. 'I need to ask him a few more questions.' So, Nice Timmy *was* avoiding her. She gazed out at the treetops, frowning. Had she allowed her focus on hat man to blind her to other suspects?

'You surely don't think he could be in any way . . . *implicated* in Elzbieta's death, do you?' asked the Monsignor. 'Because I can vouch for Timothy absolutely. He'd be quite incapable of serious wrongdoing.' He looked genuinely aghast at the idea.

'I'm sure you're right,' soothed Kershaw. 'I just want to tie up a few loose ends.'

Zielinski appeared to accept her reassurances, and seating himself behind his desk, waved her into the chair opposite. 'After morning mass, I told all the students – and the faculty – that they may be asked to provide fingerprints, or even DNA samples,' he said, regaining his usual composure. 'And I said I'd be the first to put myself forward for such tests, should the police deem it necessary.' Taking a piece of paper from a tray on his desk, he passed it to her with a grave expression.

'Great, thanks,' said Kershaw. She'd asked him for a list of all the students living in halls, divided into those with rooms in Ela Wronska's block and those living in the other four blocks. She would start by questioning those who occupied rooms closest to hers.

'How are the "crime scene investigators" getting on?' he handled the phrase delicately, as though wearing latex gloves himself.

'Nothing so far,' she said. 'Apparently, the room has had a really thorough clean.'

'That's our fault, I'm afraid,' said the Monsignor. Seeing Kershaw's eyes widen, he smiled. 'Forgive me. I simply mean that Mrs Rosiak, our cleaner, is a literal believer in the nostrum that "Cleanliness is next to Godliness". Which is good news for us, but must make things difficult for you.'

Kershaw stood to leave, but then remembered something.

'By the way, I'm going to be on *Crimewatch* tonight – mostly to talk about . . . another case,' she said. 'But they might also show a photo of Elzbieta, try to jog people's memories, just in case anyone saw anything suspicious.'

His face fell, but he opened his hand in a gesture of resignation. 'The trustees won't like it,' he said. 'But if it helps to discover the truth, then so be it.'

When Kershaw got back to the front door of Ela's block, she cursed to find it locked. Earlier, she'd got lucky, sneaking in behind one of the studes, but now there was no-one around and she didn't have Dave's mobile number. Then she remembered – she must still have the bit of paper with the access code from her first visit. It wasn't in either coat pocket, and she'd just balanced her handbag on a windowsill ready to have a proper rummage, when she spotted a guy in a duffel coat approaching.

'Excuse me,' she said, flashing her warrant card. 'I'm a police officer. Would you do me a favour and punch me in?'

'This isn't my block, I'm afraid,' he said, squinting at the keypad. 'I used to live here, last year – but they change the codes every few weeks. Sorry.'

As he walked off, Kershaw stood stock still, warrant card frozen in mid-air. Five seconds later, the contents of her handbag were spread across the doorstep and she was pulling a creased piece of paper from the debris. Smoothing it out, she replayed her first encounter with the Monsignor, remembering how he'd sketched this map to show her the way to Ela's block and, at the last moment, added the front door access code. There it was, the numbers written in his round, confident hand. She closed her eyes, trying to remember. Had he opened a drawer, checked a file before writing it down? No, her recollection was crystal clear. He'd dashed it straight off from memory.

Zielinski knew the code for Ela's block off the top of his head.

At the time, Kershaw hadn't given it a second thought, assuming the campus had a universal pass code. Now, the discovery that each block had its own unique code, and a constantly changing one at that, put the Monsignor's feat of memory in a new and sinister light. She couldn't think of a single reason why the college principal would need to know pass codes to the student accommodation. No *appropriate* reason, anyway.

Kershaw decided that Zielinski's curious failure to recognise the name of Elzbieta Wronska, his former tutee, had just acquired a new significance.

A few minutes later, she was back in the corridor

outside Ela's room, getting suited and booted again. Ducking under the cat's cradle of blue and white tape across the threshold, she saw that the girl's bed had been stripped and pulled out from the wall.

CSI Dave, who was squatting behind the bed head, torch in hand, turned to give her a broad grin. 'Come and have a look at this,' he said.

He shone his torch beam onto the rear surface of the bed head, its surface glittering with fingerprint powder. She crouched to bring her head level with his. 'You don't often see latents as perfect as that,' he said, his voice tinged with reverence. There, imprinted in the silvery dust, were the perfect impressions of four finger pads, their whorls and ridges as clear as the contours on an OS map.

'The front's had a good wipe down, but the back got missed.' He curled his fingers over the edge of the bed head to demonstrate how the prints had been left, and met Kershaw's eyes. The inference was clear: the fingerprints probably belonged to someone who'd been on top during a sexual encounter in Ela's bed.

Kershaw sat on the edge of the mattress, her heart thudding. If her hunch about the access code was right, the prints could belong to the Monsignor. She didn't quite buy him as the murderer – how would a Catholic priest get hold of an arcane street drug like PMA? – but it was still a hell of a lead. 'I owe you a big fat drink, Dave,' she said grinning. 'But right now, I've got an urgent appointment with a man of the cloth.'

Zielinski's secretary told Kershaw that she would find Monsignor in the college chapel, preparing for afternoon prayers. The place was all blond wood pews and white paint, like something out of the IKEA catalogue, thought Kershaw. Zielinski, now wearing white robes topped with a cream-coloured silk poncho affair, knelt at the altar. She hovered by the front pew, but he must have heard her footsteps because a moment later he rose, crossing himself, and turned to face her.

His smile was as confident as ever, but Kershaw thought she detected a guardedness around his eyes.

'Good news,' she said, adopting a chirpy tone. 'We've found some excellent prints in Elzbieta's room, so I'd like to take you up on your offer.'

'Offer?' asked Zielinski, his smile sagging a fraction.

'I'll give you a lift to the station,' said Kershaw, 'so you can be the first to give us fingerprints and a DNA swab.'

'Now?' he said, opening his eyes so wide she could see the red-veined white around his irises.

'We want to find out what happened to Elzbieta as soon as possible, don't we?' she asked.

Zielinski studied a roundel of coloured light on the floor, thrown by the stained glass window over the altar. 'Where did you find these fingerprints?' he asked.

'On the back of the bed head,' she said. 'Obviously left there by a sexual partner.' She jangled her car keys.

Zielinski hesitated. 'I'm more than happy to help,' he said, with something of a return to his former confidence, 'but as you can see, you've caught me just before a service.' He nodded down at his get-up. 'Let me get Mrs Beauregard to check the diary and see if we can find a slot.'

Yeah, and next time I see you, you'll be hiding behind a brief, thought Kershaw. Then what? If the fingerprints *weren't* his, that left only the access code, and given time, he could probably construct some plausible reason for knowing that. She needed to nail him right now – before he got his story straight.

Pulling a plastic evidence bag from her coat pocket, she held it up between them so he could see the map inside, and pointed to his handwriting.

'You must have been a very frequent visitor to Ms Wronska's block to know the access code off by heart.'

He stared at it for a moment, then recovered his composure. 'Certainly not. But as the head of the college, I am, naturally enough, entrusted with all the codes.'

'And you keep all six of them in your head – even though they change every few weeks?'

'I'm blessed with a facility for remembering numbers.'

Their eyes met. *Shit.* She felt the situation slipping away from her.

Then she remembered something: Zielinski's spirited defence of Timothy Lethbridge.

As though conceding defeat, she returned the evidence bag to her pocket, and saw the muscles in his face relax, just a fraction.

'Excuse me,' she said, pulling her mobile from her bag, as though it had just buzzed. She clicked on an old text message from her gym, which said her subscription was up for renewal.

She looked up at him, eyebrows raised, like she'd just had a revelation. 'Guess who wants to see me after I leave here?' she asked.

He shook his head.

'Timothy Lethbridge,' she said.

Zielinski's face slumped and he appeared to age a decade or two before her eyes. She'd guessed right – his earlier defence of Timothy hadn't sprung from an instinct to protect a student in trouble, but from fear of *what he might say.*

'The fingerprints you found,' he managed, after a long moment. 'They don't . . . necessarily have anything to do with Elzbieta's death, do they?'

'Well, no,' she said, her tone considered. 'But if their owner *lied to the police* about why they were there, I think a jury would draw its own conclusions.'

Zielinski groped for the round boss at the end of the front pew and let himself down gently onto the seat, his face as pale and sweaty as warm cheese.

Kershaw went to sit beside him. 'When did the affair with Elzbieta start?' she asked, keeping her voice matter-of-fact.

'On the orchestra tour,' he said, putting a hand over his eyes. 'Last autumn.'

'More than six months ago. How did you manage to keep it quiet all this time?'

'After returning to England, we made it a rule never to speak, nor have any contact in the daytime,' he said, reflexively pleating then smoothing the surplice over his knees. 'I used to wait till every light had been turned off in her block before going up to . . . her room.'

'And nobody ever caught you?'

'No. Except once.'

She raised an interrogative eyebrow. 'Timothy?'

Zielinski nodded. 'He knocked at Elzbieta's door late one night when I was with her. He was quite insistent, tapping and calling her name. So, in the end, she went to the door, to get rid of him.' His voice had dropped to a hoarse whisper.

Timothy's crush on Ela had clearly been of near-stalker proportions, thought Kershaw. 'That was a bit awkward. So, did he push his way in?' she asked.

'No, no. Eventually she persuaded him to go away, but she said that he kept looking over her shoulder,' said Zielinski. He looked down at his hands. 'We realised that he must have seen the chair at the foot of her bed . . .'

'Which was where you'd left your . . .' Unsure what to call the fuchsia cummerbund he wore with his cassock, Kershaw gestured at her waist.

'My sash.' He closed his eyes, a tortured look contorting his face.

No wonder Timothy's avoiding me, thought Kershaw – he doesn't want to drop his principal in it. It also explained why he had seemed so angry when he revealed Ela's rejection and her excuse of celibacy.

'Did Elzbieta ever mention a boyfriend, someone called Pawel?'

Zielinski looked up. 'She certainly knew a Pawel,' he said, hesitantly. 'When we were in Poland, the orchestra played in a place called Gorodnik. I was in Gdansk that evening, having dinner with the bishop . . .' he closed his eyes and his lips trembled. 'Does what I'm telling you . . . need to become *public*?' he asked, grasping perhaps for the first time the likely consequences of his behaviour.

Kershaw felt a flicker of pity. Then she saw Ela's coppery hair against the stainless steel of the gurney, remembered the romantic novel and the gingerbread heart in her room. Losing her parents so young, followed by the auntie who'd brought her up, was it any wonder Ela had fallen for her handsome tutor? Father figure and forbidden lover – it must have been a potent combination to a vulnerable young woman.

'If you continue to cooperate, we'll do what we can to keep the information confidential,' she said, avoiding his eyes.

He took a deep breath. 'When I went to her hotel room that night, I could see she was upset,' he said. 'She wouldn't say anything at first but then it all came out. Someone had approached her after the concert, as she was putting away her violin, a man she'd known years ago.'

'Pawel.'

'She didn't volunteer a name,' Zielinski dropped his gaze.

Kershaw paused. 'But you guessed it was Pawel – because you'd seen her tattoo?'

He nodded, cutting his eyes away from her. 'She said that he was keen to restart their friendship, but she just wanted to forget "that part of her life".'

'Was he an old boyfriend?' asked Kershaw. 'Did she meet him in London? Or on a holiday back to Poland?'

Zielinski shook his head. 'She wouldn't say any more – and I never heard her mention him again.'

'Let's get back to *your* relationship with Elzbieta,' said Kershaw, after a pause. 'When did you last see her exactly?'

He looked down at his lap. 'I have behaved appallingly.' His voice was so low she had to lean closer to hear him. Then he raised his eyes to hers and the expression in them was so desolate that Kershaw realised there was more to come – not a confession of murder, perhaps, but something almost as bad.

She had seconds to work out her next move: right

now, Zielinski's chief emotion was remorse, but his previous instinct for self-preservation could return in a heartbeat. She gazed at the golden cross atop the altar. 'Losing Elzbieta, yet being unable to confide in anyone,' she said, softening her voice. 'I should think it must have been crucifying you these past few weeks.'

'Yes, it has,' he said, following her gaze.

'Being able to talk about it at last must feel like a huge burden being lifted.'

He met Kershaw's gaze, surprised at the empathy in her voice.

'You found Elzbieta's body, didn't you, father?'

Zielinski became quite still, then let out a breath.

'She was lying on top of the bed, her eyes staring at the ceiling,' he said, his eyes still fixed on the cross. 'She was naked. Her skin wasn't quite cold, but when I checked her pulse and pupils . . . she was obviously dead.'

'How could you be so sure?' asked Kershaw – whether the unfortunate Ela really had been dead when he found her would be a matter of some significance in court.

'I was a parish priest for ten years,' he said, 'I've seen a lot of people who have passed.' His voice was steadier now. 'If I had resisted temptation, then she would still be alive, she wouldn't have been driven to do such a terrible thing.'

'What do you mean?' asked Kershaw.

'There were some drugs on the bedside table,' he said, 'and a half empty bottle of vodka.'

Kershaw remembered the post mortem. *Of course.* 'You thought she had killed herself because she was pregnant with your child.'

343

He gazed off into the darkened corners of the chapel. 'She had told me a week earlier, and I . . . didn't take it very well. I think she did this terrible thing, to spare me the responsibility, the shame . . .' He fell silent, unable or unwilling to continue.

Kershaw could barely keep still. She needed him to confess what they both knew he had done before he got cold feet.

'There's something else you need to tell me, isn't there?'

He knotted his hands together in his lap.

'It must have been an unbelievable shock, finding Elzbieta like that,' she continued. 'And when people are in a state of shock, they often do things they wouldn't dream of doing normally.' She sought his gaze.

The look in his eyes said he was ready, if she could just find an acceptable way to approach the terrible thing he had done.

'You couldn't face anyone else finding her like that, could you?' asked Kershaw. 'At the time, putting her body in the river probably seemed like the most respectful thing to do.'

Twenty-Eight

Twenty-four hours after Janusz started his trawl of building trade contacts, he got a break. A contractor called Miroslaw who was fitting out new offices in the West End said he'd heard Adamski's name mentioned as a possible site labourer in the last few days. He promised to talk to his contact and get back to Janusz.

For his evening meal, Janusz decided to make a warm potato salad to go with some *wiejska* sausage from the new *Polski sklep* on Highbury Corner.

Preparing food always helped him to think – and he had plenty to think about since seeing Elzbieta Wronska's college file.

He'd been sceptical about the girl being another of Adamski's victims – unable to see how a lowlife like him might know such a respectable girl, let alone become her boyfriend. Then, in the pub today, reading the personal background page of her file, under the heading '*Education*', he'd found the answer: '*1984-1990 – Dom Dziecka 376, Gorodnik.*'

So, that was it. After her parents died, Ela had ended up in Children's Home No. 376, in that dump Gorodnik, where she stayed till her adoption. That was where she and Pawel had met, and where they'd become sweethearts – him pricking out her homemade tattoo with a pin and a bottle of ink, no doubt, like so many kids did back then.

As he sliced the *wiejska* into fat coins, he wondered whether there could be a link between Adamski's blackmailing of Zamorski and his childhood relationship with Ela. He couldn't see one. He decided that Adamski probably read about Ela's concert in the *Gorodnik Kurier*, and on his arrival in London had looked her up at the college, perhaps in a bid to rekindle their childhood romance. Put like that it sounded almost romantic, except that when Ela turned him down, Adamski had forced her to take the shit that killed her.

Janusz took his plate of food to the sofa and turned on the TV. With the country voting for a new president the day after tomorrow, the Polish channel was broadcasting wall-to-wall coverage of Zamorski, the undisputed favourite. The cameras even followed the candidate and his wife into morning mass, an item that ended on a big close-up of his kindly face as he took the wafer from the priest's fingers. After eating, Janusz set his plate aside and tried to concentrate on the report, but after a few seconds his chin settled majestically onto his chest.

He awoke with a jolt, his pulse thumping in his ear and the hairs on his arms prickling: *something* had triggered the alarm on his autonomic nervous system. Then, he practically jack-knifed out of his seat as Copernicus jumped into his lap, purring throatily. The last time that happened, Janusz remembered, he had ended up beaten to shit on the bathroom floor. He got to his feet, feeling a twinge from his healing rib.

Not this time, sisterfucker, he thought. Reaching for a weapon, he crept across the rug and positioned himself behind the half-open living room door, his breath coming ragged and shallow.

He heard a creak as the intruder crossed the threshold and saw a head emerge cautiously past the edge of the door. The empty beer bottle bounced off the crew cut skull with a sound like a cracked church bell and he went down in a heap. With his pulse drumming in his ears, Janusz danced on the balls of his feet, ready to thump him again if he tried to get up.

'No mask tonight, *skurwysynie*?' he growled, dragging the guy onto his back by the yoke of his denim jacket.

He knocked the guy's arms down from their defensive position in front of his face – and rocked back on his heels. In place of the bunched features and close-set eyes he expected from the CCTV image of Adamski, he found a long olive-skinned face, like a saint in a medieval icon. And this guy was skinny, with arms like breadsticks; his masked assailant – and the guy he'd chased through Gdansk – had a bodybuilder's physique.

'Who the fuck are *you*?' asked Janusz, planting a foot on the guy's chest. 'Did Adamski send you?'

His mouth opened and, still winded from his fall, the guy croaked out:

'I *am* Adamski.'

The fist holding the beer bottle dropped to Janusz's side, while his brain tried to process this news.

'Bullshit.' Janusz jabbed him in the ribs with his boot.

'I came because I heard you were looking for me,' said the guy. His lumpy country accent reminded Janusz of Tadeusz Krajewski, Adamski's former employer back in Gorodnik.

Janusz frisked him roughly – he was clean – and retreated to the sofa, keeping his eyes locked on the long-limbed stranger. He indicated the armchair opposite with the empty bottle. The guy climbed to his feet, keeping a wary eye on the big man, and fingering the top of his head where the bottle had struck, backed into the chair.

'Any chance of me getting one of those?' he asked, looking at the bottle with thirsty eyes.

'*Kurwa mac!*' burst out Janusz. 'You break into my place and expect me to play fucking bartender?'

The guy shrugged. 'I heard you were looking for me,' he repeated.

Christ! thought Janusz. The guy was a real *burak* – a beetroot, a dumb redneck.

'So, don't you know how to use a doorbell, *idiota*?'

'People are following me,' he said, glancing reflexively over his shoulder. 'I have to be careful.'

Janusz scanned the guy's face. 'So you say you're Adamski, do you? Where are you from then?'

'Gorodnik,' said the guy, touching his chest and grinning with apparent pride.

'And who did you work for, before you left?'

'Tadeusz Krajewski.'

'Where is Witold Struk's house?'

The grin drooped and a shadow passed over the long face.

'Kosyk,' he muttered, fingers returning to the lump on his head.

348

Janusz frowned. If this guy had hung out with Adamski back in Gorodnik then he'd probably know this kind of stuff. Then he remembered Tadeusz and Adamski's fishing trips.

He lit a cigar. 'You caught a big fat carp with Tadeusz once,' he said. 'And gave it a nickname.'

The guy furrowed his forehead.

'No, it wasn't a carp,' he said, with an earnest shake of the head. 'It was a pike.' He grinned, revealing a gold tooth where an incisor should be. 'We called it Vladimir, for Putin.'

Mother of God! It looked like this guy was for real! Janusz tried to round up his thoughts, which were running around like a bunch of startled chickens. *If this guy is Adamski, then who is the guy in the hat? And why, in the Name of all the Saints, is he following me?*

'Congratulations,' snarled Janusz. 'You're the guy who abducted an innocent young girl so you could use her in a dirty piece of blackmail.' He took a drag of his cigar. 'The only reason I don't cave your *burak* head in is because we have things to sort out, you and I.'

His first priority was to find out where Weronika was. Maybe if he got the guy drunk he might let something slip.

Janusz got to his feet. 'Stay there,' he said, pointing a threatening finger at Adamski. 'I'll get you a beer.'

He went to the kitchen, keeping a watchful eye through the doorway, and pulled a six-pack of Tyskie out of the fridge. Seeing the kitchen window wide open, he cursed under his breath – after the last uninvited visitor, he'd started shutting it before going to bed, but dropping off on the sofa like an old-age pensioner had left him exposed. Now another bastard had waltzed up the fire escape and into his home. He slammed the fridge door. I might as well put a welcome mat under the window, he thought.

Adamski took a heroic draught of the beer Janusz handed him, then dug a crumpled pack of cigarettes out of his jeans and lit one.

'First question,' said Janusz, popping the ring pull of his can with a hiss. 'What are you doing breaking in here?'

'A friend called me to say you were asking around about me – that you're some kind of *detektyw*?' said Adamski. 'So I came to tell you to stop and leave us alone – before you get us killed!'

'*Us?* You mean you and *Weronika*?' said Janusz, incredulous. 'You're the one who threatened to kill her!'

Adamski exploded out of his seat, rage darkening his face. 'I would never hurt Nika,' he shouted. 'I'd rather die myself than let anybody touch a hair on her head.'

Janusz blew out a lazy stream of smoke and waited for him to calm down. 'Alright. Let's overlook the fact that you threatened to murder her,' he said. 'But maybe you can explain to a stupid bastard like me how using a young girl to blackmail her own father counts as *protecting her*?'

Adamski shook his head. 'I can say nothing of that,' he said in a low voice.

'I know all about it,' growled Janusz. 'You threatened to ruin him.'

'Maybe I did,' muttered Adamski, his jaw jutting mulishly. 'But everything is different now.'

Janusz narrowed his eyes. 'Something changed, after

you persuaded Weronika to leave pani Tosik's restaurant, didn't it?'

He just shrugged and folded his arms.

'You fell for her, didn't you?' said Janusz, realisation dawning in his voice. 'That must have complicated things.'

Adamski tried – and failed – to keep from smiling at the life-changing miracle that had been granted him just a few weeks earlier.

Janusz stared at him. This was turning into a night of surprises. He'd barely had time to adjust to the idea that it wasn't Adamski who'd been following him, and now the guy was grinning like a lovesick schoolboy over the girl he'd said he was ready to kill.

'Why did you threaten Justyna?' he asked, remembering the fear in her eyes that he'd failed to pick up on, the night he'd walked her home.

Adamski frowned at the name: 'That one never liked me, she was always trying to cause trouble between me and Nika – you know the type.'

'Maybe because you hit on her while going out with her friend?'

Adamski looked uncomfortable. 'That was before . . .' he trailed off.

'Before you fell in love with Weronika?'

A nod. 'You don't think it was *me* that killed Justyna?' he said suddenly, his eyes wide.

'How do you know she's dead?' Janusz shot back.

'I read about it in the paper.' His mouth twisted. 'I haven't told Nika, not yet – it would tear her apart.'

Janusz paused. He'd been convinced that it was Adamski who'd lured Justyna to her death in the Waveney Hotel, but the evidence of the CCTV footage couldn't be

351

denied. The guy in the hat had murdered poor Justyna, and whoever he was, his name wasn't Pawel Adamski.

'Tell me this,' Janusz said. 'If you love Weronika so much, why are you still blackmailing her father?'

'I'm not,' burst out Adamski. 'I want nothing more to do with him! Keeping Nika safe is more important than money.'

Janusz examined his face – and decided the turniphead didn't have the brains to lie convincingly.

'So what makes you think you're in danger?'

'After Nika left the restaurant, we rented a cottage, out in Essex.' His face softened. 'And just like this' – he snapped his fingers – 'I was happy for the first time in my life, all because of Nika.'

'Yeah, but you carried on screwing money out of her father,' growled Janusz, remembering the plasma screen and the fur coat he'd seen at the cottage.

'So what?' Pawel pushed out his chin. 'I thought he owed his daughter something for leaving her to be raised by a drunken slut.' He drank off the last of the beer and set down the empty can.

'I swear on the Holy Mother, I'd already decided to stop contacting him – forget the whole thing, start over with Nika, wipe the board clean.' He dusted one hand off against the other, a decisive gesture. 'Then these two *Polaks* turn up in the village driving a big car. They pull up next to Nika and start asking her a load of questions.' He tapped his temple, grinning proudly. 'But Nika is smart – she can tell something is up, so she runs away from them.'

'One of these men wore a funny old-fashioned hat, right?' asked Janusz.

Adamski's mouth dropped open – *like a dog that's been shown a card trick* – as the old saying went. 'How do you know that?' he exclaimed.

'I know more about this business than you think,' said Janusz, meeting Adamski's eyes. The younger man dropped his gaze.

Janusz had wondered how the guy in the hat had managed to find the cottage, but now he'd met Adamski he realised his blackmail letters to Zamorski had probably arrived helpfully stamped with a Willowbridge postmark.

'I knew they'd find the cottage before long, so the minute she told me, we didn't even pack, we just jumped in the car and left.'

'What did Nika make of that?' asked Janusz, leaning over to hand Adamski a fresh beer.

'I told her that pani Tosik had people looking for us and they might force her to go home to her Mama, so we'd better lie low. And you know what? She never even asked a single question, she just said, "Whatever you think, Pawel"' – he put a fist to his chest – 'That's how much she trusts me.' His accent was broadening as the beer went down.

Janusz processed the guy's story – so far, it fitted what he knew of the facts. 'So who was chasing you? Somebody you pissed off in the drugs trade?'

Holding up the beer can, Adamski laughed. 'This is my only drug, *kolego*.'

Janusz lit another cigar – the guy was hardly likely to admit to dealing drugs. On the other hand, with every new revelation, he sensed his theories about this affair starting to crumble beneath him. He took a deep draw on his cigar and faced the unwelcome truth. His whole investigation had been based on a series of flawed interpretations and imagined connections: the encounter with the drug dealer in the FlashKlub toilets, Justyna's suspicions about Adamski's dealing, her dying of a drug overdose. From these pathetically thin 'clues' he'd constructed an elaborate edifice which he now watched collapse in the face of the facts.

'These guys who came looking for you,' said Janusz, after a moment, 'you think they were sent by Zamorski.'

Adamski shrugged. 'Who else? He hired you to do the same, didn't he?'

'That's different. I'm a private detective, not some murdering thug.'

If what Adamski said was true, the big question was – why would Zamorski send out *two* search parties? Janusz stood up and started pacing the room.

Then it hit him.

Zamorski could never have run the risk of Janusz, or even Konstanty Nowak, seeing the SB documents that Adamski had got his hands on – because then they'd find out he'd been an informer.

When Zamorski's first search party had failed to track down Adamski, he cooked up the birth certificate story and asked Nowak to find someone who knew his way round London's *Polonia*. Although Janusz would do the legwork, Zamorski never intended to let him get his hands on the SB documents. He'd been like one of those spy drones the Americans used, a device to guide the real pursuers to their quarry. Zamorski's man – the guy in the hat – must have been on his tail from the moment he took the case.

Janusz went over to open the bay window, and leaned out, like a man enjoying the night air. Lazily scanning the road along his side of Highbury Fields, the cars under the carbon lights appeared reassuringly empty; then, blowing out a plume of cigar smoke, he lifted his gaze to the road at the far side of the green. His gaze fell on a black boxy car – a 4x4. Inside, there was just enough light from the dashboard to illuminate the outline of a man in the driver's seat. Janusz turned his head, but continued to watch the car out of the corner of his eye. After a beat, the man leaned forward, perhaps to change radio station, coming closer to the light source, and outlining for a split-second the brim of a hat.

Janusz felt his heart lurch in his chest. Did Zamorski know the sort of men he was employing? Could Poland's next president know that murder had been committed in his name? Whether he knew it or not, with a *psychol* like that running around, his daughter's life was in danger.

Then Janusz remembered the dead girl from the theology college.

'When did you last see Elzbieta Wronska?' he asked.

'How do you know about me and Ela?' asked Adamski, his can frozen centimetres from his lips.

'I know you were in the same children's home,' said Janusz, grinding his cigar out in the ashtray. 'Did you read it in the paper, about her orchestra playing in Gorodnik?'

'No, I went to the concert,' Adamski's long face broke into a wistful grin. 'You should see have seen her – she plays like an angel.'

'And when you came to England, you went to her college, made contact with her, right?'

Adamski shook his head, a stubborn look on his face.

'Come on, I know you were sweethearts back in the home,' persisted Janusz. 'You wanted to get back with her – before you started playing housey-housey with Weronika.'

'No! Ela is my friend!' said Adamski, face reddening.

Janusz took a swallow of beer. It occurred to him that the *psychol* in the hat could easily have discovered Ela's connection to Pawel and paid her a little visit, tried to get her to reveal his whereabouts. He had a sudden disturbing vision of Justyna and Ela's last few hours. The *skurwysyn* must have overpowered them, tied them up, fed them massive doses of the dodgy drugs to loosen their tongues, and after a few hours of fun, left them unconscious and dying, apparently of an accidental over-dose.

Then something else struck Janusz: Adamski used the present tense when he talked about Ela. He cleared his throat. 'The thing is, Pawel, I'm asking you all this because there's something you probably don't know.'

Pawel looked up at the older man, puzzled at the use of his Christian name.

'I've got some bad news,' Janusz went on, avoiding his eyes. 'About Ela.'

He took the news harder than Janusz could have foreseen: folding himself up in the chair and crying like a little child. Having never seen a grown man weep in that way, Janusz wasn't sure what to do. He dug out a bottle of *wodka*, put a glassful in the boy's hand, and, patting him clumsily on the shoulder, muttered a few consoling words.

Five minutes or more later, Pawel used the front of

his sweatshirt to wipe his eyes and nose as he listened to Janusz reveal what he knew of Ela's death.

When he'd finished, Pawel said, 'It's my fault she's dead.' Grief lent his long, sallow face a melancholic dignity.

Janusz felt a pang of pity. Less than an hour ago, he'd happily have given this guy the beating of his miserable life and turned him over to the girl detective. Now, he was convinced that, apart from his bungled blackmail plot, he was more or less harmless – and he seemed genuinely to love Weronika.

'Your fault why? Because it was you they were looking for?'

Pawel shook his head, eyes cast down. 'Ela would never have caused him any trouble – it was me who stirred things up, put her in danger.'

His words confused Janusz – *how could Ela cause Zamorski trouble*? It was like looking down a child's kaleidoscope: the shards of colour appeared to settle into one pattern, only to re-form into a new picture a moment later.

'If I tell you all of it,' said Pawel finally, meeting Janusz's gaze. 'Will you promise to leave me and Nika alone?'

Janusz paused. '*Tak*. You have my word on it.'

Fixing his gaze on the wall above Janusz's head, Pawel started talking, his voice so low Janusz had to lean forward to hear him.

'They put me in the home because people said my Mama and Tata were bad people,' he said. 'Maybe it was true, but at least they loved me.'

'I was so miserable there, in that place – until Ela

arrived.' A smile tugged at the corner of his mouth. 'She used to make up these stories – how we would run away with the gypsies, that we were really the stolen children of a King and Queen who'd come to collect us one day.'

Janusz recalled his own upbringing. While he'd been moaning to his mama about sweet rationing and not having enough toys, thousands of children must have endured a childhood like Pawel and Ela's.

'She looked after me like a sister. Once, when she found the big boys trying to burn me with a cigarette, she went for them like a wild boar!' Pawel's smile faded. 'She couldn't do anything about Witold Struk though.'

Janusz felt a pulse start to drum in his throat.

Adamski lit a cigarette, the lighter flame trembling. 'The first time, we were just excited to get a ride in his big fancy car,' he said. 'He drove us into the forest, and then we met *him*, waiting at the *dacza*.'

Janusz's gaze darted around the room as his brain tried to make sense of what he was hearing. Then his hands bunched, like he'd grabbed a live mains wire.

'Zamorski,' he said.

Pawel gave a single nod. 'Yes – except I didn't know his name, then.'

His voice dropped to a whisper. 'The first few times . . . nothing happened. We played checkers and he gave us things we never got in the home – Coca-Cola, chocolate, Captain Kloss comics.' He tapped some ash off his cigarette into an empty beer can, never meeting Janusz's eyes. 'He was just softening us up, to make it harder to say no in the end. Later, he would say "What about all the sweets and the toys – how else are you going to pay me back?"'

He shook his head violently, as though trying to dislodge some image.

'Every single time, I swore I would fight him, and every time I just froze, like a statue.' He pulled his jacket tighter. 'Do you know what the worst thing was? Realising that Ela couldn't protect me – or herself.'

'How old were you?' asked Janusz, his voice gruff.

'Six years old.' Pawel looked him straight in the eye for the first time since beginning his story. 'Ela was seven.'

Janusz dug his nails into his palms. 'What about the people at the home – couldn't you tell them what was happening?'

Pawel snorted. 'They all looked the other way, they didn't want to lose their jobs by pissing off an *esbek*.'

'What about Struk?' asked Janusz, after a moment. 'Was he involved in . . . the abuse?'

'No, he just played postman.' Pawel spat the word out. 'But in a way I hated him more. He bundled us in and out of that place, week after week, pretending nothing bad was happening.' He cradled his arms across his body. 'The one time I got up the guts to say that me and Ela weren't going back there, he shouted at me, told me I was garbage, just like my *straszna* family.'

Janusz had to stand up and walk around.

'What about him and Zamorski?' he said, once he could trust his voice. 'Did you ever see them exchange packages, or cash?'

'No, they hardly even spoke.' One side of Pawel's face twisted in a bitter grin. 'They couldn't stand each other. Zamorski treated Struk like a doormat – one time he slapped him, right in front of us, for forgetting to bring some magazine he wanted.'

In the SB file Janusz had taken from Struk's house, Lieutenant Struk had meticulously recorded his personal deliveries of Magpie/Zamorski's '*wyplaty*' – his wage packets. Janusz had assumed these to be envelopes stuffed with foreign currency. Now he realised the truth. The 'wage packets' had been six-year-old Pawel and seven-year-old Ela, taken from the children's home and delivered to the Bureau's star agent – *like takeaway meals*.

An image flashed up before him.

'This *dacza*. Was it by a lake?' asked Janusz.

Pawel nodded.

A view of a green-painted wooden dacza on the bank of a lake . . . set in a stand of birch trees . . . the curtains always drawn – Struk's bizarre attic gallery and the scene that he had painted over and over again.

The sense of menace emanating from the paintings, and the almost malevolent intensity of Struk's vision had puzzled Janusz. Now he understood. Struk had hated Zamorski, not for being a child abuser, but for reducing an SB Lieutenant to the role of pimp and delivery boy, and for causing his ultimate demotion. Maybe painting the *dacza* had started as a way of passing the time till he collected the children, but it had clearly become an obsession – the repeated depictions of the scene a kind of voodoo charm, an implacable oath of vengeance against his enemy.

His gaze flickered over Pawel's long sad face. 'How long did all this go on?'

'The whole summer. Then it just stopped. We never saw either of them again.'

The two men fell silent.

After a few moments, Pawel said, 'Afterwards, I would

go crazy for no reason, hitting the other kids, the teachers. A few months later, I tried to hang myself, but Ela found me, saved my life.' He lit a fresh cigarette from the stub of the last. 'It drove a wedge between us though. I knew the sight of me reminded her of . . . things she needed to forget.' Janusz nodded his understanding. 'You know, even after she got adopted by the English lady, I think Zamorski kept tabs on her, like he must have kept tabs on me. But she never made any trouble.' He thumped his scrawny chest – punishingly hard. 'It was me who had to go and wake the dragon.'

For many Polish children, it was the first story they ever heard: the tale of a dragon who had slept for centuries in a cave near Krakow, until he was roused by some curious and foolhardy children. The monster exacted a murderous revenge, killing scores of young girls, before he was finally outwitted and destroyed.

'That's why I went to the concert,' Pawel continued. 'To tell Ela I'd found out who the bastard was, this big politician who was all over the news.'

'What did she say?' asked Janusz.

'She told me to forget about it, the past was gone, there was no point raking it up. She was talking sense, but I lost my temper and shouted at her.' He pressed his fingers to his temples. 'And now I'll never see her again.'

There was no self-pity in the young man's voice, Janusz noted, only an acceptance of responsibility for what he had unleashed. 'You grew up not realising that it was Zamorski who . . . did those terrible things,' said Janusz awkwardly. 'Until Struk told you?'

'We never knew their names and as time went by, I couldn't remember their faces. I didn't *forget* what

361

happened, exactly, but I stopped myself thinking about it.' He tapped his knuckles against his temple, 'It went into a box in my head which never got opened.' He met Janusz's eyes. 'Does that sound crazy?'

'No, not at all,' Janusz said holding his gaze, thinking of the box he'd constructed in his own head for past regrets – and failings. 'So, you followed up the ad Struk put in the paper, about his antique furniture.'

Pawel nodded. 'When he answered the door I didn't recognise him. He was old and skinny.' – he sucked in his cheeks to demonstrate. 'He asked me what I thought of this guy Zamorski, who would be our next president. I told him I didn't give a shit for politics.' Pawel pinched out his cig. 'Then he said, "You don't know who he is, do you?"'

He said that Struk had scuttled down into his cellar, leaving Pawel standing in the hallway, and returned brandishing some kind of file.

'He started shoving it under my nose, gabbling on about what a terrible man Zamorski was, how personally he had never agreed with what happened.' Pawel stared up at the ceiling squinting to remember the words. 'He said if they hadn't stopped the rabble-rousers causing trouble for the country, the Russians would have invaded.' He shrugged. 'I thought he was just some crazy old man.'

Janusz nodded. After the decades Struk had spent plotting to destroy his old enemy it must have been a thrilling moment to have the instrument of his vengeance standing before him.

'He kept saying, "Look, look, there's your proof",' Pawel mimed Struk's crooked finger, his fervent prodding.

'At the top was the name Edward Zamorski, his birth date, something about Nowa Huta. None of it meant anything to me, but then he points again, and I see it – the name "Magpie".'

'Zamorski's SB codename. But I don't understand – why would that mean anything to you?'

'It was what Struk always called him, when he took us in the car – "*pan Sroka* has some new Titus comics for you today, *pan Sroka* has a special game for you to take home . . . "'

Using his enemy's secret codename in front of the children had probably given the old bastard a transgressive thrill, thought Janusz.

'When he saw me recognise the name, he laughed.' Pawel clapped his hands together once. 'And it all fell into place. The man who drove us to the *dacza* had that exact same high-pitched laugh, like a gate that wants oiling. Suddenly, I was six years old again, holding Ela's hand in the back seat of his car.'

'I started shouting at him, I don't remember what, I had him up against the doorframe.' Pawel shot his hand out, gripping the phantom Struk by the throat. 'He was saying "take the file, take the file, you can destroy him!"'

Pawel clutched his forehead, enduring some silent agony.

'There isn't a man alive who would blame you for killing him,' said Janusz.

'I didn't! That is . . . I never meant to,' said Pawel, raising his eyes to Janusz. 'He was standing in the doorway to the cellar, holding the door open with one hand,' he demonstrated with an outstretched arm, 'and the file in the other. As we struggled, he dropped it, and overbalanced.' He made a wild clutching motion with his left hand. 'He grabbed the door frame, but it gave way.'

He took a big breath and blew it out slowly. 'I was in London before I even heard he was dead.'

'But you took the file he dropped?'

He nodded. 'I couldn't bear the thought of leaving it there for anyone to read. I realised that after ruining my life and Ela's, Zamorski had gone on to become rich and famous. Somebody people *respected*.' He hissed the word. 'I wanted to make him suffer.'

'And when you started blackmailing him, he sent money,' said Janusz. 'So where did Weronika come into it? Why go after her?'

'The money didn't make me feel any better. The whole thing was just making me crazy again.' Pawel stared at the wall, lifting one shoulder.

'It was in Struk's file – that Zamorski had this little girl he adored who worked in a restaurant in England.'

It made sense. For someone with a lifetime's experience of recruiting informers it would be easy for Struk to shadow Zamorski and monitor his enemies' dealings with Weronika's mother.

'I decided to kidnap her,' Pawel went on, hanging his head. 'I'd torture him with the terrible things I was doing to her, and then I'd kill her.' He looked at Janusz sheepishly. 'I never expected her to come with me of her own accord – or that I'd fall in love with her.'

Janusz was struck by the irony of Pawel Adamski's story: after his childhood was destroyed by Zamorski, he had been saved by the love of his abuser's daughter.

There followed a long silence that Janusz was the first

to break. 'I should think you're hungry,' he said. 'I'll get you some *wiejska* – and then we'll work out how to get you and Weronika out of this mess.'

When Janusz returned with a plateful of food, Pawel took it, looking up at him with hopeful eyes. Then he slipped his right hand inside his shirt and pulled out a buff envelope. 'It's all in there,' he said.

As Pawel ate, Janusz extracted three closely typed A4-size pieces of card – still warm to the touch. Clearly the front pages of Zamorski's SB file, they summarised the highlights of the presidential candidate's career as star informer for the SB.

On the first page, the informer Magpie was named as '*Edward Zamorski – steel fabricator, Solidarnosc representative, Nowa Huta.*' It recorded Zamorski's recruitment in 1975 by an undercover SB operator, codenamed Agent *Kanarek* – or Canary. The Canary and the Magpie – *like something out of a children's fable*, thought Janusz darkly.

He was described as a '*highly-valued collaborator*' and a prolific supplier of intelligence from '*well-orientated sources*', SB-speak for his colleagues – and unwitting sources – in *Solidarnosc* and the church.

The second sheet listed Zamorski's principal targets. It included several well-known opposition figures, but the one that caught Janusz's eye was Father Marek Kuba, the courageous pro-democracy priest murdered by the SB. Beside it was the codename *Papiezek*, which had appeared so frequently in the documents from Struk's desk.

So, thought Janusz, it was the twenty-six-year-old Kuba who the SB had sarcastically dubbed 'Little Pope'. He recalled the photograph he'd seen, of friends and fellow activists Edward Zamorski and Marek Kuba at the front line of a rally, fending off ZOMO batons. He read on, heaviness gathering in his chest. Father Kuba was described as an *'anti-Soviet, anti-government, extremist; a committed enemy of socialism,'* his sermons to packed congregations described as *'material in fomenting industrial unrest.'*

The final mention of Kuba came in May 1986. After three striking steelworkers had been arrested and badly beaten, Zamorski passed the SB a juicy snippet of intelligence. Father Kuba had told him that the contents of his next sermon would go much further than the usual calls to rein in ZOMO and the *milicja*. He would speak instead of the 'moral vacuum' at the heart of communism and question the Party's right to govern. Janusz drew an involuntary breath, and raised his eyes from the document, not wanting to go on.

The entry was dated 18 May, 1986. It said that as a result of a tip-off by Collaborator Sroka, officers had secretly detained *Papiezek* and conducted a 'special interrogation'. The final sentence read: *'Refusing to recognise the objective reality of his situation, Papiezek chose instead a full immersion baptism.'* Janusz felt a wave of nausea – Father Kuba's badly beaten body had been found face down in the Biala River.

Janusz sat back on the sofa, picturing Zamorski's reliable, kindly face and wondering what went on inside that head. He no longer had any lingering doubts that the guy in the hat was acting on his boss's orders.

Pawel had finished eating and was dispatching another can of beer.

Janusz gestured to the documents. 'What were you planning to do with these?'

'I don't know,' he said. 'I don't care about any of it anymore. I just want him to leave me and Nika alone.'

Janusz ran a hand through his hair. *You'll be lucky*, he thought.

'If you're thinking you can just hand these over, bargain with them, forget it. You know too much, and whatever promises they make, they'll kill you – maybe even Weronika, too.'

Leaning forward to seek his gaze, Janusz spoke intently. 'Your only hope is to get the story into the press – but we'll have to work fast, the election's the day after tomorrow.'

Pawel stared at the floor, then nodded. 'Whatever it takes to protect Nika, I'll do it.'

'Listen to me,' he said, nodding towards the window. 'They followed you here – or maybe they've been watching the flat all along.' With a panicked look, Pawel started to get up but Janusz motioned him back into his seat. 'You should be alright going back down the fire escape, but at the bottom, climb over the wooden fence on your right – there's an alleyway that cuts down to Drayton Park.' Standing up, he pulled a wad of notes out of his pocket. 'It's five minutes up to Holloway Rd – you can get a cab there.'

'*Dziekuje bardzo, panu*,' said Pawel, his mournful gaze locked on Janusz.

'Then get yourself and Weronika straight to Luton Airport,' said Janusz, handing over most of the cash. 'Stansted's too obvious, they might be watching it – and take the first flight to Warsaw, Krakow or Lodz.'

He scanned Pawel's face – he looked like he was getting about seventy-five percent of this.

'When you land, go to the news kiosk and ask for the biggest-selling daily paper, and get a cab straight to their offices.' Janusz paused. The chances of a newspaper editor buying such serious allegations from a guy like Pawel Adamski were zero. In fact, with the election looming, it would be a huge challenge for anyone to convince them to run the story. 'Tell them everything you told me, and say that Zamorski's SB file is on its way,' he went on. 'I'll be a couple of hours behind you.'

Janusz checked his watch: it was gone 2 a.m. He decided the best course of action would be to contact Father Pietruski first thing and tell him everything. With a prominent party supporter backing the allegations, the papers were much more likely to be persuaded that this wasn't some hoax by one of Zamorski's opponents.

Pawel's face creased in a frown, 'What about Struk? Won't they think I murdered him?'

'Not once we get you a good lawyer. Anyway, right now that's the least of your worries, Pawel. The crucial thing is to get the story out there. When it breaks, Zamorski will know the game's up and stand down. Then he'll have nothing to gain from killing you – and you and Weronika will be safe.'

Twenty-Nine

Woken by the dawn light, Janusz was momentarily confused – he was a light sleeper so his bedroom windows had blackout curtains – but then he remembered where he was. After Pawel had left, he'd decided that he couldn't risk a visit from the *psychol* in the hat, especially now he had Zamorski's SB file. So he'd knocked up the guy next door, the one who worked in an art gallery. Okay, so it was past midnight, but he was still up and dressed. He seemed a bit shocked at his crazy neighbour's request to sleep on the sofa, but when Janusz explained that he'd stupidly locked himself out of his flat while putting the rubbish out, piling on the middle-European charm like whipped cream, he'd let him in.

Now, Janusz hoisted himself upright on the hard black leather sofa, cursing at his creaking joints, and checked the time: just past six. He reflected that he'd never slept under the same roof as a gay guy – a first he wouldn't be sharing with Oskar, that was for sure. Leaving the front door on the latch, he crept out in his socks and listened at his own door: nothing. He unlocked the door without making a sound.

He'd half-expected the scene that confronted him inside, but it sent a chill through him nonetheless. The place had been taken apart in the night with surgical thoroughness, every upholstery panel on the sofa and armchair slit open with a blade, and the edges of all the carpets pulled up; in the kitchen, they'd lined up the contents of the cupboards on the work surface, and emptied his coffee and flour tins into the sink. He'd clearly left just in time last night. Tough luck, *skurwysyny*. A wave of panic gripped him as he remembered Copernicus, but then he remembered putting him out on the kitchen window sill, splay-legged with indignation, before going next door.

Back in the next-door flat the hum of the power shower indicated his neighbour – *Sebastian*, that was his name – was up and about. Janusz had just finished folding up the duvet when his phone rang. *Oskar*.

'*Czesc*, Janusz.' His voice sounded uncharacteristically subdued.

'What's up, *kolego*?'

'Did you see *Crimeswatch* last night?' asked Oskar.

'It's *Crimewatch*, turniphead. No, I didn't. Why?'

'They had that lady *detektyw* on, talking about Justyna. The girl who got killed in the hotel?' Oskar's tone was starting to give Janusz the jitters.

'Spit it out, Oskar, I've got a lot to do today,' he growled.

There was another pause, then Oskar burst out, 'The guy from the hotel – it was him! The one who got me to take poor old Olek home.'

It took Janusz a while to get any sense out of his mate, but finally he pieced it together. Apparently,

Crimewatch had broadcast the shot of the guy in the hat and Oskar had instantly recognised him. It was the guy who had paid him two thousand euros to repatriate Olek's body to Poland.

'But you surely checked with the contractor at Olek's site, to see if the guy was for real?' asked Janusz, fighting a rising sense of panic.

'There was no time,' protested Oskar. 'I only got the call the day before we left.'

'What about all those official documents?' said Janusz, clutching at one last hope. 'You got them when you picked Olek up from the undertakers, right?'

A silence.

'Oskar?'

'I didn't pick him up from the undertakers,' admitted Oskar, finally. Janusz could picture his mate on the other end, shuffling his feet like a naughty child.

'Where the fuck did you get him then?!' Janusz's voice had risen several decibels.

'That guy with the funny hat, he delivered him, in a van.'

'What – to your place?'

'Not exactly. We did the handover in East Ham.'

'Where in East Ham, for God's sake?'

He hesitated. 'In the car park behind Lidl.'

Janusz groaned. This just kept getting worse. 'And this was the guy who kept phoning you when we were in Poland, right?' he asked. 'Wanting to know exactly where you were?'

'*Tak*, he was like an old woman – never off my back!'

Mother of a Whore! The fucker in the hat hadn't needed CIA-style tracking skills to follow Janusz from Islington to Gdansk. After giving Oskar a dodgy stiff to export, he had used him like GPS, calling up whenever he fancied to check their location.

Janusz shivered. He didn't even want to think about the penalty for using fake documents to export a body. He told Oskar he'd call back later. But before he'd had time to process this new bombshell, his phone started trilling again. This time the display said *'number unknown'*.

'Czesc?' said Janusz.

'It's me – Pawel.' It was Pawel alright, but he sounded in a bad way.

'They've got me and Nika.'

Before Janusz had even woken up that morning, Kershaw was on her way to his flat – and she was not a happy bunny.

After her productive day at the college, the official interview with Monsignor Zielinski had proved frustrating. As she'd half expected, the minute they reached the nick, he'd clammed up and started demanding his brief. Still, Streaky was visibly impressed at the way she'd manoeuvred him into confessing his illicit affair with Ela – and his disposal of her body in the Thames. No doubt his brief would claim he'd acted while the balance of his mind was disturbed, but Streaky and Kershaw agreed it had been a cynical attempt by the shagging Monsignor to prevent the affair being discovered. Either way, Streaky said they already had enough to nail him for 'disposing of a corpse with intent to prevent a coroner's inquest', which was apparently a pretty serious charge.

Streaky seemed to buy the scenario that poor pregnant

Ela committed suicide by PMA, and Kershaw didn't demur. But privately, the discovery that Ela's old boyfriend Pawel had looked her up on the orchestra tour to Poland, had cemented her conviction that he was involved in her death.

When she'd finally got home at gone nine, she decided to take another look at Ela Wronska's college file.

Perched at the breakfast bar eating toast and Nutella, she pulled out the clipping that Kiszka had paused over. *Kurier Gorodnik*. Zielinski's mention of Gorodnik as the place where Pawel had approached Ela gave the place a new significance. She re-read the rest of the file. And as she scanned Ela's educational background, a line jumped out at her, '*1984–1990 – Dom Dziecka 376, Gorodnik*'.

She fired up her laptop and typed '*Dom dziecka*' into a translation site, seeing the word 'orphanage' appear in the results box on her screen.

Suddenly, it all made sense. The Gorodnik link, Ela telling Zielinski that Pawel belonged to a part of her life she wanted to forget, the amateurish – no, make that *childish* tattoo on Ela's buttock. Pawel and Ela had met, and become sweethearts, in a children's home – a romance he clearly hadn't given up on – and she'd lay serious money that Janusz fucking Kiszka had worked it out long before she had.

The next morning, just before 7 a.m., Kershaw turned the Ford Ka into Kiszka's street and parked up in a spot with a good view of the entrance to his apartment block. She decided against buzzing his doorbell – if he saw her on the entry cam he might refuse to let her in. No, she'd just sit here till he came out, and catch the bastard on the hop.

'They say that if you bring the file right now, they won't hurt Nika,' Pawel told Janusz. From the difficulty he had forming the words it was clear they'd already given him a good working-over.

The last thing he mumbled out was, 'Sorry I dragged you into this.' Then one of the thugs, probably the *psychol* in the hat, took the phone.

'I tell you where to bring the documents, you leave in five minutes, you don't talk to anyone or play the hero.' His voice was flat, unmodulated. 'If we get what we want inside one hour, then it's all over and everyone can go home. If you're late, there will be consequences.' Then he gave Janusz some directions, which he scribbled on a scrap of paper, and hung up.

As it all sank in, Janusz felt a chill envelop his body. He could tell the girl detective everything, and risk a police siege that would almost certainly get Pawel and Weronika killed, or he could play delivery boy to a bunch of murdering gangsters who, once they had the documents, might easily decide to eliminate all three of them anyway. The sick feeling in the pit of his stomach told him that either way, any hope of exposing Zamorski had disappeared. However hateful the prospect of him being elected president tomorrow, the idea of disappearing to Poland with Zamorski's SB file, leaving Pawel and Weronika to be sacrificed on the altar of the greater good, was unthinkable.

'Mr Kiszka!'

Janusz whirled around at the sound of the flat Cockney vowels. The sight of the girl detective bearing down on him was about as welcome as a Russian son-in-law. He glanced up and down the street, praying to all the saints that Zamorski's thugs had given up on watching his place after finding it empty last night, otherwise her appearance might have just signed Pawel and Weronika's death warrant.

He tried to adopt a neutral expression. 'Good morning, officer,' he said, but barely slowed his pace.

As she drew level with him, her antennae started to vibrate. Kiszka looked – and smelt – like he'd slept in his clothes, and he seemed shifty and anxious, his usual cool out of the window. 'You're up and about early, you off somewhere?' she asked.

'Yes, I've got an appointment.'

She had to take two paces for every one of his just to keep up. 'You're certainly in a hurry,' she said, pulling up the hood of her black mac as some first, tentative drops of rain fell.

He caught the tone – that edge of sarcasm all cops seemed to acquire along with the badge. 'Sorry, darling, but I've got to catch the tube. I'm running late.'

Kershaw's eyes followed one of his shovel-like hands as it unconsciously touched his side – *checking for something*.

'No problem,' she said. 'I'll give you a lift. Angel or Highbury?' Pressing her key fob, a nearby car bleeped a reply. She looked up at the leaden sky and said 'Looks like it's going to tip down.'

Janusz checked his watch – a lift would save him precious minutes. 'Okay, then. Angel.' He had a hunch that if he missed the one-hour deadline, it would be Weronika who'd suffer the *psychol*'s threatened 'consequences'.

As he climbed into the passenger seat, Kershaw once

again adjusted her rear view mirror to keep an eye on him.

'So, Ela Wronska met the mysterious 'Pawel' in a children's home in Gorodnik,' she said, keeping her tone chatty, unconcerned. He just shrugged, but his eyes darted around like a pinball machine.

For a moment she thought someone had thrown gravel at the car till she realised it was hail raking the windscreen. 'And I know for a fact that Pawel talked to Ela in Gorodnik,' she said, flipping her wipers on, 'when the orchestra played there.'

All he said was, 'You've been busy.'

Janusz surreptitiously checked his watch: they were halfway down Upper Street now, about a minute from Angel.

'I think that Pawel came to London to try and persuade Ela to get back with him,' said Kershaw.

The girl and he had come to the exact same conclusion, thought Janusz – and they were both wide of the mark.

In the mirror she saw the ghost of a smirk cross his face. Why? *Because he didn't buy that scenario*, she realised.

As Angel Tube appeared up ahead she pulled up in the bus lane. He was halfway out the door before she grabbed his arm. 'Listen, I told you we got a hair from Justyna's body?' she said urgently. 'Well, we've got prints from Ela's room now, so if I can just find him I've got a really solid case.' *Okay, the prints might belong to the Monsignor, but why muddy the waters?*

Janusz met her determined gaze. Why not tell her the truth right now, see if she could raise an armed unit? If anyone could pull it off this girl could.

Kershaw held her breath: he looked like he might be about to spill the beans.

Then Janusz pictured the face of the *psychol*. And knew that he would cut Weronika's throat before the first uniform made it through the door.

The big lunk shook his head. 'Sorry, darling,' he told her, and strode away, seemingly impervious to the sheeting icy rain whipping across the pavement.

As he headed for the tube entrance, Janusz patted his side, felt the reassuring outline of the document, and checked his watch. Three stops on the Northern Line to Bank, about half a dozen on the DLR, then ten minutes on foot the other end, the guy had said – he should make it with time to spare. But as soon as he stepped inside the tube concourse the practised drone of the station announcer brought him up short. '. . . *the Northern line is suspended southbound due to a passenger under a train at Moorgate . . .*'

In the name of the Virgin! What was it with these platform divers? Why couldn't they take a nice quiet overdose at home?

Kershaw saw Kiszka do it a second time, right after he got out of the car – pat his side like he was carrying the crown jewels. An old phrase of her dad rang in her ears: *The game is afoot.*

She was still sitting there, biting her nails when her radio crackled into life and a woman's voice said: '*Charlie 1 to DC Kershaw. An urgent message from DS Bacon: please attend at J D Sports in Leyton Shopping Centre, where staff are holding an IC1 female, suspected credit card fraud. What's your ETA?*'

Thirty

Janusz took the stairs down from the elevated DLR platform at Canning Town two at a time. Checking his watch, he calculated that if the walk did take ten minutes then he'd get there with five still in hand. He congratulated himself again on his good fortune: if there hadn't been a number 43 bus at the stop outside Angel tube when the Northern Line had let him down, he'd never have made it.

He strode down Victoria Dock Road, shoulders hunched against the eye-watering wind. On his left, as the instructions had said, he passed a jumble of corrugated iron warehouses and what looked, and smelt, like a chemical factory. To his right was a desolate piece of waste ground, newly levelled in readiness for some construction project, and beyond it, the sluggish channel of brown water called Leamouth, where the River Lea widened before emptying into the Thames.

Now that he was confident that he'd reach his destination on time, Janusz started to consider what might happen there. Did Zamorski's thugs have orders, once the document had been handed over, to kill them all? He found that as much as he feared death, what really gnawed at him was the idea that Zamorski could have them all murdered and *still* become president of Poland tomorrow, with nobody any the wiser about the kind of man he was.

Passing a yard filled with yellow freight containers piled high like Lego, he took a right towards Leamouth as instructed, and found himself funnelled down an alley between the high brick walls of two old warehouses. A billboard on one wall advertised 'A landmark residential and leisure development'.

His heart was marking double time now. This was where his directions ran out – once he reached the alley the guy had said they'd come and find him. He slowed his pace. Four minutes to go. If he was going to die, he had to do *something* about Zamorski. If someone close to him, someone with clout, could be persuaded to confront him with his crimes perhaps he might crumble, withdrawing from tomorrow's election of his own accord. Father Pietruski? Probably too distant an acquaintance. What about Konstanty Nowak? The guy's charity work surely gave him some influence. But would he be clearsighted enough to accept the truth about his friend?

He made a decision. With his pulse pattering in his throat, he scrolled through his numbers and hit dial. One ring, three rings, six rings . . . and finally, Nowak's voice. Then he realised he was through to his voicemail. Before he had a chance to redial, he saw something that made his stomach lurch. Two or three metres ahead of him on the left a rusted blue metal door was set into the brick wall. As he watched, the handle turned and the door swung open with a metallic squeal. His last thought – the realisation that he might never see Bobek again.

The guy who opened the blue door was roughly the shape and size of an American-style fridge – and about as communicative. He summoned Janusz inside with a jerk of his head, and padlocked the door behind him, the graunching sound of the ill-fitting metal door and the rattle of the chain grating on Janusz's taut nerves.

He led the way through the damp-infused ground floor of the derelict warehouse, strewn with broken pallets and empty cable reels. Eyes fixed on that massive back, clad in an expensive parka jacket, Janusz suddenly pictured a bulky figure lit by orange pools of carbon light on Highbury Fields. This guy had been shadowing him, the night he went to meet Justyna!

They stopped at an old steel goods lift. 'In here,' said the man in Polish. Ukrainian, judging by the accent, thought Janusz. The Ukrainian followed him in, pulled across the huge concertina metal door as though it was a net curtain and with a clanking whine the lift began to ascend.

On the fourth floor, he nodded Janusz out. This floor had been subdivided, probably in the sixties or seventies, into smaller premises. He buzzed a camera entry phone beside a massive door – recently installed and solid steel, maybe eight millimetre. Once inside he pulled some businesslike shoot-bolts across the side and top of the doorframe.

Prodding Janusz in the back, he lifted his chin across the open plan expanse to the side of the warehouse that overlooked Leamouth. Ranks of sixties vintage sewing machines crusted with decades-old dust and cobwebs revealed the joint's former life as a rag trade factory. Janusz became aware of a strange smell hanging in the room – astringent, yet not unpleasant.

Beside the window stood a wide workbench – probably a fabric-cutting table – its surface recently cleaned, but still showing a few paler swirls of dust. On one corner lay a narrow-brimmed hat in a shiny grey fabric, the kind the girl detective had described as 'pork-pie'. A few metres away, a stack of well-worn aluminium flight cases. The *psychol* was planning a journey, thought Janusz.

The Ukrainian nodded Janusz into an office-type swivel chair on castors. The hundred-year-old glass and timber doors beside him afforded a desolate view over the fat brown serpentine coil of Leamouth, lashed by the gusting wind and spitting rain. If he craned his head he could just glimpse where it met the Thames a hundred metres away. Outside, on the ironwork balcony stood a rusted winch, relic of an age when raw materials had arrived, and finished goods had left, on ships moored below.

The door to what had probably been the factory manager's office opened and a figure sauntered out. At last, Janusz was face to face with the man he had chased in Gdansk, the man in the hat caught on CCTV in the hotel lift.

Rolling on the balls of his feet, he walked slowly over to Janusz. He swung him round in the chair to face the yellowish light from the window and looked him up and down, his crowded features twisted into an expression torn between curiosity and contempt.

He was in his late twenties, Janusz guessed, and solidly built – the trapezius muscles between his neck and clavicle humped up in the classic sign of a workout addict. But for all the physique, he had the face of a child who liked to torture small animals. The outer edge of his left ear was ragged, a big piece of cartilage gone, and judging by the redness and scabbing, the wound was recent. Janusz remembered the shotgun-toting Bielski firing at his pursuer in the woods at Kosyk, and felt a surge of ridiculous joy. *You did wing the bastard, panie kolego!*

'Why the fuck isn't he cuffed, *kretyn*?' the guy suddenly shouted at the Ukrainian, who shrugged and mumbled something. Then he turned back to Janusz, and nonchalantly pushed the side of his head with his fingertips, a gesture that was somehow more demeaning than being struck. Janusz noticed his cheeks were dappled with acne scars – probably a side effect of steroid abuse.

'Cuff him,' he said with a grin, 'but not before the old cunt hands over what we want.' Catching a whiff of something off the guy, Janusz realised it was the same smell he'd picked up before, a scent that was niggling at him, but which his brain, in its agitated state, couldn't quite pinpoint.

'I want to see Adamski and the girl first,' growled Janusz, which sent the *psychol* lunging towards him.

'You don't give the fucking orders!' he shouted, spit flying. Pulling a gun out of his coat pocket, he flicked off the safety and shoved it against Janusz's cheekbone, just below the eye. From the markings on the barrel Janusz could see it was a CZ-75, the cult Czechoslovakian nine millimetre and he could smell the oil used to clean the mechanism. A high-pitched hum filled his skull. He was in the zone now, a trancelike state where he didn't really give a shit what happened.

'Probably best not to shoot me till you know for sure I've brought the document,' he said. The guy's cat's-arse of a mouth worked angrily but after a moment he let the gun drop to his side.

Janusz hadn't given up on his plan to alert Nowak, and now an idea came to him – if he could provoke the *psychol* into attacking him, then he might be able to take advantage of the melee to press dial on his phone, which was sitting in his breast pocket, cued up on Nowak's number. If he answered – *when he answered, please God* – Janusz would start shouting his head off about Zamorski – not with any hope of rescue, but to alert Nowak to what was happening.

Seeking the *psychol's* gaze, he nodded at his damaged ear with an expression of concern. 'That looks nasty,' he said sympathetically, 'Twelve-bore?'

He ducked his head to deflect the blow, and the next thing he knew he was face down on the deck eyeballing ancient brown lino – the guy had thrown him out of the chair. Now he started kicking the shit out of him, just like he had that night in the flat, but, under the guise of curling up to protect himself, Janusz managed to press the phone keypad firmly against his chest.

Please answer. Please answer. A second or two later, through the thuds of the kicks, he made out the sound of a mobile phone ringing nearby. It seemed a simple-enough coincidence, until he heard a door open, and the ringing rise in volume.

A sense of foolishness, swiftly followed by a wave of utter desolation engulfed him. The kicking stopped, and he heard footsteps crossing the floor. Still he didn't want to open his eyes, didn't want to confront the sight he knew he would find. He was aware of being roughly picked up and set back in the chair, and finally, reluctantly, he raised his eyes to meet the clear hazel gaze of Konstanty Nowak.

'You called?' asked Nowak, looking at the display of his phone with a grin. 'Sorry, not a joking matter, I know.' He politely extended a hand palm-up, and Janusz surrendered his mobile.

The *psychol* now stood several paces behind Nowak, looking docile now his boss was in the room – like a dog that knows its place in the pack hierarchy, thought Janusz. All in a rush, he identified the scent he'd smelled on him, and in the room. *Aniseed*. And remembered that it was also the smell of anethole, the compound used to make PMA. An image clicked into the viewfinder of his memory – walking through the embassy with Father Pietruski, on the way to see Nowak, a man bowing, a gesture that had momentarily obscured his face. The *psychol*. Janusz remembered thinking the whiff of fennel was his aftershave. The warehouse must have been his drug factory – the dust on the table traces of the powdered chalk that formed the tablets, the equipment and product packed into the flight cases ready to be transported to its next destination.

His expression serious now, Nowak deftly turned the windcheater he was carrying inside out so it wouldn't get dusty, and laid it neatly on the cutting table.

'Perhaps you won't believe me, Janusz – if I may still be permitted to call you by your Christian name,' he said. 'But it was never my intention for you to be harmed – or to get so . . . enmeshed in this business.'

He perched himself on the table's edge.

'Your job was purely to find out where the boy was hiding so that we could get the file back.' He shook his head. 'It was your misfortune that he entrusted it to you. *'A poisoned chalice'*, I think the English call it.' He smiled with a dry cheerfulness and Janusz felt the last trace of hope that he might get out of this alive ebbing away. Nowak was clearly up to his neck in this shit, which meant there was no way he'd risk letting him survive.

'I was just about to cuff him,' said the *psychol*, but Nowak waved a dismissive hand.

'That won't be necessary.'

'Where's the girl – and Pawel?' asked Janusz gruffly.

'The girl is fine, Pawel less so,' said Nowak, his voice tinged with regret. 'I'm sure in your heart of hearts, you didn't really expect him to walk away from this, after all the trouble he's caused.' Janusz stared at the floor.

'But listen,' said Nowak, as if a happy thought had just occurred to him. 'I'm prepared to keep my side of the bargain and let the girl go. She has no idea who I am, and after questioning her, Radomil assures me she hasn't a clue what all this is about.'

The *psychol* grinned at Janusz and raised his eyebrows to convey how much he'd enjoyed interrogating Weronika.

'She can go back to her waitressing job under the firm impression that her boyfriend got entangled with drug dealers and paid the ultimate price,' Nowak chuckled. 'She's nineteen – in six months she'll have a new boyfriend.'

Janusz felt a wave of hatred. But he had no reason to doubt Nowak's promise to let the girl go. Why should he lie when he held all the cards?

'Now, may I have the document, please?'

Janusz opened the top buttons of his shirt, reached in for the file, and thrust it at Nowak.

'Just tell me one thing,' he said, as he watched Nowak's gaze devour the contents. 'Why in the name of all the saints do you want a bastard like Zamorski running the country? Do you get a big fat payoff or something?'

Radomil stepped forward at that, ready to bite if his master issued the command, but Nowak just smiled a tolerant smile. 'You young people think everything is about money,' he said equably. 'No, I'm backing Edward because I believe he is what the country needs.'

'A fucking paedophile who sold his country to the *Kommies*?' Janusz spat out. 'I wasn't aware they were qualifications for becoming president.'

'All ancient history,' said Nowak. 'You're an intelligent man – surely you must see that what our fractious country needs above all else is stability, a leader who can unite our ragbag of factions – church, unions . . . *intellectuals*.' As he mentioned the last group he rolled his eyes conspiratorially at Janusz. 'A strong president backed by a solid alliance is the only way to get things done. Edward is no genius, but he's prepared to listen.'

'To you?'

Nowak tipped his head in assent. 'Yes, to me, and a couple of other people who understand what is required.'

'Really – and what's that then?' asked Janusz sarcastically. Losing his temper would get him nowhere, he decided, but if he could provoke Nowak it might just give him enough time to work out a survival plan.

Nowak hesitated – then took the bait. Turning to face the window, he pointed out the cluster of cranes and high-rise blocks on the skyline that marked out the Olympics site.

'Look at that,' he said with admiration. 'The East End was a complete shit-hole, but they're transforming it – by an act of will.' He fixed his gaze on Janusz. 'All the hoopla over the sport? A sideshow. It's the roads, the rail, housing, retail – that's what will make the real difference.

'It's exactly what Poland needs – a whole new infra-structure, right across the country. Jobs for all our poor exiles stuck abroad cleaning English people's toilets.' His mouth curled in distaste, then he pointed at Janusz, 'A man like you should be doing a proper job back home, not playing *Jack the Lad* in London.'

Janusz raised an eyebrow. 'Maybe a lot of people you call exiles think of London as home now.' He realised, with a frisson of surprise, that he was one of them.

'Anyway, how do you plan to conjure up a million jobs?'

Nowak smiled. 'We've done our homework,' he said, and started to count off on his fingers. 'Within five years, there will be a comprehensive motorway network and two new hub airports; in ten years we will have regen-erated three zones of low employment: the Kashubian Lakeland, the Bialystok Forest, and the foothills of the Tatras, which will host three new cities dedicated to leisure and tourism.'

Janusz visualised the wild beauty of the national parks Nowak listed. For their 'regeneration' to produce jobs on such an enormous scale it clearly wasn't eco-tourism he had in mind – more like Dubai in the heart of Europe.

'Yeah? And who's going to fund your building spree?'

growled Janusz. 'I can't see the EU paying you to concrete over the country's top beauty spots.'

'Between you and me,' said Nowak, 'we're not keen on Poland's current obsession with Europe. "Human rights" for rapists, "health and safety", "working time directives . . . "' He paused, his eyes merry. 'The bureaucrats have taken over the asylum, no?'

Janusz frowned. Who else could come up with the sort of cash such a plan would demand? And be prepared to face down the shit-storm of criticism that the wholesale destruction of swathes of countryside would provoke, not just from Polish environmentalists but from governments right across Europe?

'The Russians,' he said, out loud.

Nowak tipped his head.

'You want Poland to climb into bed with Putin and the Kremlin? The bastards who made our lives a misery for forty years?'

Nowak pulled a tight smile. 'You know, for a relatively young man, you are remarkably conservative. But the younger generation doesn't have your baggage – they don't have a problem with our next-door neighbours.' He waved a finger at Janusz. 'Russia is awash with oil and gas profits – and all that cash needs a home. Poland is on the doorstep and a very attractive investment, if the young people can be brought home to help create the economic miracle.'

Janusz pictured with horror the class that ruled Russia – the old KGB types, and the gangster/oligarchs to whom they had gifted the country's richest assets – and thought of the journalists and other government critics who, two decades after communism had fallen, were still getting thrown in jail – if they didn't meet a fatal accident first. Then he remembered something else.

'But your father – he died in a Russian gulag.'

'Stalin saved Europe,' said Nowak with a shrug. 'After the war, he had to be ruthless, *especially* with the Poles. You must admit – as a people we've never been strong on self-discipline.'

Janusz racked his brain, trying to dredge up everything Nowak had told him during that first meeting at the embassy: how he and Zamorski had been *Solidarnosc* organisers in the seventies, had led strikes challenging the Communist regime. Facts that appeared to be borne out by the guy's biography on Wikipedia. And details such as the story of how Nowak had shared his food with the young Zamorski on the train taking them to jobs at Nowa Huta had the unmistakable ring of truth.

Something bubbled to the surface of Janusz's memory.

The SB file on Zamorski said he had been recruited by Agent *Kanarek* – Agent Canary – a codename Janusz had assumed to be a simple reference to the bird. Now he recalled that back then, conductors on trains were nicknamed 'canaries', because of the bright yellow peaks of their caps. Was it another of the SB's in-jokes? Had those *skurwysyny* in the secret police planted an under-cover SB officer on the train to Huta to befriend the young Zamorski, and amused themselves by dubbing him 'the ticket conductor'?

'How long was it after you met Zamorski that you found out about his little weakness for children?' asked Janusz. 'Or did you and your SB friends already have a file on him, when you targeted him on the train to Huta?'

Nowak just raised his eyebrows and smiled, running

a hand over his shaven head. Janusz sensed that he was caught between a desire to boast about his former career as an SB agent, and the code of silence he'd been taught.

'It can't have been much fun for Agent Kanarek, being sent off to work alongside the proles in a steel mill,' said Janusz with a half-grin. 'Did you do it for the money? Or were you like Struk – a true believer in the cause?'

'Not guilty to the last charge,' said Nowak with a laugh. 'Ideology never interested me. I'm a pragmatist.'

'So was it *pragmatic* to supply innocent children for that dirty *chuj* to abuse?'

Nowak's eyes narrowed. 'Sometimes you needed a strong stomach to stop the country from destroying itself,' he said. 'Nobody wanted an invasion – least of all Comrade Brezhnev. Think how many more innocents would have suffered and died if we'd let the trouble-makers provoke the Soviets beyond endurance.'

'And no doubt you take the same view of this scum who likes to hurt women,' said Janusz waving a hand in the direction of Radomil, who was sitting on the stack of flight cases, cleaning his nails with a penknife. 'Murder, rape . . . I suppose that's all just breaking eggs to make omelettes, in your book, right?'

Nowak glanced at Radomil. 'I wasn't aware that there had been any unnecessary impropriety,' he said. 'I don't approve of that sort of thing.'

'I'm sure Justyna will be relieved to hear it,' said Janusz.

Nowak's face darkened. 'You really are a boy scout aren't you? You hardly knew the girl, and as for Weronika, you've never even met her, yet you behave as though they're family. It's all about you, really, isn't it?' He gave a derisive snort. 'At least it made you easy to handle – when you threw the towel in, all I had to do was get Radomil to impersonate Adamski and rough you up, and suddenly it's a matter of *personal honour*.'

He stared at Janusz, his eyes hard as boiled sweets now. 'I have a theory about you, my friend,' he said, nodding to himself. 'This holier-than-thou attitude – it's all the product of a guilty conscience.'

Of course, Janusz realised, Nowak would have checked up on him. Hundreds of thousands of SB files were made public after the revolution and he'd certainly know his way round them.

Nowak had adopted an understanding expression. 'You know better than most that we all make compromises in life. If you hadn't given up your friends, you'd have ended up in prison. It would have destroyed your future.'

Janusz gripped the arms of his chair, seized by a fit of vertigo. It had been two days after his seventeenth birthday when the *milicja* had caught him spray-painting *Solidarnosc* graffiti, and taken him to Montepulich Prison. In the cells, before they started interrogating him, the one in charge had told him he had a simple choice: reveal the names of his two friends, the ones who'd got away – or leave the place zipped into a body bag.

The three of them had beaten him, stripped him, posed him like Mr Universe, taunted his skinny body, his fear-shrivelled *kutas*, and in a final act of humiliation – the memory of which he had, by an act of will, suppressed all these years – one of them had pissed on him. After four or five hours of that, yes, to his eternal shame, he had talked. He never saw his friends – Tomek and Mariusz

– again, although he did hear that they'd got off with a caution. It was only many months later that he discovered the incident had cost one of the boy's fathers, a civil servant, his job.

Janusz looked Nowak in the face. 'Going to prison wouldn't have destroyed my future – it was betraying my friends that did that,' he said. Puzzlement creased the skin round Nowak's eyes.

It was a statement of plain truth. Meeting Iza had given Janusz the will to live, had dragged him out of the deep pit into which he had sunk after Montepulich, but she could not erase the guilt and fury inside him. Were it not for his burning need to atone, he would never have insisted on going to the Gdansk demo, he would have left when it started to get dangerous – and Iza would still be alive.

He tried to imagine how Nowak's plans for Poland would play out. With so much Russian money invested, it surely wouldn't be long before the Kremlin's malign influence would be felt. It had always considered the Poles a major irritant and would welcome any opportunity to correct their misplaced affection for the Western democratic model. Then what? Laws to curtail the press? Constitutional 'reforms' to give President Zamorski ever greater power? Seeing again the expression on Nowak's face as he had scanned the SB documents, Janusz realised something else.

'A child abuser is the ideal president for you and your friends, isn't he?' he said.

He thought for a moment that Nowak was going to hit him, instead he got up from the table and stood with his back to Janusz, facing the view.

'You wanted the SB documents because they give you complete control over Zamorski,' Janusz went on. 'In case he ever gets second thoughts about your plan to sell the country to the Russians.'

Nowak said nothing for a few seconds. By the time he turned back to Janusz, his expression appeared cheerful again.

'It's a shame I can't persuade you to see my point of view – perhaps you'll come round to it when you see Poland's GDP go through the roof in five years' time.' Seeing Janusz's look of confusion, he burst out laughing. 'My apologies! I forgot for a moment that you've cast yourself as James Bond and me as the evil villain, so of course you thought that you wouldn't be leaving my lair alive.'

He leaned against the table's edge again, arms folded. 'Whatever you may think of me, I have no desire to increase the body count unnecessarily. Anyway, I arranged a little insurance policy to ensure you don't try to cause any trouble in high places.'

Janusz felt a strange mixture of feelings envelop him: a wave of relief that relaxed a hundred tensed muscles throughout his body, shot through with a thrill of fear at the mention of the 'insurance policy'.

'I am sure you've already worked out that it was Radomil who commissioned your friend for that . . . export job last week.' Nowak nodded over to the *psychol*, who was fingering his ragged ear.

Janusz gave a nod, wondering what was coming.

But Nowak paused and checked his watch. 'Excuse me, but I'm running late. Radomil, will you please bring the girl for pan Kiszka?'

Nowak turned back to Janusz. 'I'm afraid that the body you and your friend repatriated to Poland was not actually Olek Kamarewski, who lies forever in the foundations of an East End apartment block, but some unfortunate lowlife who displeased Radomil.' He put an imaginary gun under his chin and pulled the trigger, pulling a grimace at the thought of such brutality.

Bastards, thought Janusz. So he and Oskar had been duped into disposing of a murder victim, their 1600 kilometre journey filmed and documented on databases at four European borders. If he went public with the truth about Zamorski, the police would get an anonymous tip-off, the body would be exhumed and they would both face a murder charge.

Just then Radomil came back in the room, half-carrying, half-walking a slender zombie-like figure – Weronika, her wrists bound in front of her with plastic ties. As they got closer to the window, Janusz could see her mouth was reddened, swollen, her eyes above those angled cheekbones were half-shut and unfocused and judging by the rapid rise and fall of her chest, her breathing was fast and shallow. *Kurwa mac!* What had that fucking crazy done to her?

Nowak picked up the jacket he'd left on the table and slipped it on. The stocky little bald man in his cheap blue windcheater looked for all the world like one of the old retired guys you saw fishing off the harbour wall in Gdansk, thought Janusz. Nowak nodded to Radomil. 'I'll leave you to finish up here,' he said in a business-like tone. 'But don't hang around too long.' He waved a hand at Janusz, 'You can leave pan Kiszka to untie the girl.' Radomil nodded.

'Goodbye, Janusz,' said Nowak. 'I am sorry we had to meet in such circumstances.' He turned and with a cheery backward wave, he was gone.

Radomil was still holding Weronika upright against his body, one thick arm around her, beneath her breasts, her long pale hair brushing his forearm intimately. He hefted her upright and, using his free hand, beckoned casually to Janusz. But before he could get to his feet, Radomil jerked his chin out once, and Janusz felt a muscular arm lock itself round his throat. *Mother of God!* He dug his fingers into the forearm crushing his windpipe, and flung his bottom half around in a bid to free himself, sending the chair skidding from side to side. The Ukrainian cursed in his ear, but managed to maintain his grip. As Janusz fought for breath, he was aware of the distant whine of the lift motor as Nowak descended to ground level, followed, a few seconds later, by the clank of the lift gate, then silence.

Radomil grinned: the dog's master had departed. Keeping his eyes fixed on the struggling figure of Janusz, he picked Weronika up and hoisted her effortlessly onto his shoulder in a fireman's lift – Janusz heard a small gasp as she exhaled – and strode out onto the balcony. He could barely move his head but by straining right, he could just see what was happening. Radomil paused and, looking back at Janusz, tipped Weronika over the rail like a bag of cement.

At that moment, Janusz's entire perception seemed to shift, so that colours became intense, saturated . . . and every noise sounded loud and jarring, like he was locked inside one of those hip hop promos. Despite his struggle for breath, his brain became hyper-alert, too, and as he heard the splash four storeys below, which boomed like a distant explosion, he was conscious of a clock starting up in his head. She would have taken a big breath in, reflexively, at the shock of finding herself airborne, he calculated, which gave her two, probably three minutes before she started to drown, if she didn't panic and exhale on entering the water, that is. He couldn't see her being able to keep her head much above water – not with her wrists bound. As the clock's big digital display started its inexorable downward tick – 178, 177, 176 seconds – he felt an almost imperceptible lessening of the pressure on his throat as the Ukrainian shifted, trying to get a better grip. He drew a lungful of breath, felt the oxygen reaching his muscles.

The struggle must have edged his chair a few inches closer to the cutting table, because now he felt one of his lashing feet hit one of its solid oak legs. In an instant he had the flats of both size tens up on the table's edge and, with a grunt, thrust with all his strength, propelling the chair backwards on its castors with explosive force. He was rewarded by the sudden disappearance of the weight crushing his throat, and a jarring, discordant crash as the Ukrainian smashed into the windows behind. *167 seconds.*

As he hurled himself through the open door he caught a glimpse of Radomil's face, twisted with surprise, whipping round from the balcony rail. Janusz shoulder-charged him, knocking the fucker off balance, followed up with a roundhouse punch that landed right in the middle of his face. He went down and Janusz dropped his whole weight on top of him, producing a satisfying sound – the meaty snap of a rib breaking that was not his own. Feeling Radomil's right hand scrabbling beneath him, he lifted himself enough to slam an elbow down on the fucker's wrist, sending the gun skittering noisily off to the balcony's far end. He smashed Radomil's head onto the ironwork balcony floor once, twice, three times, till the eyelids drooped, then, aware that time was running out for Weronika, decided he didn't have time to finish the task, however enjoyable.

Hauling himself upright, he leaned over the balcony to scan the cappuccino-coloured waters of Leamouth, pitted with rain, and saw a pale head bob up, a little way downstream, maybe fifty metres from where the river entered the Thames and hit serious current. Below him, he saw that the riverside facade of the warehouse was clad with a network of scaffolding reaching right up to the balcony. For a moment, he considered using it to shimmy down, before dismissing the idea. No, there was only one way to get into the water quickly enough.

120 seconds. As a jet out of City airport roared overhead he clambered onto the railing and perching on the edge, calculated the drop – twenty-odd metres. Then, pinching his nose firmly, he propelled himself forward.

His final thought: *This is the last time I take a job from a priest.*

He was surprised how quickly he hit the surface, and by the violence of the impact, which was like running into a bus doing 50kph. Then there was the way the icy water thrust itself shockingly into every orifice. For a horrible moment it felt as though he would keep plummeting down for ever, but then suddenly he was shooting back up, buoyed by the three or four litres of air he'd stored in his lungs. As he broke the surface, he spun himself round towards the Thames, looking for Weronika, but couldn't see anything through the chop of murky water. Struggling out of his trench coat, he levered off his shoes – registering that the impact with the water had damaged his ankle joints – and struck out, doing a rough and ready crawl. *60 seconds.*

Halfway to the spot where he reckoned he'd last seen her, he glanced back up at the balcony, and met a sight that made him waste breath on a stream of curses – Radomil was getting up from the deck. Still slow and shaky, but how long would that last? He doubled up his stroke, feeling his chest complain at the effort, and then, as a khaki wavelet broke before him, he saw the back of a water-darkened blonde head bob lazily above the water. She wasn't moving. Perhaps she'd had insufficient air in her lungs when she'd hit the surface. Or maybe she'd been knocked out by the impact.

Let her be alive.

Another glance back to the balcony. Radomil was on his feet now, back at the rail, weaving a bit, but with the gun back in his hand – he looked like a spider in that web of scaffolding. He couldn't remember the range and accuracy of a CZ 75 but he was pretty sure that hitting a human-size target at fifty metres would be child's play.

As he got closer to Weronika, an eddy turned her round towards him. Her face was white as skimmed milk, but the eyes were half-open, lips moving. Then he saw her head start to droop forward and her eyes close. He had a sudden powerful flashback: *Iza at the demo, her white face, losing the will to live, leaving him.* A wave enveloped Weronika's face and she sank beneath the surface with a sickening finality.

Mother of God, no. Fixing his gaze on the spot, he kicked out wildly, ignoring the knifing pains in his ankles. Seeing no sign of her, he sucked in a breath and dived down, using his right arm to pull himself underwater, and sweeping his left around in a semi-circle in the hope of making contact. He opened one eye experimentally – but the visibility was nil.

He came up, praying she'd surfaced nearby, and trod water for a couple of seconds. *Nothing.* Down again, scoping out in circles from where she'd disappeared, going with the pull of the current. His hand hit slimy reed, it must be shallower than he thought. Not reed, *idiota* – hair! He grabbed for it again, caught a handful, and used his right hand to pull for the surface, the load coming surprisingly easily.

He drew a huge gulp of air, and turned the girl towards him. Her eyes were shut, her expression peaceful. Her mouth was rounded, childlike – *like Iza's.*

He slapped her face – a little water dribbled from her mouth, but otherwise it was like striking a wax sculpture. *No, not again, please God.* Then someone hurled a pebble into the water nearby. The mosquito whine that trailed it made him whip around to look up at the warehouse – where he found Radomil, both elbows leant on the balcony to steady his aim, gun pointed straight at them. Even concussed, he'd find his range soon enough. Casting desperately around, Janusz found the channel lined by vertical brick walls, wet, black, and tall as a double-decker bus – *no way out.* Then, twenty metres away, he spotted an old iron buoy, just before Leamouth entered the Thames. He struck out for it one-handed.

'Hold on Nika, hold on Nika,' he said under his breath

as they inched toward the buoy. As he reached it, he was greeted by a strident *clang!* The *psychol* was getting his eye in. He started hauling Nika's dead weight around the buoy, out of the line of fire, but then, glancing up, he saw a mystifying vision. Radomil was bending to gaze along the barrel of his gun for another shot, but he was no longer alone on the balcony – a dwarf in a hooded black cape had materialised beside him. As Janusz stared, the figure raised a silvery rectangle high into the air, and smashed it over Radomil's head. The fucker folded like a broken deck chair.

Janusz grabbed a heavy nylon rope trailing from the buoy's side and looped it around his body to keep himself afloat. Turning Nika's body around, he set her back against him, and cupping her chin to keep her face clear of the river, used his arms like bellows to force the water out of her lungs.

Squeeze, squeeze. He couldn't see her face, couldn't feel any sign of life. *Squeeze, squeeze.* Keeping up the rhythm, he craned his head around so he could see her profile, and watched a tiny dribble leave her lips, before the flow stopped altogether. She remained as still and beautiful as a statue on a grave. *No, Mother of God, no.* He turned her round and pinching her nostrils, locked his mouth onto hers, and blew gently, remembering a health and safety course back when he and Oskar built motorway bridges. *One elephant, two elephant, three elephant.* Pause. *One elephant, two elephant, three elephant.* Pause.

Nothing. He locked his mouth on hers again, but with a dragging, draining sense of hopelessness. Suddenly a jet of coppery-tasting water shot into his mouth, followed by a plosive cough. He turned her to face him, holding her head clear of the water as the fit of coughing convulsed her body and, finally, saw her eyes open, blue shot with grey, the colour of pebbles on a Baltic beach, and meet his for a moment. Then they closed again.

'Kiszka!' For a moment, he thought the voice shouting his name was in his head, but then it came again. 'Kiszka!'

He inched back around the buoy and looked up at the balcony. The dwarf had taken off its hood, revealing the blonde head of the girl *detektyw*. He felt no curiosity, only relief to see that she was talking into a radio.

Thirty-One

It took eleven minutes for the River Police Targa to speed Janusz, and the semi-conscious Weronika, upstream to London Bridge, where paramedics from Guy's Hospital, located a stone's throw from the riverside, were standing by.

They wheeled her through A&E into a recovery room, and as nurses hooked her up to monitors and stuck an electronic temperature probe in her armpit, a doctor arrived at her bedside. He beckoned to Janusz, who was hovering just outside the open door. He hobbled over on the crutches they'd given him, ungainly as a pantomime horse.

'The police say she may have OD-ed on an Ecstasy variant?' the doctor asked, squinting up at the monitor on the wall to which the temperature probe was attached.

'Yes, it's called PMA,' said Janusz.

The doctor leaned over and ripped off the thermal blanket she'd been wrapped in. 'Drug-induced hyperthermia,' he told one of the nurses, followed by a stream

402

of incomprehensible medical jargon in which 'ice water baths' and 'aggressive hydration' were the only words Janusz understood.

'Her temperature's almost 40 degrees,' he told Janusz, scanning his face to see if he knew what that meant.

He did.

'All we can do is get her temperature down and maintain blood pressure. If we can head off renal failure, she's got a good chance.'

Janusz leaned against the wall. The thought of her dying, now, was more than he could bear.

'I tell you something,' said the doc. 'If she hadn't been immersed in that freezing water, I doubt we could do anything for her.'

After Janusz had hung around in A&E for another hour, a second medic told him that the impact with the water had broken his right ankle and badly sprained the left. With one leg strapped up and the other encased in plaster to the knee, he took the lift up to the ITU to see how Weronika was doing. At the door, a nurse looked him up and down and, taking pity on the big man with the anxious eyes, agreed to let him sit by her bed for a while.

Weronika was sedated and unconscious, but he decided he could discern a reassuring trace of colour in those sculpted cheeks, and her fingernails had lost the bruised look they'd had when the river cops had pulled her out of his arms and into the boat. The funny thing was, now he could look at her properly for the first time, he couldn't for the life of him work out why she had ever reminded him of Iza. Weronika had the sharply planed, otherworldly beauty of a model, nothing like Iza's rounded, soft prettiness.

As he emerged from ITU, Janusz turned his mobile back on and found he'd got a text from DC Natalie Kershaw. She was in the hospital and wanted to see him. They met in the hospital's staff canteen, on the eleventh floor.

As he made his way towards her table next to the window, still struggling with the crutches, she looked up and they shared a rueful grin.

He lowered himself into the seat she pulled out for him. 'We make quite a pair,' he said, nodding at the flesh-coloured strapping that reached from her wrist to her elbow. 'Did that bastard hurt you?' He recalled her whacking Radomil over the head with what he realised now must have been one of the flight cases.

'No, no – he didn't come round till after back-up arrived,' she said, setting her coffee cup back in its saucer awkwardly with her left hand. 'I tore a tendon, climbing the scaffolding.'

He visualised the high sides of the warehouse, the web of slippery steel. The girl really was a *psychol*.

Studying Janusz's outfit – garishly-patterned jumper and cord trousers, presumably out of the hospital's emergency clothing store – Kershaw reflected that the man she had once thought so dangerous now looked about as fearsome as a favourite uncle.

She pushed a cup of coffee towards him, black and insanely strong, just as he liked it, and fixed him with a look. 'So,' she said, 'before we ask you in for an official interview, any chance of you telling me what the hell has been going on?'

Beyond the window the sun had come out, transforming the ribbon of river below into liquid jade. Janusz

404

took a gulp of coffee, but still couldn't wash away the metallic tang of river water.

'You've got the CCTV and forensics to prove that this . . . Radomil guy murdered Justyna, right?' he said, flexing his fingers so the joints popped.

'Yes,' she allowed. 'But I've got no idea *why* he killed her.' He'd been carrying a passport – and the Polish police had faxed over a lengthy rap sheet. Radomil Janowiak was a career gangster in the synthetic drug trade, who'd narrowly escaped conviction for the rape of a fifteen-year-old girl in Warsaw the previous year, after the girl unaccountably changed her story.

He fiddled with the spoon in his saucer. 'And I'm guessing you found another of his victims, in that warehouse?'

'Pawel Adamski? What was left of him, yes.' She blinked, trying to clear the image. 'On the floor of the men's toilets.' Adamski's passport had been lying in a pool of half-congealed blood under a urinal.

'He'll have Radomil's DNA all over him,' said Janusz. The guy wasn't the kind to delegate the violence – he enjoyed it too much.

He fell silent. Pawel's death would come as a devastating blow to Weronika, if she survived the PMA overdose. He remembered the story Pawel had mentioned, about the children who woke the dragon. If only the dumb *burak* had stopped blackmailing Zamorski when he fell for his daughter, maybe the two of them might have escaped, started a new life somewhere.

'As for the religious girl, Elzbieta, he murdered – I've got nothing that would help you with that,' he said, shooting her a look from under his eyebrows.

She shrugged. It was obvious where he was going with this.

He stretched his plastered leg out, wincing. 'The way I see it, darling,' he said, 'you've already got the guy nailed for two murders and an illegal drug factory. Sure, I'll make a statement about how he tried to kill Weronika, too. But I can't see what else you need from me.'

Kershaw shifted in her seat. 'What was Adamski's role in all this? And the girl's?'

Ever since the police boat plucked him out of the water, Janusz had been wondering whether to tell the girl about Konstanty Nowak and Zamorski. But what solid evidence did he have against either of them, when all was said and done? Ela and Pawel, the only two people who could testify to Zamorski's crimes, were both dead. And the SB document that could prove the entire conspiracy was in the hands of Nowak, who would dangle it over the head of his creature, the president, for the rest of his political life.

'What does it matter?' he shrugged. 'You've got your murderer.'

'Maybe, but I think that bastard Janowiak was acting on orders.' She stuck out her chin. 'And I think you know who was giving them.'

He met her gaze. 'And we both know that you never catch the big fish,' he said, throwing a weary hand up in the air. 'This is the way the world works.'

She bit her thumbnail. 'If Radomil does decide to talk, to give up his boss, would you help me then?'

He was about to tell her that wasn't going to happen, the guy wasn't the type to spill his guts, but then he scanned her intent little face, mouth set in a determined line.

'Yes, I would.'

She gave a single, satisfied nod.

He had a hand on the crossbar of his crutch, ready to lever himself out of the chair, when she leaned across the table and put a hand on his forearm.

'Do you remember me saying that I thought Justyna's killer left your card in her mouth, as a kind of message to you?' she asked.

He nodded.

'Well, I think that was another thing I got wrong.'

She saw Justyna's face again, cheek pressed to the mattress, forefinger laid across her lips – a gesture which, at the time she had put down to chance. Now she believed it had been a deliberate sign by the dying girl, telling police to *look in her mouth*.

'I think she put the card there herself, when she realised Radomil was going to kill her,' said Kershaw. Janusz met her steady gaze. 'It was her way of telling you what had happened – because she knew she could trust you to bring her murderer to justice.'

By the time Kershaw got back to the nick, DI Bellwether's Volvo was parked up in its usual spot. According to Bonnick, right after his arrival he'd summoned Streaky to the eighth floor, and she'd barely had time to make a cuppa before the phone on her desk rang, too.

'Sit down, Natalie,' said Bellwether, from behind his desk, indicating the vacant chair next to Streaky, who, she noticed, had put on his suit jacket. 'I hear from DS Bacon that you've been rather busy the last few days,' he said, setting both hands on his armrests.

'Yes, Guv.' Kershaw slid Streaky a sideways look – *was*

407

this going to be a herogram or a bollocking? – but she couldn't read his expression.

'You've got a good case against this priest character . . .' the DI went on.

'Monsignor Zielinski.'

'Zielinski, yes – for the disposal of Elzbieta Wronska's body.'

He consulted a notepad on his desk. 'Plus a suspect in custody for the murder of the man found in the warehouse toilets, and the murder of the girl in the Waveney Thameside Hotel. And let's not forget his portable drug factory.'

She allowed herself to relax a fraction. *Herogram.*

Bellwether looked up and smiled enigmatically. 'He's quite a catch, this Radomil Jan-ow-iak,' He rhymed the middle syllable with cow.

'It's Yan-ohv-iak, Guv,' said Kershaw.

Streaky shot her a warning glare. 'Whatever,' said Bellwether, his smile evaporating. He leaned forward and put both elbows on the desk. 'Here's the thing, Natalie. We all want to put the bad guys behind bars, but the way you've conducted this investigation has been inappropriate and wholly unprofessional.'

Make that a bollocking.

As Bellwether started turning the pages of his notepad, Streaky used his little finger to dig wax out of his ear.

'Failure to attend a job in Leyton . . . A complaint from Traffic about a private car with a Met logbook on the dash dumped in a bus lane in Islington . . . failure to consult DS Bacon before deciding to follow this *Kisszaka* character . . .' Streaky shot her a look, in case she was planning to give him another pronunciation lesson.

'There just wasn't time, Guv. It was a spur of the moment decision,' she said, trying to keep her voice steady. 'If I hadn't jumped on behind him there and then when he got that bus I'd have lost him.'

'And what about when you got to this warehouse? What on earth did you think you were doing?' he said, his tone becoming incredulous. 'You know the procedure – you should have called for back-up, not risked your life scaling four floors of wet scaffolding!'

'I *am* an advanced climber, Guv,' said Kershaw, pulling an apologetic grimace.

Bellwether continued as though she hadn't spoken.

'And perhaps you could remind me, Detective Constable,' he said, tapping his pen on the desktop, 'of the standard procedure when a police officer encounters a situation involving firearms?'

Fuck. 'Guv, it would have taken half an hour, more maybe, to get CO19 there,' said Kershaw, aware of a pleading note entering her voice.

Bellwether put the tips of his fingers together and fixed her with a steely look. 'I'm also interested in how this Kiszka got stopped at Stansted,' he said. 'Special Branch can't find anything official on the system. Any ideas?'

Double fuck. She opened her eyes wide and shook her head. By the sound of it, at least Jason had covered his tracks after slipping Kiszka on the watch list.

Bellwether sat back, shaking his head. 'When I first joined CID, the place was full of detectives who displayed a blatant disregard for the rules. They thought police work was all about boozy lunches with informants and getting physical with suspects,' Streaky sucked his teeth disapprovingly. 'I'm glad to say that attitude is largely ancient history nowadays,' he continued, with a glance at the Sarge.

'As a modern police service we have to be rigorously professional – the public has a right to expect us to observe the rules and regs, and to follow *all the proper processes,*' he said, tapping out each word with his pen on the desk. 'This is a twenty-first century capital city, not the bloody Wild West!'

Bellwether squared his notebook on the desk and lined his pen up along the edge. 'I am suspending you forthwith, pending investigation by Divisional Professional Standards. My advice is that you use the time to consider whether you possess the right attitude to be part of the Met, let alone CID.'

Triple fuck. As she and Streaky left Bellwether's office, Kershaw was aware of a buzzing in her ears and a numbness enveloping her fingers and toes.

'Well, that went well,' said Streaky.

'It's not fair,' she protested. 'If I hadn't done what I did that girl would be dead! And probably Kiszka, too.'

Streaky stopped mid-corridor and whipped round to face her, his chin already reddening.

'You know what you are, don't you, Kershaw?' he jabbed a finger at her. 'You're *job-pissed.*'

She stared at her feet. A job-pissed cop was an over-excitable sad case who'd become hopelessly obsessed by their work, usually because he – or she – had sod-all else going on in their lives.

'It's one thing being job-pissed in *Traffic,*' said Streaky, dismissing an entire department with a wave. 'So what if a few motorists doing thirty-four in a thirty zone get tickets. But in CID, it's a *fucking liability.*'

A passing civilian carrying a box file shot the big ginger bloke and the short blonde a curious look.

'Yes, Sarge,' she muttered. But Streaky wasn't finished.

'I'll bet that most of your brilliant deductions about this case have turned out to be a Load of Old Bollocks, haven't they?'

She gave a half-nod – he was right about that.

'And d'you know what?' he went on. 'If you'd kept me in the loop, instead of going off on your own private ego trip, we could have put the lid on this *before* villains started throwing girls in the river!'

Kershaw bit her lip hard enough to bruise it.

'You've got to learn you're part of a team, not the Lone fucking Ranger!'

Breathing heavily, Streaky hitched up his suit trousers.

'Right then,' he said, calming down. 'If you take all that on board, then one day, you might just make a passable detective.'

Their eyes met.

'Sorry, Sarge. And . . . thank you.' She felt an absurd rush of pride. *Streaky rated her!*

Back on the fourth floor, the Sarge barged through the door to the office. To her horror, the place was heaving – Browning, Bonnick, the civilian officer Toby Brisley, and – just her luck – Ben Crowther, too.

'Chin up,' said Streaky to her under his breath, before clapping his hands and addressing the whole room. 'DC Kershaw here will be taking an unforeseen sabbatical from CID to catch up on the daytime TV schedule,' he said, with a sarcastic grin. 'So to see her off, we're all going down the Drunken Monkey for what I believe the boss-wallahs call a "*working lunch*".'

'I'll get my fags and meet you boys at the lift,' he shot her a sly look, 'but Spiderwoman here says she'd rather take the drainpipe.'

She was lifting her coat from the hook when she heard Ben's voice by her ear.

'Bad luck, Nat,' he said softly, reaching past her for his jacket. She took a breath and turned round.

'Listen, Ben,' she said, her gaze hovering around his mouth. 'I'm really sorry about the other day, I behaved like a total numpty.' She gave a backward nod and dared to meet his eyes. 'I let Browning get to me, wind me up about the night we . . . went out.'

'Hey, don't stress about it,' said Ben, eyes crinkling at the corners. 'Streaky dropped a hint that something like that had happened.'

He helped her on with her coat.

'Streaky as a relationship counsellor, what a thought,' said Kershaw. 'Not like we count as a relationship!' she trilled, back-pedalling madly.

Ben just laughed. 'Maybe he could have his own reality show, advising star-crossed lovers.'

'His top tip for healing rifts – take the little lady for an Indian.'

'Or, if it's really serious, a slap-up meal at Romford Harvester.'

They stood there grinning at each other. I'm finally getting the hang of this apology business, thought Kershaw.

'I had a really nice time the other night, Natalie,' said Ben, straight-faced now.

'So did I, Ben.'

'Really?'

'Yeah, really.'

Ben brushed an invisible mark out of the sleeve of his jacket. 'So, after this piss-up . . . I don't suppose you fancy getting something to eat?'

What the hell, she thought, *one of us could always get a transfer.*

'That would be lovely.'

Thirty-Two

Janusz stood at the polished walnut bar of the Polish Hearth Club, ordering drinks for himself and Father Pietruski. Kensington was a bit of a *schlep* and the place wasn't exactly cheap, but they'd agreed to meet here for the same unspoken reason – it was a nice quiet spot for a discreet conversation. As the white-waistcoated bartender prepared his order, Janusz studied the oil paintings of Poland's past presidents that lined the walls of the high-ceilinged Georgian salon. After the Nazi invasion of 1939, the Polish government's cabinet-in-exile had continued to meet in this room – right up until the first democratic elections in 1989. Now the next time he came here he'd see that bastard Zamorski's mug staring down at him: although the polls only closed an hour ago, everyone said he had it in the bag.

Janusz carried the drinks to the corner table – a precarious manoeuvre given his knee-high plaster cast. After telling Pietruski the latest news on Weronika – the doctors said she was out of danger – he had barely begun to relate Pawel Adamski's revelations about Zamorski when the old man raised a hand to stop him.

'You can't close your ears to this,' protested Janusz in an angry murmur. 'That bastard's probably president by now – and the church helped put him there.'

The priest closed his eyes. The old guy was looking fragile since this business, thought Janusz with a stab of anxiety.

'I know all about it,' said the priest quietly.

Janusz stared at him.

'But before you start thinking that I, or the church, had any part in this wicked *konspiracja*, it was the poor young man himself who told me the story.'

'Pawel?' asked Janusz, incredulous. 'When?'

'The night before last, before he came to you – he presented himself at the church, just as I was locking the doors.' The priest stared at the table. 'I could see he was in an overwrought state, so I agreed to hear his confession.'

The priest pulled a hand across his forehead, as though to erase what Pawel had revealed that night in a confession lasting two hours. 'From what you said on the phone, you are already aware of Zamorski's wicked depravity against helpless children,' he said, his face hardening. 'But what Pawel wanted to talk about was the violence he himself had unleashed, by his lust for revenge.' He let out a wintry sigh. 'He wasn't a bad man, at heart. I only hope that my words that night were of some small help to him.'

They sat silently for a moment, both thinking of Adamski's wretched childhood.

'What do you intend to do – about Zamorski?' asked Janusz.

'What can I do?' asked the priest, turning weary eyes on him. 'You know that I cannot break the seal of the confessional, even after death. And the church is hardly in a strong position to accuse anyone of such a crime,' he said, raising a skinny old hand in a gesture of defeat, 'even if we could produce a single scrap of evidence against him.'

So Zamorski was going to get away with it, thought Janusz, and unless Radomil could be persuaded to turn informant on his paymaster, so was Nowak. Then he remembered something he had to break to the priest.

'You know it was Zamorski who betrayed Marek Kuba?'

'Betrayed *Marek*? Are you sure?' asked Father Pietruski, eyes wide with shock.

Janusz nodded. 'It was all in the SB document. Zamorski warned them that he was about to give some big sermon, even told them where to pick him up.' He slumped back into his upholstered chair, feeling suddenly weary. 'He might as well have been his executioner.'

Suddenly, the sound of tinny cheering rang out, a jarring note in that hushed setting. The barman, who had turned on a tiny television behind the bar, evidently at the request of a group of drinkers, smiled apologetically and reduced the volume to a whisper. Janusz and the priest felt their gaze drawn to the screen, which showed celebrations getting underway at Renaissance Party headquarters.

The piece cut to a shot of Zamorski, impeccably suited, casting his vote earlier that day, looking calm and in control, as a banner at the bottom of the screen ran an exit poll prediction saying he would receive 65 percent of the votes cast.

An explosive sound of contempt from the big man

sitting with the priest drew some surreptitious looks from the bar's other residents.

'With both houses behind him, he could be in power for a generation,' said Janusz.

'I'm still close to some *Solidarnosc* people – good friends of Marek,' said the priest, tugging at his earlobe. 'Some of them have *Partia Renasans* connections. It's only right that they should be told the truth about Zamorski.' His lips trembled at the memory of his fellow priest's brutal death. 'For all the good it will do.'

As the two men drank in sombre silence, Janusz felt a sudden impulse to cheer the old guy up. 'I'm having a visitor over in a couple of weeks,' he said, his voice gruff.

'Marta?' asked the priest, his eyebrows shooting up.

'No, father. Bobek.' Janusz felt his mouth twisting into a foolish grin. 'He's coming to stay with me for a few days.'

The priest's face brightened, but then he frowned. 'Should you be taking him out of school?'

He gave the old man a caustic look. 'I'll set him some maths problems, alright?'

After Father Pietruski left, Janusz settled down to get comprehensively drunk, but ten minutes later, a loud voice shattered his reverie.

'*Czesc*, sisterfucker!' bellowed Oskar, hurling himself into the seat the priest had vacated.

'Put a sock in it, Oskar,' Janusz murmured. 'You're not on site now.'

'Sorry, everybody.' Oskar made an expansive gesture that encompassed the room. Seeing people's attention fixed on the TV, he craned round Janusz's shoulder to squint at the screen. 'What's going on?' he asked Janusz, then his eyebrows shot up. 'Don't tell me I'm missing Eurovision?!'

'You're not serious, Oskar?' said Janusz, watching his mate upend a tiny silver-plated bowl of nuts into his mouth. 'You must know there's an election on.'

'Oh, *politicians*. You won't catch me voting, it only encourages them,' he said dismissively, spraying nut fragments over the table. '"It takes two to lie – one to lie and one to listen."'

'Who said that?' asked Janusz.

'Homer Simpson,' said Oskar, with the air of someone quoting an unimpeachable source.

'Anyway,' he said, dusting salt from his hands. 'Are you going to get me a fucking drink or shall I just die of thirst here on the carpet?'

As Janusz paid for the round, he wondered briefly whether he should tell Oskar about the murdered gangster they'd unknowingly delivered to Poland in place of Olek, but decided against it. With Radomil – and the gun that had probably dispatched his victim – in police custody, he reckoned Nowak's insurance policy had expired, and telling Oskar anything he didn't strictly need to know was a risky strategy.

Nine quid poorer, Janusz returned to the table bearing the drinks.

'So, *kolego*,' said Oskar slyly. 'Guess who turned up at the Stratford café today?'

'Who?'

'Oh, only Kasia,' said Oskar swirling his drink round.

'Yeah?' said Janusz, pretending to look at the TV, aware of a fluttering sensation in his stomach. 'How's she doing?'

Oskar leaned toward him. 'She's left that club!' he said in a piercing whisper, 'where she does the *striptiz*!' A few heads turned at nearby tables.

'Yeah, I know – her boss told me,' said Janusz. 'He overheard her talking to Basia – they're opening a nail bar in Warsaw.'

Oskar shook his head slowly, his face a chubby roundel of pent-up glee.

'And you're meant to be the big detective?' He shook his head pityingly. 'Since when did Ray start speaking Polish, *idiota*?'

Janusz realised Oskar was right, for once: Ray did only know about three words of Polish. The whole thing had been a malicious wind-up, no doubt to pay Janusz back for telling the punters there were hidden cameras in the peepshow booths.

'She's opening a nail bar, alright, but not in Warsaw,' said Oskar, 'in *Stratford*.' He chuckled delightedly.

'She told *you* all of this?' asked Janusz.

'Why not?' protested Oskar, then shrugged. 'Okay, so maybe she came in looking for you. She asked when you were coming back from Poland.'

Janusz fought an urge to phone Kasia there and then – knowing that Oskar would never let him live it down.

'Anyway,' Oskar went on, 'I didn't come all this way just to sort out your sex life. I've got a brilliant idea for an import business.' He leaned toward Janusz. '*Antique woodstoves*,' he whispered.

Oskar rapped out a celebratory tattoo on his mate's plaster cast. 'You and me, *kolego*, we're going to be zloty millionaires!'

419

Epilogue

GLOS WARSZAWY

PRESIDENT DIED 'BY DROWNING' – A NATION MOURNS

The Government has declared three days of national mourning after the shocking death of President Edward Zamorski, who was elected in a landslide vote four weeks ago. President Zamorski's body was found among reeds on the eastern bank of Biala River yesterday morning, and police sources confirm that he died by drowning. A note found on his body suggests that he took his own life for personal reasons. By a poignant coincidence, the President's body was recovered from almost exactly the same spot as that of Father Marek Kuba, the pro-democracy cleric abducted and murdered by members of Sluzba Bezpieczenstwa in 1986.

World leaders have joined to offer tributes to a national hero, a man who was a beacon of courage and integrity.

Acknowledgements

Although many of the bigger historical events in this book are accurately described, it is largely a work of fiction. Readers interested in reading more about the *Solidarnosc* story or about Polish history in general might try some of the following works that played an invaluable part in my research.

SOLIDARITY – The Polish Revolution, by Timothy Garton Ash. Yale University Press 2002.
The Magic Lantern: The Revolution of '89 Witnessed in Warsaw, Budapest, Berlin, and Prague, by Timothy Garton Ash. Random House 1990.
God's Playground – A History of Poland: Volume II: 1795 to the Present, by Norman Davies. Oxford University Press 1981.
The Polish Way by Adam Zamoyski. John Murray Publishers 1987.

I'd like to give heartfelt thanks to my husband Tomasz, whose experience of growing up in Poland and living through the Solidarity era brought the historical record to life for me – sharing his memories of everything from the titles of children's comics to street demos and black market smuggling exploits. The list of others who helped with the Polish research is too long to detail fully here but a special mention is due to my parents-in-law, Slawek and Barbara, and to Kasia Kaldowski who dug deep into Polish customs and sayings for me, as well as correcting some shockingly poor grammar. Many thanks, too, to pathologist Dr Olaf Biedrzycki for unlocking the secrets of violent death, and to the police officers who helped me get 'the Job' right, especially the ever-helpful Detective Sergeant Paula James.

I'm grateful to my dear friend Selina O'Grady who read the book in draft and offered such sound advice, and to my longstanding champion Joan Bakewell whose encouragement and support meant – and means – so much to me. Huge thanks, too, to fellow writers Emlyn Rees and James Craig who showed such generosity in their vocal enthusiasm for the book during its journey to publication.

Above all, I must thank Laetitia Rutherford and Ivan Mulcahy at my agency MCA for all their input to the book and for investing so much time and belief in me as an author. It is due to their efforts that *Devil* found such an excellent friend and champion in my publisher, Scott Pack.

And finally, a thank you to my mother and father who, from the very start, gave me the gift of loving language and the stories that it weaves.

Find out more at: www.anyalipska.com